KT-425-608

PRAISE

"Effortlessly blends the brutal and the tender, the dark and the light. Aector McAvoy is a true original. So is David Mark."—**Mick Herron, author of** *Dead Lions*

"McAvoy must be one of the most fascinating fictional detectives out there – a true original. This is an intoxicating brew – Catholicism, travellers, underground fight scenes, the mob – and rumbling through it all like a bear with a blush is DS Aector McAvoy. Superb writing. A truly fantastic read."—**Michael J. Malone, author of** *A Suitable Lie*

"To call Mark's novels police procedurals is like calling the Mona Lisa a pretty painting. Beautifully crafted, filled with flashbacks, horror, angst, and chilling detail, this one is his most complex and best yet."—*Kirkus Reviews* **(starred review)**

"[A] strange but compelling brew."—**Thomas Gaughan,** *Booklist*

"A police procedural thriller that pulls no punches... Another terrific mystery/suspense novel by a master of the genre."—*Midwest Book Review*

"There seems to be no end to the vile deeds to be encountered in [Hull]."—*The Wall Street Journal*

"Hurry up and read the first three novels in this amazing series, because the fourth installment featuring the huge and huge-hearted Aector McAvoy is the best yet... Author Mark creates vivid, poignant characters that drive this series, from the complex McAvoy to his gypsy wife; from the tenacious Pharaoh to various supporting saints and villains. The ending is a stunner."—*The Cleveland Plain Dealer*

"Mark's excellent fourth novel ... weaves a complicated web of deception, betrayal, and violence as the action builds to a stunning conclusion."—*Publishers Weekly* **(starred review)**

"A dark, bloody, twisting tale of love, hate, and greed you can't put down."—*Kirkus Reviews* **(starred review)**

"Det. Sgt. Aector McAvoy is recovering from tragedy, living with his young son in a flat near the burnt skeleton of his old home and easing back into work with what should be a straightforward investigation of suspected police wrongdoing. But it leads him to some very bad guys. Fourth in a dark and much-starred series." *—Library Journal*

PRAISE FOR *SORROW BOUND*

"Each McAvoy novel has been dark, but *Sorrow Bound* goes beyond dark to near-apocalyptic. Mark pulls it off, though, and fans of the giant Scottish detective will lose sleep reading this one."*—Booklist* (**starred review**)

"Mark adroitly weaves all these threads together during a sweltering Hull summer full of lowering clouds but no rain, 'a feverish heat; a pestilent, buzzing cloak.' The physically imposing Aector, a terrific lead, hews closely to the rules. Well-fleshed out supporting characters round out the cast."*—Publishers Weekly* (**starred review**)

"McAvoy is a sure bet for fans of dark crime fiction set in Britain. Mark is particularly skilled at brief, effective characterization and at establishing an ominous, suspense-ridden setting in which his hero must struggle to reconcile his concept of justice and his admirable integrity with the evil that men do. VERDICT: A satisfying read-alike for fans of Peter Robinson or Val McDermid."*—Library Journal*

"Compelling characters and a knotty mystery make the third from Mark (*Original Skin*, 2013, etc.) stand out from other procedurals."*—Kirkus Reviews*

PRAISE FOR *ORIGINAL SKIN*

"Dark, disturbing and gripping... Graced with a complex plot and stunning imagery, *Original Skin* stands as a worthy successor to Mark's debut, *The Dark Winter*... Readers who revel in thrillers marked by intelligence and originality will celebrate the continuation of a fresh and fascinating series."—*Richmond Times-Dispatch*

"Compelling ... Richly satisfying and told with remarkable flair, [*Original Skin*] confirms Mark as one of the darkest of the new faces in British crime writing, and not one to miss."—*Daily Mail* (UK)

"Sophisticated plotting, in-depth characters, and sharp dialogue elevate British author Mark's gritty second police procedural featuring Yorkshire Det. Sgt. Aector McAvoy. Mark expertly brings together two seemingly unrelated investigations while weaving in McAvoy's devotion to his young family and sensitivity to the Roma background of his wife, Roison, whose extended family becomes involved in his inquiries. Fans of John Harvey and Peter James will find much to like."—*Publishers Weekly* (starred review)

"A dark and nasty police story with strongly drawn characters, an unsettling story, a twisty plot, and a surprising ending... Snap it up."—Examiner.com

"McAvoy's second is an excellent police procedural featuring sex, violence, and complex characters who are quirky but likable."—*Kirkus*

"Readers will immediately be drawn to the compelling, contradictory personality of McAvoy. Grade: A."
—*Cleveland Plain-Dealer*

"Equally good read as a stand-alone or as the second in a series, Mark's fast-paced police procedural featuring a likable and compelling main character is sure to keep fans of dark UK crime fiction entertained."
—*Library Journal*

PRAISE FOR *DARK WINTER*

"David Mark's British police procedurals are a wholesome corrective to cop novels starring prima donna detectives who single-handedly solve major murder cases. Sgt. Aector McAvoy, the 'gentle, humble, shy giant of a man'... is clearly the hero of this brawny series set in the north of England... But Mark surrounds his Scottish detective with fellow officers who make vital contributions to the case and are interesting in their own right."—*The New York Times* **Sunday Book Review**

"British crime reporter Mark's outstanding first novel, a suspenseful whodunit, introduces Det. Sgt. Aector McAvoy... Readers will want to see more of the complicated McAvoy, who well deserves a sophisticated and disturbing plot."—*Publisher's Weekly* (starred)

"[A]n impressive debut. John Harvey readers should take note."—*Booklist* (starred)

"With a poetic intensity in its prose, an unpredictable plot and a Scottish detective, Mark's novel gripped me from its opening pages."—*Milwaukee Journal Sentinel*

"It will not be long until new voices in the genre are hailed as the 'next David Mark.'"—**Bookpage.com**

"Fast moving and tightly plotted, with strong characterization and a likeable protagonist, this is an extremely promising debut."—*The Guardian*

"A promising debut by David Mark... certainly provides a trip to Hull and back."—*The Telegraph*

"A fantastic debut of a police procedural series that takes place in northern England. Just as Detective Sergeant Aector McAvoy seems to be able to put himself in the mind of a killer, David Mark has developed his characters so completely that the reader can almost put himself in the mind of McAvoy as he is connecting dots that no one else even sees. McAvoy may be a gentle giant of a man but he is also determined to get at the truth even if his job is in jeopardy. Luckily, he finds a believer in his boss, another dedicated officer who also is fighting to keep her job."—**Nancy McFarlane,** *Fiction Addiction*

"An exceptional debut from an exciting new talent. David Mark is an original and captivating new voice."
—**Val McDermid**

DARKNESS FALLS

ALSO BY DAVID MARK

The DS McAvoy Series
Darkness Falls
Dark Winter
Original Skin
Sorrow Bound
Taking Pity
A Bad Death
Dead Pretty
Fire of Lies
Cruel Mercy
Scorched Earth
Cold Bones

Standalone Novels
The Burying Ground
A Rush of Blood
Borrowed Time
The Zealot's Bones

For Steve P. A good man.

I had a dream, which was not all a dream.
The bright sun was extinguish'd, and the stars
Did wander darkling in the eternal space,
Rayless, and pathless, and the icy earth
Swung blind and blackening in the moonless air;
Morn came and went – and came, and brought no day,
And men forgot their passions in the dread
Of this their desolation; and all hearts
Were chill'd into a selfish prayer for light.

From 'Darkness', by Lord Byron (George Gordon)

"The dog that digs deepest finds the bones."

Gypsy proverb

Prologue

Shane is feeling good. Shane is feeling great. Shane is feeling downright *smashing*, now you're asking. There's a giddiness to him; a fizz – a general sense of ebullience and *joie-de-vivre*. Shane is rather proud that he knows the phrase *joie-de-vivre*. A horse of that name had won a minor steeplechase at Uttoxeter in 2005 and earned a decent payday for the Francophiles swigging their supermarket champagne in the county stand. Shane's own nag, Maple Stirrup, is still running.

Shane had learned that *joie-de-vivre* means 'joy of living', and is French. Shane can understand the joy of living, if one is French. They have very good bread. Shane also knows that to be a Francophile means to love French things. Shane struggles to understand how that lends itself to 'paedophile'. He doesn't love 'paedos' at all.

Shane is standing in the kitchen of his small flat. He rents the top floor of a narrow, red-and-brown house halfway along an overcrowded terrace in Hull's grandly named Garden Village. A damp, anaemic-looking sunlight oozes in through the porthole that Shane has cleared in the grime which varnishes the kitchen window. The filth now stains the sleeve of his dressing gown. The gown, once white, is now largely sepia toned and mottled with assorted stains. Pizza, at the lapel. Piss, at the hem. Ella... *everywhere*. The garment hangs loose, cordless. He is naked beneath – his rotund belly nosing through the curtains of his robe like the head of a bear snuffling in through a tent flap.

Shane whistles as he pads across the kitchen. It's a new song – something about poking faces. He likes it. Likes the video too. He opens the refrigerator door. Considers the possibilities. The top shelf is all spices and pickles. He likes his food hot, does Shane. He cannot taste very well. His nose has been broken and broken again, and his sense of taste was wiped away along with the snot and blood. He has to squirt obscene spurts of super-hot sauce onto his daily tin of baked beans if he wants to be able to receive any pleasure from his food. The sauce makes his nose run and his eyes water but he enjoys both feelings. It is the closest he gets to crying.

Shane scans the contents of the other shelves, looking for something befitting his lady-friend. The thought of her warms him. Excites him. Delights him. Fills him with so much *joie-de-fucking-vivre* he wants to rub himself against the kitchen wall. She's in the bedroom, spooned up on her side, cradling the space he has just vacated. Worn out, poor thing. Already missing him. Deserves a treat.

He allows his thoughts to linger. Sucks his cheek as he considers his lover. She's definitely not his usual sort. She's a bit out of his league, if he's honest with himself, and he always tries to be. He knows he's not the best-looking lad. He sometimes catches sight of himself and cannot help but be disappointed in his likeness. He's ungainly. He can't help but see himself as a bit... well, *mismatched*, as if he were a person put together from the unwanted bits of other people. He doesn't like to analyse himself too closely but he does wonder whether it is a sense of general futility that stops him taking any care over his personal hygiene. A washed pig is still a pig. One of his friends told him that and had expected him to laugh about it. He could be mean, sometimes, could his friend. Thought he was just being funny, but some of the barbs struck home. Last summer Lewis had told him that he looked as if somebody had stepped in his face while it was still hot. That had upset Shane. Upset him so much that Shane had been forced to follow him home and stamp on his cat. Things had been OK after that. He'd even commiserated with his poor friend. Who could do such a thing? Who could treat an animal like that? Shane had been rather proud of his performance. Mum always said he could have been an actor, if he'd had the discipline and could read well enough to learn his lines.

Shane looks up at a sudden sound from the window. Rain. Later afternoon rain, hitting the kitchen window. He hadn't noticed the coming of the rain or the darkening of the sky. He has been marvellously indolent today. It has been a languid, lazy, sensuous day, for him and his lady-friend both. These past days have flowed over one another like a shoal of silvery, slippery fish: a glorious tumult of pleasure. He cannot remember eating very much but he is not particularly hungry. He smokes sixty cigarettes a day and they suppress his appetite. He is obese largely because of the pills that the doctors insist he takes. Weight gain is a side effect. So too is nausea. Headaches. He hears ringing sounds in his ears when he takes them too late in the day. He can't hear the sounds now so he presumes he has taken them already. Perhaps this morning. He seems to recall having risen from his bed already today. Had there been a visitor? Perhaps one of his friends had come to call. Shane is not popular, not like Lewis, but he doesn't suffer for company. His friends frequently pop over to play computer games or watch a porno or to cut up their powders and potions on the low coffee table in the living room. Sometimes they bring him lager or shoplift him a six-pack of Lion bars as a thank you. Shane likes Lion bars. He hopes his mum will get him a Lion bar Easter egg this year. Last year she got him a posh one, from the fancy chocolate shop. With his dead taste buds it had been like eating slime.

He closes the fridge door, tutting at himself. He'll have to get better at taking care of himself. He needs to clean the place up a bit. Buy some groceries. Some fruit and veg, maybe. A toothbrush. Toilet roll. There's never been much point, living on his own. But since meeting his new friend he has become aware of his own shortcomings. His house is filthy. Grotesque, even. There is a patch of carpet in the living room that has begun to rot down through the wood beneath. There had been a cat's litter tray there when he moved in and he had taken to using it himself when he was too pickled to make it to the bathroom. It smells bad. Sometimes he can't sit in the lounge without two twists of dishcloth up his nose, reclining in one of the mouldy, pilfered deckchairs that face the cracked plasma TV.

Shane was delighted to find that his new friend had been into the same things he was. She'd been too polite to mention the smell as they sat together in their matching chairs, watching as he blitzed through the levels in *God of War III*, hacking and slashing through a great swathe of monsters.

She'd been impressed with his speed. Didn't flinch at the more shocking visuals that flickered on the cracked screen. Limbs ripped, heads removed, bowels gutted – she had sat and drunk it in. She'd been the same when he slipped the disc into the DVD player. Hadn't offered a word of protest as the screen filled with skin.

Shane becomes aware of a new sound: something irritating, just at the edge of his perception. He wonders if it's the rain, coming down harder now, turning to snow, the way it did in January when the world turned white.

And then he hears his name.

"Mr Cadbury, this is the police, sir. Could you let us in, please – we really would like to talk to you…"

Shane is not used to being address as 'Mr Cadbury'. He does not really care for the name. At school, people called him all manner of names, each inspired by some form of chocolate or confection. He has answered to Cocoa. To Shit-Kat. Fudge-Packer. Willy Wanka. He hopes his girlfriend has heard him being addressed with such respect and reverence. He doesn't mind being her bit-of-rough but if they are to have a future together he will have to become a little more refined. He's quite excited at the prospect. He's always wanted a reason to improve himself. He doesn't know very much about her yet, but he fancies she will object if he continues to wipe his arse on the shower curtain.

Another voice now. Low. Soothing – the sort of voice you might use to pacify an angry dog.

"Shane, my name is Aector. Hector, if it's easier for you. It's Scottish. Your friend Lewis said you were the chap to talk to about something really quite important. I don't want to bother you but if you could just open the door for a moment I can get out of your hair."

Shane considers it. On balance, he fancies it would be rude to turn down such a reasonable and politely made request. He is the sort of chap who might help somebody out. He is the sort of gentleman who would make room in his schedule so as not to inconvenience somebody unduly. And his voice had been nice. Soft. Sort of up-and-down, like a friendly giant in a fairy tale.

"Won't be a moment, pet," he shouts through to the bedroom. There's no response. He smiles as he imagines her dozing, dead away – no doubt dreaming of the life they will make together and the things they will do when her batteries are fully recharged.

His bare feet squelch across soggy carpet. He takes a handful of his gown and wraps it around himself. Unlocks the door and pulls it inwards.

On the doorstep stands a tall, broad police officer. He has red hair, damp at the fringe and temples, and a neat beard. He's wearing uniform. So are the two men who stand behind him, their hands to their noses and mouths, each taking shallow breaths and flinching as the haze of flies rise and settle, rise and settle – making the pile of rotting food and slippery bin-bags seem as though it may be alive.

"You're a big man!" says Shane, looking up at the officer. He has brown eyes. Sad eyes, really, like a cartoon cow. "Are you strong? I bet you're strong. There's a man on *World's Strongest* who looks a bit like you. He's foreign. Are you foreign?"

"I'm Scottish," says the man on the doorstep, gently. "Have you been to Scotland?"

Shane thinks hard about the answer, wanting to get it right. "I think so. We went ice skating, once. A day trip. When I was at BridgeView. It was nice. Tell me your name again."

"It's Aector, Shane. Aector McAvoy. You can say 'Hector' if it's easier."

Shane licks his lips. Tries it the proper way, with a little cough in the middle. He smiles, hugely, when he gets it right. "Aector," he says, again, and sticks out a large, dirt-smeared hand. "I'm Shane."

The big police officer takes Shane's hand without hesitation. Shane feels the strength in his grip. He senses how much restraint he is using. How much work is going into not squeezing his grimy, fleshy paw. He appreciates it.

"Who are these two, Aector? The coppers behind you?" He peers past the big man's shoulder, at the two constables. One has turned a funny colour: a weird marbling of grey-and-green, like moss on an old stone wall. The other is glaring at him, his eyes tiny pin-pricks, radiating a kind of bad energy that makes Shane think of the way roads shimmer with heat haze on a hot day. He doesn't like them.

Aector is speaking again. Shane reminds himself it's rude to ignore somebody when they are trying to be polite. Tunes himself in to the right frequency.

"…I'd love to see your place, Shane. Those stairs almost did me in and a sit-down would do me the world of good. We could even stick the kettle on, eh?"

Shane makes a show of considering it. He doesn't have a kettle, as far as he can remember. But he does like the big police officer and wants to be liked in return. He wonders if his girlfriend will object to these unexpected guests. Hopes she won't make a fuss about it. He's heard that girlfriends can moan if their needs are overlooked. He wants to be a good boyfriend. Wants to get everything right.

"It will have to be quick," concedes Shane. "I've got a lady-friend." He gives a wink, two old friends, talking. "Proper looker. Goer, too. Got better things to be doing, if you know what I mean."

The police officer gives a nod. Manages a little smile. Follows Shane into the flat.

"Sorry about the state of the place," he begins. "I've been meaning to sort some stuff out but you just don't get the chance, do you? Life's a full-time job."

Behind Aector, the policeman with the hard eyes is muttering. Coughing now. Raising his hand to his mouth and retching.

Aector ignores the man, who strikes Shane as unnecessarily rude. He gives Shane a kindly smile. "What's your lady-friend's name, Shane?" he asks, softly.

Shane hesitates, unsure if he wants to reveal too much. But the giddiness rises up and he finds himself talking, the way he had when Lewis popped by earlier and asked to meet the new lass he had bragged about over the phone.

"It's Ella," he whispers, quietly. "Goes nicely, doesn't it? Shane and Ella."

There is movement behind the big man. The copper with the hard eyes pushes forward, growling something unfathomable, but Aector puts out a hand and holds him fast, his arm like a fence-post.

"Is she here, Shane?" he asks, quietly.

Shane nods, eager to please. "Bedroom," he says, motioning over his shoulder towards the closed door. Its whitewashed surface is covered in scribblings – graffiti, a multi-coloured diorama of obscene words and pictures, each made more grotesque by the childishness of the hand.

"Keep it down," mutters Shane, as he opens the door, beckoning the police officers behind him. "Poor love's exhausted..."

Shane stands aside and allows his new friend to squeeze past him, his big frame part-in and part-out of the room. Shane is close enough to feel him stiffen, as if an electrical charge had just surged through his body.

Shane looks past him, considering again the feast for the eyes that his lady-friend is serving up to the newcomers. He's a lucky man. Luckiest man alive.

Aector's voice, low, his breath hot, up close to his left ear. "What have you done, Shane?"

Shane bristles. He doesn't like the big man's tone. "She's mine," he says, petulantly. "She was a gift."

Sergeant Aector McAvoy looks back at the mess on the bed. Sees rags. Torn silk. Empurpled, ivory limbs, swollen as if drowned. And red. So much red...

His hands tremble as he reaches for his radio. He pauses, forcing himself to breathe. To take shallow breaths. To stay professional. To do what must be done.

He feels the reek of her climb inside him. Tiny particles of violated flesh and spilled blood flood his mouth and nose.

"I'm sorry," he whispers, and the words come out in a rush. "I'm so, so sorry."

Beside him, Shane Cadbury puts a blood-smeared hand on his blue sleeve. "It wasn't me," he says, moodily. "She was a present, I told you. Can you go now? Can you go...?"

McAvoy keeps the tremble from his voice as he speaks.

"Sir, this is Sergeant McAvoy. We've found her. Found Ella."

Shane scowls: a toddler robbed of a favoured toy. "She's mine," he begins. "Can't I keep her...?"

And then Police Constable Poyser draws his baton. Yells, all spit and rage. Comes for Shane like a crazy man, swinging wildly, promising to kill him, to kill him properly, to put him down and keep him down and pound his bones to dust.

"No," says Shane's new friend, Aector, wrapping a big left arm around him and turning his back on the police officer. "No, you don't get to have him..."

Shane listens, cosseted in the comfortable, warm embrace of the nice police officer.

Listens, as the blows fall like rain.

I

It's Sunday, February 5 2012.

11.58 p.m.

The car park on the north bank of the Humber Bridge – the *Christian* side of the river.

Owen Lee, Press Association Hull and East Riding correspondent, gathered like a fist in the driver's seat of a 1986 Vauxhall Cavalier: Elastoplast-brown. Not a classic. Not vintage. Just knackered, and old.

Me.

I'm not crying. I want to. I'd fucking love to. There's a peach stone in my throat and cold grit in my eyes, but the tears won't fall, so I just pull anguished faces and rub my face with my gloved hands.

The dark crescent beneath my right eye sings with pain as I jab my thumb into it. I do it again. And again.

The car radio gave up years ago, so I'm listening to the tinny sound of Johnny Cash on a portable CD player, circa 2001. I don't want the violation of putting the earphones in my ears, so I've left the crappy square of plastic and wire on the front passenger seat, sitting on a mound of takeaway boxes and old newspapers, the cords dribbling over the edge of the seat – teaching the weeping willow how to cry.

I'm cold. The heater's been broken for years. Normally would I sit and bitch about the East Yorkshire weather, but tonight the cold is almost reassuring. The goose pimples on my skin are a physical reminder of the unpleasantness of it all; the sheer intolerability of life improperly lived.

Not long now. Minutes, maybe. Then the rush of air and the smash of water and the absolute perfect nothingness.

I purse my lips and push another lungful of pain into the air. Each breath becomes a cloud, gathering as steam from a kettle, then disappearing into ribbons and nothingness.

I look at my watch. Seconds from midnight, just like the whole human race. I realise I'm not going to die on February 5. I won't make it to the bridge in time. It'll have to happen on February 6. The sixth day, of the second month, of 2012. Rain is forecast. Dark skies and high winds. Snow's on the way. The trial is starting at Hull Crown. Ella Butterworth's killer, Shane Cadbury, sticking to his not-guilty plea despite all the evidence to the contrary.

I try harder, desperate for meaning. It must matter. It *must!*

Three-and-a-half weeks since Jessica left me. Two-and-a-bit months since we flushed the clotted lumps of our child down the toilet in a mush of reds, of sodden tissue and swirling water. Couple of years since Kerry stuck a needle in her arm, and a dagger through Dad's heart. Just over a year since the monster in Mam's tit ate her up, pulled out her hair and wrapped her in a pine box that weighed less on my shoulders than the burden pressing against my chest.

Three months until my thirtieth birthday.

February 6.

Just a day.

The day I'm going to die.

I step out onto the tarmac and a sudden gust of frosty wind fills the car and blows my scarf up over my face. The wind is stirring the leaves and bullying the trees ringing the car park, muffling the roar and rush of the occasional car moving across the bridge overhead.

As I straighten myself up and adjust my clothes, the hunger in my gut reaches a tendril towards my throat, and I belch, sourly, my mouth filling with the taste of bile and bitterness. I've barely eaten in weeks, and sickness has become a constant. I vomit at thoughts I don't like, at new situations and pressing engagements. It's a nervous condition, so the doctors say. I've disassociated myself from my own body. My gut belongs to my head, and my head doesn't belong to me. I wipe my mouth, and spit.

A few street lamps are still on, casting a sickly sodium glow over the dozens of empty parking spaces. I'm parked close to the woods, near the admin offices. Twelve hours ago the place would have been buzzing, despite the weather. The Humber Bridge Country Park. The eastern edge of Yorkshire. Kingston upon Hull. Hull. 'ull, to its friends, if it had any. A city hungover from the days when it was the world's biggest fishing port, and metal trawlers would leave St Andrew's Quay to travel to distant waters and return laden with a silver bounty that would feed the nation, and make fat men wealthier. All terraced streets and neighbourliness, kids in bare feet. Clouds from the smokehouses mingling with the damp and the fog, clinging to donkey jackets and headscarves and trickling into swampy lungs. Lads stinking of skate and haddock with a wedge of cash in their pockets. All long gone, now. Those times that brought wealth and loss. When lives were snuffed out by a wave and wives dreaded the sound of the chaplain's feet on the cobbles. The houses remain, but the city is on its arse. Empty houses, smashed windows. Lorries belching fumes and children who can't read. New office blocks standing empty and shopping streets boarded up or burning down. Yesterday's generation pining for the days of the fishing industry the way a battered wife forgets her abuser's sins and yearns for his return. A journalist's paradise. A murder a month, and some of them fabulous. Schools at the arse-end of the league tables. Hospital bandaged in scaffolds and tarpaulin to try and stop any more roof tiles striking the patients who huddle in the doorway, sneaking a fag while supporting their frail bodies on the stand of an intravenous drip.

My city. Trapped in its grip, like a wasp held inside a shot glass, all broken limbs and tinfoil wings, buzzing and striking an invisible barrier, drowning in sticky syrup and fading breath.

Here, eight miles up the road, it's a different world. The Country Park. Deep lakes, green with algae and punctured by fallen branches that poke through its surface like so many blades. Fifty-foot limestone cliffs, dirtied by moss. Well-groomed forests of ash and sycamore, parted like Brylcreem-ed hair with manmade paths and helpful rails. Jess and I used to walk miles in its cosy embrace, holding hands as we ambled between the trees. I can see it now, clear as what's in front of me. See us laughing. Reciting baby names. Listing holiday destinations and favourite meals. Wrapped up in the bollocks of it all. Me, talking and planning and pretending and unburdening. Her, listening and nodding and pretending, and wishing I was normal and loving that I wasn't; ever walking on the rice paper and eggshells of my temper.

My watch beeps suddenly as night turns into morning.

It is the day of my death.

I lock the car and drop the keys into the depths of my pocket, where they find a comfortable spot between my notebook, cigarettes and mobile phone. Johnny Cash is trapped inside the car, still warbling away on the passenger seat, sat proud on a mound of yellowing newsprint that carries my name.

I look up at the bridge, then turn my head to the right where the footpath that Jess and I used to take is shrouded in darkness. The woods have no shape. They are just a black mass – all whistling sounds and shaking branches, snapping twigs and falling leaves. They hold no danger for the damned. A man in pursuit of his own death doesn't fear ambush.

Turn, and head towards the forest. Even as I duck beneath the dark, tangled branches I ask myself what I'm doing. I've played out this journey countless times. I'm supposed to be walking towards the footpath that runs along the bridge. I'm supposed to be smoking a cigarette and counting my steps and putting distance between myself and the shoals of sharp-toothed sadnesses that swim behind me. Instead I'm walking away from the water, ducking under branches, crunching over damp wood.

In moments the woods have swallowed me up. I can hear my boots rustling through the wet leaves and keep a hand on the rail as the footpath starts to descend. The forest is black and cold, and I can sense eyes upon me, hear the scrabbling claws of the creatures who live in the dark. I feel as though I am walking inside myself.

My footsteps are becoming heavy, my coat starting to stoop my shoulders. Despite myself, I'm starting to feel nervous. My eyes are watering, forcing me to close them for longer and longer moments, inviting slumber, wrapping sleep around myself as a blanket against the cold.

I am lost now, lost in the darkness. I reach out my hand and feel the knobbled bark of a tree trunk. I suddenly realise my feet are wet, that water has soaked past the lip of my boots. I splash backwards, onto soft ground. My right boot slips and my knee hits the wet ground, hard. My teeth bang together and I mash the side of my tongue. I can taste blood. I spit on the forest floor, raising a gloved finger to my mouth. Even through the leather I can feel the wetness.

Now the tears flow. My throat coughs up a lump and I spit it on the forest floor as salt water runs down my cheeks.

I don't sob. Instead I hold myself still, fists balled, teeth locked, as the tears pour down my face.

Crying for what I am, for what lives within me. For all I have failed to do.

My cheeks feel raw as the wind slices against the wetness and I wipe my face dry with the back of a glove. I screw up my eyes, peering again into the gloom. There are vague shapes, but nothing more. I take a tentative step and realise my boots are now on soft leaves, rather than the hardness of the path. I shuffle forward again and strike something firm. I curse and stop again. My grand gesture, my heroic death, is becoming farce. I need to find myself before I can kill myself. Muttering, I remove my glove and plunge my hand into the pocket of my coat, searching for a light. After foraging through the assorted crap, I grip the Zippo lighter that I'm usually too lazy to fill. I pull it free and spin the wheel. There is a tiny spark but the flame is swallowed by the wind. I curse and cup the lighter with my hand, trying to shield it from the gusts that seem to be growing stronger, whisking the detritus of the night. The flame catches hold but disappears again when I take my hand away. Third time lucky, I think, and then chastise myself for optimism.

I flip the wheel on the Zippo and there is an explosion of light and power as my world is turned red, orange and vermillion.

It takes me a moment to realise that the blaze of light was accompanied by sound, and came not from my hand. I hold the lighter aloft, my movements slow and sluggish, as though wading through syrup. Everything has slowed down, become heavy, drugged.

Inexorably, as though the thought is carrying a burden, I realise I am not alone.

There are lumps in the darkness, lumps of flesh and bone.

The shapes become figures, human figures. They are real. More tangible and touchable than my visions.

And like a face forming in flame, one of the lumps becomes a man. His arm is outstretched, a shadow, a blot of richer darkness against the black. He is holding something in his hand. The other shape is shorter, lower down. A few feet away from where I stand, open mouthed.

He is sagging slowly, falling like a building, collapsing in on himself. I expect him to shatter on impact as he hits the forest floor.

Then the standing man is turning, looking at me, as I hold my tiny flame. His arm drops and I hear an intake of breath, and a curse of exclamation as the flame is extinguished. There is another explosion of light and sound and something whistles past my cheek. I jerk my face away but there is a heat that rocks me and, in an instant of adrenaline, wakes my will to live.

My senses are suddenly alive as the tumblers of understanding start to fall into place and I realise that I am being shot at, alone in the dark; that a stranger is about to rob me of my grand gesture, and end my life in a way I have not condoned.

I am suddenly very much alive. Alive and angry.

I have fantasised about my death for so long that my life has become precious to me, the one thing I control and own, and I will not have it defiled by another.

Instinct and fury take me over and I am suddenly charging forward, lunging at the spot of darkness where I last saw the figure. I roar and leap, arms outstretched, a wounded tiger, and collide with a block of flesh.

Legs and arms entangle.

Hot breath, chaos and confusion and a hand pushing against my face.

We are tumbling now, rolling in the dirt, enmeshed in one another. The man is strong, all wiry muscles beneath the bulk of his clothes. He is on top of me but I have his wrists and we are flailing at one another. He is stronger than me, too strong, and pulls an arm free, bringing his fist down in my face. There is a meaty thud which only angers me further and I bring my knee into his back. He pitches to the side and I roll free, kicking out at the darkness. Then a flash of face, like a sliver of moon, flits by close to my own, a glimmer of snarling white, and there is fist in my gut and I am on my back again, pinned under his weight, gazing up as this stranger throttles me with gloved hands.

I am lying on another mound of flesh and clothes, fighting for life on a mattress of death.

My hands scrabble in the mud and dirt, rake through wet leaves as the pressure builds in my throat. His face is close to mine, his mouth open, teeth bared... Then I feel it, hard and metallic.

Raw, cold power.

I grab the object with my hand and swing it hard against his head.

There is a grunt. A moment of incomprehension. Then he slumps forwards and falls to my side.

And I am on top of him now, astride his chest, holding the gun in my hand, pointing at this stranger's face as he lays unconscious in the dirt and darkness. I'm panting, breath as heavy as the wind.

Gripping the gun between hands that don't shake.

Hands that feel strangely comfortable around the sturdy handle.

I look down at the two mounds of skin and cloth. The one I have fought with is still breathing. He is about my age, and scruffy, unshaven, with curly hair. Rough. The other is younger. Spotty and pock-marked. A third eye stares out from the unlined whiteness of his forehead, clotted with blood and matching his lifeless gaze.

I retire from myself, and allow the thing within me to take over. I see myself search the older man, tentatively pushing a hand into the inside pocket of his leather jacket.

I pull out a rolled-up freezer-bag of white powder, and a wad of cash, thick as a Brontë novel.

In the space of but a moment, my life, and death, everything has changed. Everything! The fates that have thwarted me, that for so long pissed on the enthusiasm that used to blaze within me, have interceded at the last, and hauled me back. For as I strolled towards my death, they handed me a chance to change it all. As I prepared to throw myself into oblivion, the world decided it was a more interesting place with me in it. The fates conspired, and handed me all I ever asked for – a fighting chance to change things. I am a man who does not value his life, and who longs for death. I am a man without belief, and unencumbered by conscience. I am suicidal with a bellyful of rage and regret and agony and misery and so much fucking hate, and now, with a weapon. I feel like I've found a magic lamp. A man can truly change his stars – with a gun, a packet of powder and a wad of cash.

I look at the gun, slide the clip from the butt, and count out six bullets. Some of the grooves in the clip are empty and I catch the tang of smoke and cordite as I hold it to my face.

So many memories.

Each bullet glints in the darkness, a wicked, gold-toothed smile.

And suddenly I am laughing, laughing in the dark, as I slide the clip back into the gun, and pocket it. I feel around on the ground for a suitable rock, and raise it above my head as the future stretches away like some beautiful white road or a sliver of silver moonlight, promising exotic journeys and a blissful destination.

The universe has given me six shots at happiness, and I'm going to take them.

Blessed and pardoned for what I'm going to do.

I'm not going to waste a shot now.

I bring the rock down.

And it begins.

2

Aector McAvoy jerks awake, sitting up so quickly that it seems for a moment as if the bed has been travelling at speed before coming to an abrupt stop. He pitches forward, grabbing at nothing, a single word trapped in his throat.

"*No!*"

He claws at the chill, dark air. Raises a big, sweat-greased palm to his forehead. Shivers, gasping for breath.

"No," he says, again, as he catches the lingering scent – that trace of spoiled meat and dead lilies, rotten fabrics and sour, unwashed skin.

He lowers his hand and presses it to his big, bare chest. Feels his heart, banging, banging, thudding against his ribcage like a lunatic nutting the door of a padded cell.

"Christ," he whispers, and glances around in the darkness, instinctively afraid that one of the other boarding school boys will report his blasphemy. He swallows, drily, and gets a hold of himself. He's home. He's in his own bed. It's been fifteen years since he last slept in the bunks of the posh private school that his mum's new husband sent him off to when he became an imposition. He's a grown man. A police officer. A sergeant. Decorated for bravery. He's a husband. A father. He's a big, strong man and he doesn't need to be afraid. And she's here, beside him, beautiful as sunlight, even in the dark. She pours into him like honey.

"*Roisin...*"

He feels her fingers, cold and soft; her warm breath on the side of his face. He feels her press her forehead to his shoulder; rub her face against his arm as if blotting an impression onto the canvas of his skin. Gradually, his breathing slows. The dark room becomes familiar.

Here.

Hull.

Home.

The little semi-detached on the new-build estate at the north of the city. The half-finished bedroom: gaudy patterned wallpaper and fairy lights, a big pink-and-white wardrobe groaning under the weight of sparkly shoe boxes.

Her. His *Roisin* – the same way he is so very much her *Aector*. His wife. Stroking his skin. Whispering to him. Telling him that it's OK, she's here; that there's nothing to be afraid of.

And then he is lying back down, his head on her stomach, her hands in his hair, and she's singing, softly, in the voice that fills him with honey.

"*In Dublin's fair city, where the girls are so pretty...*"

Movement, in the bed. Then Fin McAvoy, three years old and built like a bread oven, is wriggling up to where Mummy and Daddy are snuggling, and he's giggling to himself as he slithers up his mum's small, warm frame and thuds against the enormity of his dad: six foot six of muscles, pale skin and red hair.

"Mammy singing?" he asks.

"Trying to," says Roisin, softly. "Trying a few things,

Sonny-Jim. Trying it on with your father, as it happens, but there's no chance of that now you've stuck your oar in."

"Me not got an oar."

"Daddy has," a giggle in her voice. "Daddy could row us home with it."

"Mummy silly. We are home. This is home."

"Yeah, Mummy silly. Mummy really fancies a giggle. Wants to lay on her back and laugh until she shakes."

"Daddy would like that too."

Fin McAvoy has only just turned three but he knows that Mammy sometimes says things that are funny, and rude, and that make Daddy blush. It's too dark to tell if this is one of those times, but he knows that beneath the blankets, they're holding each other close and that they are smiling, brightly, into the dark.

"Daddy have nightmare?" he asks, gently.

McAvoy nods. Sits up. Reaches out and finds his son and pulls him closer, pressing their heads together as if transferring a thought. "Just a dream, son. They're silly things, dreams."

"I have dreams," confides Fin. "Like Daddy."

"Everybody dreams," says McAvoy, and presses his head into his son's curls, blocking out the last trace of the scent that plagues him. "Some people remember them perfectly. Others don't. I don't really remember mine. They fade away really quickly. I just get funny feelings for a while afterwards."

Fin looks at his father solemnly, nodding his understanding. "Was it the lady?"

McAvoy freezes, his mind filling with pictures as the fading dream surges back to fill his vision. Suddenly his whole world is *her*: his nostrils clogged with the smell of spoiled meat, his vision nothing but torn silk and sticky blood. He wraps his arms around Fin. Holds his son until the moment passes.

They have been getting worse, these visions. As the court case has inched closer he has found himself thinking more and more of the dead girl he had so hoped to find alive. Has found himself thinking of Shane Cadbury – the plump, slow-witted sex-pest who had plunged a knife into her again and again and laid her out in his bed like a trophy. He has never truly felt clean since that day. He knows that scents are particular, that each aroma is made of tiny fragments of a source. Each time he smells Ella Butterworth, he remembers that she drifted inside him. She has done more than climb under his skin. She has made herself a part of him. Her body, corrupted, defiled, is within him. She is his responsibility.

Roisin rolls over and flicks on the bedside lamp. She looks at them both, sleepily. Her dark hair hangs in thick curtains across her tanned, delicate face. She's still wearing her fake eyelashes and last night's make-up and lip gloss, making her look at once dishevelled and glamorous. McAvoy smiles, helplessly, as she stares into him, radiating a love and desire that finds its mirror image in the intensity of his own, doe-eyed gaze. They have been married for three years and still they take one another's breath away.

"Mummy's got no pyjamas on, Daddy."

"I noticed that, son. That fact really did catch my attention."

"We have breakfast?"

"I think it's too early for breakfast, Fin."

Roisin snuggles in to the two loves of her life. Whispers something in Fin's ear that makes him giggle. Then he slithers out of bed and runs, heavy-footed, towards his bedroom, closing the door behind him.

"What did you offer him?" smiles McAvoy, as she climbs astride him, grinning, her sparkling fingernails forming a garnet necklace upon his chest.

"He gets an ice lolly for breakfast," she murmurs, breathily.

"That's a high price to pay," says McAvoy, distractedly, as his world becomes paradise. "Am I worth it..."

"Priceless," whispers Roisin, closing her eyes.

An hour later, and McAvoy is sitting at the kitchen table, sipping tea from a mug the size of tankard. He's wearing a battered rugby shirt with a pair of pyjama trousers, and staring somewhat vacantly through the rain-spattered kitchen window towards the little garden at the back of the house. To McAvoy, a Highlander, this is the Kingswood estate. To Hull residents, it is North Bransholme – a continuation of what was once the biggest council estate in Europe and a name laden with negative connotations. It's a typical new-build: small, near-identical properties lining a seemingly endless parade of cul-de-sacs and quiet roads. It's not the sort of place that either McAvoy or Roisin would call their forever home, but it suits them for now.

They hope this year will finally give them the second child they have been yearning for. Roisin has endured a succession of miscarriages. The doctors cannot understand why and have tactfully suggested they celebrate their child and curtail their attempts for a larger family. Roisin won't hear of it. She is from a Traveller family and has always imagined herself having lots of children, just like her own mum and dad. She has only just turned twenty-one and still entertains visions of having five or six kids running around her feet by the time she hits thirty. McAvoy, a decade her senior, would give her the moon if she asked for it, but each new pregnancy terrifies him as much as he delights in his wife's happiness.

His instinct is to protect her – to do everything he can to spare her from any harm, to insist she go to bed and stay there, doing nothing, and to remove all potential harm from her life. But she will not hear of it. She is a strong, fierce, independent Traveller who won't so much as allow her husband to dry the dishes or make himself a cup of tea, despite his protestations that he wants to do his share. She has her code and he respects it, even while beating himself up each day, feeling guilty right through to his bones that he is some unreconstructed Neanderthal, sitting with his feet up while his pretty, too-young wife vacuums under his feet and brings him home-baked cakes from the kitchen. He has voiced these concerns to Roisin, who habitually responds by laughing at him, calling him an idiot, and then kissing him hard enough to dislodge a tooth. She loves him fiercely. Loves him harder than he ever imagined himself being loved.

He drains his tea. Looks through the open kitchen door to where Fin, in his dressing gown, is sitting watching a wildlife programme while eating a Rocket lolly. McAvoy smiles. Remembers the bargain that Roisin struck with their son, and luxuriates for a moment in the memory of her.

She's upstairs, singing to herself in the shower. He can just make out the soft lullaby of her voice. He wonders whether Fin would be OK for a little while – whether she would appreciate him coming to soap her back, and knows at once that she would. They are addicted to one another.

"Daddy…"

McAvoy returns from his daydream to find Fin holding out his mobile phone. It's the work one – the one that rarely rings. It has been charging in the living room.

McAvoy feels his cheeks begin to burn. He feels as though he has been caught out – interrupted doing something he shouldn't have been. He has always blushed. He's the only copper he knows whose face colours at the merest mention of naughtiness or impropriety. The beard covers the worst of it, but bare-cheeked he flushes scarlet. Roisin, who was only a child when they first met, is of the opinion that it is the sweetest thing she has ever seen. McAvoy, who has endured three decades of taunts, is less keen.

"Hello, Detective Sergeant Aector McAvoy, Major Crime Unit…"

Saying it aloud makes him feel rather proud and a total fraud all at once. For the past few months he has been a member of the elite unit led by Detective Superintendent Doug Roper. It is a position he requested, cashing in his one favour with the Divisional Commander, earned by virtue of finding the body of Ella Butterworth and detaining the man who killed her. He had been under the impression that Roper was the best of the best, and wanted to learn from somebody with one of the most impressive clearance rates in the service. But Roper has side-lined him with a series of secondments – loaning him out to other departments or lumbering him with dispiriting admin tasks. McAvoy is by no means too proud to do what he is asked and has taken to filling in his worksheets in triplicate in case the originals are lost, but he is beginning to feel paranoid that Roper is doing more than teaching him the importance of due diligence. He feels deliberately excluded. Roper didn't pick him, and Roper doesn't want him. These past months he has been ping-ponging between departments – cyber-crime, domestic violence, fraud. He has become a master at databases and spreadsheets and has felt more like an accountant than a police officer. He hasn't complained, has just got his head down and done his best, but this is not the job he hoped to do when he quit university and applied to join Cumbria Constabulary at the age of twenty-two.

"Hello? Are you the big chap? Scottish? Came to visit us when we had the break-in? You left a card. Sorry, sorry, should have said. Sharon Menzies. I run the tea room at the Humber Bridge. You came and gave us some leaflets…"

McAvoy remembers her. Forties. Brunette. A warm sort: welcoming, kind – the sort who fosters troubled kids and manages to get them through their GCSEs and doesn't let people say she's an angel because she's got no time for that sort of touchy-feely nonsense. He'd been sent by the Assistant Chief Constable to give a talk on crime prevention after a couple of scallywags broke in to one of the units at the Country Park. She'd refused his offers to pay for his own cup of tea and slice of lemon drizzle cake. Shit, he'd known that would come back to haunt him…

"Mrs Menzies, yes. This is DS McAvoy. How are you? I recall you saying your husband hadn't been well. Sciatica, was it? Hope he's doing better…"

He glances up as Roisin enters the kitchen, wrapped up snug in a leopard-print dressing gown and Ugg boots. She's towelling her hair dry, smiling at him. She smiles well, a dazzle in her eyes that outshines her bright white teeth. She always seems pleased to see him. He has to look away. She looks so young. Too young, he thinks. He has never reconciled himself to their age difference. She was seventeen when she climbed into his bed. He was twenty-six, and had just broken up with a woman ten years his own senior. He has spent endless hours analysing what it all means. Roisin, always able to put him back together again, has told him time and time again that he has nothing to reproach himself for. She wanted him and she made it happen. She'd loved him from day one, and wasn't going to wait another moment. He proposed the minute she told him she was expecting their son. Trudged onto a halting site on the outskirts of Doncaster and asked Papa Teague for his daughter's hand in marriage. Him. A copper. A fucking copper! The wedding had been small. Papa Teague had given his blessing to the union but he was damned if he was going to show off about it.

"Look, Sergeant, this is probably just my lad being silly – our Kieran, he's not gone in today – teacher training, or something, so he's with me, and he gets bored the second you switch off his Nintendo, so he went for a bit of a walk in the woods while I was opening up, and…"

McAvoy hears something in her voice. Something like fear.

"Carry on, Mrs Menzies…"

"Well, he's all for calling 999, but that seems a bit over the top for something that's probably nothing, but I

remembered you and I had your card and you were so nice
to talk to…"

McAvoy rubs his hand over his face, smoothing his
beard. *He should tell her to call 999*, he thinks. *Should do
things properly…*

"It's just, our Kieran, he's really adamant. Is that the right
word? Adamant."

"Adamant about what, Mrs Menzies?"

Her words come out in a rush, bats gushing from a
cave. "He says he's found a body. In the woods. There's
a shoe sticking out of a bush. I asked him what he was
talking about. A shoe's a shoe – not a body. And he told me
I was daft and explained himself, like. Said that the shoe
was attached to a leg, and the leg was half buried under
some leaves. He swears blind, Sergeant. And he would have
stopped me, wouldn't he, if he were just being silly? I told
him – I said I was ringing you, and he said that was good.
He's got a face like a ghost, Sergeant. Have I done right?
I don't want to go down there. Is this your sort of thing?
Have I done right?"

McAvoy breathes out, slowly. Glances at the clock.
It's 7.58 a.m. he's on-call this week, primed to go to Hull
Crown Court to deliver his evidence if the case against
Shane Cadbury goes that far. Chances are, he'll plead guilty
long before that. If he were to phone this one in, deliver
it up to Roper on a plate, perhaps he'd get a chance to be
involved. To prove himself. He despises himself at once
for the thought. If there is a body, it means somebody has
suffered. It means grief. Bereavement. Pain. To think of it
as an opportunity for advancement is grotesque. He looks

down at the floor, ashamed of himself. Feels Roisin move close to him and put her hands in his thick red hair.

"You did right," he says, softly. Then: "I'll be there as soon as I can."

3

Me. Awake... wide awake, eyes like peeled pears...
taking stock... remembering, remembering...

And I'm fumbling in yesterday's muddied, bloodied
trousers for my phone.

Finger like a knife, stabbing at the numbers.

Humberside Police Voicebank.

Two rings, then a *click*.

Recorded message.

Usually handbag snatches and indecent assaults.
Enough for a sixty-word news-in-brief on a slow news day.
Occasional gem. Maybe the odd grandfather scaring off
burglars with a bedside lamp. Once in a while an update on
a stalled murder case, a re-appeal for witnesses, an excuse to
drag better stories from the archives and give them a polish.
New intro, new quote, ten paragraphs of background.

Always Dave's voice on the line. Inspector Dave
Simmonds, twenty-eight-year force veteran. Skinny lad.
Family man. Good mate. Good contact. Always gives me
first question at the press conferences. No dress sense.
Sponsored by Jack Wolfskin and Gore-Tex. Likes hiking.
Yorkshire accent, always friendly. Playing the game.

"*This is Inspector Dave Simmonds in the Humberside Police press office. Good morning. The time is 8.17 on the morning of the 6th of February. If you keep listening I've put a few incidents on the media-line for the North Bank. Quiet night on the South. We have a sex attack in Bridlington, an entry by deception in Driffield and a theft of a pedal cycle on Greenwood Avenue in Hull. On a general note I would like to warn yourselves and the public that the roads are exceedingly icy today and already we've had reports of people driving too fast for the conditions. Five cars came off the A15 northbound between Barnetby Top and the Humber Bridge before 7 a.m. Nobody injured, thank goodness. I would suggest people only go out in their cars if they absolutely have to. Inspector Pinkney from our road safety division is available for interview. On another note, most of you will be aware that the trial of Shane Cadbury starts today at Hull Crown Court. I have been informed that the entire Butterworth family are going to be there, supported by our family liaison officers. Detective Superintendent Roper intends to be at court for the duration of the trial and either myself or press officer Gemma Tang will also be in attendance. As per usual, we will not be commenting on the case until after the verdict is returned, at which time, photographs of the defendant will be made available. We're expecting a lot of national press interest so I would suggest local press get there early if you want to guarantee a seat...*"

No mention of bodies in the woods. Too early. People still too dozy at this hour. Not me. I'm wide awake and buzzing. My eyes are bullet holes.

I pull my shirt off the back of the radiator and slip it on, enjoying the warmth. Patterned black tie still in a noose. Slip it over my head and pull it closed, two buttons down from my collar. Black trousers. Italian leather shoes. Gold chain and chunky identity bracelet. Sovereign ring on my right hand. Quick once-over with the electric razor, careful not to touch the sideburns. Brush my short hair with my hand. I always look more like I should be standing in the dock than sitting at the Press bench.

Step back...

Crunch.

I've stepped on crushed glass. I'm standing on a picture. Jess and me, grinning at the camera from the top of Mount Vesuvius, toasting our engagement with a half-bottle of red plonk. Sunny day. Faces gleaming with the exertion of the climb and the heat of the Neapolitan summer. I'm smiling wider than she is. I look good with cut-off jeans and a muscle-shirt, sun-tan and a henna tattoo on my arm. She's got a bare midriff, a blouse tied beneath her little boobs, and shorts to match mine. Doc Marten boots and a bandana over her black hair. There's a wisp of smoke climbing up from the volcano's crater behind us. A German guy with a walking stick took the picture, just after I got up off my knees. We got a round of applause from the other tourists. Jess was embarrassed. I loved it.

I pick up the picture from beneath the fractured glass. Yesterday I put my fist through it, swept my arms along the mantelpiece, thrust a boot through the vase on the coffee table. An empty bottle of Southern Comfort put paid to the glass presentation case in the alcove, and my model cars are all over the floor. The ornamental Samurai sword that used to be mounted by its side is now embedded three inches into the doorframe. My coat is hanging from its handle. Stuffing is spilling out of the slash-wounds on the sofa. My solitary award for journalism, a giant winged Pegasus on a plinth of open newspapers, ceramic and weighing over a stone, is peeking out from the shattered remains of the television screen. There's blood on the hardwood floor.

Clean up later. Not important.

No food in the kitchen. I've let supplies run down. You do when you're planning to kill yourself.

Coat on. Powder in one pocket, cash in the other, both pleasantly heavy. Neither have been counted. I feel some strange aversion to dissecting these gifts into numbers and weights, figures and pounds. I don't want to seem mercenary.

I grab a notepad from the cupboard by the sofa and thrust it into the waistband of my trousers. Pick a packet of knock-off Polish cigarettes from the pile. Seize my bag. Sling it over a shoulder. Hug my arm to my chest and feel the pleasing weight of the gun in my inside pocket.

Out the door, down the stairs. I throw a quick glance over my shoulder at the apartment block I call home. Edge of the city centre, opposite a church I've never been inside and a theatre that only gets a full house when it's playing something the audience has seen before. There's a little courtyard garden up ahead: dead leaves and monochrome rose bushes.

The ground is greasy under foot, but I grip with my toes through the slick soles of my shoes, and fall into a rhythm. It's freezing cold, but I'm feeling something, somehow... new. It's a prickliness across my back and a kind of gentle warmth in my belly. I feel taller. Stronger. Recharged.

The gun, clinking against my ribs with every stride.

And me, thinking: manic and hungry and scared and on fire...

Six bullets.

Six shots at happiness.

4

The Guildhall clock is halfway through its 9 a.m. carillon as I jog across Alfred Gelder Street towards the Hull Crown Court. *Oranges and Lemons*, say the bells.

Sky up above the colour of school socks.

Rain on the way.

Couple of vans parked on the kerb, satellite dishes on their roofs. TV lot are here, with their good suits and perfect enunciation and their unnerving ability to look sincere when they're going live to the studio.

A honk of a horn: commuters losing their shit as they inch forward in insulting increments, fighting for a space, fighting each other, fighting the world and losing...

Three photographers in joyless bobble hats are huddling by the steps, looking at the backs of their cameras the way people are starting to look at their phones. I recognise them all. Alan from the *Hull Mail* greets me with a nod of his head, sending his thick bifocals an inch down his nose. Garry, from the *Yorkshire Post*, mutters a greeting from between his beard and his hat, and Dean, one of the local freelancers, gives me a smile. They all look chilly and put-upon, but have the air of those who have practiced being cold over the course of the last thirty years, and have learned that moaning is a leisure pursuit and better enjoyed over a pint.

"Going to be a bumpy ride, this one," says Alan, blowing out a cloud of smoke. He is cupping his dog-end in his hand, embers towards his palm, as though concealing it from prying eyes.

I insert myself into the huddle.

"A week at least," he continues. "Even Roper's starting to get jumpy. Reckons Cadbury might plead manslaughter and the CPS will agree."

I give a snort and shake my head. "No chance. They've got his DNA. They found her in his flat. Houdini couldn't escape from this one. The family would bloody riot. And Roper doesn't get jumpy. Cadbury did it."

"You know that and so do I, but you know what juries are like. Law of averages, innit? You get twelve people together, one of them's got to be a fucking idiot. Could be worse. We've got a backgrounder ready to go."

"He won't plead," I say. "He's nowt to lose."

Alan gives me a knowing smile. "You haven't done your backgrounder, I can tell."

"I have," I say, forcing a smile. "Blinding stuff."

"Bollocks. Mum won't talk, we don't know Dad, and we've all got the same stuff from the victim's family. What have you got that we haven't?"

I try to look as though I'm sitting on a blinding exclusive. "Have to wait and see," I say, smugly.

He shakes his head, not buying it. "You've got nowt."

Somebody in a suit crosses the brick forecourt carrying a briefcase. The three snappers turn, lift their cameras, reel off a couple of shots, and then turn away. In unison, they peer at the tiny digital viewers on the backs of the cameras. Happy, they let them drop.

"I take it they haven't arrived yet then?" I ask, lighting a fag, back to the wind.

Garry shrugs. "Family? Haven't seen them. Coppers might have sneaked them in the back but I doubt it. They've been champion up until now though. Can't see them suddenly playing silly beggars, unless that lass in the press office has told them to clam up. Anyway, Wendy said she's going to bring me down a holiday snap of Ella for the backgrounder."

"That's the mum, yeah?"

Garry nods. "Yeah. Nice lady. She's keeping the whole family together. Copper told me she hasn't even cried yet. Not like the dad. He's aged twenty years since this happened. Honestly, when you see him it breaks your heart."

"Him that identified her, wasn't it?" Alan again. Everybody's pretending they know more than everybody else. It's all part of the game.

Garry looks at him like he's slow-witted. "No, none of them had to. How could they? Her face was such a mess they had to use dental records and her jewellery. Poor lass. Such a pretty girl."

It's one of those unspoken rules in journalism: an unacknowledged box-ticking exercise that news editors run through when deciding how many column inches to give to a murder, and the ensuing trial. The pretty ones are always front page news. A good family helps too, whatever the hell that is. You really hit the jackpot when they're pretty, and blue-eyed, and white, and middle class. Those are the stories that really gets Middle England tumescent over its Alpen. As a reporter for the Press Association, I'm above such considerations, but I moonlight with half a dozen different agencies, altering my style and nudging the facts into different shapes depending upon the requirements of the different newsdesks. I can be *Daily Star* in the morning, *Telegraph* of an afternoon and *Socialist Worker* of an evening. It can make a chap with one or two loose wires feel positively schizophrenic.

"Surprised he didn't get away with it on an insanity plea. Been in more nut-houses than a hungry squirrel." Garry again.

Me, shaking my head. Then, casually, unable to resist showing off: "I'll be getting chapter and verse on all that later on. Seeing his mother this afternoon."

A few whistles and nods of a job well done. "Where d'you find her? Haven't got a bloody word with her. Told young Tom to fuck off, and we don't let Tony H near women, as a rule. They tend to call the police."

I give a smile and gesture at myself. "Talent and charm, lads."

We start to laugh, as Garry snorts and calls me a flash bastard.

I gesture at the TV crews. "See they've made the effort then. Didn't give a damn when she was missing, did they? Always the same. We do the donkey work then they swoop in with their cheque books out and fuck it all up for the rest of us. I guarantee you they'll be here for day one, sod off, then back for the verdict."

Garry gives a shrug and sucks through his teeth, no doubt searching for a drop of residual Stella Artois. "If it was London they'd have been all over this from the start. Eighteen-year-old girl in a wedding dress cut up in an alleyway 100 yards from her own front door? Kiddy-fiddler in the dock. Would be a bloody swarm of the bastards if it was London."

"Some new faces," I say nodding at two TV people, fiddling with equipment with freezing fingers. One is a black lad in his late twenties, the other a middle-aged woman, wearing a stripy ski hat with tassels hanging down below her matching scarf. I size her up. Londoner. Money.

"Oh you'll love this," says Alan, suddenly gleeful. "They're with Roper. Supercop's having a TV documentary made on him."

"You're joking! Christ, he does himself no favours does he?"

"Aye, one of those fly-on-the-wall jobs. Some satellite channel following the investigation – Roper as the star. We carried a piece on it last week, but a lazy bastard like you won't have bothered picking up a copy."

"Jesus. I bet he's loving that."

"Turning into a proper celebrity, our Douglas. He gets fan mail every time he goes on Crimewatch. Must be hard for him to kick the shit out of suspects when they're asking for autographs."

I stamp on my cigarette butt, and realise that for the last five minutes I've felt good. Felt at home. Haven't thought about the loaded gun in my pocket or the blood on my hands.

"Reckon I'll get on inside then. Leave you to freeze to death. You staying long?"

"Staying for the duration, I think. I'll check with the desk in a few hours."

I give a smile and trot up the steps, pull back the glass door and stride in. There are two security desks, one to the right and one to the left. Jim, the old guy with a grey moustache and a rattly cough that can clear a room, is at the one on the left. He takes the job seriously, so I ignore him and turn right.

Sally the security guard is smiling as I approach. She's sweet on me, is Sal. Thirty-one, buxom, with short red hair and glasses, she's managed to turn me into her ultimate fantasy figure in the three years since I first started idly chatting her up. She's become useful since then, always letting me know if the case I'm after has changed dates or location, or if the families of crime victims have slipped out the back to avoid photographers. She buys me little things once in a while and sends filthy texts when she's been alone with a bottle of Lambrini, but she's a decent lass, and worth the hassle. It doesn't take much to keep her interested, and she never makes me empty my pockets as I pass through the metal detectors. She's also the only security guard in the building under the age of sixty.

"Morning, princess," I say as I breeze through the gates. There are three loud beeps from the metal detector, but nobody says anything. Security is a joke. We reckon the contract has been franchised to Al-Qaeda.

"Morning, Owen," she says, blush already creeping out of the top of her navy blue uniform. "Big day – quite the circus. I tried to save you a seat but the usher said it was first-come-first-served."

"Story of my life," I smile, and then lean in to whisper in her ear. "I'm never first to come."

She giggles, and blushes, and I'm about to give her a little cuddle when I remember the gun and decide not to risk it. "Is he here yet?" I ask, quietly.

"The defendant?"

"Yes, Shane Cadbury. He's coming from Wakefield Nick, isn't he? They'll never get him here on time. Never bloody do. Judge Skelton goes spare with 'em every time and they still turn up half an hour late."

"The family haven't turned up yet either. If you want to go for a coffee I'll give you a shout when they arrive." She smiles at me, eager to please. Then she spoils it, cocking her head and looking all wistful and sincere. "Everything sorted out with your sister?" she asks.

She may as well have slapped me.

"Same bloody story," I say, automatically. "Don't worry about it."

I curse myself. Christ, why did I tell Sal about Kerry? Why tell anyone? I don't know if I'm ashamed of Kerry, or ashamed of myself, or if there's no shame there at all. I don't know if it's all my fault, but I do know it's my responsibility.

"I'll get it sorted," I mumble, mostly to myself. I turn away as I say it, so she doesn't see the look that crosses my face as I think about my little sister. The baby of the family and its brightest star, right up until the moment I did what I did.

She's smacked up to the eyeballs, most days. Bruises around every vein. Hasn't eaten anything but cigarettes and cheap alcohol in weeks. She's wretched when I think of her. Painfully thin. Blue veins traceable through translucent skin.

Ribs cutting her from the inside. Nothing in her eyes. She's drooling, gently, into her blonde hair; legs draped over her landlord's shoulders or wrapped around her dealer's waist.

She's almost slid too far, has Kerry. She's almost beyond my reach. Almost too far gone to pull back.

Suddenly my head is full of her, full of images that the pills have always succeeded in keeping blurry and peripheral.

Kerry. The bright girl with the high cheekbones and strong, slender limbs, who loved animals and birds and flowers and trees, and who wanted to save the world, and who loved her brother more than anything. Kerry, who didn't turn from me when I did what I did. Kerry, who tried to keep us all together, and who found that the occasional spliff helped her keep her own monsters quiet. Kerry. Who got in with the wrong people when her brother was away, and never really came back.

"I'm off next week, if you want to pay me a house call," says Sal, with the same hopeful expression she has used on me for as long as I've known her.

"I'll think about it, princess," I say, with a wink that chases away my thoughts. "I'll think good and hard."

I let my hand brush her waist as I turn away and head up the winding stairs to the first floor. She wriggles like a happy cat.

The stairs are in the middle of a circular room. Consultation rooms, corridors, and the courtrooms, all lead off the main landing. A big window faces out onto the street, with a row of padded seats in front of it, and a metal headboard that makes quite a noise when you smack it as you sit down. Circular padded chairs, all facing outwards, are arranged haphazardly across the rest of the floor space.

The place is almost deserted at this early hour. I smile hello at a couple of ushers in their black gowns as I tramp over to the window and stare out past the centuries-old splendour of St Mary's Church and its bell tower blackened by the smoke and fog.

I stare down at the forecourt, where three of the *Hull Mail* reporters have joined Garry and the others. The *Mail* always sends reporters mob-handed for the big cases. I'll be doing this on my own. It took me a long while to persuade the Press Association there was a need for an office in Hull, but after they spent most of the previous year sending lads over from York and Leeds to cover the umpteen murders that had taken place, they decided it would be cheaper to have me based here full time. I don't have an office, and the long-promised laptop has yet to arrive, so I do things the old-fashioned way, with a notepad and a telephone, ringing my stories across direct to the copytakers. I've only been on the payroll four months, but they seem happy with me. The money is steady, and a damn sight better than when I was freelance; a hooker without the benefits of a pimp.

I slump down in one of the chairs, careful not to bang my skull on the inexplicable metal head rest. Pick up somebody else's *Daily Star*. Look at the headlines. Feel my head fall and the familiar synapses of depression and despair flaring in my skull. Such insipid shit. Such bland and meaningless fucking bollocks, and me a fucking star at creating it. No-mark celebrity shags another. Reality TV show nobody cares about might be rigged. Politicians lying. NHS failing to meet targets. Police raiding the wrong mosque and now appealing for calm in the Muslim community. Shit without flavour. Pain without feeling. Death, documented by people who don't know how it tastes.

I light a cigarette, and allow myself the ghost of a smile as I flip the wheel on the Zippo lighter, and let the sensation catapult me back to the mayhem of last night. I don't flinch from the memories. The shudder that passes through my body is exhilarating. I move my arm and through the lining of my coat, allow the gun to fall into the crook of my elbow. I hold it like a cuddly toy, a source of comfort.

I could have been dead today. I could have been floating down towards the Trent with mud in my pockets, my face white and bloated, leaves in my mouth and dirt in my hair.

5

"I've never heard that word before," says McAvoy, a little awestruck, a little afraid. He glances across at Roisin, hunkered down inside the collar of his waterproof. She's driving, jewelled fingers on the steering wheel, staring across the big empty car park, her vision given bars by her big false eyelashes. The windscreen wipers screech across the rain-smeared glass. It's a less offensive sound than the stream of Traveller invective that she unleashed at the Boothferry Road roundabout not long before.

"Which word?" she asks, amused, and flicks a glance in his direction.

"Most of them, actually," says McAvoy, considering. Roisin is rarely given to temper but when the outbursts come, it seems that somebody has mixed magnesium with potassium chlorate. She explodes, and burns out with an extraordinary intensity. McAvoy finds it frightening and volatile and absolutely beautiful, just like the rest of her. He treats her like a rogue firework: afraid to go near without a bucket of sand. She frequently tells him he's an eejit, shaking her head at a joke that only she seems to understand. McAvoy, already baffled that somebody like her could truly

48

love somebody like him, hopes that whatever the joke is, it continues to please her.

"What was it I said?" she asks, with a smile that it is safe to approach. "It just comes out, like the songs I sing Fin. It's in your soul – you know. English is the wrong language for a Traveller – we're poets."

"I think I picked up 'dinlaw', 'bawlaw' and '*transpirate mish*' and I know enough to guess I shouldn't ask for a direct translation."

Roisin grins. McAvoy puts his hand on hers and gives it a gentle squeeze. Rolls her wedding ring around under his big, clean fingers. It was her grandmother's, given to McAvoy to present to his bride when Papa Teague saw the pitiful specimen that McAvoy had used all of his savings to acquire. The ring on her finger is three hundred years old, studded with rubies and sapphires. He's always afraid somebody will see it and presume him to be a successful, wealthy man. When he pictures himself – bumbling, clumsy, inert with indecision – he is painfully aware how poorly he measures up.

He looks across at the woods that ring the car park and feels his chest clench as he considers what he hopes to find within. He wonders what it says about him, how despicable a person he must be, that he sees a potential death as an opportunity to curry favour with the boss who values him so little. He hears himself start to prattle. "I can drive back, if you'd prefer. The traffic at this time of day – well, I'm still getting used to it. There doesn't seem to be any sense to the way they built this city." He shakes his head. "Newland Avenue – the one with the nice cafés. Rumour has it they got the plans for the parking spaces upside down. Outside Sainsbury's you have to go past the space, then indicate, and reverse it at a 270-degree angle. I'll take you there. It's very entertaining…"

Roisin laughs, all lip gloss and white teeth. She has a stud in her top lip and a succession of large hooped rings in her dainty earlobes. She's wearing a top that doesn't cover her midriff, beneath a velour tracksuit top. McAvoy, sitting in the passenger seat in a blue Tesco suit and shabby raincoat, feels like a carthorse next to a unicorn.

"Have we been here?" asks Roisin, pulling in. She glances across the mostly-empty car park at the hugeness of the Humber Bridge. "We've walked that, I remember. Was I pregnant? Bloody freezing but an amazing view. Aye, we came here. Cliffs and trees, yeah? You told me about the cliffs. They're white and made of chalk, which is why the locals call it Little Switzerland. See, I remember stuff. I love it when you tell me things."

"Really?"

"Yes, ye fecking eejit."

McAvoy looks into the back seat, where Fin, strapped into the car seat, is looking around, mildly intrigued. He catches his dad's eye. "Did Mammy upset the other driver?"

McAvoy nods, and puts a finger to his lips. "It was the other driver's fault, Fin. Mammy is an excellent driver. He shouldn't have been so worried about his precious Audi. As Mammy told him, there was loads of room."

"Too right there fecking was," growls Roisin, re-applying lip gloss in the rear-view mirror. She smacks her lips, then blows her son a kiss. Then she gives her attention to her husband. "Go on then. Be a police officer. Do your questions and stuff. They're ladies – you'll have them eating out of your lap."

McAvoy feels his ears go pink. "It's hand, Ro…"

"Aye, whatever," she grins, and gives a full, throaty laugh. She leans over, quick as a kingfisher taking prey, and kisses him full on the mouth. He feels her warmth. Tastes her. Feels her climb inside him and settle down: a fox slinking into the warmth of a familiar burrow.

The cold wind swirls around him as he makes his way across the car park towards the row of units. There's a little shop, and an information centre, but they're both closed for the winter. The café is the only building with its lights on. There are some white plastic tables dotted around outside for anybody keen to sit in a car park in the drizzle, but none are occupied. He can make out a couple of customers inside: hunch-backed, windblown characters, protecting plates of fried food and mugs of tea as if they were vultures guarding a carcass.

The door opens. Framed in the warm yellow light that spills from the café, is a small, dark-haired woman. She's the same height as Roisin, but more amply proportioned. She's got a cigarette in her left hand and a Styrofoam cup in her right. With her big sunglasses, leather jacket and biker boots, she looks like a hungover rock star. She inches her dark glasses down her nose as she considers him. He notices bangles on her wrist. She's wearing hooped earrings too, though they are not as extravagant as his wife's. She doesn't look dissimilar to Roisin's mum, though he decides he should keep this, and every other helpful observation, to himself. He suddenly recognises her. He's seen her before, bustling her way out of a meeting room at Queen's Gardens, glaring at a manila folder held in fingers locked as if in death. It's something about the set of the jaw. She's attractive, though he hates himself at once for allowing the thought to occur. She's a senior officer from across the river. Grimsby Nick. Ran a CID unit looking into cold cases until budget cuts put a stop to it. Took time out just as he was arriving in Hull – some 'unnamed personal drama' that stalled a stellar career. He stops as if confronted by a childhood hero.

"You're a big old piece of policeman," she says, sucking her lower lip and nodding, approvingly. "I've been reading your name off your business card. Still can't get it right, so I'll call you 'Sergeant'. You can call me 'Guv' or 'Boss', or 'sweetheart' if you want a swift headbutt to the groin."

McAvoy feels all the breath rush out of him. He's used to feeling out of his depth, but in the presence of this small, daunting woman, he's absolutely drowning.

"I'm Aector McAvoy," he says, and is pretty sure he's right. "The owner – she called me – said there had been an unusual discovery…"

She gives a bark of laughter. "Unusual? Yes, that would be about right, Sergeant. Two bodies, one with a bullet in his head and the other without much head to speak of? Yeah, that's pretty unusual."

McAvoy takes a moment to process things. If he were wearing a hat, he would take it off and clutch it to his chest. His face becomes solemn and filled with sadness. He licks dry lips, and looks down at the floor.

"Ha!" laughs the DCI. "Jesus, Sergeant, did you go to Stagecoach as a child? Best bloody amateur dramatics I've seen in an age."

McAvoy snaps his head up, a hard look briefly gripping

his face before he can get it under control. He suddenly remembers her name. Patricia. Patricia Pharaoh.

"There is a fatality, then?" he asks, quietly. "I advised the owner to dial 999 but she was most insistent it wasn't anything to worry about so I said I would take a look…"

She shakes her head at him, sunglasses slipping down her face to reveal piercing blue eyes, and the darkness beneath. *She doesn't sleep much*, thinks McAvoy, automatically. *And there's pain there…*

"Well, you'll be delighted to hear that I've also had a perfectly good day ruined. I only wanted a pissing cup of coffee to wash down the ibuprofen. Then the young lad's asking when the big police officer is going to get here and whether he can go back to look at the body, and despite my absolute desire to scurry out and leave it to you sods on this bank of the river, I felt duty bound to ask the questions that a good police officer should ask. Such as 'what fucking body?'"

"And you got a reply?"

She drops her cigarette and grinds it out. McAvoy notices the mud and leaves on the flanks of her biker boots. "Just what I needed after the weekend I've had. Followed the lad down to the most sorry excuse for a pond you've ever seen. Rummaging about in the undergrowth like a tramp looking for a place to build a second home, and there they are. Poor bastards."

"You've called it in?"

She chews her lip, staring past him. He follows her gaze and realises she is looking at the people carrier, where he can just make out the shape of Roisin, rocking extravagantly to whatever CD she has put in the player. He looks back and sees the accusatory frown on the DCI's face.

"Roper's team, aren't you?" She wrinkles her nostrils, sucks her teeth. "What a waste. Had a quick glance at your file when they gave me your card and said you were making your way over as if you were the bloody sheriff. You've done some good work. Big brain, from what I can tell. Helped with some very difficult cases. Friends in high places and enemies in even higher ones. What a fascinating chap you are. Shame you've wasted your one favour on hitching your wagon to that bent bastard."

McAvoy looks confused. "I don't understand..."

"Well, that's one good thing, at least," muses Pharaoh, lighting another cigarette and pouring the last dregs of her coffee onto her boot then rubbing the toe against the rear of her dark jeans. "Most of the blokes who've worked for me would rather die than say they don't understand. Not many of the ladies willing to admit to it either."

"Should I go?" asks McAvoy, looking pained. "You've obviously got this under control..."

She laughs, big and loud and seemingly quite happy with the question. "Fucking hell," she says, puffing out her cheeks. "I bet Roper bloody loves you! No wonder he's got you out on loan to any department with a shitty job that needs doing. You're not his type at all."

"What type is that?" asks McAvoy, before he can stop himself. He wants to know about the two dead men.

"Bastards, normally," muses Pharaoh. "Ambitious, dickled, right-wing, misogynistic uber-cunts who'll do whatever he tells them to do and then lie about it afterwards if it helps them slip up the greasy pole behind him and pay a few quid off the mortgage on their Lanzarote timeshare."

McAvoy recoils, raising his hands. He glances back to

the people carrier and the safety offered within. He hopes Roisin will come and ask him if everything's OK, then slip her hand into his and take him home. He bites down, back teeth mashing together, wishing he were a better man or, at the very least, a less feeble excuse for one. He stands still: a schoolboy waiting to be told how many times he must write out 'I must not be useless' on the blackboard.

"That the missus, is it?" asks Pharaoh, chattily. "You know there's an asterisk next to your name in your human resources file, don't you? And if you happen to enter your good lady's name into the PNC database or HOLMES, it comes up as flagged. You need to be an assistant chief constable to view the record of your Roisin. You really are a fascinating chap."

McAvoy rubs a hand over his face. Something sticky catches his thumb. He realises he's wearing pink lip gloss. He turns crimson. Dies a little inside.

"In answer to your question, McAvoy, I have indeed called it in. But I've done the sensible thing of leaving a message on a phone that I know won't be checked for at least a couple of hours. That means I am absolved of responsibility and don't have to get sucked into the investigation. So, if you want to be Roper's good doggy for the day and get into his good graces, you can tell him you've got a case that looks like it could have headlines aplenty, and you know how he likes his headlines. He might even give you a few slices of packet ham while he tickles your tummy and rubs behind your ear. He's like that, is Doug. As for me, I get to go home, and deal with my own shit, safe in the knowledge that I did my duty."

McAvoy watches her mouth move as she talks. Stares

into her blue eyes, peeping over the top of her frames. He sees a flicker of something: an intelligence, certainly, but something more. Something that tells him that she's playing a role. There are tears inside her: tears unspilled. His compassion overwhelms him. He lowers his voice, cocks his head, gives her his full focus, as he remembers why she took the leave of absence. Her husband. An aneurysm. Left in a near-permanent vegetative state but clinging onto life. And her. Four daughters and a stepson to raise. He understands why she wants no part in an investigation over this side of the river. She has too much to do.

"Why are you telling me?" he asks, gently. "Surely I'll have to explain that I saw you here. You're telling me that you've purposely avoided involving yourself. You clearly hate Roper and his unit, yet you're handing him a double murder. And you don't know me at all and yet you're talking to me like I've personally affronted you. Is there something wrong? I'd be glad to listen. I'll call it in, and we can go and talk. I can see you've been crying... I'm OK at listening. My wife says I am..."

Pharaoh glares up at him, a sheen of moisture veiling her blue eyes. She looks at him the way Roisin often does: baffled and exasperated, unsure whether to throw something at his head or bite his lip.

"You're an interesting man," says Pharaoh, shaking her head. Then she walks past him. "Tell Roper you saw me and that I told him this was more up his street than mine. And tell your wife to start dressing you as if somebody loves you. That suit's too small for you. And so's she."

McAvoy stays silent. Watches her storm across the car park towards a little two-seater convertible. She pauses, momentarily, by McAvoy's people carrier. Gives Roisin a stare that she returns. Shakes her head, and trudges on.

McAvoy watches her go. Wonders what the hell just happened. Then he pulls out his mobile, takes a breath, and calls Doug Roper.

"Sir, this is McAvoy. Yes, that one. The sergeant. Erm, I think, well…"

He clears his throat. Closes his eyes. Winces, as the words come out in his low Scottish accent.

"We've got a murder."

6

The lads from the *Mail* appear at the top of the stairs. Tom, Tony T and Tony H. Tom's a young lad, first job out of college. A middle class southerner, he's doing his best to fit in with the pack and laughs along at in-jokes he doesn't understand, but has an eye for a good story and a nice turn of phrase.

Tony T has been at the *Mail* for an age. The running joke is that he's approaching the end of some unique prison sentence, imposed for a despicable crime. Mid-fifties, he's one of those blokes who earns more than the editor because he joined the company in the days when journalism was well paid, and has watched his salary creep up ever since, on a contract written in stone. It's been a long while since he was bothered about being any good at his job, but he knows Hull better than anyone. He's one of the few *Mail* reporters I'm ever likely to bump into in the pub, but can become a little maudlin by his third pint. His wife and daughter died within weeks of each other about ten years ago – wife from cancer, daughter from three bottles of paracetamol. We indulge Tony T for his moments of despondency. He doesn't do much. Picks and chooses his jobs, and takes pleasure in fuck all.

Tony H is something altogether different. He belongs to an age when reporters smoked cigarettes without filters, bashed out genuine stories on Imperial typewriters that made the floor shake, and when 600 words of half-decent scandal could bring down governments. When readers actually believed. He looks sepia. Black suit, white shirt, black tie, ashen face. Dirty mac. Yellow fingers. The only thing missing from his general appearance is a trilby hat with a 'press' ticket stuck in it. He's a walking cliché, a proper ducker and diver, a wheeler-dealer, a heartless, compassionless hack who's always one last warning away from losing his job. He's an utter wanker and I like him immensely. Any decent story the *Mail* ever runs comes from Tony H. He arrived in the city six years ago after leaving a paper in the Midlands under a cloud, and within days had found out the name, address and inside leg measurement of the thirteen-year-old boy rumoured to be providing a service to the then-assistant chief constable of the local police force. Tony H's legend continues to grow. The villains in Hull think of him as more of a threat than the coppers. We usually share information if we turn up on the same job, which we frequently do.

"Owen Lee the Lonely," says Tony T with a smile, as though he's the first person to think it up. "You're up early."

"Well Simmo told us local lads to get a good seat, didn't he? Good old Simmo. Always thinking of us."

"You consider yourself local, do you?" asks Tony H, showing teeth the size of tombstones.

"I've got a foot in both camps, mate," I say. "Local contacts and national interests, community stories with national acclaim. Best of all possible worlds, Rat-boy."

"Fuck you, Voltaire. Nice shiner."

Tony H and I grin at each other, and young Tom looks nervous. The three lads slump down into the seats beside me, one on either side, Tom furthest away. He's the only one who bangs his head. I remember the days.

"Looking flashy," says Tom.

"That's me."

"King of Bling, ain't you," smiles Tony H. "Terrified of magpies."

"Doesn't hurt to look good."

"Wouldn't know."

"Court One, is it?" asks Tony T.

"Yeah, we should all fit in OK." I say. "Judge Skelton. Won't take any shit."

"Going to be a bloody circus," points out Tony H, gleefully. "What did you bring?"

"Oh shit," I say, suddenly remembering that the stakes in our long-running competition have risen dramatically over the course of the last few court cases. "Forgot, mate. What about you?"

Tony H reaches into his inside pocket and pulls out a cut-throat razor and a toy hand grenade. There are whistles of appreciation as he says "Beat that".

We've been playing this game for a while now. Court cases get fucking boring after a while so we like to pretend we're terrorists. It started when a young lass from the *Grimsby Telegraph* got into court with a fruit-knife in her handbag and mentioned it to me and Tony. We wondered how far we could take it. We knew security was shit but we really wanted to push it. We've been getting more competitive ever since. Tony brought in a rocket launcher he had made out of the insides of toilet rolls a few weeks back. Security didn't say a word.

Young Tom, who wants to show willing, pulls a hammer out of his coat pocket. "What do you think of that?" he asks.

"Fucking hell," we all say.

"Put that away, you daft bastard," says Tony H, pissed off. "Christ, you're not all there, are you?"

Tom sulks, and wonders if he misunderstood the rules.

Tony winks at me, then says: "Did you hear Cadbury sacked his barrister not three weeks ago? Got a last minute replacement."

"Oh aye? Who?"

Tony H grins and lights a Hamlet from the tip of his last one. He blows a smoke-ring which drifts away and expands to frame the 'No Smoking' sign. He strings out the moment. "Your old mate. Tin-Tin Choudhury."

Oh fuck.

"Seriously?"

"He might be bringing you your thank you card."

I give in to a rueful laugh. "As long as it's got a fat brown envelope inside. By Christ I earned it. Fucking hell." I spit the words and think about the implications. "Well there go my chances of getting a copy of the opening defence statement. Or a chat with Cadbury when he gets sent down. Fuck."

Tom looks for a moment like he's about to put his hand up and ask a question, but stops himself when he remembers he's a big boy now and is allowed to speak to the naughty men without getting told off. "You got history, have you Owen?"

I sigh and stub out my cigarette on the underside of my boot. It's still encrusted with mud. "Nothing a little bullet in the brain wouldn't sort out," I say.

Tin-Tin Choudhury: the barrister responsible for the biggest embarrassment of my professional life. I picture him, floating there like the Cheshire cat. Face an amalgamation of Saddam Hussein and Bagpuss. Body like a bag of custard in a three-piece suit, or in Choudhury's case, a three-piece suite. Poirot moustache. Trumpet-player cheeks. Hair dyed bottle-black under a blood-red turban. Shoes shiny enough to see up junior solicitors' skirts. White teeth. Likes to play with a cricket ball while he's thinking. Fat. Monstrously fucking fat. Polished. Syrupy. Kisses women's hands when introduced. A fucking crook.

Four years ago, when I was still working at the *York Evening Press* and knackering myself and my car with the daily journey through to York, Choudhury fucked me over. Richie Prospect, a local lad and king of the daytime quiz show, was up at court charged with a fairly nasty attack on a young girl. Prospect, he of the orange tan, capped teeth and infinite smugness, was unbelievably guilty. The police had his teary confession, and they had the sworn testimony of umpteen ex-girlfriends about the weird games he liked to play in the bedroom. But Prospect had Tin-Tin Choudhury. He rubbed his jewelled hands together and rose to the challenge. Prospect pleaded not guilty. Tin-Tin strung out the legal wrangling, got adjournment after adjournment, while the screams of the press reached fever pitch. Entire teams of reporters were taken off-diary, and digging into Prospect's seedy past became a full-time job. I got the lot. By the time the trial came, I knew everything from Prospect's dick size to the wattage of his microwave. I was just itching to go to print with it. The trial lasted a fortnight, punctuated by the most cut-throat defence case ever seen at York Crown Court. It didn't do any good. By the time the jury retired, it was clear that Prospect was going down. Then Choudhury had his master stroke.

Me.

The jury retired on a Friday at 2.30 p.m. – the worst time imaginable, missing any useful deadline, and threatening to spill the case over into the next week. I couldn't see the jury coming back with a verdict that day, and made a judgement call. I went to the pub. Choudhury saw me leave. He caught me on the way out, and suggested I give him my business card. Out of the goodness of his heart, he promised to let me know if the jury suddenly came back. Two hours later, he called. Choudhury told this panic-stricken, hapless reporter that I had missed the verdict, and that Prospect had been convicted. He offered to bail me out, gave me details of the sentence, and waited patiently by the phone, feeding me details, as I cobbled the case together.

It all landed perfectly – just in time for the evening deadline. I told the newsdesk it was over, sent my story – and told the IT department to launch my background features onto the website, detailing every sordid encounter in Prospect's past, safe in the knowledge that there was no jury to prejudice and no risk of contempt of court. I sat back, feet on my desk, proud of a job well done, and waited for the plaudits to roll in. Then the phone rang. John, a decent freelancer from York who died a couple of years back, asked me what the fuck I was playing at. The tumblers of recognition began to fall into place, as the agony of comprehension poured ice water into my veins. Choudhury had played me. The jury hadn't come back with a verdict at all. They were still deliberating. I had just released months of work into cyberspace, labelling Prospect every variety of pervert. I had just been fucked, and my ass, busily augmenting and diminishing from the size of a manhole cover to a poppy seed and back again, was suddenly all too aware. Other news sites spotted the story and lifted it. Within an hour, half the country had seen or heard all about Prospect's past, while the jury were still sitting in their cosy room trying to decide if he was guilty of anything whatsoever. Of course, the entire case collapsed. Choudhury argued that his client could never get a fair trial. I was roasted by my bosses and the Press Complaints Commission until my brain was running out of my ears. Of course, I fought my corner, pathetically pointing the finger at Choudhury; even making a complaint to the Bar Council, but nothing stuck. I kept my job by the absolute skin of my teeth. When Prospect was finally sent down for raping a teenage girl, I was there in the press box to watch. By then, even Choudhury wouldn't go near him. Those in the know, knew. Knew exactly what Choudhury had done. He had made his point. He had pulled a stroke so beautiful, it made him want to pull and stroke. And when he finally saw me again, eyes meeting as we crossed paths one cold November day at the Old Bailey, he had the temerity to smile, raise an eyebrow, and turn away. It was a wound that had never healed.

I let the weight of the gun rest on my arm.

And stroke it like a puppy.

7

Getting bored of small talk, now. Of Tony's tall tales and Tom's questions. They're running over the details of the case in voices too loud and too unfeeling, oblivious to the milling crowd around us, waiting for their own trials and hearings to begin – unused to this. Unaccustomed to the violence that we chronicle daily, and to which so many of our number have become immune.

I want to distance myself from them. I find myself scanning the faces in the crowd, the cheap shirts and ties, the tracksuits, wondering if any of them knew her, if they loved her, if they can hear Tom setting out the details of the autopsy at maximum volume.

I stand, stretch, feel the pressure of the gun and the notebook.

Walk away, through the bodies, no direction but somewhere else.

"Now there's a shite for sore eyes. Looking good, sunbeam."

A voice that likes the way it sounds kicks me in the side of the head. I turn and see Detective Superintendent Doug Roper treating me to his very best smile. Supercop. Shirley fucking Temple. Celebrity copper and tabloid darling. Thirty-nine. Expertly-trimmed moustache, with a tuft beneath his lower lip. A tan he's worked at. Six foot one, straight-backed, but casual. Eyes that twinkle like the last embers in the hearth, and with about as much genuine warmth. Smile like a string of pearls, and a smirk like a bear trap. Leather, knee-length coat, brown Ben Sherman suit and Gucci loafers. A cloud of Aramis. The faintest whiff of violence, and cunt.

"Now then, sunbeam, you here on time, are you?"

"I wanted to give myself the best possible chance to get close to you, Doug – I knew there would be an admiring throng."

"Ah yes, it can be distracting. Told them to give me a moment's peace, actually. They've thronged off to do whatever throngs do. Nice to have a bit of peace – a bit of one-to-one time with a sophisticated gentleman."

"Kind of you to say so. You're looking good, though you know that, of course."

"Not so bad yourself, son. Bit rumpled around the edges, few creases that wouldn't sit well on a chap like me, but you just about pass muster. Few bruises though, lad. Bit of yellow under the old eye, there. Bit of a scuff on the right hand too. You been up to mischief, Owen?"

We stand, inches apart, enjoying the game. He likes me about as much as I like him, but we engage in pretence because we both suspect we might not like anybody else very much either.

"So," I say. "This going to be a walk in the park?"

"Doesn't do to count your chickens," he says, talking into my eyes in that way of his, where you can see your own reflection floating, as though trapped, on the blue irises.

"The Butterworths are in with a couple of my lads and it doesn't half bring it home how important this one is. Got to get this monster put away, sunbeam. Got to."

"Come on, Doug, you don't need to give me the speech. The cameras aren't on you. We both know he's going down. It's open and shut."

"Wish it was," he says, taking a tin of cigarillos from the inside pocket of his leather jacket and lighting one with a match he has ignited on his thumb in a deft and slightly showy motion. "He's got Choudhury, now, hasn't he? Which means all bets are off. And if what we're hearing is right, we could be in the shit."

"Can you say?" I ask, wondering if I should pull out my notebook or keep it chatty. "You know we can't write anything that might fuck up the trial so there's no harm."

The grey sky beyond the glass suddenly darkens further, as if the sun just shivered and closed its eyes. A heavy rain begins to pummel the windows and the walls and we have to raise our voices to be heard over the tattoo that the raindrops are drumming on the roof.

"You'll find out soon enough anyway, laddo," he says through a delicate puff of smoke. "There's a so-called witness that has suddenly appeared. You know Lewis, the lad who told us where to find Ella? Well he got sent down a few months back for some minor stuff, and this witness that Choudhury's come up with was Lewis's cellmate for a few weeks. We have a feeling this lad is going to tell the jury Lewis confessed all to him. Bragged about framing his thick mate. Could be enough to create a reasonable doubt."

"Fuck."

"Fuck indeed."

I lower my voice, two old friends having a chinwag. "If I was in your shoes I might be tempted to find this new witness and explain the importance of all this to him. Might be tempted to persuade him of the joys of silence."

"Would love to, my friend, but Choudhury's got him secreted away somewhere safe and plush and, besides which, I'm an honest copper and wouldn't dream of trying to get away with such a thing." He twinkles, then adds: "Might get found out."

We stand and brood in silence for a moment, then he says: "Still, it's all good copy for you boys, isn't it?"

"You know this one isn't like that," I say, feeling the hint of sickness rising in my throat. "Ella was an angel. We all want the right man put away. The Butterworths don't deserve this."

"Nobody deserves this," he says.

"Some do," I say, quietly. "You know that."

"Catch you later," he says, with a wink.

There's a prickling starting to spread all over my back. I don't like this. My teeth are hurting. My jaw tight and wired. Cadbury needs to go down. He must. The Butterworths need justice. This case has affected us all. I wrote metres of copy when they were searching for her. Tony and me had been out for a drink not more than a mile from where the attack happened that very night, and we both felt real closeness to her family as soon as we knocked on their door and they invited us in to share photo albums and drink sweet tea and eat their biscuits and talk about their daughter while a monster was brutalising her corpse not far away. They're good people. Their daughter an innocent. In most murder cases you can rationalise it. You can tell yourself that the victim shouldn't have got in that car, or acted that way, or raised their voice at the wrong person, or acted like a slag. But Ella was sweet. She was good and caring and pure, and loved her family and her cats and her fiancé, and she squeezed her wicked thoughts until they disappeared, and she lost her life because she was an angel who stumbled onto a demon's blade.

I think of the funeral, of the bright flowers and the kisses on the cards and the family sitting rigid and regal as the packed crematorium seemed to shudder from the weight of grief in its guts; as the hundreds of mourners, drawn black and grey in savage pencil strokes, wept and wailed and choked back snot as the priest said his words, and how we chuckled, rueful and relieved, as Ella's sister told stories of mischief past, and how tears ran down cheeks and onto notepads and into microphones as we listened to Robbie Williams's voice oozing from the stereo as Ella passed behind the purple curtain and into the flames to the sound of her family's strangled cries, and the words of her favourite song.

I duck into the toilets. Two suits are at the urinals so I head for the nearest of the three cubicles. Sit down on the plastic seat with my head in my hands. The weight in my pocket clinks against the porcelain. Instinctively I look up, as if there might be a shooting gallery of faces peeping over the door

I sit back on the toilet seat, back straight against the cistern, and close my eyes, breathing slowly, as though listening to music.

I hear the voice of the gun. Retrieve it, carefully, as if handling porcelain.

It's black. Gleaming. Rubber on the handle, writing on its side.

For a moment, through the haze of my half-closed eyes, the markings become three distinct words.

KILL THEM ALL...

8

Court One.

    10.26 a.m.

Four minutes to kick-off.

Still no sign of Cadbury.

Families packed in behind me. The hiss of pop bottles opening. The bleep of mobile phones being switched off.

Hands being held. Words of comfort. Wendy in the front row, next to her husband, Arthur. She, regal in a green suit. Made up. Hair permed. Putting on a show. He, shambolic. Jogging pants and a jumper under two coats. White hair. Face red. Eyes the colour of brie. Puffy. Broken. Decent bunch. Poor but proud. Working class. Real class. Some bitter, some hateful. All missing a piece of themselves. Trapped like spiders beneath a glass by the barriers of their loss. Not touching each other. Torn apart by grief.

I'm silent. Drinking it in. Second seat from the right, four feet from the glass partition which separates the decent folk from the accused. Burly security guard in a pressed white shirt. No defendant yet.

Paul from the BBC on my right. Indira from one of the radio stations to my left. Coats still on. Cold inside the courtroom, with its pale walls. Wooden benches and hard seats. Extra seats laid on. We're crowded in, touching elbows, balancing notebooks on knees. Only six hacks can fit behind the actual press bench. We're twisted. Swivelling to face the judge's bench, perched up high at the front. No judge yet.

Below is the court clerk. Roy. Scouse lad. Knows his stuff. Grey pinstripe under his black gown. Salt and pepper hair peeping out from the sides of his curly wig.

Flanked by an usher – thirties, brunette and dumpy, looking like Harry Potter in her black cloak, and a logger – ancient, pale suit, Royal Navy tie, lines in his face that he could keep his spare change in – preparing to fall asleep on his court tape recorder.

Then Choudhury. A blob of silk. Leering over the junior barrister at the bench behind him, and the solicitors behind her. Cricket ball, rolled lasciviously around his palm. A lot of touching. Every word accentuated with a hand on a shoulder or arm.

A pain in my chest just looking at him.

Prosecutor at his side. Elegant. Tall. Straight back. Glasses. Must be fifty-plus under the wig. Crisp seam in his black trousers, shine on his black shoes. Reading through his opening statement, glancing back at his junior, a younger man, to check the occasional fact. Limbering up. Ready to go the distance in a case that could make him.

More solicitors further back. Then coppers. Assistants. Hangers-on.

Evidence bags stuffed under desks. Files. Bundles of folders, law books, stacked like rocks in a dry-stone wall. Jugs of water and tumblers marbled with limescale.

Jury benches still empty.

Different, this time. I've covered hundreds of court cases.

Become immune. This time, I feel it. We all feel it. The whole city gives a damn, this time.

Door opens to my right, behind the glass. Heads turn. Voices drop. Another security guard. Fat. Old. As intimidating as lettuce.

Then comes Cadbury. The man of the hour. The Killer. The Monster. The Chocolate Boy. The Accused.

Late twenties. Round face. Belly hanging over cheap blue jeans. Short-sleeved white shirt untucked on one side. Stains on the front. Goatee beard and two earrings. Tattoos on his forearms. Hair short and unbrushed. Face blank. Staring ahead. Takes his seat between the security guards.

Words from behind me. Mutterings of contempt, of raw hatred.

Wendy and Arthur twisting to see.

Me in the way. Trapped in the glare. Their stare is a flamethrower. It roars through me like white light. It fixes me into my seat. Strips me bare. I expect my misdeeds to be played out on the wall behind me.

I sag, exhausted, as they turn away.

A knock on the door.

Rat-*tat*.

Judge enters. Swish of purple and red. Thin man, stern faced. No nonsense. Street map of capillaries splashed across his nose. Takes his seat. Glances at the papers on his desk. Business-like nod. Already spent half an hour talking to the barristers in his chambers. Refused to be delayed by legal argument. Wants to start today. Finish Friday.

Looks up.

Ready to rock and roll.

"Gentlemen. Shall we have the jury in?"

More bustle. Ushers banging through side doors. Shouts from other rooms. Judge talking. Me staring at the rich splatter-pattern on the curve of my boot. Picking at it with a fingernail.

Red.

Jury enter. Rag-bag bunch. Some in suits. Young lad with a mullet haircut and skinny arms. Couple of mumsy types in polo necks. Gangster-looking guy in a black suit and turtle neck. Gold bracelet. Pensioner with thick glasses. A woman I recognise from a night in The Manchester Arms. The manager from the bookies down Whitefriargate, looking annoyed to be here. All the same expressions. Nervous. Excited. Eager to find out if they'll make the final twelve. Irritated to be here but too curious to leave.

Names called.

Twelve answer and come forward. Always one attractive lass in a jury. This one's about thirty and blonde. Too much eye make-up. Snuggly jumper but a bare stomach. Dirty look about her. Something in the way she carries herself. The type to slap on a bit of roll-on deodorant in the morning rather than have a wash. My type. One to watch.

Always one fat bastard. Always one sensible type who's brought his own notebook. Always a scummy fucker in jogging pants carrying a Netto carrier bag.

The pride of the English legal system. Would lose a pop-quiz against a brick. Can't decide on pizza or Chinese most nights but allowed to pass a verdict on a murder.

Confirming their names now. Taking the oath. Some voices falter. Some can't read the words on the card. Sweet lady with glasses drops the Bible.

Words from the judge. Telling them about their important duty. Playing the kindly role. Making them feel important.

Cadbury tugging at his beard with his right hand. There's a rosary wrapped around the pudgy mitt, clutched tight.

Me. Rolling dried blood between my fingers. Looking around and thinking of murder.

Monsters starting to giggle behind my eyes.

Feeling hysterical. Oppressed. Grinding my teeth. Suddenly overcome. Over-wrought. Looking down, staring at nothing, ground opening beneath my feet. Legs jiggling up and down. Biting lumps of plastic off the Biro between my teeth.

Hungry. Hungry for something.

And the prosecutor is on his feet. Distinguished. At ease. Elevated above the baseness of the actions he is describing.

A voice rolled in brandy, matured in oak barrels, describing horrors unimaginable, filling the courtroom with blood.

Rain.

A hard, persistent drumming on the glass ceiling – angels weeping for a defiled sister.

9

McAvoy stands facing the wind, face so pale it could be reflecting moonlight. He can hear his own heart beating. Can feel his pulse against the strap of his watch. A sharp, diagonal rain comes in from the water and finds the gaps in the canopy of trees, which conspires to soak him while giving the illusion of shelter.

Behind him a tangle of trees and thorns. Sycamore, ash. A holly bush, the remains of a den built by children some time over the weekend. Inside, two dead men. They look like lifeless birds in a ravaged nest.

In his ear, repeating like the sound of an old locomotive, Roisin's words as she departed. "You're good at this. Believe in yourself. You're a good man. A good man. A good man…"

McAvoy chews on his lip. He feels sick. In his nostrils, the smell of Ella; the memory of her; the sensation of her drifting inside him and taking possession of his flesh. He cannot smell the dead men behind him. They are still fresh. He has glimpsed little of them since taking up his position a little back from the footpath, his back to the big chalky cliffs and the tree roots and creepers that snake over and through them like veins.

"A good man," he whispers, and rain sprays from his

lips. He does not know if he believes it. And even if it were true, he wonders whether it marks him out as a good police officer. He has been told for the past decade that he is 'too soft', 'a pushover', a 'sucker for a sob story'. One sergeant, early in his career, told him without malice that the police service was no place for 'bleeding heart liberals' and warned that he would get a reputation as a 'do-gooder' if he continued taking things to heart and trying to make a real change in people's circumstances. McAvoy has mulled over the accusation for the best part of a decade and still can't work out how doing good could merit derision.

"This better be good, Jock! I'm piss-wet through here. Dripping like a fucked fridge!"

McAvoy turns at the sound of the voice. Coming down the wooden steps, clinging onto the greasy handrail and scowling into the downpour, is Detective Inspector Julie Stace. She has a homely, almost mumsy look about her, as if she might work in a pre-school, spending her days singing songs about silly wombats and helping toddlers find missing socks. McAvoy knows that the appearance is misleading. With her sensible bobbed haircut and librarian-style spectacles, she has been under-estimated by many an opponent in the interview room. Each has found, to their cost, that the small, soft frame serves as a cashmere mitten around a steel claw.

A step or two behind is Detective Constable Duncan Slater. McAvoy doesn't know either particularly well but in Slater's case, he can't help notice that 'a step or two behind' seems rather fitting. He's a large, lumbering sort, workshy and happier doing as he's told than offering anything in the way of creative thinking. He's middle-aged and the muscles that marked him out as an athlete in his youth have loosened like old elastic and to McAvoy's eye he looks like a taxidermist's early work: disjointed and inexpertly stuffed.

DI Stace fixes McAvoy with a glare as she crosses the ground between them. She's wearing green wellington boots that are several sizes too big and they slip forward and back as she slips and slithers her way through the mud. "The boss said you'd killed a couple of people. Wanted us to help you make it look like an accident. That right?"

McAvoy can't seem to work out how to reply. He had an opening line prepared but he can't extract it from the swirl of his thoughts. Instead, he steps aside, a little theatrically, and points at the white training shoe which pokes out from between a mesh of branches.

"Ah," says DI Stace, scowling. She looks up at him. Cranes her neck, and takes a step back. "This is what you do, is it? On your days off. I thought you were building a new database, or sticking paper snowflakes to the windows at HQ, or something. We could do without this."

Slater looks past him. Turns up his nose. "He'll want it," he mutters, half to himself. He gives a disinterested look at McAvoy, and then at DI Stace.

"Yeah?" asks DI Stace. "Tell him, then."

"He won't be up until after the opening statements. He's got the camera crew with him. He'll want to make it look right. Dramatic."

A decision has been made. McAvoy looks from one to the other, wondering what will come next. He has a pained, fluttering feeling in his chest. He wants these officers, these elite detectives, to pay some heed to the dead men in the tangle of branches and thorns. He wants their murders to be acknowledged, their endings mourned.

"Couple of bad lads, by the look of it," says Stace, angling her head. She reaches out to move a branch, and McAvoy stiffens, forcing himself not to grab her hand. She notices. Arrests her forward motion and gives him a smile that dies well before her eyes.

"He said you wanted in. Be part of things. That true?"

McAvoy nods: a child being promised a sweetie if they own up.

"This?" asks Slater, scornfully. "Two bad lads in the woods? Druggies, probably."

McAvoy finds his voice. Wherever it has been, it has brought back something cold, and dangerous, like the growl of distant thunder. Not many people have heard him speak this way. "Druggies, Detective Constable?"

Slater doesn't catch the warning tone in his sergeant's voice. He laughs, openly. "All very formal, aren't we, Mac? Just call me Dunc."

McAvoy looks down at the floor. "Druggies, Dunc? What does that actually mean?"

Slater laughs again, looking over at DI Stace, who is fiddling with her mobile. "Drug addicts, Mac," he says, openly mocking. He sticks his tongue in his lower lip. Slaps at his forearm as if trying to raise a vein. "Scum. Wastes of space."

McAvoy's eyes become pin-pricks, his pupils boring into the forehead of the amused DC. "That's your considered opinion, is it, Detective Constable Slater? These men are drug addicts? Beneath you? An inconvenience in your day?"

"Why are you getting bothered, mate…?"

"Why am I getting bothered?" McAvoy feels a patch of prickly heat spreading across his back. "Why do the deaths of these men cause me concern?"

"OK, Mac, don't split your knickers over it… what do you want me to do, bring a fucking wreath?"

Two circles of colour bloom on the whiteness of McAvoy's face. He alters his position, cocks his head, his eyes carving a circle in the junior officer's face as if with a blow torch. He forces himself to take a breath. "Those trainers, DC Slater. They are Nike Air Yeezys. They cost more money than most people see in a week. And they are mint condition, save the mud and blood. People with a drug dependency will sell their own skin to get their hands on the drug of choice. Those trainers would buy enough heroin to kill an elephant."

Slater shrugs. "OK, so one's a buyer, the other's the dealer. Got out of hand, killed each other. Job done. Fuck, you don't have to be so prissy. Why are you always acting like a preacher? Guilty conscience, is it? Something to make up for?"

"Dunc," says DI Stace, quietly, typing out a text message. "Don't be a dick."

"Who's he to fucking talk to me like that…?"

McAvoy steps forward, fast on his feet for a big man. Slater puts his hands up as if he's about to receive a blow, transforming from aggressor into scalded spaniel in the time it takes McAvoy to close the distance between them.

"I'm a sergeant," he says, voice soft as silk. "I'm *your* sergeant. And you'll damn well listen to me. Roper may be happy with you treating murder victims like slaughtered cattle but you will afford these men some respect and you will do the same with me. You're not 'Dunc', you're not one of Roper's good old boys, you are a detective constable on the Major Crimes Team and you will never use the word 'druggies' around me again..."

DI Stace looks up from her phone, a half-smile playing at the corners of her mouth. She considers McAvoy as if seeing him for the first time. Licks raindrops from her lips. "That'll do, pig," she says, with a laugh. Then she holds out her phone. Roper has been listening at the other end of the line.

McAvoy takes the phone. Holds it to his ear.

"All right Mac?" asks Roper, a grin in his voice. "I heard we had a couple of dead druggies..."

10

"Ladies and gentlemen of the jury. My name is Timothy Anderson and I represent the Crown in this case, assisted by my learned junior, Mr Figgis. The defendant, Shane Cadbury, is represented by my learned friend, Mr Choudhury, who sits to my right, and Miss Hall, who is seated immediately behind him.

"At the time of her murder, Ella Butterworth was eighteen years old. At around 8 p.m. on Thursday, January 27th of last year, Ella was at the home she shared with her family on Rufforth Garth on the Bransholme estate in Hull. She and her younger sister had been trying on their dresses, ready for Ella's wedding, which was scheduled for two days later. During the course of the evening, a glass of red wine was spilled on Ella's dress. Ella's mother, Wendy Butterworth, suggested taking the dress straight round to her aunt's house, approximately 500 yards away, on the next Garth. Her aunt had a reputation in the family as always knowing what to do in a time of crisis. Very upset at what had happened to her dress, Ella decided not to waste time by getting changed, and ran from the house, still wearing her wedding dress and veil. She left her shoes in the house, and ran barefoot. Wendy Butterworth had gone to get her coat from an upstairs room, but by the time she came downstairs again, Ella had gone, leaving her sister alone in the living room.

"Wendy Butterworth would not see her daughter alive again.

"Ella arrived at her aunt's home, but nobody was home. Witnesses recall seeing Ella knocking repeatedly on the door, and looking very upset. After ten minutes, Ella left, heading back in the direction of Rufforth Garth. By now the time was around 8.15 p.m.

"By tragic coincidence, the defendant, Shane Cadbury, had been visiting friends in the Bransholme area, and was making his way back to his home in Hull's Garden Village, along the same route as Ella. Some time around 8.20 p.m., Ella was lured into an alleyway off Scampton Garth. In that alleyway, Shane Cadbury attacked her with a large knife. Forensic evidence later showed that the weapon was most likely a 'kukri' – a curved utility blade that we commonly associate with the Nepalese or Gurkha military regiments. In a frenzied, brutal and sustained attack, he stabbed her more than forty-seven times to the head, back, chest and stomach. He used such force that the knife repeatedly went right through her body. For more than a minute he plunged his knife into her, over and over again. The knife has never been recovered.

"Cadbury then walked to the next street, and broke into a Ford Fiesta belonging to a Mr Arthur Kirkhope. He drove the car to the end of the alley, bundled Ella's body onto the back seat, and drove her back to his flat on Berkshire Street, near Summergangs Road. Cadbury then dragged Ella's dead body from the car to the front door of his property, and carried her up the stairs. A neighbour remembers seeing Cadbury struggling with somebody in his arms, but from their vantage point of 100 yards away, assumed it was one of his friends, who may have been drunk.

"Cadbury then carried her into the bedroom of his flat, returned to the car and dumped it a mile away, at The Lambwath public house, on Lambwath Road. He then calmly walked back to the flat. He stopped to talk to a friend, Jonathan Sugg, at the end of his road. Mr Sugg questioned the blood on his clothes, and Cadbury said he had been in a fight. He was said to be 'totally calm'.

"Cadbury then returned to his flat. Cadbury then had sexual intercourse with Ella. Quantities of his semen were found inside her. There is evidence to suggest that this sexual activity was repeated over the course of the coming days.

"Cadbury then set about cleaning the flat in an attempt to dispose of what must have been a large quantity of blood.

"When Ella did not return home, her mother began telephoning family and friends. Those calls met no success.

"The Crown's case is that Shane Cadbury, at the time he inflicted those wounds, intended to kill Ella Butterworth, and is therefore guilty of her murder.

"My task at this stage is to give you an outline of the evidence which you will hear during the course of this trial. In that way, when the evidence is called before you, either from the witness box or when it is read, you will have a framework in which to put that evidence.

"Ella Samantha Butterworth was born on the 5th of June, 1992. She was the oldest of three sisters. Ella was of very slight build, and at the time of her death was just over five foot tall, and weighed fifty-two kilos. She was a very attractive girl, with shoulder-length brown hair, with blonde streaks. At fifteen years old, she began a relationship with Jamie Thornton, who was in her drama class at school. Very much childhood sweethearts, the young couple were happy together and recognised as deeply in love, and on her sixteenth birthday, they were engaged. Ella then began a drama course at Hull College, while Jamie took an apprenticeship in stage lighting, which allowed him to save money for a deposit on a house, and for their wedding.

"Shane Cadbury, the man in the dock behind me, is twenty-six years old. At the time of his arrest, he weighed twenty stone. He is six foot three inches tall and of considerable physical strength.

"Since January 2007, Shane Cadbury had been the tenant of the Berkshire Court property, where he lived alone. Cadbury lived upstairs, and at the time we are concerned with, the other flat was unoccupied. Cadbury was unemployed, and claiming disability benefit. He had few friends, and spent much of his time in his flat, watching videos and playing on his PlayStation. A considerable quantity of pornography was discovered in the flat, along with a sketchbook of graphic and explicit sex scenes, that he had drawn himself. A journal of short stories, many pornographic, was also discovered. In that journal, Cadbury fantasised about having sexual intercourse while dismembering and decapitating a beautiful woman.

"I now turn to deal with the movements of Ella and the defendant on the night of her death. On that fateful day, Ella had returned from college to the home she shared with her mother, father and sisters. Jamie Thornton had also been staying at the property with Ella's family for several weeks past. After the family ate a meal together, Jamie said goodbye to Ella and walked to The Ship Inn, at Sutton, where he had arranged to meet friends. He had arranged to be out of the house so Ella and her sixteen-year-old sister Stephanie could try on their dresses for the wedding, which was booked for January 29th. Ella's father took the family dog for a walk, so the girls could get ready. He and Jamie left the house at around 7 p.m. The youngest sister, Tara, was staying at a friend's house.

"Ella, Stephanie and their mother spent an hour making last-minute plans for the wedding and tried on their dresses. Despite being asked to take them off so they would not be dirtied, Ella and Stephanie were so enjoying themselves in their dresses, they kept them on as they sat at the kitchen table and planned seating arrangements, giggling as they looked forward to the big day. Stephanie then knocked over a glass of red wine, which dribbled over the left leg area of the dress. Ella burst into tears, as did Stephanie, and their mother tried to sponge off the stain, but could not. She quickly suggested they take the dress to Ella aunt's house, her father's sister, Joyce Butterworth. Ella ran from the house, in the dress and veil, and barefoot.

"That same evening, Shane Cadbury had been visiting friends at Manston Garth, Bransholme. He had spent the evening eating a takeaway and watching a horror movie with Steve Venables and Daniel Lewis. The defendant had drunk at least three cans of lager that evening. He left at round 8.20 p.m., after falling out with Daniel Lewis. They had argued over Mr Lewis's intention to propose to his girlfriend. The defendant tried to talk him out of it, and became insulting towards Mr Lewis's girlfriend. The defendant eventually stormed out of the house in, what the Crown suggests, was a state of temper. The route that would take him from the property back to his own flat unhappily coincided with the route Ella would take from her aunt's house back to Rufforth Garth.

"Cadbury's path crossed that of Ella Butterworth's in a dark, unlit alley, just two streets from her home, with the most tragic of results. We contend that Cadbury used a large curved knife that he was fond of carrying to inflict the fatal wounds. That knife has not been recovered, but we suggest the stabbing only ended when the tip of the knife broke off in the brick wall that he pinned her against as he murdered her. You will be shown the sharpened sliver of this murder weapon doing the course of the trial.

"Ella's screams were overhead by several nearby residents but, as you will hear, they thought it was simply the sound of children playing.

"Within half an hour, Ella's mother had become concerned. She telephoned Joyce Butterworth but got no response. She then walked to her house, but there was no reply when she knocked on the door. She then walked to The Ship Inn, where she saw Ella's fiancé, Jamie Thornton, and explained that Ella could not be found. Together they searched nearby streets and started making telephone calls to Ella's friends.

"By this time, we suggest that Ella Butterworth had been murdered, sexually assaulted, and her body was in Shane Cadbury's flat.

"Eight days later, and following a police appeal, detectives received a telephone call from Daniel Lewis. He had been to Cadbury's flat the day before in an attempt to reconcile their friendship. Cadbury allowed him into the living room of the flat and the two patched up their differences. During the course of the afternoon, Cadbury had taken a trip to the bathroom, and Lewis decided to pop into Cadbury's bedroom to look for a video they could watch together. As he walked through the door, he saw the decomposed, violated and blood-soaked body of Ella Butterworth, laid out on the bed. She was still wearing her wedding dress, which was now red with blood. The top had been pulled down to expose her breasts.

"Mr Lewis ran from the flat in a state of shock. He ran back to his own home, where he drank a great deal of whisky and passed out. He woke the next day, sickened and disgusted at what he had seen, and telephoned the police.

"Almost three weeks later, as the city united in a desperate search for a missing daughter, Police Sergeant McAvoy, together with Police Constables Dicker and Poyser from Humberside Police, followed up the call, which had been mislaid among the huge volume of documents and potential leads. Cadbury let them into the flat, and immediately pointed them towards his bedroom. Sergeant McAvoy entered the room. He saw what Mr Lewis had seen, but by this time, Ella Butterworth had been decapitated. Cadbury was immediately arrested. Due to the extreme nature of the wounds to her body and the presence of a footprint on the collarbone, we grimly suggest that Cadbury used his bare hands to remove Ella Butterworth's head.

"The officers were overcome by a stench they described as being like rotting food.

"As the officers waited for scenes of crime officers and

lead officer Detective Superintendent Douglas Roper to arrive, Cadbury began to talk about Ella and what he had done. He called her 'his girl', and spoke of her sexual prowess, and how she had been a gift from the devil, just for him. He spoke normally and without emotion.

"Scientific investigation of the alleyway found a large quantity of blood. Slash and scratch marks consistent with a frenzied attack were found on the wall. The car in which Ella was transported was also recovered. More blood was found on the stairs leading to the defendant's flat, and in the living room and bedroom.

"The knife used to inflict the wounds was most likely tossed into the drain, but despite an extensive underwater hunt, has not been recovered.

"During police interview, Cadbury declined to answer all questions bar one. When asked why he had killed her, he said he did not. He said he found her dead, and looked upon her as a gift.

"The Crown says that the defendant is responsible for the murder of a gentle, loving and fragile young woman, and that he is guilty of murder. Thank you."

Enough for a splash. Few decent quotes and a bit of gore. Have to make a judgement call on the grisliest stuff. A bit much for some readers, not enough for others. I'll leave that to Neil on newsdesk. Let the bastard earn his pay.

Good stuff, though.

Hard.

Nasty.

Easily digestible. Good versus evil, beauty and the beast,

all boiled down to 600 words. A bitesize morality tale with a punchy headline.

My sort of caper.

Cadbury looking at his feet as the details poured out. Breathing deeply as Anderson talked about her nakedness, spoke of violation and depravity and made it sound like poetry.

Reporters pulling faces and trying to keep up as we scribbled shorthand. Putting asterisks next to the choicest quotes.

Sickened for a moment, then down to business.

The copy running through my head like a mantra.

Bored by 11.30.

Looking up and around and inside.

Spinning in my seat as two detectives slip quietly into the courtroom and whisper in The Flash's ear.

Thirty seconds of eyebrow raising.

Conversation behind a palm.

Then Roper getting up, nodding to the judge.

Sliding out of the courtroom in a swish of leather.

Acolytes riding his coat-tails.

Me mulling it over.

Judgement call.

Twitching.

Up.

Bowing.

And out the door.

II

Clive Sullivan Way, 12.15 p.m., heading west out of Hull towards the country park.

Two bodies found in the woods...

Taking it easy, careful of the speed trap round the bend past the pharmaceutical warehouse. Bastards have already got me twice. Six fucking points and £120. Entering the sixty zone now. Flip a finger to the coppers in the van as I pass the camera, and floor it.

Waters of the Humber, brown and choppy to my left. White caps on the ripples. Paper chase of gulls, squabbling over shit, a taste of things to come.

A fast eighty in the rain.

Only one wiper works, so I'm leaning across to the passenger side and peering through the gap, carved in the waterfall running down the windscreen.

Cigarette smoke clinging to my damp clothes.

Johnny Cash dead beside me.

Passing the Arco warehouse. Christmas lights and a fat Santa Claus on the roof, still promising presents as the year moves towards March.

Thinking of Christmases past. At Drayton. The country estate we called home. Dad, the gamekeeper for a poor boy done good. So much less than he deserved. I get heartburn when I think of those days. That time. That Christmas. Mulled wine and eggnog, carols and bad sweaters. The winter shooting party, and the one that would come six months later under a blazing sun. Of that day. Mam and Kerry in the cottage; me and Dad, men at work. Serving the rich men. In among them. Mingling. Not exactly beneath, but a step down, and to the left. Feeling like the guttering on their mansion, the shingle on their drive. Me, a child, with watery grey eyes and a good right hook, sniffing the Bloody Marys on their breath, and watching, as Dad thanked them for the grubby notes they stuffed in his waxed jacket.

Remembering myself, nine years old, in the back of the jeep. Dad winking, to show it was all OK, and me knowing it wasn't. Trying to work it out. Trying to fathom why we lived in the cottage, and Mr Blake, with his red nose and fleshy lips and lecherous hands, lived in the Big House. Wondering where his magic lay. Why our presents, once opened, were so clearly shop-bought. Why I recognised them from last year's January sales. Why Santa loved the Blakes more than us, when they already had so much. Sniffing spent cartridges, the earthy, sharp tang of gun smoke. Cheek tugged and hair ruffled by fat men in tweed. Shiny coins dropped in my pocket. The occasional hand on my arse. Sometimes wondering if Dad served them because they were better than him, or because of the powerful, shiny thing in their hands.

And later, bouncing back to the cottage in the old 4x4, resting my head on the dead grouse, listening to Dad talk about football.

A Volvo estate suddenly honks loud and long as I drift

into the inside lane, and I open my eyes with a jolt, lighting a cigarette, chewing the top off a bottle of Nurofen and gobbling three down, as I press the accelerator hard and tear through the curtains of rain.

I pass a lorry. In the dirt on its back end, somebody has written: *"Please overtake quietly – refugees asleep."*

Mobile phone tucked under my chin, spouting nonsense to a copytaker: last of a dying breed.

"Right, read that third para again, will you? Yeah. Ta. Right, scrub that bit. OK, first para again. Ready? A teenage girl was brutally murdered while wearing her wedding dress then decapitated and sexually abused – two days before she was due to marry her childhood sweetheart. New paragraph.

"Ella Butterworth's dead body was repeatedly molested by her alleged killer, Shane Cadbury, twenty-six, in the days after her death, and body parts were found more than a mile away. Her body... shall we say 'the bulk of her body?'... is that too harsh? OK, leave it as is... Body was discovered in Cadbury's flat in Hull's Garden Village, where the accused is said to have carried her after murdering the 'angelic' teen in a frenzied attack in an alleyway near her home.

"Right, then it's as it was. Remember the inverted commas around gentle and fragile, yeah? Oh, I took them out did I? Stick them back in. Cool. Whack that over to the desk and stick my mobile number on top. Tell them I'll let them know how this body-in-the-woods thing turns out. Nice one. Cheers, princess. Ta'ra."

Bang. Job's a good 'un.

Hang up and dial the police voicebank again. Heard it three times already but it doesn't hurt to be thorough.

"This is Inspector Dave Simmonds in the Humberside Police press office, the time is now 11.37 on the morning of February the 6th. This is an appeal for information over a suspicious death. This morning, at 9.15 a.m., police received a telephone call from a concerned local business owner at the Humber Bridge Country Park, near Hessle, who reported the presence of a body in a dense patch of woodland. Police immediately attended the scene. Two bodies were confirmed. Scenes of crime investigators are now in attendance and the park has been closed to the public. I am now on my way to the scene. I would like to stress that we are at a very early stage in the investigation, and I know you will all want identifications as quickly as possible, but that could take some time due to the nature of the injuries. We are treating both deaths as suspicious at this stage. A murder enquiry has now been launched. Thank you."

Pull off at the roundabout, past the foody pub overlooking the water, and the carved grizzly bear, down Ferriby Road. Trees either side. Leafy, even in bleak midwinter. Big houses. The smell of money.

Know the road like the palm of my hand.

Copper in a yellow jacket standing by the entrance to the Country Park. Huddled in his jacket, collar up.

I slow down and wind down the window. He ambles over. Young lad. Earnest face. Don't know him.

"Park's closed, mate," he says.

"Yeah, so I heard," I say, smiling. "I'm with the Press Association, mate. Have the pack arrived yet?"

"Pack?"

"Press pack. Heard we've got a murder."

"You're the first."

He's leaning in the car window now. Christ he's young. Doesn't look like he even needs to shave every day. Pink cheeks, blonde hair. Bit fleshy. A human Battenberg.

He looks wet through. His whole head is in the car, helmet touching the roof, rain dripping from his chin. He's looking for warmth. Smiling. Obviously lonely. I dare him to mention the knackered windscreen wipers.

"Simmo around?"

"Simmo?"

"Inspector Simmonds, mate. Skinny fella. Press officer. Of a sort."

"Oh yes, he's just arrived."

"I'll see him in the car park, will I?"

He looks worried, and withdraws his head.

"I haven't had instructions yet. Best you wait here."

"Oh, fair enough mate, but there's going to be a pack here before too long and we'll be blocking the road. Last time we had a spot of bother in the country park we set up shop in the car park. As soon as Simmo gets his bearings it'll all be sorted. Tell you what, I've got his mobile number in my phone. I'll give him a call."

The lad sticks his tongue in his cheek as he thinks. Then he shrugs again.

"OK, go on through."

I treat him to a warm smile, and drive on.

I turn left into the overflow car park and pull in close to the gates. The rain is easing off but it's still miserable beyond the glass. The trees that edge the car park stand tall and brooding, their tips stretching upwards to puncture the grey clouds which hang low, like a hammock holding a fat man, over the park.

I get out of the car, and as the rain and the wind grab at my coat-tails and the crows and the seagulls scream overhead, there's a moment of clarity and astonishment, as though a normal person has suddenly taken a look at the world through my eyes.

Hours.

Just a matter of fucking hours since I was parked up, not more than a hundred yards from here, yearning for death.

Hours since I was smashing in a stranger's face with a rock.

It's a funny old world.

12

Standing beneath a striped golfing umbrella, the collar of his leather jacket turned up and his hands deep in his pockets, Detective Superintendent Doug Roper is enjoying the rain. *Very cinematic*, he thinks. *Very noir*.

"Sir."

Roper's standing on a thick tree root, slick with moss, watching the forensics team erect a white tent around the two corpses. The TV crew are being kept back until he's got to grips with this. Doesn't want there to be any unforeseen balls-ups. He needs to come across as confident, together, unflappable. Caring, but not soft.

"Sir. Excuse me. Detective Superintendent Roper, sir."

He turns at the rumble of the low, deep voice. There's a Scottishness, in there, but it's refined, like good whisky. He's had a good education, this one. Learned to speak the Queen's. Roper's been through his personnel file with a red pen and committed the details to memory. He's a clever sod, his new sergeant, but there's no cunning there. Sensitive, too, but without the guile to use it to his advantage. He's dogged, certainly. Diligent. Handsome sod, too, under the blush and the beard. Big lump of a thing. Six foot six and a Viking look about him, if Vikings were given to shyness and didn't swear in front of the ladies. He's not the sort of chap Roper would have picked for his team, but the sly sod banked a favour when he found Ella's body last year and Roper couldn't think of a good reason to refuse his request for a transfer to the Major Crimes Unit. He's kept him out of the way for months, giving him every kind of pointless, tedious task he can come up with, but he's still got a zeal in his eyes that turns Roper's stomach. He'd have loved to have been there when he found Ella. He's got it on good authority that there were tears running into his beard as if from a tap. Still wouldn't let PC Poyser put the boot in, though. Stood his ground and kept his two constables from laying a single finger on Cadbury; standing there, blushing, arms folded, tears and snot and steam rising from his face and the knot in his tie half strangling him, letting Poyser strike him like a drum. All to save a sad sack of shite like Shane Cadbury. It doesn't make sense to Roper. There hadn't even been a TV crew handy to capture his display of morality.

"You talking to me, son? Sorry, it's the accent." Roper licks his lips, remembering a joke. "Did you hear the one about the Scottish mafia don? Made people an offer they couldnae understand…"

McAvoy gives a dutiful smile. "Very good, sir."

Roper rolls his eyes. "Not much fun in you, is there, son? Learn English from Jeeves, did you? Lighten up, lad."

"It's a crime scene, sir," says McAvoy, quietly. "Two men are dead."

"Yes, but you're not. I'm not. And we'll solve it. There are reasons to be cheerful."

Roper smiles, broadly, as he watches McAvoy struggle

to find the appropriate expression. It's like watching a cat chewing a toffee. He seems to Roper like a visitor from another planet: as if Spock had fathered a child by a big ginger yeti. He doesn't seem to understand how adults communicate with each other. Never gets the bloody joke.

"Go on then," says Roper, sighing. "Tell me."

McAvoy nods, gratitude etched into his face. "Sir, the big one's still got his watch. No wallet, but that's a nice piece on his wrist. Expensive. I think we can discount a robbery. At least, not an opportunistic one. And I've been speaking to one of the park wardens. Got a list of descriptions of people who use this area regularly. Joggers, dog walkers and whatnot. There's a remote control car club use the car park on a weekend..."

Roper treats his sergeant to his best smile.

"Hector..." he begins.

"Aector, sir. Hard to say, I know. I don't object to McAvoy."

"Fucking big of you, lad."

"Sir?"

Roper shakes his head. He wonders if it wouldn't be easiest just to wire some money into the big fella's bank account from an anonymous source and get him suspended while subject to investigation. He might just be a liability. He hasn't got the hint he's not welcome. Too fucking earnest by half, thinks Roper. Big clean hands and a scrubbed neck. Always first in and last out. Real ale man. Never going to be one of the boys. The other lads and ladies in his part of CID know how to play the game. They leave it to Roper. They deal with the robberies and the straightforward rapes and the unglamorous shit, and they let Roper solve the murders, and they don't ask questions and they smile at his jokes and they stay the fuck out of his way. But the Jock is different. He turns up at crime scenes to see if he can help. Drafts suggested working practices in his own time. Cross-references filing systems. Builds new databases on his home computer so staff can share knowledge and make suggestions. There's something unnervingly wholesome about the cunt.

"You could be right, Sergeant," says Roper. "You get back to the ranch and start working the database. See if you can find any other robberies where something valuable was left behind. Get on to the remote control club. Check their members for any dirt. Nationwide search. Give Interpol a tinkle, too. Mention my name."

McAvoy, with mud up to his shins and his feet swimming inside his black shoes, gives a puzzled look. "I'm not sure that the watch being left behind is a signature, sir. I don't think they left it on purpose. I just mean they didn't take it. Or want it. And I was thinking of the car club as witnesses rather than suspects, sir. But…"

"No, it's something worth considering," says Roper, charming. "Case like this, we want to cover every angle. You're the computer whizz, anyway."

"You're sure you don't want me here, sir?"

"I'd love to have you here, sunbeam, but you'd be helping the investigation a lot more working the database. The DI is on call if I need anything specific, and you'll be the first to know if we need anything. You get on back. It's a horrible day."

McAvoy stands, shivering and cold. His cheap fleece is wet through and his suit is damp underneath. Another drip of rain runs down the back of his neck. When are you going to learn? he asks himself. They're trying to get rid of you again. Want you out of the way. You're not one of them. You're not one of Roper's boys. Do you even want to be? You've heard the whispers. You've glimpsed something in the way he does business. Give them a bit of publicity and it goes to their head. They think they're untouchable.

No, he tells himself, sharply. Give people the benefit of the doubt. That's what makes you good at what you do. You think the best of people and give them a chance. Innocent until proven guilty. And Roper's conviction rate is top-notch, he thinks. Keep plugging away. You'll get there. You'll show him what you can do…

"Yes sir," says McAvoy.

"Good lad," says Roper, watching him slurp his way through the mud and back to the path. "Miss you," he says, under his breath, as McAvoy reaches out a hand to help up the big, bright-eyed PC who's slithering around in the mud at the edge of the perimeter.

Roper considers young Sam. He's got plans for the lad. Eager to please, none too bright, and happy to hurt those whom Roper deems deserving. Big baby face and innocent eyes, and bad all the way through.

Could be a godsend, all this, thinks Roper. Tie up the Butterworth case and sort this out inside seventy-two hours and it's TV fucking gold.

He shivers under the umbrella and stares out as officers in luminous raincoats tie police tape around trees. Christ, this could be good. Could be a real hit. Real nasty, by the looks of it. Could be gangland. Everybody likes gangland, don't they?

One of them, the scruffy lad, has got a bullet in his head. Tough luck, son, thinks Roper. Could have been worse.

The other one's not even human anymore. His head's almost gone. It's just bone and pulp, and a swamp of blood-red leaves.

The scruffy one couldn't have done it, he thinks. Hasn't got the strength or the venom, by the looks of him. Smackhead, too. Couldn't lift anything heavier than a needle. No, he thinks, the bigger lad probably shot the scruffy one. Drug deal gone wrong, maybe? Could be. Who killed the big lad, though? Somebody he was with? Somebody he trusted? A partner? Christ, it couldn't be a stranger. Nobody could stumble on this and then do this much damage. This was somebody who came here to kill, and did it royally.

"Sir, the press are arriving."

A young female officer, dripping with the cold and with flushed pink cheeks, is shouting at him from the pathway. He gives a smile.

"Anybody I know?"

"Tony from the *Mail* just pulled up, and Owen Lee from the Press Association has been and gone."

"Fine. I'll be out to see them in a tick."

Been and gone? Quick off the fucking mark, that one. So sharp he might cut himself. You'd never know his past to look at him, either. Never know what he had done. Not unless you're Doug Roper, he tells himself.

He pulls another cigarillo from his coat pocket and lights it. Runs through a quick mental stock-take. Anything to ruin his mood? Any little problems? Oh yeah. *Minns*. The bodybuilder. The cellmate. Choudhury's star witness. Could fuck it all.

Shit.

Roper sucks his teeth. Considers his options and finds that most of them are very much to his taste.

He steps off the root and onto the wet soil, with its carpet of leaves. Takes a step and feels his loafer nudge something hard.

Roper reaches down and gently slides his hand under the leaves.

His fingers close on metal.

It's good to be me, he thinks.

Quietly, discreetly, he pulls out the gun, and slips it into a clear plastic evidence bag. He puts it in his pocket.

Behind his eyes, wheels are turning.

Can't waste a moment like that, he thinks. Need an audience.

Besides, it could come in handy.

He turns and walks away.

There's a spring in his step.

13

Simmo spots me as I walk into the main car park. There are a few police cars, parked up here and there. Roper's Jag is next to the forensics van, just begging to be keyed. There are some coppers milling about, trying to look busy, and a bloke from Supercop's documentary crew sits pulling on some wellies in the back of a Range Rover, but nobody pays me much attention.

That's all going to change.

Simmo gives a wave and plods across to meet me. He's got a hiking jacket on over his uniform, and is wearing a woollen bobble hat instead of his cap. Well-pressed trousers with shiny knees, tucked into well-loved welly boots. He mimics a shudder as he gets close, and we shake hands. I'm still wearing gloves.

"First again, Owen?" he asks, with a smile.

"You know me, mate. Can't help it."

"I thought we'd have the place to ourselves for a while yet. Everybody being tied up with the Cadbury case and all that. Always nice to know where you and Tony H are."

"Yeah, I struck lucky. I saw a couple of the coppers leave the courtroom in a hurry and popped out on the off-chance.

Checked the voicebank and suddenly my day's even shittier than it was this morning. Fucking trial of the century and now a double bloody murder. Should make Roper's documentary a little juicier."

"Aye, it looks like it could be a big one for you, this. One of them's been shot by the looks of things, and the other's had his head stoved in. Really bad. Really."

"Fuck."

"Aye, fuck indeed. Between you and me, like."

"Oh yeah. Christ, though. What can you say on the record, then?"

"It's so early we can't really say owt. Victims of a violent death, that's about it. Roper might be willing to talk to you in a couple of hours, but you're going to get wet. I'd stay in your car. You won't get near the scene."

"In the woods, is it?"

"Yeah, a few hundreds yards in. Reckon it happened last night. It's a bit off the beaten track, but you couldn't hide two bodies in there without somebody seeing."

"Were they hidden, then?"

"Well, they were covered over a bit, right in amongst this real tangle of trees. It's a horrible place for the forensics boys to be working. Soaking, they are."

"Couldn't happen to a nicer bunch."

"No."

We laugh at that, and Simmo removes his glasses to wipe the raindrops from the lenses. He looks weird without them, almost cadaverous. If you didn't know Simmo you would think he was severe, harsh, patrician-like. Long nose, high cheek bones, thin eyes, grey hair. But he's a deflated fat man.

By nature, Simmo should be twenty stone, red-faced and jolly, able to balance a pint on his gut; the sort who roars with laughter at everything from a filthy joke to a dog's fart. A fast metabolism robbed him of his birth right.

"What you going to be doing?" I ask as I debate my next move and a gust of wind plays with the tails of my coat. There's a metallic noise as the gun bangs against something in my pocket. Simmo is too busy shuddering to notice.

"I'll hang about a bit then head down to Hessle. Get a cup of tea. There's that sandwich shop on the main street in Hessle, isn't there? They do that baguette with the caramelised peppers and onions." He gives the matter some consideration and makes a conclusion. "The day could be a lot worse."

I give him a friendly pat on the arm, and saunter back to the car. My coat is billowing in the wind, and I'm vaguely aware that I'm looking good.

Step back inside the Vauxhall. Trap my coat in the door and crush the fags in the pocket. Curse, and get over it.

I lie back in the driver's seat, and close my eyes.

I'm tired now. My mind has always worked at two distinct paces, and it wears me down, despite the adrenaline that's carbonating my bloodstream. My thoughts arrive like they're driving between speed bumps, roaring between obstructions, then slamming on the brakes and easing over the hurdles, speeding and slowing, speeding and slowing.

I look up.

It takes a moment to register what I am seeing.

There.

Just above the level of the trees.

A security camera.
Pointing at the car park.
Clicking.
Whirring.
Like me.

14

Iopen my phone and glance at Jess. The pain of staring into those eyes is duller than before, as though somehow muffled and muted by the weight of all the other thoughts lining up like stacked towels in my mind.

I allow myself a moment, a fluttering of wings in my chest and a tongue of sickness on my thorax, then I'm scrolling down to Tony's number.

The briefest of chats. Excitement in his voice, something shrill and anxious in mine. Arrange to meet up later.

Then on to the newsdesk. Neil Grange, the northern news editor, his two bellies divided by a belt, nether regions a bulging mass of flesh, pressing against his cream slacks and forcing his grey jumper to ride up. Moustache and bulging eyes. Panicky. Takes it seriously. Thinks I'm too reckless and doesn't like the way I talk to him, but hasn't yet fathomed a way to make me care.

"Neil, mate. It's Owen. Got the court copy, did you? All cool? Well that's up to you. I thought we'd try making it sound interesting for a change. No, that's your call. You get paid more than me. Anyway, there's been two murders. Two bodies in the Country Park by the bridge. Well no, you're right, they could be suicides. Whatever. Well look, it sounds interesting so I'll send you some stuff. That laptop would be a help, if you ever get round to it. No, I'm sure you're busy. Anyway, I'll keep you posted. What? No I can't get there. I'm doing this. And the trial. Got that backgrounder lined up for later. I'm not omnipotent, am I? You show me how, then. No. No. Fine. Bye."

Fucking prick. One for the list, definitely.

Open the inbox in my phone. Read Jess's last message again. Three days ago, now. Three days and still the words make my face twitch and fists bunch.

So many tears, inside one girl...

I pull some faces and light a cigarette but I'm not enjoying it and I'm pissed off, so I decide to explore the wound, and call Kerry.

The payphone on the landing of the house where she has a room is answered by a Kurdish-sounding man. I'm pretty good at telling the difference. I can mumble an introductory salutation in Albanian, Serbian, Arabic and Bosnian, having made it my business to get myself on good terms with the influx of asylum seekers and migrants who flooded into the city a decade back. It's done Hull a power of good, though it hasn't been without trauma. I covered a riot a few years ago that started when a gang of Bosnians and a gang of Serbs all decided to attend the same family fun day at their local pub, and things turned sour. Ended with half of West Hull being sealed off, and got worse when some daft bastards with white skin decided to get involved and got their heads kicked in. Other daft bastards with white skin took umbrage at this, and some poor Kosovan who had nothing to do with it got himself spread across a good swathe of the city centre. Relations are still in decline.

Personally, I couldn't give a fuck where people come from, and reckon their life must have sucked if they think that life on Spring Bank in Hull is a better option.

"*Bayanit bash… tu chawai yi?* I was hoping to speak to Kerry, dark hair, slim girl, if you could give her a knock…"

The Kurdish chap hangs up when I switch to English and I sit, grinding my teeth, more pissed off than before.

The phone rings, and I recognise the number as Lenny's. She's called half a dozen times already today, and I keep ignoring her. I don't want to think about Jess, or hear Lenny's fears. I ignore her, and it stops, so I just sit there for a while, thinking of green painted walls and pale curtains and leather straps and soft toys and pills and shocks and pills and treatments and diagnoses and Mam's tears and Dad's guilt and Kerry's hand in mine.

It rings again, Kerry's number. I answer it immediately.

"Kerry?"

"Owen," she mumbles, like a drunk. "Hey you."

"Are you all right? You left a message last night. Sounded like you were freaking out."

"Did I?" she asks, vague and blurry. Her voice a ghost. "I don't know." Then, with a start. "Owen, I need some money. I need…"

"No, Kerry. I can't."

"Please." Whiny, like a child asking for sweets.

"I can't let you poison yourself anymore."

"You've got your poison," she says, anger in her voice. Desperation too. "You're an addict too."

"Kerry, you're going to kill yourself…"

"I will if you don't get me what I need." She's crying now. Snotty and pathetic. So far removed from the little girl who used to hold my hand in front of the painting, that she's almost unrecognisable. Almost.

"I'll be round tonight," I say, shaking my head, and feeling each of her tears fall upon my defences like acid.

"Hope so. But don't promise. I hate broken promises."

"I love you," I say.

The line goes dead.

Almost without warning, a great surge of emotion rises up from within me, pitching me forward as surely as a breaking wave. My head fills with images of Jess. Of the love of my life. Of the girl I drove away because I couldn't stand how hard she loved me. I think of the skinny, broken, tearful mess she became. That I perhaps turned her into. Broken and miserable and weak. Living for the moments of compassion and tenderness I would sometimes throw her, if the breeze in my mind was blowing the right way.

Tentatively, as if probing at a painful tooth, I start thinking of happier times. I think of sunny days. Throwing stones in the water and holding hands. Me, listening as she prattled on about people at her work, suggesting colour schemes for the dining room. Me, trying to be entertaining, desperate each time her smile failed. Her, talking about babies and the future, trying to disguise her questions over my fidelity. Dark fears dressed as jokes. Me, promising all, denying more. Me, telling her that I need nobody else, that she's all I want. Her dissecting my answers. Finding meanings that weren't there. Her, crying again. Always crying. Jess. The girl who loved me to the end, the end of us, the end of her suffering and the doubling of mine. The girl who is missing. Gone from my arms. Taken.

I get out my phone and text Lenny. Tell her to try Jess's

friends in Nottingham, and send her the number. Tell her that it might be worth her driving down there. That Jess used to go there sometimes, when we fought. I apologise for ignoring her, and tell her when I get a moment, I'll have a ring round a few other people. I tell her not to worry, then feel ice in my stomach as my mind conjures an image of what could have happened to her.

No, I say, shutting it down, and I grip the gun through the material of my jacket, holding it like a talisman and feeling its strength flow into me. No, don't…

15

"...no, I'm back at the office. Setting up the incident room. It's important. Useful. Honestly, this is the best place for me. I wish I could be there but this could be the opportunity, you know? Who did? Roisin, she's a senior officer, a decorated senior officer, she wasn't looking at me like anything. Contempt, perhaps. No, I didn't notice. She's not a woman, she's a police officer. Yes. I'm not getting into this conversation – everything about you is perfect. Of course. Like there's no tomorrow, I swear it. You'll make me blush. You will. The plastic's melting, I have to go..."

McAvoy hangs up. Holds his hand in front of his mouth until he's sure that the smile has disappeared behind a cloud. Gets a grip on himself. Sits, quietly, unobtrusively, waiting for somebody to tell him what to do. Nobody looks his way. Nobody gives a damn.

McAvoy's grown used to his own company since he ditched the comfortable camouflage of uniform and moved down the corridor to CID. It's not that they don't like him. They just don't know what to do with a man who cycles to work and loves his wife. Who brings home-made soup in a flask each day to save himself the prices at the canteen. Who arrives early, stays late, doesn't swear and won't use the office phone for personal calls. Who doesn't surf the web unless it's work-related. Calls people by their full rank and smiles when he mentions his wife or son.

Months after being unveiled as the new boy, McAvoy knows he's the loose stitch in Roper's tightly-knit team. The unknown quantity. Mentally bracketed by the others as a computer geek, paperwork junky, oddball and anal retentive.

They've tried, of course. Tried to help him chisel his way through the invisible barrier that keeps him apart from the rest of them. Even given him nicknames.

Mac.

The Highlander.

The Flying Scotsman.

None have stuck.

They've played jokes, too. Left a raw chicken breast in his desk drawer when they found out he was experimenting with vegetarianism. Superglued his fountain pen to his keyboard. His coffee cup to his coaster. His coaster to his desk. Left his mobile number on a toilet wall under the legend '*Jock Sucks Cock*'.

All good, clean, workplace stuff.

They've watched his reactions, and despite his attempts to laugh along, he's come up short.

Been dismissed as a do-gooder, know-it-all and pain-in-the-fucking-arse.

He's never been any good at all that blokey stuff. Never really felt comfortable with the back-slapping and the swearing and the burping of pop songs down the boozer. All the talk about tits and arses. Fifteen pints and a fight. Then being sick and starting again. He doesn't doubt that he and his father could drink each and every one of them under the table given a bottle of whisky and a log fire, but he isn't the competitive sort. He wants to fit in, but for the right reasons. Wants them to indulge him in his idiosyncrasies because he's good at what he does. Wants to hear them whisper that McAvoy might have his own way of doing things, but that he gets results.

He likes it when Roisin calls him a maverick. He's never imagined himself as such, but somehow she's right. He *is* the loose cannon. He is the one who does things his own way. By doing things properly, by the book, deliberately, methodically, legally, he's become a trouble-maker, and been pushed to one side.

He takes a swig of carrot and coriander soup. It's got chilli in it and makes his nose run and his cheeks flush, but he can feel it warming him through. Doing him good. Lifting the damp, corpse-tainted air of the Country Park from his raw lungs.

He's used to the cold, of course. Accustomed to it. His skin has been toughened by two decades of working the land. But the weather in this city chills him to the bone. It makes his marrow seem soggy with ice water. The air, laced with a grey, insidious mist, makes him cough and his eyes drip and seems to sap the strength and stoop the shoulders. A year after arriving in Hull, with little Fin only just turned two, he wonders how long it is since he last saw sunlight. Wonders what this place is doing to him. To his family. He feels like a figure in a still-damp watercolour. Sees the people around him in greys and washed-out swirls of dirt. It sometimes feels like living inside a rain cloud. It's a hard place to find the motivation to be different.

To do your job.

To get on.

To shine.

Even the victims seem somehow accepting.

People cudgelled in the street.

Grandads beaten up for asking a teenager to get off their front wall.

The owners of burgled homes and firebombed restaurants.

All seem to have a shadow in their eyes that suggests they knew it had been only a matter of time. That everybody gets it, at some point. That it could have been worse.

There's a weariness to this city. A lethargy. He sees it as a man made old by hard work: coughing up lumps of gristle and weak with emphysema, limbs riddled with arthritis and only bitter memories in its eyes.

He finishes the soup, and mops the bowl with a hunk of Roisin's home-made bread. Thanks her, in his mind. Pictures her smile. Spends a moment enjoying the image of her and Fin, picking herbs, rolling pastry, seasoning the meal that he won't be home in time to eat.

Turns back to the computer screen and flicks through the files in front of him. Cross-references database after database. Does everything he has been asked to do. Completes every pointless task. Watches the windows grow dark and the reflection in the glass more vivid. Tries not to glance at the clock on the wall. It's not his way to criticise. Even when he returns home long after his loved ones have gone to bed, he climbs in beside them and holds them tight, and thanks God for what he has. The ethic was drummed into him by his father, on the croft they farmed at Wester Ross in the far north of Scotland. Five hectares of land and a white-washed stone cottage half an hour's walk from the nearest B-road. A childhood spent preparing to take over, of letting his hands grow used to the feel of feed buckets biting into his palms, of frost crystals splintering beneath his Wellington boots, of being too cold to breathe and too tired to stand, and knowing that only by keeping going, and sowing, planting, feeding, slaughtering, would his family be able to eat. Then boarding school. A new life, with a mother who didn't know what to do with him and a stepdad who offered nothing but money. He's never fitted in anywhere since. Not at university. Not out there in the big wide world. And he can't go home again. Not now. Not after what happened when he chose the old family croft as a safe place to disappear with the teenage Traveller with whom he had fallen desperately in love. Not after the bad men came, and left blood on the whitewashed walls.

After a while, he looks up from the computer for the screen-break that the clock in the corner of the monitor is telling him he is due. He blinks and casts his eyes around the long, empty office. Messy desks. Dusty computers, rarely switched on. Evidence bundles and rain-spattered files spilling off desks and under tables.

He wonders where they are. Which avenues Roper is following up. Who's in the frame. Whether they'll even bother to tell him.

A flash of anger followed by customary reproach and regret...

Roper.

The man who charged Shane Cadbury with the murder of a young girl. A girl whose stench is still in McAvoy's nostrils. Whose decomposing flesh seems to be continuing its ruination inside his throat. Whose smell masks the scent of his wife's perfume, his son's freshly-washed hair. Whose face seems to stare at him from every computer screen and newspaper, noticeboard and magazine rack.

A face he didn't see, the first time they met, because her head had been removed by the butcher who stood there beside him.

Shane Cadbury.

A look of longing upon his ugly, moonish face...

The phone begins to ring in Roper's empty office at the far end of the room, and McAvoy instinctively keys in the number into the pad that transfers the call to his own phone.

"Humberside Police CID. Can I help you?"

The line is crackly. Hard to make out, as if the person at the other end of the receiver is outside, buffeted by angry winds.

"Doug, that you?"

"Detective Superintendent Roper is unavailable. Might I be able to help?"

"Doug? Doug, I'm losing you..."

"Sorry, this is a terrible line, might I be able to ring you back..."

"Doug, look, it's Paul Gosling. Tech unit for Thames Valley. I just heard the news. I'm sure you're up to your eyes with this double murder so I'll keep it brief..."

McAvoy hears another roar of wind. Tries again to interrupt but is drowned out.

"The Cadbury case, yeah? I heard it's all systems go. What did you do with the tech report?"

"I beg your pardon?"

"The tech report. About the mobile number? The ghost messages the lads did for you? Was it nothing, after all? I wouldn't be asking, but they were wondering if you'd got to the bottom of it. They aren't cheap, these boffins, so I hope they were worth your while. We don't normally follow up, but the Butterworth case affected everybody. Even down here. Getting the right man means a lot to everybody..."

McAvoy finds himself breathing harder.

Ella: like fingers down his throat.

He reaches into his pocket for his twisted handkerchief pouch, fat at one end like a comet, an elastic band wrapped around the crushed spices Roisin picked and mixed for him, when he first began to complain that the smell of Ella's memory wasn't going away.

He breathes it in.

Loses himself for a second in rosemary, sage, marjoram, picked with hands that can make him feel wonderful, safe, beloved...

"It was just that with the other stuff we were surprised you went with the murder charge, but look I know you know what you're doing..."

McAvoy sits and stares, listening to the wind whistle down the phone, wondering if the gale will mask his Scottish brogue. If he can sound as swish and glamorous as the man whose face is more famous than the villains he catches. Wonders if he should. If it's right. If he's letting curiosity get the better of him. Indulging himself. If he's guilty of conceit for daring to second guess such a decorated officer.

But he remembers Shane Cadbury's face.

And Roper's, that night.

When he had found her, on the bed, in the bloodied gown.

He remembers that feeling, that certainty, unequivocal and deafening.

He didn't kill her.

Took her, but didn't stick the knife in.

"Paul," he says, talking through the handkerchief and the herbs. "Can you send that report to me again...?"

16

3 p.m. Hessle foreshore.

Three clapped-out motors and an ice cream van spread out on the concrete car park.

Wind.

Rain.

The bleakest of midwinters. Each gust of wind more pissed off and miserable than the last.

The sun giving up and letting the grey clouds and the darkness swallow it whole and pull it, inexorably, below the brown waters and the white caps and the frothing waves.

The street lights and headlamps opening their eyes.

Waiting.

Watching.

Drinking it in.

Looking at the Humber. My old friend. A strip of shingly beach and then the muddy waters. A shimmer to the brown surface today, as though somebody has jostled a cup of cold coffee.

The Humber Bridge overhead. Tonnes of metal twisted into a thing of beauty, its peaks and troughs precise and perfect, resembling a reading on a heart monitor.

The door creaks open on the other car, three spaces to

my left, and Tony H gets out. He walks towards me, neck sunk into the collar of his dirty cream mac. Eyes darting. Hands in his pockets. Naturally shifty. He once appeared before a judge to explain a story he had written and was ordered to bring his transcript of an interview. He produced perfect shorthand notes on beer mats and the backs of bank statements. He can write in his pocket with a stub of pencil lead under his fingernail. Everything is a prop for Tony. He can wrap Hull around himself like candy floss around a stick. He's a fucking rat. Feral, and fag-stained. My mate.

He raps on the roof of the car before he pulls open the passenger door.

"Fucking hell, it's pissing down." He throws himself down hard on the passenger seat. He crushes an old burger box and puts his boots all over my cuttings collection, but doesn't seem to notice or care.

"All right, Rat-boy?" I say, pulling out a cigarette. "It's funny, but your mum's dry as a bone when I fuck her. Still, she does insist on up the arse."

Pleasantries exchanged, I offer Tony a fag and he accepts. He pulls a Hamlet box from a pocket and slips the cigarette inside.

"What are the headlines, mate?"

He sinks back into the seat and stretches his legs, arching his back like a yawning cat, then he begins rummaging in his pockets. Eventually he finds a Gregg's chicken and ham pasty. The bag is grease stained, and gives off no steam. The coat was probably manufactured around the pasty.

Tony gives a little yelp of triumph as he roots in the bag, and takes a big bite.

"Right, I've spoken to the desk and the young lad's been

keeping an eye on the trial. Nowt better than we've already got. The mum's going to be giving evidence first thing tomorrow. Then Lewis. Choudhury's going to eviscerate him. No steer yet on whether Cadbury's going to give evidence. Fucking big bugger, wasn't he? Could snap a girl like Ella in half with those big shovel-hands of his. How he's pleading not guilty I don't fucking know. Funny one, this, ain't it? Was looking back at my notes and I reckon you and me couldn't have been that far off when it happened. Remember, when all that stuff about Two-Jags Prescott came out and we were up in Sutton, outside the gates waiting for a chat with his missus, freezing to death. He might have walked right past us. Makes you think, doesn't it? Anyway, we splashed on this morning's opening. Not bad stuff. I saw yours on the wires. Decent write. So much to squeeze in the intro, wasn't there? The family must have been stapled to their seats not to storm the cells and rip his bastard head off. I don't know how much they know about his past but when it comes out we're looking at more fireworks. How many times has he been banged up for sex crimes? Fucking nonce. Shagging little girls for years."

He finishes the pasty and looks around at the mess in the car. "Owt to drink?" he asks.

"Should be an old Lucozade under your chair. I might have pissed in it once or twice though."

"Nectar," he says and reaches under his seat. His hand emerges with the bottle and he twists the top off. There is no hiss. He takes a glug, gives a shrug, and ploughs on. "Right, this bollocks up at the Country Park. I've spoken to my guy and he reckons it's going to be a fucking blinder. Roper was kind enough to give me a steer. It's looking like a drug deal gone wrong. They haven't got an ID for either of them yet, but it shouldn't be long before it's all formal. One of them's got needle tracks up his arm and the other's got 'dealer' written all over him."

"So have they killed each other, then?" I ask, all innocence.

"Doesn't look like it," says Tony H, lighting a Hamlet. "Early doors, but the science boys reckon the gunshot victim died almost instantly. That means somebody else must have battered the other one's brains in. He's a big fucker though, so we might be looking for a hard case."

I stare out through the glass, unsure what face to pull. In my head, the arcade-game and slot-machine jingle; metal on metal on metal. This is how my brain responds to the absence of my medication. Audible hallucinations. Nausea. Strange, high, keening diphthongs of sound felt but not truly heard. I can taste blood. Taste metal. It feels as if my mouth is full of bullets.

Tony gives me a look and raises an eyebrow. Our quid pro quo relationship requires me to give him something useful, and at the moment I've got nothing. I try and finesse some bullshit, to shake glitter onto a turd.

"I've had a chat with one of my tame sergeants and got pretty much the same," I say, stifling a cough as I breathe in a lungful of Tony's cigar. "But it looks like they might have the killer's car on CCTV. There's a camera in the trees in the car park, and there's no way that whoever did this went there on foot."

Tony nods, and rubs a finger across his yellow teeth. There's a squeaking sound, like a snooker cue being chalked, and he looks down at the digit. He rubs whatever he's found on the under-side of the passenger seat. "Yeah,

I heard something like that. Apparently, they've found one car abandoned a few streets away that might belong to the guy who had his face smashed in. The bloke who got shot probably took the fucking bus. Fucking chav bastard. I suppose if he was high enough, he might have flown."

We fall into silence and stare at the water, brooding on how to take the next step with minimal effort. We're supposed to be competitors, but work better as a team. I always keep something back when we meet up for our clandestine, grubby little chats, but he does the same to me. There's always been something between us, a weird bond of drink and debauchery.

"What's your next move then?" he asks, absent-mindedly pulling up his shirt to examine his chest. He licks his finger and gives his nipple a rub. It's yellow, like a spot. "I'm hoping for a name by five-ish. Roper is going to call me, so I'll let you know."

"I reckon I might go for the CCTV angle. See if I can find out where the tape is stored and get a look-see."

"Happy fucking hunting. Roper will have this locked down pretty quickly. He's got his 100 per cent clean-up record to think about."

"Is he still claiming 100 per cent?"

"Aye, he's found a way of ignoring that debacle last year. He'll still tell anyone who'll listen that he's never lost a case."

Tony looks momentarily bitter. We both know the case he's talking about: an attack on a Hessle Road prostitute that was almost unprecedented in its savagery. Caron Cross. Sixty-three. Every bone in her face was smashed. She looked like a rotten apple when they found her, but she pulled through. A city council contractor, Denis Johnstone, was charged within days. He was in the area at the time of the attack, been spotted on CCTV moments later, and his wife had given evidence that he had come home covered in blood, but Johnstone's defence team managed to convince the jury that he had actually been busy beating somebody else up at the time. The crime he admitted to was nasty, but not as barbaric as the hell that was visited on Caron. There was a lot of evidence to suggest that the investigation team had known about the other incident and tried to shush it up, and Roper's reputation took a hit. It's the only crease in his Armani suit, but it does piss him off. It pisses off Tony a good deal more. He's been keeping Caron's bed warm since she got out of hospital.

"What's the rest of the day got in store, then?" he asks, fishing for that little bit more than he's ever likely to reel in.

"Remember, I'm seeing Cadbury's mam? And I'd better pop in at my sister's, give myself a dose of misery."

"Things no better, are they not?" he asks, shaking his head, and for a moment, genuinely concerned. "Such a shame. She's a lovely lass. I know I've only met her a couple of times but she seemed such a sweetie. Shame you can't just blow that fucking landlord's head off."

"It's not just her landlord, mate," I say, grabbing the steering wheel, hard. My knuckles go white beneath my gloves. "It's her fucking dealer too. She's shagging him, y'know? Reckons he's her boyfriend, gonna make it all better. Called Beatle, or some such shit. They all need fucking doing. You met him that night in Sailmakers, when we were trying to get some food down Kerry and she was pretending she was clean. He wasn't happy. Ugly prick in tracksuit bottoms and a baseball cap."

"Maybe. Dunno. Don't think he rings a bell. Be nice to put him out of the picture the way the Yanks do, though, eh? This is England though, Owen. If we were in America you could nip down the corner shop and buy a fucking Uzi. Do the both of them. And Choudhury. Christ, you could clear out half the baggage in your life. Cheer yourself up a bit." He laughs, and scratches at his cheek. Delicate flakes of skin float into the air. One settles on the dashboard. I half expect it to begin evolving before my eyes. A few million years, and Tony's DNA could be approaching that of a human being.

I smile at him, and blink, to distort the look in my eyes. "I bet it's more difficult than you think."

"I dunno, mate," he continues. "The Americans seem to just point and pull the trigger. We've got to content ourselves with glassing people. That's what makes this country wonderful."

We both laugh, and Tony turns his head to stare out the window. He doesn't want to get back out of the car. The weather is too miserable. The storm isn't angry. More suicidal.

"Oh fuck it," he says, and opens the door. The wind charges in and whips up a maelstrom to match the one in my mind. "I'll call you later."

He stumbles out and runs back to his car, jacket over his head.

The sky is almost black now, marbled with the grey of the storm clouds and the purple haze of the chemical plants at the estuary's mouth.

Pull out my phone. Trying to get ahead of the game.

Scroll down and call Roper. He answers on the fourth ring, fashionably late.

"Now then, sunbeam," he says. "You not fancy the trip to the woods?"

"Popped up and back again," I say, smile in my voice. "Nothing to see. Figured you'd give me preferential treatment."

"You've got my mobile number. What more you want?"

"The lot."

"You'll be lucky. Don't know much myself yet. Give me a bit of time and I will. You reckon this will go national?"

"Definitely, if you give me it first. I know you're a busy boy, but ask Simmo to give me a bell as soon as you get anything. Day or night. I don't sleep much."

"Nightmares?"

"No. Your lass keeps me up."

We laugh, two blokes, pretending to banter. Pretending to like each other.

"All I can tell you is it's almost certainly drugs-related. We're looking at CCTV footage now, but without much success. It could be a gang-style execution, how about that? Worth a headline?"

"Belter. Stay in touch."

"Do my best."

Click, and he's gone.

I'm alone, watching the last of the lights come on.

The bridge illuminated. A pathway of yellow bulbs, beckoning me like a moth.

Watching the water.

17

Tony calls as I'm on my way to see Satan's mum, stuck in traffic on Holderness Road. McDonald's on my right, kebab shop on my left. Grotty end of town. Stout young mothers with knocked-off pushchairs; old blokes in comfortable slacks and Dunlop trainers, pottering down the pavements, waiting for the chippies to open. Soaked through and wind-blown. Pale faces and grey eyes. Garish under the street lights. A land of people who don't brush their hair at the back.

The darkness is almost iridescent. Multi-coloured, like a pigeon's neck.

Jess's picture, lighting up.

Tony's mobile number illuminating the screen.

Me. Too busy to deal with him: "Tony, mate. This going to be good?"

"Fucking corker, lad. Just got off the phone to my mate in CID. No formal ID until first thing, but they know 'em both. The one that got shot is local, some shitty little dealer from Orchard Park. Real ratty fucker. Record as long as my knob. Twenty-three-year-old, called, hang on a sec... Daz Norton, that's it. Lived on Gildane, off Danepark. Not exactly classy."

"Is that near the cop-shop? Where they found that lass a couple of years back?"

"Aye, that's the one. Anyway, doubt we've lost a brain surgeon there. Got shot in the face. Not much of it left. The other one, though, he's the real deal."

Eager now, but trying not to sound it – waiting for the name of the man I killed, scribbling in shorthand on the back of a betting slip.

"He's a Leeds lad. Proper gangster by the sounds of it. Alfie Prescott. Thirty-three. Fucking headcase from what my mate says. Works for some other nutjob in Leeds. Something Petrovsky. Getting it bottomed out as we speak. You know those Dutch lorry drivers, got sent down a few months back. The ones on the ferry? Got about sixteen years apiece for all the charlie? Well Prescott was named as the guy who set it all up. Could have connections right up to the big players in Holland. Did a stretch for GBH a few years ago. Doesn't even try to act legit. Known as a problem-solver. Coppers were fucking terrified of him. Anyway, he got his head ventilated with a rock by the looks of things."

A tremble in my throat, nails eating into the palms of my hands.

"Wonder what he was doing around here then. Your lad say?"

"All I got was a feeling. If this little weasel was a foot soldier, a crappy little pusher, he might have pissed off the wrong people. Maybe Prescott was here to do him, and got jumped straight after. Any luck, we'll have a fucking gang war before the end of the week."

"Fuck."

"Indeed."

"What's next then? You going to knock the family? Name him?"

"Trying to get it confirmed from another source now, but the desk are jumpy. Probably hang fire until the morning. You?"

"Follow your lead, mate. I'll let the desk know, make myself look good, like."

"You owe me one."

"You owe me one more."

"Laters, mate."

"Aye, cheers."

Switch the phone off. Stare at the scrawl on the betting slip.

Notice I've drawn a tombstone.

Look up at the sound of honking from behind. There's a gap in the traffic ahead of me. A cyclist nips into the gap from the pavement to my left, darts behind a bus. He turns his head as he disappears out of sight, and for an instant his face is a tapestry of blood, his features twisted and obscured beneath the thick fluid. Eyes empty, teeth dropping into the black cavity of his ravaged throat and jaw.

Then he's gone, and I'm looking at the roadside again.

I release the handbrake and ease forward, rubbing my eyes.

18

Detective Superintendent Doug Roper sits on the edge of his desk like a funky newsreader and casts his eyes over a report he's read a dozen times. The cameras are rolling, so he makes it seem like he's fascinated. Cocks an eyebrow, like he's seen something everybody else has missed. Nods, gently. Hint of a smile.

"Cut," says whatshername. "Perfect," she adds, as if he didn't know.

He asks for a moment to himself and leaves the room. In a moment he'll have to put a warm hand on the shoulder of the ugly bastard downstairs who just identified the body with the bullet hole in it. Have to pretend he gives a shit. That he somehow cares that the world is shy one more useless prick.

Interesting, though, he thinks. Bit of a surprise to hear the name. Been a silly boy, ain't you, he says to the dead. Could all work out nicely, this. Few phone calls, little bit of pressure, delicate prod and poke. Couldn't have asked for more.

Time to drop the gun, he thinks?

No, he decides. Always nice to have a trump card.

Surprise about the other one, though. Big fucker. Hard as nails. Couldn't have gone down easy.

Might be worth throwing the press a bone. Let somebody in and bank the favour. Owen? Fuck that. Arrogant little shit. Never looks away. Always meets your eyes. You wouldn't know it to look at him, would you? Wouldn't know what he did.

Tony H, he decides. Bring in the rat.

So much to do and so little time.

His mobile rings and he sees that it's McAvoy's number. He titters, as he imagines the poor cunt still plugging away at the computer, trying to track down every member of the national remote control car club. Got his moment in the spotlight, didn't he? Found Ella's body, made the arrest. Promotion and a transfer. Onto Supercop's team. But not one of the boys, yet. Doesn't know when to leave well alone.

The phone stops ringing, eventually.

Roper strokes his moustache. Breathes deep as he does a round-up of things to worry about.

Still no word on the cellmate.

A lesser man would get twitchy, he tells himself.

A lesser man wouldn't have got this far, he replies.

19

Twenty minutes later. Third in line in the queue for chips. Last in line, truth be told.

The smell of fried fish. Grease. Bleach. Lights too bright. Doing to my eyes what a low buzzing would do to my ears.

Me feeling peculiar. Floating above it all, looking at myself through a telescope.

Trying to tear my eyes away from the woman behind the counter. Mid-forties. Big hair. Batter blonde. Gold earrings. Maybe four foot ten if she's wearing heels. Busy. Boisterous. Soft cheeks. One tooth too many in her top row. Pink tongue. Wrinkles at her eyes. Too much mascara. Smoker-pink cheeks. She's not fat but could do with being wound tighter from the top. Breasts four inches lower than they should be. Just soft lumps, visible through her T-shirt and striped tabard.

She moves away from the counter, tray in hand, and picks up a newly fried piece of haddock from the stack behind her. Places it on a mountain of chips. She does it right. Perfect. Probably very Feng Shui. She shakes on salt and vinegar without being asked and starts to wrap it.

She's wearing leggings. Black. White trainers and slouch-socks. Hasn't even looked at me yet.

I turn my head away, stare at the patterns in the perm of the pensioner in front. She just wants chips. Done in a moment. The woman behind the counter treats her nicely. The old dear blathers on about the weather. Tells her she's going to her daughter's for Sunday lunch and she's almost got all of the shopping done. Calls the younger woman Lena as they chat. Doesn't ask her what she has planned for the big day. Lena smiles at her as they talk, gives nods of encouragement. Knocks a few pence of the price. Won't hear of her paying the full whack, but tells her not to tell her friends. Calls her Flo. Flo grins like she's won the lottery and tells me Lena's got a heart of gold. She says it almost sadly. Puts the parcel in her shopping bag and totters to the door.

Lena watches her go. Waves. Gives a little smile. Looks up and raises her eyebrows. They need plucking.

No recognition.

No interest.

"Yes love?" she says, encouragingly.

I drink her in for a moment.

"Mrs Cadbury?"

She flinches at the name. Her mouth straightens into a thin line. Her hands go straight into the pockets of her tabard, like a cowboy going for his six-shooter, and she steps back from the counter.

"Owen Lee," I say quickly as she begins walking around to the open hatchway. "From the Press Association. You said you could spare me…" I fade out as she marches around the counter, disappearing for a moment as she passes the jar of pickled eggs. A foreign-looking guy peers his head over the fryer, further back in the shop. He's young. Maybe my age. Olive-skinned and stubbly. I size him up and fancy my chances.

She emerges on the tiled shop floor and carries on past me to the front door, pulling a bundle of keys on a curly pink cord from the pocket of her tabard. She shoves one in the lock and turns it. I see her face reflected in the glass of the rain-lashed front door. There's anger in her eyes. Passion. Uncertainty. She looks like she's in the middle of an argument with some offending husband and can't decide whether to fuck him or leave him. I know the look well.

She flips the sign on the door to 'closed' and turns back to me. She wipes a hand on her apron and comes forward. She's even smaller than I thought. A quarter of the size of the vast brute she gave birth to a quarter of a century ago. He must have sucked her dry.

"You had to pick teatime, did you? Busiest time, love."

"Sorry," I say, floundering. "I could come back…"

"No, you're here now. Savio!" She shouts over her shoulder to the young man, not taking her eyes off mine. "I'm shutting for a few minutes. You go and see how much scampi we've got left in the freezer. Then take your break." She raises her hands and gives a shrug, then mutters, almost to herself: "Not exactly bloody heaving anyway."

She points me through the hatchway and the kitchen to a side door. She puts a hand on my arm as I pass, to steer me, and I have to stop myself jolting at the contact. I'm led down a corridor. I find myself wishing she'd take my hand, and let me float behind her like a balloon on a string. I'm gazing at my feet as I walk, my boots leaving wet footprints on the blue patterned carpet, getting dizzy in the swirls.

The carpet comes to an abrupt stop at the foot of the

stairs. The patterns don't match up as it starts up the single flight.

I hold the bannister as I follow Lena. Her arse is three steps in front of my face, and I'm feeling weird, trying to think of something to say. She's muttering about excusing the mess and hoping we can keep this brief.

I close my eyes and bump into a wall, knocking a pencil sketch of a horse and hounds askew. Lena looks at me and I mumble an apology, and then I'm bumbling into the darkened living room, plonking down on a rocking chair too close to the electric fire. It's the only light in the room.

"Are you all right, love?" she asks with genuine concern. "You don't look too good."

"Really?" I say, squinting up at her. "You look fantastic." I smile as I say it to let her know I'm not a twat, but I sense it looks like a grimace, and stop. I purse my lips to fight down the nausea, and wish she'd offer me a glass of water.

Lena looks taken aback but not offended. She unfastens her apron and pulls it over her head. She lays it down on the sofa and sits next to it, hands clasped between her knees. She doesn't seem to mind the half gloom, but it's too heavy for me. I can't really make anything out. There are lumps in the darkness. I can see the shapes of pictures on the wall but not their contents. I can't get a sense of my surroundings. There are squares of deep jet against charcoal.

"Any chance of a light on?" I hear the whine in my voice as I say it, and give a cough. I give myself a more manly lilt as I carry on. "I look better in the light."

Lena gives a shrug, gets up and switches on the big light. It's garish. There's no shade. A single bulb hangs in the centre of the room and its glow is harsh, aggressive.

Lena returns to her seat and gestures up at the light. "I never have it on myself. I like it cosy."

The brightness hits me like a slap. I let my face become charming, open my eyes wide and fix them on Lena, giving her a shake of the head and a gentle smile. "I can see again."

"It's always so bright in the shop," she says, by way of explanation. "I get these awful headaches. I just use the telly and the fire when I'm up here."

"Even for reading?"

"I'm not much of a one for reading. I used to read the *Hull Mail*. But then it got too hard."

"Too hard?"

"All the nasty things. All the violence. When you live alone you don't always want to know there are psychopaths walking the streets." I hear it as *cycle paths*. I always do.

"There's just you, then? No man around."

"No, not for a while." There's regret in her voice. Acceptance, too. "Never had that much luck with the buggers." She looks me up and down for the first time and I can sense her weighing me like a fish. I'm happy to play up to it, to be on display. There's a certain quality to her gaze. Perhaps a hunger. She doesn't seem as defensive as I'd feared. I might be done in half an hour. Maybe less. Say my goodbyes and then go and visit my sister. Work out my frustrations.

I look around the room as I stick a hand in my pocket and retrieve my notebook. My fags are in the way and I pull them out and lay them on the arm of the chair. Lena looks at them and I offer her one. She nods furiously. I half get out of my chair to reach across to her and she does the same. We meet in the centre of the room, half-crooked. I light hers first, but the lighter dies before my own ignites. I start patting my pockets with the unlit fag in my mouth. Lena takes the end between finger and thumb and leans forward, pressing the glowing ember of her own cigarette to mine. I breathe deeply and our eyes lock, only inches apart. We both smile, and then she's embarrassed and retreats to the chair. I do the same, feeling better.

The room is almost bare. Neat. Simple. Brown carpet, Ikea rag-rug. Old-fashioned sideboard against one wall. Portable TV next to the fire. A frosted glass window set in one wall, next to a bare white door. Floral wallpaper on the chimney breast, pale pinky colour on the others. Half a dozen birthday cards on the mantlepiece over the fire. All of its bars glowing red. All of the pictures on the wall are classless classics. Monet's lilies. Cezanne's bathers. Van Gogh's chair. Ophelia, floating in death.

No photographs.

"Right," I say, suddenly business-like. Making a start on the pre-prepared bullshit. "As I explained, what I'm wanting to do is put the other side of the story. So often with these high-profile court cases, the accused is demonised to such an extent that nobody ever stops to think that they're still a human being, or asks themselves what tragedies in their life led them down a certain road. As you've no doubt seen, your Shane has already been portrayed as an out-and-out monster. What I want is to get a piece written from your point of view, looking at his childhood, his background. As I've promised, we won't identify you. It took a lot of courage for you to call me, and believe me, we'll respect your wishes. Now I've done quite a lot of research already and I know about which schools he went to, getting expelled at fifteen, floating between a few jobs and apprenticeships, and then..."

"And then?"

"Well, and then, erm, the problems. The convictions. We'll come to that later though. For now, it's his childhood that intrigues me. Do you want to talk me through it?"

"Where do I start?"

"Well, am I right in thinking Shane was an only child?"

"Yes."

Wait for more.

Nothing comes.

"And his father?"

"Not around."

She's looking down, now. Seems to be chewing on something but there's nothing in her mouth. Picking at a stubby hangnail on her right hand. Scratching a spot on her hairline. All the little twitches that seem to bring comfort in times of strife. Grieving mothers, angry fathers, broken loved ones turned inside out with emotion; they all give the same performance, and I conduct it like an orchestra. I've seen it all before. It's punctuation for their pain. As much a part of the dance as my soft voice, my understanding eyes, warm palms laid on their cold hands – giving the odd choke on a syllable as I lay myself bare and share their pain, pretending to give a fuck about their little Jimmy.

"Lena," I start...

"I'm sorry," says Lena, suddenly looking up at me. Eyes the colour of stone-washed denim fill with apologies and shame. She looks at my notebook as though it's a doorway she's afraid to pass through. It feels conspicuous in my hand. My pen is cumbersome, an irritation; a lance held between finger and thumb. All at once I'm horribly aware of myself, of her, of the nature of our association. We're not friends. Not colleagues. Not lovers. I'm a stranger asking questions in her living room and idly wondering if her cunt smells of haddock or cod. It all feels real, as though I'm actually living my own life.

She leans forward in her seat, like a jockey. Elbows on her knees. Rubs her hands on her leggings.

I put the pen down.

Lower the notebook like a sail.

Stand up.

Cross the room.

Take the seat next to her on the sofa, close enough for my hand to brush the soft hairs on her bare arm.

And she starts to talk.

It's fucking good.

Dynamite copy.

Revelations and remorse. Anger at herself. At me. At her son and the devil that sired him.

Disappearing into her bedroom more than once; returning with hankies, touched-up make-up, a lop-eared stuffed rabbit that she asks me to put on Ella's grave.

Say I will.

Probably won't.

By the time I start writing things down, she's opened the drinks cupboard and we're necking Taboo. I've told her about Jess. Kerry. Created a fictional brother who died of leukaemia. Given her absolution and held her as the sobs came.

Cherry-picked from her pain until pound signs danced in my eyes.

20

Back in the car, scribbling in the dark.

Getting it down while it's still fresh and raw.

Before it gets swallowed up and diluted.

I have to get Cadbury out of me. I don't want his secrets to meet my own.

As twisted child abuser Shane Cadbury begins a life sentence for an horrific murder, reporter Owen Lee spoke exclusively to his mother about how she feared him even as a child...

There is little about Lena Winstanley to suggest she once gave birth to a monster – a violent sexual sadist who butchered and decapitated a young bride-to-be in her wedding gown and kept her corpse for his own sick pleasures.

Petite, polite and proud of the fish shop she runs in her home city of Hull, East Yorkshire, Ms Winstanley, 44, is a popular member of her community and a good friend to her neighbours and customers.

But Ms Winstanley has a secret she hoped to hide from the community she calls home. 26 years ago, she gave birth to Shane Cadbury, the man whose horrendous slaying of young Ella Butterworth shocked the city and led to a high-profile court case which this week ended with Cadbury being sentenced to...

At the culmination of the trial, Presiding Judge (**check name**) Skelton labelled Lena's son a "**wtvr he fukng calls hm**."

The jury, who wept as they were showed photos of the beautiful and innocent young victim, were told how Cadbury had a long history of violence towards women and had spent time in young offenders' institutes and adult prison for vile sex attacks on children.

Ms Winstanley, who adopted her mother's maiden name when Cadbury's crimes were first exposed, said last night: "Every young girl who gets pregnant is afraid of how their child might turn out, but they do the best they can and will stick up for them regardless. I did that for so long. I kept saying people got it wrong, that it wasn't his fault. But I was lying to myself. He was an animal, and when I think of what he did to that young girl, I can't stand to look at myself in the mirror."

Lena was just 17 years old when she fell pregnant during a brief relationship with a visiting seaman. A much older man, he beat and raped her when she told him she was expecting a child, and then left the city.

Lena believed she had miscarried in the wake of the attack, but several months later discovered she was still pregnant, and it was too late for the termination she admits now she desired.

Disowned by her family, Lena struggled to raise Shane on her own and debts forced her to move to a succession of flats around the city.

She said: "I tried to give him what I could, but I couldn't work because there was nobody to watch Shane. We were together all the time, and he was a hard baby. He didn't sleep much and he would scream like no other child I knew if he didn't get what he wanted."

Shane grew into an even more difficult child, who earned a reputation as a neighbourhood bully.

She said: "Parents were always knocking on the door and saying he had been attacking their children. He didn't really play with them, so they would call him names, and then he would get them, one by one. He was a big boy."

A poor performer at school, who suffered from what Lena now believes was Attention Deficit Hyperactivity Disorder, Shane was frequently in trouble. He began smoking at nine years old, when he was also involved in a physical confrontation with a man who was then Lena's partner.

She said: "He hated the man I was seeing. He didn't want to share me. He would pretend he was ill if he knew I was supposed to be seeing him. My friend stayed over one night, and Shane came into our room and attacked him with a hammer. It was like something from a horror film. He was shrieking and crying and trying to kill him."

Following the incident, Shane withdrew into himself. He became fascinated by the occult, and in his teenage years spent most of his time in his bedroom, sketching images of women in horrific poses and listening to music.

When he was 13 years old, he was expelled from school and charged with indecent assault after molesting a younger girl in an empty classroom.

A similar incident followed at his new school, and he was sent to a young offenders' institute. When he was released, he was a much more sociable person, and found a group of friends from the surrounding East Hull estate, but they barely went to school and spent most of their time at an older friend's home, watching pornography and horror films.

By now an obese but muscular young man, Lena came to fear her son.

She said: "He was still my son and I loved him but I was becoming so ashamed. I couldn't make excuses. He would tell me that the girls had wanted it, or that he was being set up, but it was happening all the time. He would watch girls from his bedroom window and I would know what he was doing to himself. It was vile, but I couldn't get through to him. He ignored me, and was always out with older mates.

"The police were constantly knocking on the door. He was getting done for theft and assaults and drinking more and smoking cannabis, and I didn't know who he was. He'd come home while I was asleep and draw symbols in red paint on the wall, just to scare me.

"He wouldn't get a job, and just drifted. I could go weeks without seeing him, and then when he was 22 I just reached the end of the road with him."

At 22, Cadbury was arrested and charged with raping the eight-year-old daughter of one of his friends. Remanded to Wakefield Prison, he bullied other inmates and was frequently in trouble.

At the trial, where his counsel told of his drug addiction

*and low IQ, he spoke only to confirm his name, and his
conversion, through the prison chaplain, to Catholicism.
Conflicting reports and a mix-up over forensic evidence
meant the charge was reduced to indecent assault. He
entered a guilty plea to the lesser charge and spent 14
months in prison.*

*Upon his release, he made no attempt to contact his
mother, who had now opened her new business.*

*She said: "Despite the trouble he's been in I know he
feels no guilt. I know he has done truly evil things and I
can't stand the thought he was once a part of me.*

*"When that young girl was missing I had this feeling,
this hollow, empty feeling, that he was involved. I was
just waiting for it to be confirmed. I'm not his mother.
He's taken my life too. I was his first victim."*

Bang.

Job done. Most of it true and all of it juicy. Exclusive.
Mine.

Gun in my waistband, humming, softly.

Jobs to do, people to see.

Needing a drink.

The press of flesh and stink of ale.

Need to fish in the sea of humanity.

Reel something in.

21

"*Good evening, this is Inspector Dave Simmonds on the Humberside Police media line. The time is now 6.57 p.m. on February 6. Just a brief update, as promised, on the ongoing inquiry into the two suspicious deaths at the Country Park. Many of you have been calling me to ask me to confirm two names that are currently doing the rounds. As I've explained, until all of the families have been informed and certain forensic tests completed, I will be unable to release any identities and would request that you do not print any names in association with this case until we are ready to formally release them. I can only say at this stage that a post mortem examination has been carried out by Professor Murray, that's John Murray, with an 'h', and spelled M.U.R.R.A.Y, before you ask, of Sheffield University, which showed that one of these men died from a brutal and sustained attack, and that the other met their death as the result of a gunshot wound. This is now a murder inquiry. There will be an informal press conference at Priory Road police station at 9 a.m. tomorrow. I am aware that many of you may be covering the Shane Cadbury murder trial at the moment and I'm sorry for the inconvenient time, but Detective Superintendent Doug Roper is heading this investigation personally and unfortunately this is the only time he will be available. Further to the questions I have been asked about the CCTV tapes which cover the car park, I can confirm that yes, a tape has been recovered and will be viewed by officers. I would like to thank you for your patience. I will update this media line as soon as I am able to do so."*

8 p.m. One elbow on the bar at the Tap & Spile on Spring Bank. Full of disenfranchised liberals seeking asylum and finding solace in conversation with the like-minded; the lefties who don't want to admit they're getting secretly pissed off at the amount of olive-skinned faces on the street beyond the leaded glass.

Decent boozer, this. Walking distance from the *Hull Daily Mail* main office. Quick stroll from Kerry's. Never more than two feet from a fuck.

Busy. Must be sixty people milling about in the two rooms, spilling beer on the wooden floors, squeezed in at tables and leaning against columns, shredding the labels off bottles of Budweiser, and building pyramids with beer mats on the varnished tables. It's a theme pub, and the theme is drinking and having a laugh. Mixed crowd tonight. Students in corduroy flares and tiny tops, middle-aged women in jeans and Monsoon dresses, blokes with long hair and leather waistcoats, old blokes nursing a pint of Smooth and talking about the rugby. Lots of ornaments and knick-knacks on the walls. Turn-of-the-century bottles and tin cans, huge keg of beer standing in the centre of the back-bar. Got a yellow feel about the place. Got a good reputation for music, too. Holds the infamous 'Tap on Wood' acoustic competition every year. I caught the final a couple of years back, when one of Kerry's mates came second, losing to a skinny bloke who did a ballad version of 'Ace of Spades' to end his set. It was a good night. Kerry hadn't unravelled yet, though some of her stitching was beginning to come loose. She still believed, then. Still wore the CND badge and posted leaflets through doors for the Legalise Cannabis Alliance. Still ate food when she needed to, rather than when she remembered. Still had arms that didn't look like tea bags. Still laughed at what was funny, instead of giggling at silence and empty air. Still worked at the animal shelter and spent most of her wages on toys and treats for the cats that nobody wanted. Still called Dad every couple of days. Still kept her legs shut until somebody opened them nicely. Still my sister.

I take another gulp of lager, and make room at the bar for a middle-aged woman in leather trousers. She thanks me with a smile.

"Getting pretty crowded," she says, motioning over her shoulder at the crowd while trying to catch the attention of the barmaid by waving a £10 note. I look at her hand. Risen veins snake over pale skin like tree roots.

"Band on, is there?"

"Yeah, King Rollo. Blues lot. Really good." She has to shout over the noise of the crowd, and opens her mouth wide. I can see the fillings in her teeth.

"Aye? Has he got a ponytail?"

"Yeah, that's him. I'm a bit of a groupie. Me and a few mates follow him everywhere."

"Come far?"

"Hornsea." Fifteen miles up the coast. Bridlington's middle class half-sister. "There are a dozen of us tonight. My round.

Oh, hiya. Four halves of Stella, two lager and lime, three Diet Cokes, a vodka tonic, rum and coke, and an orange Reef, please. Phew, got that right. And you?" She looks at me, gesturing at the drink in my hand.

"Oh. No, I'm fine, thanks."

"Sure?"

"Well, if you don't mind? Cool. Bell's whisky, please. With ice."

The barmaid starts putting the order together while I run an eye over my new friend. She's late thirties. Short dark hair fluffed up and ruffled. Round face. Brown eyes. Gap between her two front teeth, like Madonna. Hint of a double chin. Tits worn well in a black top, with a pendant hanging in her cleavage. White blouse worn over. Quite chunky round the middle. Big arse. Black boots. She's sweet, like a sex symbol in a Disney cartoon; an alluring mouse, maybe.

"Thanks," I say, downing the whisky as the barmaid places it in a beery puddle in front of me, and diluting the burn with another gulp of lager. "You need a hand to carry the rest?"

She gives me what she thinks is a twinkle of the eye and says: "No, I'll do it in shifts. Give me an excuse to keep coming back."

I finish the drink while she's still looking at me, and turn my back, ordering another lager from the blonde barmaid. I'm served before anybody else. When I glance back over my shoulder, the woman is already retreating into the crowd, with an added swagger in her hips. She's definitely got an hourglass figure, but it's got too much sand.

I bite the top two inches off my next drink, hoping it will

work like medicine. I'm starting to feel faint, as though my head could float from my body.

There's a vibration in my pocket as my phone rings. I look at the screen and see the number is being withheld. Ramming a finger in my ear I flip open the phone, and strain to hear.

"Owen Lee," I say, raising my voice over the rumble of the rabble.

"Owen? It's Simmo. You free?"

"Pub. Working hard."

"Tough old life."

"Think I've earned it today. You've got to organise a better system. You can't go having double murders on the first day of a trial. And not on a Monday when I've got a bitch of a hangover."

"I'll have a word. See if we can't spread the juicy crimes and retributions over the course of a year. In fact, fax me a copy of your holiday schedule for the next twelve months and I'll distribute it around the criminal fraternity."

"You're a good man, Simmo."

"I aim to please. Anyway, just checking in with a few titbits, if you're interested."

"You know me, mate. Always like a bit of a tit. That's why me and Tony are mates."

"Well, when you see him, give him a good-natured slap from me," he says, a mild note of irritation creeping into his voice. "He's always a pain in the arse but he's gone into overdrive on this one."

"So which way does Roper's nose think the breeze is blowing?"

"It's too early to say, Owen, and I mean that. He asked

me to give you what we've got, but that's fuck all. You'll be the first to know when there is something concrete."

"I never need concrete. Sloppy cement is more than enough." I'm shouting as I talk, trying to make myself heard over the noise of the bar, and I'm getting a few looks.

Simmo senses I'm losing interest and fills up the silence with speech. "Well, at the moment you could do worse than following up the drug deal angle, with a smattering of gangland culture thrown in," he says, and quickly begins to warm to his theme. "No doubt you've heard the names that are doing the rounds. Well, they're spot on. And one of them is somebody West Yorkshire Police know very well. A real proper villain. Muscle for hire. Quite a bright spark, too. Inventive. Used to rob banks when he was younger but after he got out of Wakefield Prison he had what some would consider a bit more class and clout. He leathered the head doorman at a club in Leeds that belonged to a real nasty piece of work, and came to the attention of a lot of big names. Got offered a few jobs with the big leagues, but didn't like to be tied down. Got himself a nice little number doing the occasional piece of work. Cash-drops, the more dangerous deal, that sort of thing. But he found his niche in punishment beatings, and worse. The lads in West Yorkshire have him down for at least three murders last year. Remember that bloke whose body they found in a suitcase in the car park at Ferrybridge services? You remember, they still haven't found the head. Well they reckon that was his handiwork."

"Nice chap, then. Christ, you're really going to waste man-hours solving his death? Somebody's done you a favour."

"No doubt, but we've got that old public duty thing to worry about. Not a problem in your line of work, I realise."

"Yeah, yeah," I say, suddenly bored, feeling too hot and jostled in the confinement of the bar, but not wanting to leave in case the tit who's staring at me takes it as a victory.

"Anyhow, past few months he's been almost exclusively on staff for Mr Petrovsky…"

"Petrovsky? Remind me." I know Simmo's trying to pretend he knows all about the big boys of the criminal world, but we both know he's only just found all this out.

"Russian bloke in his sixties. Doing time for shooting a copper who gave him a speeding ticket, and still running things. Got a lot of fingers in a lot of pies, but it's mostly drugs and illegals. There's barely a ship arrives in Hull that hasn't got some of Petrovsky's merchandise on board. And a heck of a lot of Kosovans, Albanians. Even a few Ukrainians, for old times' sake. Not one to cross. Our boy has basically been making sure people still realise Petrovsky is the boss. Could be out on appeal before long and wants his business to still be there. Laddo was making that happen. Been putting dents in faces. Making sure people don't take liberties."

"And is that why he was in the woods with the other bloke, you reckon? Sorting out a problem for the boss?"

"It's definitely a possibility. The other chap was a bit of a nobody really. Been done for dealing a couple of times but there was never anything to suggest he was into anything major. Maybe he was playing out of his league and got caught out. Might have been cutting his crack with brick dust and baking powder. Maybe he just said the wrong thing. Roper will find out. You know what he's like."

I feel a dig in my ribs. It's not a gentle gesture. Somebody pissed off; somebody out to make a point.

My right hand drops into my coat pocket, and closes on the gun. I keep Simmo pressed to the left side of my head, which is wet and sweating, like an open oyster stuck to my skull. I feel ten feet fucking tall. Ten feet of shit and misery, but ten feet nonetheless.

"You picked the wrong fucking horse, lad…"

I stop, mid-flow, as I stare into the face of an angry blonde. Eleanor. Lenny, to her mates. To Jess. My Jess. Best friends since school. When Jess left me, it was to go and stay at Lenny's place, a ground floor flat on the edge of the city centre. I often imagined them living out a Manhattan lifestyle, all red wine from big glasses and Doritos in a bowl, *Sex and the City* DVDs and fluffy pyjamas, scented candles and delicious gossip. It was Lenny who came by for Jess's stuff when we split, who had brokered meetings and financial settlements. She thinks she's tough.

"Owen? Owen, you still there?"

Simmo's voice is chirruping in my ear, but I ignore him.

Lenny is staring at me, hard, waiting for me to finish my call. She's angry. Intense. If her eyes had teeth they'd have swallowed half of my face by now. I'm staring back. Tongue stuck to the roof of my mouth. A deluge of memories swamps me, images of happier times.

"Won't be a tick, princess," I say.

"Princess?" Simmo's voice in my ear again. "You sound busy. I won't hold you back then. Look, I'll see you at the press conference in the morning, and I'm not sure what you can do with this at this time, but a couple of officers have viewed the CCTV. It's really poor quality, but it shows there was a car in the car park at the time that we reckon all this happened."

"Poor quality? I thought you could get cameras that can read the brand name off a packet of cigarettes from the top of a block of flats."

"Yeah, you can, but this is your absolute basic one. They only put it in because they were getting trouble with blokes meeting up in the toilets after dark and doing the nasty."

"Nice."

"Quite. Anyway, we can't get a number plate but we can get a vehicle type. It's a Vauxhall Cavalier, real old piece of crap. Mid-Eighties. Not even a classic. Can't be many of them around so it shouldn't be long before we find who it belongs to. Could be nothing to do with all this but it has to be a priority as a line of enquiry. We'll be putting out a press release in the morning. We're going through the database now. I'm sure I know somebody who drives one but my brain just isn't in gear tonight." Simmo stops, as Depeche Mode give way to James Brown. It's an eclectic jukebox.

"All right?" asks Simmo.

I've been silent for a few seconds, watching Lenny go through her repertoire of facial expressions. Eventually, she'll have to smile. She looks good tonight. She's twenty-eight. In good shape. Likes floaty dresses and leg warmers. Pale skin and rosy cheeks. Rings in the shape of flowers and butterflies. Beautiful smile when she unshackles it.

"Cool, mate," I say. "Thanks for that." I'm surprised by how little I care. "Owt else useful?"

"Just that whoever did this has more to worry about than the coppers. Petrovsky's not going to be happy to have lost one of his boys. The other one's a nobody, but the big lad? Let's hope the killer's got some bullets left."

"Reckon he can handle himself. See ya later."

"Yeah, bye."

I close the phone slowly, and slip it into my pocket, where it clinks against the gun. It's a reassuring sound and sensation, playing just for me.

"Hi, beautiful," I say. Once upon a time, I'd have greeted her with a kiss on the edge of the lips and a hug, taking my time to breathe in her perfume and press her tits against my chest. Don't think she'd appreciate it now.

"Your phone is working then," she says.

"What?" I ask, thrown.

"I've been calling you back all day. I was telling myself that your phone must be broken. I've already tried her friends in Nottingham. I'm not stupid. They haven't seen her." She sounds scared and angry.

"Maybe she just needs her space," I say, hopeful, and cling to the thought like a lifeline. "I bet you she's there and told her friend not to say. She buggered off one night when we were together and her friend swore blind she wasn't with them. I went and knocked on the door and guess who fucking answered?"

"But her friends are my friends. They know me. They wouldn't lie to me."

I shrug, suggesting that I don't want to hurt Lenny's feelings.

"Why don't you go down there. You're obviously out of your mind with worry. Be best to put it to rest."

"I don't know." Then, hopeful, wide eyed: "Why don't you come with me? We can compare notes, have a think…"

"I can't, Len," I say, terrified at the prospect of even thinking about Jess, and where she might be. "You go. They'll talk to you more than they'll talk to me."

Lenny puts her head to one side. "You don't care. You never cared."

"What are you talking about. I'm sick with worry…"

"Bollocks. She's missing and you just care about yourself."

"What do you want, Lenny?"

"I want to know where she is. She didn't come home."

"When?"

"Last night. After she met up with you."

I frown, not having the first bloody clue what she's talking about. "I never saw her last night."

Lenny shakes her head angrily and opens her mouth in stages before she speaks, as though it's climbing stairs to do justice to the size of her fury. There's spit dangling between her top and bottom teeth. "Don't lie to me, Owen. She said! She said she was going to see you. I couldn't stop her this time."

Her voice has gone from an angry whisper to a semi-shout, and we're getting a few looks. I'm feeling self-conscious and my sides are starting to prickle with sweat again. I fear my face may be red.

"Lenny, I honestly don't know what you're talking about."

"Owen, don't do this! I got in about ten-ish yesterday and she was just pulling her coat on. She was going to see you. I didn't even get any time to talk her out of it. When she didn't come home I figured you'd just worked your magic but she still isn't back. She had her… I think she was carrying her… Fuck, I don't know. Over her arm, you know. She was manic. Oh I don't know." She stops, deflating, looking down at her feet as though the answers may be there. "I'm really worried."

Silence. My brain whirring. Trying not to let my feelings reach my face.

Lenny looks up, directly into my eyes. My reflection is a pencil sketch, all black outline and shading. I'm colourless, empty, just waiting to be rubbed out. I pinch the bridge of my nose, fighting the image. When I open my eyes again, Lenny's face is close to mine, and I see a crowd of mildly diverted spectators staring over her shoulder. I realise I'm losing this, and spread my arms expansively, banish the blood from my cheeks and feel the sickly paleness melt into my face. I settle back into my skin.

"I was in the pub till gone eleven last night," I say, softly, as though lulling a baby to sleep. "I haven't seen Jess in days. It's too fucking painful! And you keep such a close guard on her brain, she wouldn't have come to see me even if I'd asked. She was the one who said it was best if we didn't even try to be friends. You've cleaned the place out of anything she might need. Last I heard you were setting her up on fucking dates. You reckon she'd suddenly just come running if I called?"

"Yes! Just because she can't stand you doesn't mean she's not in love with you. Why do you think I keep such a close eye on her? It's because the second I turn my back she's sneaking out the house to see you or trying to send you messages. She's written and deleted more bloody messages to you than I can keep count of. Christ, you know what she did on Saturday? She went and picked up her wedding dress! The one she told you she'd cancelled. The one she said she would never wear? She picked it up and brought it home. I found her, crying, sobbing that you, fucking you of all people, would never see her in it."

"Hang on," I say, starting to shiver, as though blanketed in a wet towel on a cold day. "I can't be held accountable for what she does, Lenny. I want to see her in that dress. I always did. That's why I proposed. I didn't want her to cancel the wedding. I didn't want it to end. It just couldn't continue, or so she said. I couldn't be what she needed. I was killing her, and dying from the pain of it. And we both feel worse when we're apart. I'm so fucking confused. Why are we apart, Len?"

"Because it's best for everyone," Lenny cries, exasperated, astonished at my ignorance. She doesn't seem to know how stupid she sounds.

I run my hand over my brow. It's like stroking wet porcelain. "Look, honestly, I never saw her yesterday and never contacted her." I suddenly look concerned. Then: "Try Nottingham. Honestly. Call me when you get there. She'll just be getting her head straight."

"Or she's copped off," says Lenny, letting a sigh turn into a half laugh and almost halving in size as the weight of righteous indignation escapes with a rush. "I can't… I just don't know, Owen. You made her so happy, and so sad, and she doesn't see what you are, not really…"

I pull a face, suddenly bored, and not really in the mood for hearing any more about how shit I am. "You're a good friend," I say, quietly, then lean in, and let my lips touch her ear. "Don't blame yourself for losing track of her…"

Lenny's eyes fill with tears. She gulps, once or twice, and then throws her arms up and pushes herself away, storming out of the pub through the throng.

I smile at my own reflection, but there's no pleasure in it. I'm the worst man I've ever known. I should be floating downstream towards the River Trent, muddy water in my lungs and absolute nothingness in my bloated eyes.

And then I'm just drinking, and thinking of dead bodies and criminals and bullets and victims, and the unfairness of it all. Thinking of the people charged with finding justice for the innocents, and their unsuitability for the task. Wondering at the madness of the world we have created and my hatred of my place within it.

Taking solace in alcohol.

Drinking until I'm numb.

22

"Daddy brush?"

Fin McAvoy looks at his father through a veil of frothy soap. He's been told that brave boys and girls tolerate the stinging sensation in their eyes. He's stoic in his tolerance of the discomfort, squinting up at his dad as the suds drip down his face.

"Brush, son?"

"Yep. Mammy say it punk. What punk?"

McAvoy, damp to his waist, smiles indulgently at his son. As instructed, he takes the soft Mason-Pearson hairbrush from the window sill, and begins to brush his son's soft, red curls into a mohawk. Fin, as instructed, sits quietly.

"This is the look you're going for, is it?" asks McAvoy, softly. "Suits you. I'm not sure my dad would have approved of this. Did I ever tell you that my dad used to cut my hair. Your Uncle Duncan too. He used the same scissors that he used on the sheep. Can you imagine that?"

McAvoy doesn't await a response. He disappears inside his own head for a moment, remembering the croft. Himself, Duncan, his big strong dad, making a living from the land in a little white-painted croft not far from Loch Ewe in the Western Highlands. The memories are never entirely happy. He has never forgiven himself for taking his mother's offer. She walked out on his father when McAvoy was only five years old. At ten, she came back. Told him she was remarrying. A wealthy man; a man with connections. He was welcome to come and take advantage of them. Welcome to make the best of himself. His brother, his father, his teachers – they all told him that there would never be an opportunity like this. That he owed it to whichever deity had given him a big brain then dumped him in Aultbea. He did what everybody seemed to be telling him to do. He's regretted it ever since.

"Look good, Daddy?"

McAvoy considers his son. He's brushed his curls into a magnificent peak, sticking up as if greased with hard butter. McAvoy grins, indulgently. Lowers his forehead to Fin's and tells him, in a quiet voice, that he is what life is for.

"Jesus, I'm sorry…"

McAvoy turns as Roisin scurries into the bathroom, unfastening her dressing gown. She gives him a look – desperate, beseeching – and then she is lowering herself to the toilet seat.

McAvoy looks down to the floor. Closes his eyes. Prays, and wishes, and wonders which has more potency…

Roisin looks between her bare knees. Raises her head and gives McAvoy a look. Then she shakes her head. "Gone," she says, quietly. "I'm so sorry…"

McAvoy holds himself together as if afraid he were made of sugar. He walks to his wife on his knees. Puts his head against hers. "It's not your fault," he says, softly. "Oh Roisin. We should stop. This isn't fair…"

Fierce, face flushed, she shakes her head. "No," she says,

and rubs her face against his shoulder. "No, we keep trying. Whatever happens, we don't give up."

McAvoy strokes his wife's hand. Looks away, as she rises from the toilet seat, and looks, dejectedly, into the bloody water. She says a small prayer. Fastens her gown. Presses herself to McAvoy. Sniffs, and wipes the tears from her eyes.

"Looking good, boyo," she says, to her son. Fin is making no complaint about the goose pimples which pattern his flesh. He knows Mummy is sad. Knows that Daddy would slice off a limb if it made her pain go away.

"Me a punk," says Fin, cautiously. "Me in Prodigy. Me Twisted Firestarter..."

Through the tears and the pain and the desperate desire to make everything different, Aector and Roisin McAvoy hold their son, and weep, silently, for the child that will not be.

"I'm sorry," says Roisin, again.

At her side, her husband wraps his arm around her waist. He can find no words of comfort. Just holds her, and hopes it is enough.

Knows, to his bones, that it is not.

23

9.17 p.m.

Owen Lee, Press Association Hull and East Riding correspondent, staggering across Spring Bank.

Rain; an upright sea.

The night, dark and unforgiving: all neon signs and dirty yellow street lights. Circles of illumination as cars swish by. Me in the spotlight. Horns honking.

Too much blood in my head. Face feeling full. Fit to burst.

Passing the pizza place at the top of Kerry's street. Bright inside. Too bright. All white walls and photographs of fried chicken and lasagne. Pizza boxes stacked behind the counter. Vaguely ethnic guy in a white T-shirt talking to two teenagers in the warm. Looks inviting. Friendly. Sort of place that beckons you in on a wet February night.

Staggering on down Morpeth Street.

Sick with hunger. Sick with drink. Sick of myself.

My coat heavy with water, pulling me down. Bent over, mouth open, eyes glazed, working my jaw in circles to relieve the pressure in my head. Fear my ears may pop. Or my eyes.

Halfway down the street, trying to focus. Walk into a wheelie bin and fall over.

Cars parked along the length of the street. None with a registration plate less than three years old. White vans. One by my head.

Kick open the gate to Kerry's place. Pain. Think I may have twisted my ankle. Think I might do it again.

Front door wide open. Light on in the hall. Bare bulb, no shade. Migraine exploding behind my eyes. Wet, muddy palms screwed into my face. Shapes moving behind my eyelids. Colours around the edges of the picture, moving rhythmically, delicately. Black kaleidoscope. Central flame, now. A perfect circle of white darkness, glowing among the blurs.

Sliding up the wall. Moby CD playing in a downstairs room. Dusty carpet, edged with cobwebs, turning to sludge beneath my feet.

First floor. Stop moving. Payphone nailed to the wall, impeding my progress.

Bumble around it. Half blind.

Fingers scrabbling at the doorframe.

Door swinging slowly open.

Pictures of Audrey Hepburn on the wall.

Lights bright.

Sofa-bed, still in sofa form, draped with an Afghan scarf. Coffee table, covered in paper, ragged envelopes, empty bottles of 7Up. Foil dishes. Dirty teaspoons. Personalised coffee mugs bearing other people's names.

Kerry, laid out on her back, head draped over the far arm. Wearing nothing but a faded grey T-shirt. Riding up.

Hairy legs. Filthy soles to her feet.

Eyes closed. Nobody home.

Man in blue overalls, standing over her.

The names of the Hull City promotion-winning side of 2004, winding around his neck.

Pants around his thighs.

A look of acute surprise creasing his face as I crash into the room.

Alcohol in my system igniting like brandy in a frying pan. Flaring blue.

And as I'm rising to my feet, listening to his protestations of embarrassment, his apologies, his shame, I'm piecing it together.

Thinking "money lender". Debt collector. Bailiff. Popping round to collect a payment, and leaving a deposit instead.

And I'm barrelling into his chest, pinning his arms beneath my legs, nutting him silly, tenderising his forehead, laughing as he uses what little consciousness he has left to try and find a way to fasten his pants.

Me, sitting on his chest, down behind the sofa.

Kerry still not moving.

My hands at his throat, thumbs wedged between the central defenders and last season's midfield general.

My face impassive as I throttle the life out of him.

Watching his face turn blue.

Hearing his feet drum on the carpet, the rhythm reminding me of an old C&W tune Dad used to play over and over again on long car journeys back from the hospital; Kerry and me humming along on the back seat, playing games, counting horses and pylons, listening to Mam and Dad talking about wallpapers, about new stair carpets, about my grades and medicines, about itineraries, and how to squeeze museums, galleries and beach days into one week in Cornwall. Telling us to keep the noise down. Always watching me in the rear-view-mirror, always keeping a suitcase between Kerry and me. Mam reading one of the leaflets they had given her, listing which food colourings I should be kept away from, and which signals she should come to recognise as an indicator of looming violence.

Me, gulping down mouthfuls of air.

Eating his soul as it leaves his body.

Thinking: *I'm getting better at this*.

24

Peaceful, now. Lights low. Tie-dyed curtains pulled to. Low thump of bass coming from somebody's CD player. Like a heartbeat.

Me, wrapped in an Afghan scarf and fading adrenaline. Warm and damp.

Bailiff still on the ground, eyes open.

Kerry not moving. Breathing like a hot bullmastiff.

Me on the floor with my back to the sofa, legs drawn up. Smoking a cigarette. Calm. Concentrating on every breath. Counting them. Eyes open as I breathe in. Closed as I exhale. Exhausted. Weary to the bone. Starving. My vision bobbing as if I'm in the ocean, looking at the room through waves that push and pull, lift and break.

Not much left here now. Everything of value sold or taken. Still cluttered, but with nothing. If you tidied away the crap the place would be empty. Kerry's life. Kerry's home. Kerry's creation. Kerry's world. Not Kerry's fault.

I pull myself up to my knees, and then stand, shakily, feeling the blood returning to my legs. Pins and needles jabbing my feet.

Things to do. Got to clean up my sister. Got to eat. Got to stop all this. Got to keep going.

Feel like I've been breathing in paint fumes. I know what I've done, but it's not real. Even the body at my feet seems somehow removed. Staged.

The bathroom's at the bottom of the corridor and I make my way to it, locking the door behind me. Light on. Off-white suite, lemon walls. No panel on the bath. Ring around the enamel. Half-finished tiling job. Squelching over green lino and a rotting pedestal mat.

I turn the cold tap on full and hold my face under the stream until my head is numb. Mouth under the tap, drinking and slurping. Slightly minty flavour in my mouth as I lick the tap.

Drying myself with the hem of the scarf that's still around my shoulders.

Walking back into Kerry's place, still dripping.

She hasn't woken. Neither has he.

I kick the door closed behind me, and push the TV up against it. Best not to be disturbed. Business-like, I cross to the small kitchen area in the far corner of the bedsit. Two-ring hob and a dirty rectangle where the fridge used to be. Door hanging off the solitary cupboard. Nowhere to hide a body. Bin-bag full of dirty clothes.

Hands on hips I look around, willing the bare walls to suddenly yield an empty cupboard or a waste disposal chute.

Kerry gives the faintest of groans and I smile down at her as though gazing at a contented baby. I'm consumed by love for her, the need to protect her. I want to tear my skin off and drape it over her as a shield. She's an innocent. Mine. My responsibility. Something Jess could never understand.

I take the hem of her T-shirt in my hand and pull it up

to her face, wiping her eyes and cheek, the folds at her neck. I'm looking at the body I've exposed. I see the bones pushed up tight against her belly, and skin like candlewax. Bruises in the crook of each elbow, drilled with holes. Veins standing out on her breasts, nipples flaccid and shapeless. Chipped nail varnish, long since applied.

Hurriedly, I pull the T-shirt down, and squat down by her face. She's still beautiful, to me. Ears like a pixie, pierced a dozen times. Button nose, full lips. She shaved her head a few months back and it's still short and ragged, with twin beaded rat-tails hanging down at the front. Her mouth's open, and I catch a glimpse of her teeth. They look like toffees, and are starting to rot. The smile of a smackhead.

I stroke her cheek gently with the back of my hand and then slide my arms under her, one under her head and the other cupping her arse. I ease her off the sofa and carry her to the door. She's almost weightless. It's like carrying a ghost. She doesn't wake as I lay her on the floor and cover her with the duvet.

The bailiff's not that big of a guy, and I figure he'll fit where I'm going to stick him. I pull the cushions off the sofa and grip the metal frame of the bed inside, pulling it out and unfolding the legs, propping them up among the detritus of the coffee table. A space appears inside the sofa. To me it seems coffin-shaped. Naturally, as though I've done it a thousand times, I put my hands under the armpits of the bailiff, and heave him into a standing position. It's hard going, and I'm consumed with a fit of giggles as the words "dead weight" appear in my head and beat like a drum. In stages I get him to his feet and myself to mine, and drape him over my left shoulder as though burping a toddler. I can feel his erection prodding my hip. With my free hand I push the wire frame of the bed into the air, and bundle the bailiff into the gap created. His legs don't go in. I try to bend them at the knee but they seem stiff and it creeps me out, so I just kick at him until he squeezes into the gap, then drop the bed back down. I nudge the coffee table out of the way and the legs of the bed hit the floor, then unfold the mattress out over the frame. In a second, the bailiff has gone. Out of sight, out of mind. Problem solved.

I pick Kerry up again and feel her begin to stir. I lay her down on the sofa, still bundled in the scarf. I step back, and slip off my coat, jacket and boots, switch off the light and lie down beside her. I spoon up behind her and let the heat from her body warm mine, a fiery aching suddenly spreading into every limb.

My arm around her waist, nose at the nape of her neck.

Dick squashed up against her left buttock.

Room spinning. Eyes heavy.

Falling asleep with my naked sister on top of a corpse.

Gazing at perfect blackness behind my eyelids.

Monsters nowhere to be found.

25

Two hours later, and we're snuggling. Little cold nose in the crook of my neck, rasping gently against my stubble. Hand on my chest, fingering my hair. Breath slow and soothing. Her on her front, leg draped over mine, drawn up, like a dog pissing.

She's awake, but fighting it. Knows she's got to come down and doesn't want to. Hanging on to sleep. Me too. Liked it there. Dark. Uncomplicated. Silent.

Trying to keep my eyes closed, but the lids slide upwards, slowly, like a lift carrying a fat man.

Open into grey.

Still dark in the room, but dark with shapes and lumps. Possibilities.

I stifle a groan as I realise I haven't changed during the night, and I still have to face every day with my own mind.

"I knew you'd come," whispers Kerry, so low and breathy it comes out in a rush and I feel the breeze on my cheek. "I needed you."

"I'll always be here, princess," I say, without thinking. I'm pre-programmed to say this shit, regardless of the truth. "I'll always look after you."

She starts to wriggle, like a baby with wind. Fluttering,

groaning noises escape her lips. Her hand leaves my chest and I feel her rubbing her eyes, massaging the bridge of her nose. "Ugh," she says, and starts to sit up. "Just urgh."

I put a hand on her bare shoulder and pull her back down to my chest, resting my head on her soft, short hair. She doesn't resist. I kiss her on the top of the head, and wrap an arm around her shoulders. With my other hand I pull the scarf up, over our heads, and we're in a warm little cave, where I can only see the tears that sparkle in her eyes, the hints and shadows of her face. It's nice. Our voices are soft, like a spoken lullaby. We're safe in here, on top of a corpse.

"You got somewhere to be?" I ask softly. "Let's just chill."

"I'm all for chilling," she says, sibilant, like a tyre swishing over a wet road. "You're not normally a fan."

"I am. I want the easy life. I've just got responsibilities."

"You're too tightly wound to chill, Owen. You even sleep aggressively. Do you still sleep with your arms folded?"

"It has been mentioned. That's the way I was shown."

"At the hospital?" Her voice is cautious. An ember from an old fire suddenly begins to smoulder in mine.

"Yeah. Never really broke the habit."

"What's the thinking behind it?"

"Christ knows. I just did as I was shown."

"They probably didn't want you touching yourself."

"Probably not. Didn't work though. You just get somebody to do it for you. Maybe that's what they were hoping."

I hear Kerry smile. "You're never short of offers, Owen. Jess didn't know what she was letting go."

"She didn't let go, Kerry. I set her free."

"Did she want to go?"

"She said she did. Can't really blame her, but I do."

"I'll miss Jess. She was fun. Don't think she really liked me though. Think she thought I got in the way."

"I remember moments when she liked you a lot, and I remember moments when she wished you were dead. I remember all of our moments."

Silence for a little while, then, timid, she says: "Do you still see her?"

I close my eyes and breathe deeply. My hands are shaking.

"Sometimes," I say. "She still appears when I'm tired. Or stressed. I can control it though. She doesn't tell me what to do."

"I envied you, you know," she says, quietly. "The things you saw. I sat and stared at her too, and she never spoke to me. Never moved."

"You don't want what I've got, Kerry. You don't want to see what I see. Or do the things I've done."

"You've paid for what you've done. You were taken away from us. From me. And I never really got you back again."

"You paid too. You paid too high a price."

"You did it for us. You were ill. She was whispering in your ear. I know how it is to be addicted to something that's killing you, Owen. Something dreadful but mesmerising."

"She was the only one who understood…"

"I would have understood if you let me in. You were my big brother. And after the accident, you just…"

"It's all in the past now, Kerry. Think of our happy times…"

"I think of them before I fall asleep and it makes me feel like you're here."

"Sometimes I am. Sometimes when you feel there's

somebody else in the room, watching over you, listening to you breathe, it's because there is."

We lie in silence. I can hear the lady's voice, telling me of St Peter, denying his Lord three times before the cock crowed. She is angry and hurt, and I shake her away.

The CD downstairs changes to something harder, and the volume cranks up. I strain to hear the words. Placebo, I think. Something about friends in need and friends with weed. Couldn't agree more.

"I got a bad feeling last night," she says, gently, as though the words are coming from far away. She's talking in washed-out watercolours. "After we spoke. You sounded…"

"Sounded what?"

"Like you used to. Sort of, you know, empty. Hollow. Waiting to be filled up with something you could use as fuel. I thought you might hurt yourself."

I shush her with a kiss, and stroke her cheek. "It was a bad night. It's a bad time. I think about things too much, you know that. I still want to bury my head in mud to stop the noise of my brain. That hasn't changed. Pills don't change that. Nothing changes that."

"You are still taking them, though. You have to. You know what happens…"

"I'm cool, baby. I'm your big brother, remember. Fucking invincible."

"Those things I said last time, Owen. About not needing you anymore…"

"You were out of it. I'm amazed you even remember."

"Sometimes my head gets like yours."

"Nobody's got a head like mine, mate. I'm blessed."

Silence again, broken only by somebody else's music,

and the gurgling in our bellies. After a while, the stomach rumbling becomes funny.

"Peckish?" I ask, laughing.

"Sick with it."

"Pass my phone."

Kerry slides down my body and slithers onto her knees.

I hear Kerry rummaging through my pockets.

Coat pocket.

Shit.

Fucking gun.

Fuck, fuck, fuck.

Kerry suddenly shuffling back, into my arms as I kneel on the bed, falling back with me, phone in hand, giggling.

Me, laughing with relief.

I breathe deeply, pain in my sinuses, heart pounding. Flip the phone open. Switch it on. Girly jingle as it chirrups into life, then searches the sky, starts to ring.

"This is the Vodafone voicemail service. You have two new messages."

"Owen, it's Lenny again. Listen I know we had words before but I'm getting really worried. She's still not home. I believe you if you say you didn't see her, but that means she could be anywhere. Look, please give me a call. I'm sorry about how I spoke to you. I know things aren't easy for you at the moment and you miss her, but... oh I don't know. I don't know what to do. Please give me a call. OK? Bye."

Message left at 9.37 p.m. To return the call, press 5.

"How do, mate. Tony. Sat in the Tap like an arsehole. You coming? I'm struggling a bit, to be honest. Desk don't want to go in too deep on the gangland shit but they're going to have to if this Petrovsky starts making waves.

Anyway, might see you in a bit. There's a press conference at Priory Road tomorrow so I'll see you there if not tonight. Take it easy, mate. Laters."

Best not think about it. So I don't.

Kerry rolling a cigarette in the dark.

Me, scrolling through my phone for the number of a pizza place. Ordering a large ham-and-pineapple without being asked. Give the address. He doesn't get it first time, so I spell it. Tell him in Italian instead. Doesn't help – he's Tunisian. Couple of cans of pop as an afterthought.

Hang up, snuggle down.

I pull Kerry close, taking the cig from her and breathing deep.

"Fifteen minutes, he reckons. Pizza man."

"Cool."

Silence again. Comfortable. CD player drifting into uncharted territory; something I don't recognise. Feeling old.

Kerry playing with her hair, moistening her lips and spitting bits of tobacco.

"You're such a lady."

"And you're a gent."

"If the girls at pony club could see you now…"

"They'd be jealous. I'm in bed with you."

"People will talk."

"They always did."

"Fuck them."

"I always did."

"I remember. Vicky liked you almost as much as her horse."

"Neigh, lass."

We laugh, gently.

"I haven't killed those brain cells yet. The ones from when we were little."

"Me neither. They sometimes get a bit lost in there, but I know we were happy once. You without smack, me without, well without whatever the fuck it is I take to get by. It's a sensation, somewhere inside me, floating around like a dust mote in the sunlight."

"I love it when you talk like that. You should never have stopped writing. Proper writing I mean."

"And you should never have stopped being you. Christ, princess…"

"Don't. I know."

"But you've fallen so far, and you're still in there, just trying to break out…"

"I can't do it, O. I can't live and not be numb. Neither can you. I need the veil. I need this."

"But Kerry…"

Cold fingers, clamping over my mouth, shushes in my ear. I deflate, and hold her close.

"One day," I start to say, and trail off.

"One day we'll both get there. You're not exactly on the right road either."

"But I hide it better."

"You think so?" Incredulity in her voice, toes rubbing my bare shin.

"Better than you. You just need an old greyhound and a can of Special Brew and you'll be all you ever wanted to be. Is there a fucking school for you people? Fuck, it's a good job Dad's too far away to see this." I sound angry, but I'm not.

Kerry tenses in my arms, thinks about what I've said, and sags. It'll be a few hours before she needs another hit, but already she's feeling itchy, and I sense her fingers start to scrabble at her thin arms, then the rustle of her fingernails in her pubes.

"Yeah," is all she can say. She shrugs, lying down, distance between us.

I let out a half laugh, feeling bad. "Sorry. Tough love."

She reaches out for me. "I like it when you love me hard."

"You're not allowed to say that anymore," I say, disconsolate, turning her lunge for me into a cuddle. "What about this dreamy new guy, the man who's going to make it all better? Whatshisname. Beatle?" The name is like a piece of shit in my mouth that I have to spit out, and Kerry notices.

"He's got something. Plans. He's a lot like you."

"Fuck off."

"No, really. He's got a bit of style. Ambition. And he wants to take care of me."

"He's a dealer, darlin'. He can't take care of himself."

"He's more than that. And anyway, he's not a proper dealer. He just gets bits of stuff here and there."

"Oh yeah, I forgot his main occupation. Signing on."

"You've never liked my boyfriends. Beatle's different. Honestly. You should get to know him. He would make a better impression. He knows what you mean to me."

"I'd kill him."

"No, Owen. You'd get on. He's really funny, and he's like, got this infectious laugh, and enthusiasm. Sometimes I'm high with him before I even shoot up. That has to be a good thing."

"You're in love with him? It's only been a few weeks."

"No. Well, maybe." She sounds shy, like a schoolgirl talking about a boy in chemistry class who saw her knickers when the wind blew. "He says he loves me."

"What can he offer you, Kerry?"

"He says he's going to give me the world."

"Well it's mine and he can't fucking have it."

"He's better than you think, Owen. He looks after me. He wants me to quit this shit as well. And he's strong, despite what you'd think to look at him. Couple of days ago we were down Princes Ave and these lads in a Land Rover pulled up and one of them tried to drag him in, and he got away from them. Stood up to them. He wasn't even bothered. Said it was just some people trying to scare him over some little deal, and they could fuck off if they thought he was scared. Just let it wash over him."

"Oh he sounds peachy."

Then: "What have you told him?"

"About what?"

"You know, Kerry."

"Nothing, Owen. The past's the past. I would never tell a soul about that. About you. We've fallen far enough, I swear."

Silence again.

Me, thinking about it.

Frowning in the dark.

"Where is he now, then? This Beatle? Is it with an A or an E, by the way? Is he a bug or a walrus?"

"I think it's with an A, but I think it's actually supposed to be an E, the way it's meant. He's out. Busy bee. Just taking care of a bit of business. That's what he says. I think he likes to say it."

"Deal business?"

"*Business* business." Her voice cracks, and I realise she's missing him. Might even be concerned. I make a concession to human decency and don't push.

"Do you remember that game, Kerry?

"Which one?"

"The gun game. When we were little."

"You mean the bullet game? Yeah." Kerry is smiling again. "You've got a gun with two bullets in it and you have to decide who to shoot and why. Yeah. I still play it."

"Me too."

"I remember you always used to say if you had two bullets you'd shoot Ms Start twice, just to be sure."

"Yeah, I hated science."

"Then there was the doctor. Finnegan. You wouldn't even waste a bullet on him, you said. And if you did, you'd insert it manually."

"Lovely idea," I say, laughing gently.

"And that bus conductor who was mean to Mam. And Mam, sometimes."

"It wouldn't have made any difference. The bullets would bounce off."

"Yeah."

"Yeah."

Laughing, then wistful. Both in a rainstorm of memories and regrets.

"It's not so easy, you know, princess," I say, under my breath, deadening the words on the fuzzy crown of her head. "You don't get many shots in this life. Shots to change your world. Two bullets in your gun is simple. It's specific. It's two wankers who've pissed you off. A hundred bullets and you climb a tower and just start taking pot-shots. Law of averages, innit? Throw a rock in the air and you'll hit someone guilty. But imagine six. You've got this chance. It's a lottery ticket. Three numbers come up and you win a tenner but you're almost regretting your good luck cos it isn't good enough. How do you decide? How do you take those shots and take them right? You find yourself not wanting to waste them. So you don't. You bank 'em, and you bash somebody's brains in with a rock or you strangle the bastard, and you keep your gun in your pocket for when you need it. Or when you want to use it. And as long as you've got it, you know you're untouchable."

Silence.

Said too much. And not enough.

Me tense, waiting for reaction.

Body taut.

Kerry breathing heavily again.

Asleep on my chest.

Rat-tat-tat-rat-tat-tat.

Knock at the door. Business-like, practiced.

Pulling on my trousers, throwing the scarf over Kerry.

Rummaging in my coat pocket.

Gun in my hand, soothing the panic.

Upright. Deep breath.

Holding the gun behind my back as I open the door a crack and the light of the hall throws a frame around me.

I look into the face of Detective Superintendent Doug Roper.

26

He's changed his clothes since this afternoon. Black suit, now, with a barely visible purple pinstripe. Black shirt, open neck. Neat row of surfer-style beads around his throat. Black leather jacket, with barely a raindrop on the lapels. Had a shave, too. Widened the divide in his moustache and pointed the bit beneath his chin.

Young copper from this afternoon behind him, holding an umbrella, giving a wide smile of recognition.

TV crew behind, crowding onto the landing. Black lad holding the boom. Cameraman obscured beneath a giant leather trilby and a hiking coat. Filming merrily.

Five in total.

Bullet to spare?

File the thought.

Roper's face rippling as he sees me, like he's sucking a lemon or about to come.

Words dying in his mouth.

Wheels turning in his head as he tries to figure it out. Why. Why I'm here, bare-chested, raising an eyebrow in his face.

"Owen?" Taken aback and not liking it. "You live here?"

"Evening Doug. Y'alright?" Nod to the others. "No, mate. Sister's place. The fuck you doing here?"

Keeping it light. Laughs in our voices, like two old friends bumping into each other somewhere unexpected.

Then, softly: "You after me?"

Roper shaking himself cool. Pupils expanding, like ink dropped in water.

Runs a hand over his mouth and deposits a half-smile.

"No, no, I'm looking for a Lee…" stops as realisation dawns. "Ah. Small world."

"I'll say."

A painful, drawn-out pause. It's all a little awkward.

"What for?" I ask, confused.

"Best we come in."

Roper can't decide if he wants a scene. Would make good TV. Already he's rehearsing his lines in his head. Probably got a script in his pocket. Been practicing his menacing glare and compassionate tilt of the head all day.

"No, tell me why you want her."

"Is she in, Owen?" A touch of steel to the voice.

Kerry's hand suddenly around my waist, her face poking over my shoulder. Wearing my shirt and pulling it down.

"What do you want?"

Him, flipping a switch labelled 'charm'.

"My name is Detective Superintendent Doug Roper," he says, fixing his eyes on hers and attempting to smoulder. "I'm with Humberside Police. Just ignore these people behind me. I need to…"

"Cut! Christ, sorry about this but it's much more realistic if you don't mention that we're here. Just act as though we're not. Do what you would normally do and we'll just blend into the background." An arm on Roper's elbow as she makes her point.

Roper rolling his eyes, giving me a wink to show he knows this is all bullshit, then turning back to Kerry.

"Sorry about that. Yes, as I was saying…"

"No, Doug. This is fresh. First time. You've just knocked on the door. Laddo's opened it, sister's come out, you break the bad news…"

"Flora!" he says, disappointed.

"What? Oh, sorry."

Roper's head in his hands. Turning to Kerry with a shake of his head. Dismissing any further instructions from the camera crew with a wave of his hand.

"Ms Lee, it really is best if we come inside. I'm investigating two murders and I think you may have some information which could prove useful. I'll try not to take up too much of your time."

"What's going on?" Me again, squeak in my voice, like a finger rubbed on dry teeth. Goose pimples on my flesh. Breathing fast. Kerry's hand tightening around my waist.

Both of us stepping back to make room.

Retreating back to the bed.

Gun in my fucking hand!

Looking down at it, then up at Roper.

He hasn't noticed. Eyes everywhere but here. Drinking in Kerry's life then burping up assumptions.

I drop the gun gently. Push it under the sofa. Have to give it some welly, as its progress is impeded by a dead body.

Kerry shuffling back on the sofa-bed. Face pale.

Rubbing her arms.

Me perching on the edge, blinking as the young cop switches the light on and we're bathed in nasty light.

TV crew squeezed in the doorway.

Roper sitting down next to Kerry. Surreptitiously checking he doesn't sit on anything nasty, then giving her his full attention.

"Ms Lee…"

"Kerry." Automatic.

Smile of gratitude. Nod. "Kerry, do you know a gentleman called Darren Norton?"

A second's puzzlement. "Erm…"

"You might know him as Beatle?"

"Oh." Big smile. It freezes. She's torn now, a dutiful drug dealer's girlfriend and a well-raised gymkhana champ who once won a rosette for growing a sunflower. Not knowing which is the right answer. The right persona. Looking at me and getting a shrug. "Yes? Yes. He's my boyfriend."

"Kerry, I'm sorry to tell you this but Darren Norton's body was discovered in the Humber Bridge Country Park this morning. He'd been shot. I'm investigating his murder, along with that of another man, who was found at the same time. I need your help to try and get justice for Darren."

My eyes two perfect smoking gun barrels.

Kerry's searching for mine. Filling with tears. Fingers instinctively clutching at the crook of her arm, longing to fill it with delicious poison. Cake crumbs under her skin.

"What? No! He can't be…"

"His brother positively identified the body this morning, Kerry. I'm very sorry."

"No. Owen, tell him he's wrong." She's imploring me

to take the pain away, but all the magic's gone from my wand and I just sit there, looking at the floor, picturing the moment I finally met her precious boyfriend; a patch of shadow in the darkness, falling into mud and leaves, a hole in his head and a bullet in his brain.

Kerry – wiping tears, sniffing, dabbing at her nose with the sleeve of my shirt. Sniffles, but no sobs.

Roper pursing his lips, nodding to the young cop in the direction of the kitchen, urging him to go and make a cup of tea.

Film crew zooming in. Microphone boom snaking across the room above my head like a dinosaur's neck, peering down at Kerry as she loses herself in thoughts and miseries, cross-legged, staring at her lap, tail of my shirt puddling in front of her dignity.

Young cop, staring at the draining board and looking for ingredients. Giving up and pulling a face that suggests he'll be wiping his feet after he leaves.

"Kerry."

Roper, soft of voice and watery of eye.

"Kerry."

Her looking up. Light catching the blackheads on her nose. Putting one of her plaited rat-tails in her mouth and sucking on the end. Spindly legs and arms like twigs stripped of bark.

"Kerry, do you have any idea why Beatle would be at the Country Park late last night?"

Looking at me again, knowing that this is the sort of shit I can wade in without dirtying my socks.

"Tell him the truth, Kerry," I say, soft as her face. "You can't drop him in it now."

Kerry adopting the pose. The dance of grief. Picking it up lovely.

"I don't know." Voice like a weeping wound. "He didn't say where he was going."

"When was the last time you saw him, Kerry?"

"Yesterday morning, I think." Face creasing with the effort of recollection. "It might have been the day before."

Roper moving closer and placing a hand on hers. Me shuffling away.

"Tell me what you think I need to know."

And she does. Doesn't even take any charm to pick the lock. Opening up to Roper's probing like scrunched-up silk.

"I know he was a dealer," he says. "I know he was a bad lad. But he didn't deserve this and I'm going to catch whoever did it. You can help."

She's his now. Lured into his camp without even a look in my direction.

"He didn't get scared, y'know," she says, earnestly, sniffing, taking the cigarette that Roper has produced and ignited without request or ceremony. "But he was excited. Working on something that was going to make it all better. But he didn't speak about it, I swear."

"It's OK. Just tell me what you know." So gentle. So delicate. Such a fucking pussy. "They tell me you meant everything to him. How long had you been together?"

Kerry smiling, all girly, through the tears. "Just a few weeks, y'know, but it was real. Soon as we met it was just, like, we'd always known each other, y'know."

"Where did you meet?"

"William Booth House." Homeless hostel in town.

Kerry's occasional home, when she can't remember where she lives. "He was staying there for a night and we just got talking and sat together in the park for ages. He was so clever, and really kind to me. He had a real something about him, a real spark. His life hadn't gone the way he wanted it to, but his dad used to…"

"Yes, I heard. So it was love at first sight?" Smile in his voice. Might be genuine.

Me, shaking my head and scowling at the floor.

"I think so." Giggling again. "He said he wanted to make my world spin in the opposite direction. And he did."

"Wine you and dine you, did he?" asks Roper. I'm the only person in the room who notices the trace of irony at the corners of his eyes.

"It wasn't like that. But he brought me things. Held my hand. Took me for walks. Looked after me."

"Gave you drugs?"

Pause.

Kerry testing the edges of the man-trap and deciding she doesn't fear it.

"Sometimes. But he didn't want me doing so much gear anymore. We only smoked a bit of dope together, took the odd E. But he didn't go near smack. Hated the stuff."

"But he sold it."

Kerry shrugging. Roper accepting her acceptance.

"Did you know he had enemies, Kerry?"

"We had a bit of bother a while back with some people shouting at us but he wasn't bothered. And the other day… well, some lads in a Land Rover gave him some aggro. But that was nothing. Barely mentioned it again. But I suppose when I think about it he was a bit jumpy. When we were in the pub he used to watch the door, always sitting with his back to the wall."

"You noticed that, did you?" Roper asks, surprised. Doesn't seem interested in the Land Rover.

"It reminded me of somebody." She looks at me for the first time, and I smile automatically.

Roper takes his hand from hers and removes the cigarette stub from her mouth. Extinguishes it on the sole of his boot.

Playtime over.

"You see, Kerry, Beatle had some very dangerous enemies. Beatle had been a very bad boy. He'd started working for somebody that a bottom-feeder like Beatle had no right to work for. Beatle should have stuck to selling barbs and wraps to schoolkids. That was his level. It was his place in the world. He had no right to step into the world he stepped into."

"What?" Kerry confused now, looking around for a friend, wanting the tenderness back. "What d'you mean?"

"Beatle had stopped being freelance, pet. Beatle was on the payroll for a very bad man. And Beatle, God bless his ignorant fucking cotton socks, didn't realise what a bad move it would be to cream a little off the top. And today, Beatle has a big fucking hole in his head."

Kerry's face twisting into tears, like a sponge being wrung. Me moving forward without thinking. Melting. Arms around her shoulders and pulling her in.

Looking up at Roper.

Glare that could turn a desert to glass.

"Enough."

"Job to do, laddo. Murder to solve. Two, actually. Bonus.

And princess here might be able to help. You know the score."

"And what, you reckon my sister killed him, do you? Shot him in the woods and battered his mate to death? Christ, she can barely remember her own fucking name most of the time. She can't raise a glass to her lips without stopping for a rest."

Wry smile from Roper.

Silence, again.

Tension like fog.

Just him and me staring at each other.

Doug breaking first, giving a nod to the young copper to stand down.

"Fair enough, Owen. It's a lot for the poor girl to take in. Sorry to have to break the news like this. I'll get back in touch when she's had time to digest all this."

Kerry looking up and half-smiling. Polite, despite herself.

Me and Roper standing up, both still on guard.

He can't resist it. Gives me a look.

"Seems that you're your usual well-informed self, laddo. Surprised you didn't break the news yourself, if you know everything. Must have come as a shock for you too."

Kerry's head spinning in my direction. Cameraman repositioning himself and zooming in on my face.

Could be the money shot.

"What?" Poor retort.

"About Beatle. You're on the story, know the names."

"I just knew him as Beatle. Didn't put that on the voicebank, did you?" My smile looks like a snarl.

"Maybe not. Still, cracker for you, ain't it? You going to let her stop crying before you get your exclusive interview with the victim's girlfriend? Or do the tears add to the piece?"

"You can fucking talk," I say, pissed off, nodding at the camera team.

"Yeah. I can."

"So many ways of saying nothing. Must be so proud. Got to bring in a TV team just so it's worth your while to open your mouth. Must be quite sad, constantly having to validate your existence like that, not being a real person unless there's an audience to watch the performance."

"But I do things, lad. And you just write about them."

"And what have you done? Haven't even got a reg number for this Vauxhall you're chasing, have you? Haven't got a fucking clue. You're telling her you're going to catch him? Bollocks."

"I will catch him, son. I catch them all."

"You couldn't catch syphilis, pal. Not unless your wife let you back in her bed."

Frantic coughing from the young copper as the laugh rattles his throat.

Sniggering from the sound man.

A little intake of breath from the director, an excited slurp of air, as she realises she's making classic TV.

Kerry chewing on her knuckle.

Me smirking, arms outstretched, daring him to bring it on.

Doug frozen, trying to work out how Supercop would react at a time like this.

Roper moving at last, nodding to the others to wrap this up. Pressing a card into Kerry's hand.

"I'll see you again," he says.

"I'll see you out," I say, and hold the door open.

Camera drops. Microphone retracts.

The film crew are muttering among themselves as they file down the corridor, and I spot some patting of backs.

Young copper goes next, raising an eyebrow as he passes my face. It's a friendly gesture, as if we're mates. I can't return it.

Roper last of all. Stops in front of me, face close to mine.

"Balls, lad. Fucking big ones. I wouldn't want to piss me off."

"Press conference at nine? Can't wait."

Five seconds of eye contact.

Then we both smile.

Just the two of us, loving it all.

"Should be a cracking show," I say, friendly.

He nods enthusiastically and we walk together down the corridor and stairs. "Oh aye. Just watch the cracks about the missus next time, eh?"

"Yeah, sorry fella. You can win the next one."

"I will, don't fret."

We're at the door. He pulls it open and lets the storm in, the darkness and the flashing lights. "See you tomorrow?"

"No doubt. Trying to do this and the trial is a fucking ball-ache."

"Worse for me. Ella's fiancé's on the stand. Choudhury's going to eat him up. Defence should start day after tomorrow. He's got a psychiatrist reckons Cadbury's so-called confession is worth fuck all. Then there's the cellmate. You know juries, and Choudhury's basically written his script for him. If Cadbury walks..."

"He won't. He did it."

"Maybe."

Stops.

Said too much.

"Look after your sister."

"Always will."

And he's gone, in a swish of coat-tail.

Me, standing on the step, bare-chested, watching his car move off, thanking fuck that I parked the Cavalier a few streets away.

Smiling as it passes the white van; its owner stiff beneath Kerry's bed.

Shivering as I realise they've all gone.

A car engine. Thick, expensive tyres on wet tarmac…

Land Rover coasting past me, slowly – a hulking lad in a tracksuit top at the wheel, following Roper. Passenger: a skinny guy with style.

Staring at me.

Forming a gun of finger and thumb.

Pulling the trigger as they pass by.

And I'm standing there; cold and exhilarated. Glad to be alive. Thinking one word, over and over.

Petrovsky.

27

McAvoy wishes he were the kind of man capable of acting on impulse. He saw a film once on an aeroplane (his first trip abroad, to a honeymoon on a Greek island, where his pale Celtic skin peeled off like wallpaper), in which the lead character was urging another man to throw caution to the wind. Saying that sometimes, it was better to rush in headlong, than dally with strategy. The advice had jarred strongly with his father's words.

Slow and steady wins the race.

Look before you leap.

Fools rush in where angels fear to tread.

Don't be a bloody fool.

If you marry that gypsy bitch you'll never hear another word from me.

He stands outside the tidy three-bedroomed house, a bundle of documents under his arm, and feels an overwhelming urge to ring Roisin. To get permission. To be told, again, that he's a good man. A policeman. That he's just doing his job.

The paperwork in the manila envelope seems to sting him. Each word on the printed page feels like another brand. A lash on his skin. An accusation that he has been a peripheral part of an investigation which is trying to convict the wrong man.

He holds the scented handkerchief to his face again. Breathes deep. He wonders if her photograph will be staring down at him. If he'll be able to keep his feet when the nausea comes. If he'll drop to his knees and throw up his lunch in the living room of the Butterworth family home.

He doesn't know what he wants more. To knock on the door and ask the dead girl's parents for a quiet chat, or to turn and run. Get back to his computer files and the glorious feeling of disassociation that comes with investigating through a keyboard and a screen.

He turns away from the property. Finds it too painful to look.

From the files, McAvoy knows Ella didn't grow up here. She and her family had lived a few streets away until she was in her mid-teens, before upgrading to this nice, functional, ex-council property, with a sparkly pebble-dashed frontage and cheap double-glazing that seem to jar, at once twinkly and thickly dull, in the glare of the street lamp and the veiled moon.

He wonders how long it's safe to stand here, across the street, inside the piss-stinking telephone box, getting his courage up and working on his story. Wonders if he's aroused suspicion. What he'll do if a squad car pulls up. What he'll tell Roper, about why he was standing across from the Butterworths' family home, with a dossier of evidence that is starting to suggest Shane Cadbury might not have killed their baby girl. That Doug Roper might have taken the easy option. That the real killer might still be on the streets with a weapon in their pocket and bad intentions on their mind.

He rehearses the lines in his head. Wondering whether it is ever acceptable in the eyes of God, in the eyes of his father, to tell a lie.

"Mr Butterworth... yes, hi... just for the sake of completeness... I'm eager to go through a few items in your statement... just check the facts..."

The door to the phone box swings open and McAvoy spins round, a deceit forming in his mouth, his papers clutched to his chest; a picture of guilt and remorse.

"We told you, no more bloody comments!"

Ella Butterworth's father is framed in the doorway. He's angry, but with it is a colossal tiredness. An exhaustion. The air of a man who has fought many enemies, and knows that weight of numbers is soon going to bring him down.

"Leave us alone," he says, weakly.

McAvoy tries to pull himself together and reaches into his pocket for his warrant card. He holds it up, trying to find the muscles in his face to twitch out a smile.

"I'm Detective Sergeant McAvoy," he stammers, then takes a breath. "Hector," he adds.

Arthur Butterworth gives a slow nod. Tries to look apologetic and gives up. He's wearing a cheap, charity-shop overcoat, jogging pants and shoes. He's got a scarf around his neck and wisps of wool are attaching themselves to his unshaven, pale face.

"Sorry," says Arthur. "Thought you were another reporter. It's not as though we haven't been good to them. Given them everything we have. What more is there to say?"

The question is so immense that McAvoy can find no words.

Under his arm, the folder burns guiltily, but he ignores it, and finds Arthur's eyes with his own.

"Sorry, I was just passing this way and wanted to check everything was OK. I've been involved in the investigation and wasn't sure if the family liaison officer was still assigned…"

Arthur nods and steps backwards, allowing McAvoy to extract himself from the phone box. He feels suddenly shivery as he steps into the cold, misty dark.

"Diamonds, they are," he says, softly. "Family liaison team. With us even before Roper found her. Kept us going. Can't speak highly enough of them. Nowt else for them to do now, though, is there? Just got to get through the trial, and then it's done."

McAvoy looks at the house across the street. There are still no lights on inside.

"Your wife home?"

"Yes. Just having a quiet few minutes."

"The light's off. I wasn't sure if you were in."

"What's the point in switching it on?" Arthur doesn't say it, but McAvoy hears the sentence, in his skull: "What's the point of anything?"

"Sorry if I scared you," says McAvoy.

"No, no, it's nothing. Pleased you care. I was just off for my walk and saw you and figured you were another reporter. Nobody else ever uses that phone box. When she was missing, they would stand across the road from the house and ring us, asking to be allowed in. Must have figured the caller display unit would seem more friendly if it were a local number instead of a mobile. The things they tried! One lad came to the door and reckoned he'd torn his trousers and wanted to know if we had a needle and thread. The missus let him in and next thing he was pulling pictures off the wall! We gave them what they wanted in the end, of course. Don't know if we did the right thing, now. Every copy of every paper has the same picture. The one where she's smiling, sort of looking over her shoulder. God, she was so happy that night. She had a real talent, y'know. If she put herself forward a bit more she could have been a star. When she won that singing competition in the *Hull Mail* I thought I was going to burst with pride. She was so happy. Deserved it all. Judges all said it wasn't just her looks. Had such a talent. Such a talent…"

He drifts away, lost in himself, mummified in misery and loss. Consumed with the grief of a man who knows his baby was being butchered while he downed a pint in the pub.

"Which way are you heading?" asks Arthur, suddenly. "I don't mind a bit of company, once in a while."

"Of course," says McAvoy, falling into step beside the older man as they plod through the cold and the dark to the end of the street. They don't speak much as they wind their way through the estate. Arthur's breath sounds pained. Difficult. McAvoy finds himself offering Roisin's services.

"She makes this toddy which really cuts through the gunk in your chest," he says. "Tastes wonderful too."

"Knows her stuff, does she?"

"Oh yes. We've only got a little herb garden but she's been raised with all this stuff. Knows which leaves can cure what ailments. Honestly, you tell her you've got a broken leg and she can find the right flavour mint-leaf to fix it."

Arthur gives in to a smile, but his mind is clearly elsewhere. He doesn't care about his chest. His pain. He relishes it, and will end it, when this trial is over. When the Chocolate Boy is behind bars.

They are already in the alleyway before McAvoy realises where they've been heading.

Arthur stops. Puts his bare hands on the rough bricks.

"This is where the knife blade broke off," he says, softly. "Went right through her. They never found it, you know. Of course you do, what am I saying?"

McAvoy doesn't know what to do. He wants to put a hand on Arthur's arm. Tell him he understands. But it would be lies. All he knows of Ella Butterworth is what her corpse looked like. How her rotting cadaver smelled when he opened the door. He doesn't remember her first steps. The first time she flashed the smile that would light up the newspaper stands.

"Just seconds, they say," he's muttering. "A couple of seconds either side and their paths would never have crossed. She'd have come home. Had a cry about the dress, but we'd have fixed it. Silly thing to get upset about, but I suppose she wanted the fairy tale. Wanted it to be perfect."

McAvoy nods. Summons up the courage to pat the older man's back. Gets no response.

"Bad timing, they say. Silly thing to die for, isn't it? That's the bit that gets me. I know Cadbury's not all there, like. Got the screws loose. But how do you see a pretty young thing and go from giving her the eye to cutting her up? That's what I don't get. God help me, when she was missing I had all sorts of images in my head. I reckon I always knew she wasn't coming home. But for it to be a stranger? For it just to be bad luck?"

He sniffs, but he's too used to these feelings to give in to more tears. "That's the hard part. Knowing his face was the last thing she saw. She's never had a hand raised against her in her life. Never said a bad word about anybody. She was beautiful. She had such a good heart."

Arthur turns. Fixes McAvoy with a look from beneath eyelids swollen with the effort of blinking back a never-ending agony.

"You got kids?" he asks, suddenly.

"A boy," he replies, grateful to know the answer to at least one question. "Fin. Just a toddler. We're trying for another but maybe it's not meant to be. Fin's enough, whatever happens."

"Nice age," he enthuses, smiling without showing teeth. "Treasure him."

"I do."

"You can never keep them safe enough," he says, looking at his feet. "Christ, you can't know how many times I've wished it was me instead of her. Anybody but her. I'm her father. I'm supposed to keep her safe."

"You can't blame yourself," he begins, but it's feeble.

"I don't," he says. "Not really. I blame Cadbury. He's the one who did it. That much was clear from the first time I met your man Roper…"

McAvoy feels the pain in his gut. The sensation of falling. Of nausea. He smells the old man's rotting daughter in his throat. Wants to steady himself against the wall but fears he'll feel her blood on his palm. Wants to ask. Ask how it would feel if he learned that somebody else had stuck the knife in. That Roper had taken the easy option. Taken it easy and nabbed himself a headline. Arthur saves him from himself.

"I had my doubts, of course," he says, talking more to himself than to the policeman. "You go through everybody in your mind. Try and imagine the unthinkable. It wasn't that long before she went missing that we had those hassles with the kids in the neighbourhood, bouncing on the cars, making a show of themselves. And then there was that chap who Ella convinced herself was spying on her. I still don't know if that was true, but her mum had no doubts she saw somebody at the window that night. I called the police, like you do, but they couldn't find anybody. I only bothered because Ella had told me about these funny messages she'd been getting. You can convince yourself of all sorts, though. Wendy even reckoned some of her tights had gone from the basket, but that's how it builds. You scare yourself..."

McAvoy can't breathe. He looks at the spot where Ella Butterworth lost her life and turns to her father. Listens to him spill his guts about another line of enquiry the investigation had ignored.

Finds the strength in his mind's eye, to take notes.

The stench in his nostrils.

The feeling in his belly.

He's out there.

The man who killed her.

We've got the wrong man...

28

Give yourself an Oscar, thinks Detective Superintendent Roper. *A-grade performance, that. Fucking beautiful.*

He skips down the stairs and enjoys the slick, graceful sound his shoes make on the linoleum. Swishes down the corridor, coat-tails billowing. Alone, and still making the effort to look good.

Add that one to the repertoire, he thinks. Actually had him thinking I was surprised to see him there! Like I didn't know. Like I'm not Doug Fucking Roper. Little tit.

It's all coming together, he thinks. All the little pieces. And I can knit them into something beautiful. Documentary crew were creaming their knickers. Can edit out the insults. Some of them stung.

Flies in the ointment, though, sunbeam. Still got to find this witness. Can't screw the trial. Can't let the Chocolate Boy melt. You got a little physical with him in the interview and there could be repercussions. Don't need that, he thinks. A little bit of reputation is one thing, but a blemish on the record could spoil things royally.

Pulls his phone from his pocket. Quick call to McAvoy, the rising star. Hope the cunt's asleep, he thinks.

Answered on the sixth ring.

"Sergeant. It's Roper. The girlfriend. Yeah. Pick her up first thing. Wait until her brother leaves, though. I don't want there to be a scene."

Oh Doug, he thinks. You are a card.

29

She cried for two hours after Roper left, snottering and muttering into my shoulder, begging to be held and then pushing me away.

I was glad to escape, happy to jog the half mile to De Grey Street and fork out for a foil wrap full of poison; pressing three grubby notes into a grubbier hand, the gun back at Kerry's flat for fear of temptation during the transaction.

I wanted to look away while she shot up, but couldn't move my eyes – fascinated as the rock bubbled on the spoon, as the blood misted the chamber of the syringe, and the delicious smack charged into her veins.

Me, wiping the drool from her chin.

Laying her down and watching her sleep; cuddling my hand to her face.

Slipping away in the darkness.

She'll be out for hours.

I miss the coat more than I miss her. The gun is too obvious in the inside pocket of my suit jacket, my fags and notebook too cumbersome in my trousers.

And I'm cold. Shivering in the fine drizzle of the grey morning.

7.22 a.m., Tuesday, February 7.

Tramping up Spring Bank. Back towards The Tap.

Pop into the little café near Kwik Fit and order a tea with two sugars, warming my hand on the polystyrene cup.

Sipping tea and feeling it sting my teeth. I order a teacake and stand, waiting.

"Excuse me, have you finished with the *Mirror*?"

I turn around and a big lad with a stud in his lip and short, bleached blonde hair, is pointing at the newspaper I've inadvertently leant on. "Help yourself," I say, handing it to him. He takes it, gratefully, and orders himself a ham salad sandwich, in a broad Hull accent.

"Bit fancy," I say, conversationally. "More fried pig trotters and giblet ciabattas in here."

"I look after myself," he says, smiling. He's youngish and there's a bit of a softness to his movements and a slight pouting of the lips that I take as distinctly homosexual.

"I can see that," I say. "Which gym you with?"

"Used to go to the Holiday Inn," he says. "Left there a few months ago and just been doing my own thing since then. You into lifting, are you? You look in good shape."

"I do my bit, when I remember. The workout's the boring bit, though, isn't it? I just go for the sauna and the Jacuzzi. Chill out a bit."

"I know what you mean. Love the lifting though. Working up a sweat."

I sip my tea and he glances over the sports pages. His sandwich arrives before mine, but he doesn't find a seat immediately. He stands, looking at me. I sense he's lonely.

"You want to join me?" he asks, and there's a look in

his eye that suggests he'd like to do more than chat about weightlifting.

"Sorry," I say, and mean it. "Got to be at work. Another time, though, eh? You a regular here?"

"No, never been in before. I'm staying at the hotel down the ways there and their idea of continental breakfast is a fucking croissant and a roll, so I came out to get myself something. I can come back though."

"If you like," I say. "You sound local, though. Why you staying in a hotel."

He goes a bit coy, and I help him out by saying: "Boyfriend kick you out?"

He gives a smile and shakes his head, tapping the side of his nose in a conspiratorial gesture. "I can come back tomorrow if you want to continue this conversation..."

"Might see you around," I say, as my teacake appears in a greasy bag on the counter-top.

"I'm Minns," he says, and the name flows over me without being snagged.

"A pleasure," I say.

Out the door and into the rain.

The fumes.

Darkness like rancid fruit.

Suddenly not hungry anymore.

I drop the teacake in an empty bin outside the corner shop.

Onwards and upwards, jangling sounds right in the centre of my head.

Not giving a shit as I pass the two coppers and scene of crime van down Jamieson Street and get into the knackered, beige, Vauxhall Cavalier that every copper in East Yorkshire is looking for, and failing to spot.

Flip Johnny Cash out of the CD player and slide in a bit of Prodigy.

Waking up properly and swilling my mouth with tea.

Juggling a notebook, polystyrene cup and unlit cigarette.

Into first, second, third.

Roaring up Spring Bank at sixty, an hour before gridlock.

Light it up.

Breathe deep, to my toes.

Twisted Firestarter.

30

T wenty minutes later.
   Road slick beneath the tyres.

Looking in the mirror, I notice that my stubble's become a beard. I look like my dad, but with something added and a lot taken away. Thinking of him feels like a pint of cold Guinness on an empty stomach, and I pull back from the memory.

I let my brain drift down familiar, well-worn tracks. Remember his hands, those big hands and the tiny cigarettes he cupped within them; those fingers the colour of over-ripe bananas.

Drifting into Cottingham for the press conference. Still dark.

Round a roundabout, down a side street. Park in a cul-de-sac, under a tree, outside a big house with an unkempt garden. Children's swing and a slide on its side. Soaked fluffy rabbit, sinister on its back, abandoned on the front step; glassy eyes staring up at the tumbling sky.

Cottingham. Britain's biggest village, according to the sign and the bullshit. Town, really. Quite well to do. Few chain shops, decent pubs, nursing campus. Big bastard of a police station, next to the site of the new cemetery. Fields, here and there. Rural, after a fashion. It all looks the same.

A sigh, then out the car. Not raining, exactly, but the air's wet.

Freezing. Wishing I'd brought my coat. Feel naked without it.

Fags and notebook tucked under my arm, inside my suit jacket.

Gun in my waistband, pleasantly uncomfortable.

Bit of a walk ahead, through the town and down Priory Road, fields full of horses either side.

Passing houses, stepping between dark shadows and circles of streetlight, then drifting into countryside.

Today's the day, I think. *Today's the day you all get to see who I really am.*

"More than a hundred blows," he reckons. "Pathologist couldn't tell which bone fragments came from the front of his head and which from the back. Powder and mush."

"Brick, wasn't it?" Scruffy lad from a radio station, standing with us without being asked.

"Rock. Boulder, actually. Smashed his fucking head in."

We all say: "Nice".

8.54 a.m. Priory Road Police Station canteen. It's been cleared for the press conference.

Me, Tony H, Steve from *The Mirror* and Aled from one of the Leeds news agencies, leaning on the snooker table and talking death.

Big room. Modern. Rows of chairs facing a table, in front of the Humberside Police crest.

Place is filling up. TV crews fiddling with tripods, checking levels, getting in each other's way. Cockneys talking into headsets and mobile phones.

Kids from Yorkshire radio stations, dressed in Punkyfish and corduroy, looking lost.

Microphones on the table, sticking out in all directions, like spears repelling a cavalry charge.

Proper reporters lounging at the back, sharing with our mates.

Knowing it's all bullshit. Surprised to see so many faces for a routine press conference. Isn't even silly season. Plenty happening.

Train crash in Oxfordshire last night, I'm told. Nutter drove the works van onto a level crossing. Four dead and plenty injured. Enough for six pages. Another Leeds United player arrested for butt-fucking a teenage girl in the lift at Elland Road.

Business as usual.

Tony H sucking the chocolate off a Twix and scowling at Steve, who's stolen his thunder by sharing the details of the post mortem.

Raining in sheets now, soaking the news vans parked on the field beyond the glass doors.

I missed the worst of the downpour.

Charmed life.

Black circles around my eyes.

Waiting for Roper.

"I wonder what they were doing in the woods, though. Lover's tiff?"

Laughs all round.

"It's a theory. Has to be drugs though. You know the Petrovsky line, yeah?"

"Fuck yeah. Checked the cuttings and we haven't had much on him. Not exactly a Kray though, is he? Not a household name."

"No, but this guy's got the potential to be a Bond villain. We could make him anything we want. Can't exactly libel the evil twat, can we?"

"True. How you playing it, Owen?"

"God knows. I'm struggling to get worked up about it, to be honest. A druggie and a headcase take each other out and they waste my taxes trying to catch someone for it? Nobody ever stops and wonders whether it's worth the bother, do they? Be nice if just once, they said, 'Who gives a fuck about this one' and spent the money on, I don't know, me? Makes as much sense…"

Raised eyebrows.

Realise I barked it. Said it like I meant it. "Sorry, was in my *Daily Express* mode, there. Give me a moment, I'll *Guardian* it up for you. Yes, shocking, terrible – probably had an awful childhood, poor lamb. I blame the cuts to social care. Call this a coalition government? Clegg's nowt more than a sock puppet…"

Relief all round.

"Remind us why you haven't got your own column," says Tony H, lightening the mood.

"Doubt this will be worth the trip," says Aled, nodding expansively. He's come over from West Yorkshire for this, on the off-chance one of the nationals will have neglected to staff it. Busy thinking of ways to make his copy unique. "Still, everybody loves Roper, don't they? Always good for a line or two."

"I bloody don't," I say, wanting to tell somebody about his visit to Kerry's, and deciding against it.

I amble over to speak to Trish from one of the local TV stations, but she's busy getting an earful from a producer on her mobile, and after a few seconds standing waiting for her to finish and sharing a conversation of facial expressions, I decide I look like a twat and head for the door.

Cigarette. Fingers. Lighter. Lips.

Inhale. Absorb.

Shivering, blocking the doorway, staring at the car park and the grass, wires snaking around my feet.

There's a barrel-chested bloke in a well-pressed suit leaning against the wall, taking deep breaths of cold air. Big lad, looking lost. He's a redhead with pale skin and freckles. Probably about my age, though better looked-after. He sees me and moves along the wall to make room. He looks familiar. Definitely a copper, but I can't place him.

"Fag break?" I ask.

"Fresh air, actually," he says, and his voice is a low, soft, Scottish brogue.

"Yeah? Sorry if I'm spoiling it for you. Do you want me to put it out?"

He pauses, as if unsure how to respond. I can see him working things out. "That's rather up to you. My wife's a smoker. People should make their own decisions."

I smile, politely. His manner is a bit disconcerting. I have an overwhelming desire for him to like me. He's got big sad eyes, like a cartoon cow, and there's something about his manner that makes me think he should be wearing a hood and sandals and trudging along a pilgrim trail. Maybe it's the voice, I think. Or the stillness. Or maybe I'm just going mad.

"Which paper are you with?" he asks.

"Press Association," I say.

"A fine organisation. No frills. I presume this will be going national?"

"Oh yeah. Big story. Should get Roper a few headlines."

He raises his eyebrows and gives a little smile. "He will be pleased," he says.

We share a look that says we both know Roper and the things that make him tick. He thaws a little.

"Oh aye, he's not averse to seeing his name in lights," I say.

"No, he's certainly got a profile."

"I'd love to see his psychological one."

We laugh, making friends, two blokes together. Then he back-pedals, as if concerned he's given too much of himself away.

"It's important, though," he says. "The media can play a crucial role in any investigation…"

He sounds like he's reading from course notes, and I lose interest. He seems to sense it.

"I'm sure he does it out of decency and a burning desire for justice," I say, dripping sarcasm. "Not just so he can see his face on the telly and lick the screen."

He doesn't reply. Just stands there, looking daft and nervous. I feel for him. I can't imagine how it must feel to be almost inert with indecision and self doubt. I sense a pathological willingness to please. I sense that if I made a gentle jibe about his roots or his hair, he wouldn't sleep tonight for wondering what I'd meant by it. Wouldn't fit in with the press crowd, I decide. Not one of the boys.

He makes to leave, then stops. "You're covering the trial as well, are you?"

"Oh yes. Busy bee."

"What do you think?" His big face is earnest and genuinely interested. I'm taken aback to be asked. Reporters don't often get a chance to offer opinions to anybody who isn't part of the hack-pack.

"He's going to go down," I reply. "Roper wouldn't have let it get this far unless he was sure. I've heard about this witness but I reckon Cadbury's a good bet."

"I didn't mean about being found guilty. I meant about being responsible."

I pause, smoke in my mouth and throat. I give him a puzzled glance, and he tries to laugh it off. It comes out as a high-pitched cough. He's got no style at all, this one. But there's something in his eyes that makes me want to pat him on the shoulder and tell him he's a good egg. Picking on him would be like kicking a puppy, and I haven't done that in years.

"You not on the same hymn sheet as the boss?" I ask, journalist reflexes kicking in, nose for a story, ear for a yarn.

"Best get back inside," he says, then extends a large, clean hand. I take it and am surprised at the roughness of the skin. It's weather-worn and used to hard work. Like Dad's.

"McAvoy," he says. "Sergeant."

"Owen Lee," I reply.

His face freezes. For a second various expressions seem to duel on the large canvas of his face. Then he nods and turns away, stepping back inside the police station.

I'm puzzled, for the briefest of moments, then forget it and try to enjoy the last of my cigarette, looking around at nothing very much. I notice a fair few uniformed coppers milling about out in the rain. Yellow coats, hunched at the shoulders. Loads of them, now I look again.

They're looking at me. Glancing over shoulders, throwing sly eyes. Milling about, like they're trying to appear relaxed.

More, by the gate.

I can see arms being raised. Fingers to earpieces, walkie-talkies to mouths.

And I'm feeling paranoid. Trapped. Set up.

I can feel every bump and prickle on the gun's handle, pressing into my back. Can hear the wet thump of a skull cracking; the hiss and squelch of a thorax being pulped.

And I'm trembling. Dropping my cigarette. Bending to pick it up but feeling a constriction as the gun digs in, and stopping, hunched, halfway to the floor.

I want to stay here. Trapped between moments. Hiding. Each foot on a different road.

A sudden movement to my left. People taking seats, switching off phones, rolling cameras.

Those young enough, angle one leg across the other, notebook on thigh.

And I tumble, still shivering, to a seat at the back, plonking down next to one of the assistant press officers. Juliet. Forty-six and blonde. Moderately well-kept. Designer glasses bought cheap from Asda. Trouser suit in a tasteful green.

And then Roper is here. A swish of leather and a cloud of Aramis; camera crew and two sergeants following like apostles.

Looking bright. Well-rested. In his element, here. Cameras. An audience. A chance to perform. Probably nipped into the toilets to touch himself up beforehand.

Flops into his chair like a dandy. White shirt and matching white tie today. Black pinstripe. Tan shoes. Chunky knot in his tie.

Leaves an empty seat beside himself.

I put a heading on a new page of my notebook, and the date, but the letters blur as I look at them and I don't know if they're shorthand or longhand.

Me smashing my eyes shut, scraping the top layer off my tongue against my teeth. Whimpering, quietly. Pen leaking ink onto the page.

Everyone straining for a better view, as though Roper's a fucking rock star.

Sip of water. Flash of a smile.

"Good morning. Thank you for coming. I'm aware that it was quite short notice and many of you have to cover the ongoing trial at Hull Crown Court, so I'll keep this brief. It's been a long twenty-four hours for everyone."

Another sip of water. Scans the room. Spots me. Smiles.

"As you are all aware, two bodies were found yesterday morning in the Humber Bridge Country Park. One had been the victim of a bullet wound, the other a particularly savage attack. It should be mentioned that the injuries were some of the worst ever seen by experienced members of this police force. Our inquiries have quickly identified a vehicle that was parked in the nearby car park around the time we believe the killings took place, which was shortly after midnight. Unfortunately we have no registration plate, but we believe the vehicle to be an early-Eighties Vauxhall

Cavalier. We are currently searching a large database of vehicles, but I would urge anybody in the East Yorkshire area who drives such a car to contact myself or my officers so they can be eliminated from our enquiries. The names of the victims have already been made public and I don't propose to waste your time by going through it all again. However, I am concerned that people understand what a horrific crime has been perpetrated and feel that can be best illustrated by providing some more information about one of the victims. Darren Norton was just twenty-three when he was killed, two nights ago. He was originally from Goole, but had lived in Hull since leaving school at sixteen. He worked for a time as a porter at Castle Hill Hospital, and as a barman onboard one of the North Sea ferries for several months. He was known as an aspiring DJ, and had a younger brother with whom he was no longer in contact. Yes, I can confirm that at the time of his death he was a registered methadone user who had struggled with a heroin addiction for some time, but he was nonetheless a victim of murder, and those who knew him have painted a picture of a caring, intelligent, ambitious young man. His family are understandably too upset to comment, but Darren's girlfriend has agreed to read a pre-prepared statement to help with the investigation. A copy of the statement will be handed out when she has finished and she will not be answering questions. Thank you."

My heart, bouncing off the inside of my skull and dropping through my arse.

Door swinging open to my left, and Kerry shuffling in. Family liaison officer supporting her arm. Same grey T-shirt. Face white as angel-wings, eyes like a snowman.

Floaty skirt and flip-flops. Shaking. Small. Disintegrating. Wrapped up tight in her brother's coat.

High as a kite.

Roper, clearing a path to me with his eyes, and winking.

Tony H looking up, seeing Kerry, and spinning round to me as though he's on a spit. Eyebrows in his hairline.

Me melting into my chair. Ashamed. Humiliated. Beaten.

And suddenly, so very fucking angry.

"Fuck you, Roper. Fuck you!"

Out of my chair, picking it up by a leg. Hurling it at the crest behind his grinning, smug head.

Roper not moving as the chair ricochets off and the crest topples over behind him.

Everyone ducking. Girls shrieking.

Film crew swinging their lenses in my direction.

Me kicking over a camera, shoving Aled, bundling past the same young copper who, yesterday, seemed to want to be my friend. Times change.

Out the door and into the rain.

Coppers running towards me on all sides.

Me reaching for the gun.

Slipping on the wet grass, soaked through. Everything slick. Oiled. Coppers' feet going out from under them as they reach me and slide by. Melee in the car park. Wet hands in my face. Me, fighting on my back. Faces and boots and nasty yellow raincoats. Grunting and swearing.

Mud wrestling. Me, a giant bar of soap in the bath, popping out of clutches and squirting into gaps.

Back on my feet and running.

Blood thundering in my head. Tears on my cheeks.

Six bullets lining up in my mind, pleading to be used.

Looking back as I run, at the faces at the canteen window, at the rolling cameras. The coppers sprawled on the floor.

Roper's voice crackling on the radio.

"Let him go."

Through the car park, up the road.

Running from myself.

Heart beating. Brain banging.

Crunching out a back tooth and spitting it out. Gruesome trail of spit and blood on my suit. Sticking my tongue in the hole and getting off on the agony.

Rain falling like a guillotine.

31

I can't get my teeth into the vein. I'm a yapping dog trying to bite through a football. The flesh keeps sliding away from my gnashing teeth.

There's something thick and buttery at the back of my mouth. My throat's closed up; the screams and tears twisting it shut.

Tears soak my face and shirt. Snot runs into my mouth. There's gristle in my back, my neck, scaffolding my stoop over the steering wheel.

Noise like a rumbling stomach escaping my lips, a ululating whine that makes my eyes twitch.

Sinuses tingling.

Chewing on the wrist of my right hand. Grabbing the biggest vein between my front teeth and pulling, tearing. Gnawing. Grunting.

Blood escaping the frayed graze. Bubbling up and spilling out as I chew deeper. Taste of meat filling my mouth. Claret soaking my cuff.

Can't even formulate thoughts. Can't analyse or introspect. Can't talk myself through. Just lumps of sound, banging in my head alongside song snatches and film dialogue.

Roper. Kerry. Beaten. Jilted. Her, taken from me. Her, acting without asking. Led by another. Directed. Twisted. Bodies. Gun. Drugs. Duty. Kill. Kill. And Jess. Christ, I want Jess.

Fighting the traffic and losing.

I'm staring out the side window, still chewing myself like a teething baby.

The cars have their headlights on half-beam, bringing more shade to the gloom. Mine aren't switched on. I don't want to extinguish the dark. It's where I live.

Fuck!

Cursing my temper. My lack of control. Why didn't she ask me if she should do it? Why didn't Roper give me a fucking courtesy call? Why did I let myself show? Knowing, now, that I must be truly nothing, that I must be the fucking joke I always feared. I should be striking fear into people's very souls. But nobody's frightened of me. Nobody even thinks of me at all.

I spit on the inside of the window and wipe it into the steam on the glass. It's gruesome with pink, frothy blood.

Flick on the lights. Half-beam. Full.

Me, lighting a fag. Blowing on the ember.

Turn the cigarette around in my fingers, insert it, ash first, into the black hole of my gob.

Press the hot embers into the gap where my tooth was.

If I scream, I'll fail.

Penance. Absolution.

Whole body vibrating with agony. Grit.

Smelling my burning skin.

Into the wrong lane.

First, second, third, fourth.

Cars swerving. Horns honking.

Me in a bubble of pain. Protected, in the knowledge it can't get any worse.

Fuck the gun.

I'm a bomb.

32

"Went well," says the young copper, standing at the urinal and talking back over his shoulder as Doug Roper washes his hands in the sink.

"Oh yeah," he replies. "Peachy."

Roper's not ready to congratulate himself yet, but things are panning out perfectly. Superiors happy with the way things are going. He's got evidence that's only a casual drop and an easily-wrung confession away from a conviction. The Cadbury trial just about on track, when the pieces fall into place. And now Owen, fucking himself royally for the world to see.

"She gone?"

"Who? The girlfriend? Yeah, got a squad car to drop her back at that shit-tip of hers. I'll go back and get the statement signed when you tell me what it should say."

He's learning quick, this one, thinks Roper. Not quite a protégé, but certainly a useful lad to have on side. Looks chinchilla-soft, but he's already shown what he can do when his blood's up, and he's ever so keen to learn from his hero.

"When are we going to have him in then?" asks the young lad, eager to please.

"Laddo? Don't worry, son. I've got plans. Got the call this morning. Minns has been spotted."

"How do you keep it all in one head, sir?"

"You've either got it or you haven't, sunbeam."

"Have I, sir?"

Roper says nothing. Just thinks: *We'll know by tonight*.

He walks back down the corridor past the canteen and up the empty staircase to his office. He'd insisted on a room with a view, and the large glass window stares out across farmers' fields and pastures filled with grazing, shaggy-legged horses.

He shuffles papers for a while, watches the horses in the hope that two of them might have a shag. Draws something pornographic on the cover of a mauve file in his in-tray, then picks up his phone and tells reception that they can tell the film crew he's ready for them again.

Sometimes, he thinks, in these bored moments of waiting for the world to catch up with his thoughts and for his prey to fall into the traps he has dug, he wonders what it would be like to be a normal person. A Mr Average. A DS McAvoy. He shudders the thought away.

Impossible, sunbeam, he thinks, and cups his balls, as if testing a melon for freshness. *That would be a world gone mad*.

33

10.17 a.m.

Owen Lee the Lonely, jogging up the steps to Hull Crown Court.

Only one news van today. Nationals bored already.

Me in my second best clothes. Soft grey suit with a sky-blue lining. White shirt. Leather gloves. Knee-length, battered leather jacket. Receipts from four years ago in the pocket: admission for two to the amphitheatre in Verona; large cheese and tomato pizza, two bottles of Bud and a cooking apple soaked in rum and powdered sugar.

Remembering the jewels in Jess's eyes, catching the light of ten thousand candles. Her, shivering, goose-pimpled, snuggling into my broad arms as the tenor's voice soared in the cashmere darkness.

Through the door, lost in memories, regrets.

Scary Sal, lighting up as she sees me.

"Late today."

"Busy man, Sal. I spread myself thin, but some people want butter both sides."

Umpteen beeps as I step through the metal detector. Jim looking on.

"Missed much, have I?"

"Don't think they've started yet. Cadbury's late again. You weren't here for the mum's evidence, were you?"

"No. Heard it was pretty raw."

"Very. Did herself proud though. What's today?"

"Think we should be on to the fiancé, and then it's showtime. Cadbury's mate – the one who found her body. Rumour is, Choudhury's going to try and pin it on him. Young lad did a bit of time a few weeks after the body was found and somehow, Choudhury's got his cellmate onside. Going to say he confessed to everything. Bit of DNA to back it up. Tin-Tin's going to make this his finest hour, the crooked bastard."

"Fireworks, then?"

"Like the sky when I make love to you, princess."

I feel the heat of her blush as I turn away and head up the stairs, steeling myself, ready to face the eyes of my little world.

Nonchalant. Carefree. Shitting myself.

Whole fucking bench of them, facing the stairs. Tom and Tony T. Steve. National lads. Radio jokes. Nudging each other and pointing with their stares.

Me, shrugging. Searching for a facial expression.

And then Tony H appears. Melting out of nowhere, all long face and yellow teeth. A vampire forming from a cloud of mist.

Taking my elbow, and leading me away.

Gossip and glares, burning the back of my head.

He says nothing until we're tucked in a corner. He's half hidden by a potted plant. I'm in the shadow of the toilet wall.

Checks over both shoulders. Ducks his head, then he's off.

"She's all right, mate," he says, face earnest. "She said her piece and then left. Nobody bothered her. No questions. Just a statement, if you're wanting it. Picked you up a copy."

Me silent. Glowing, somewhere between my dick and my belly, in the knowledge that I have a friend.

I nod, try and articulate something, but I don't know what to say. Don't know how I feel. I have a hard enough time remembering my opinions without remembering my reasons for them.

He shakes his head, puts an arm on mine. And says: "Fuck, mate. I'd have lost it too."

I shrink as my breath escapes; like a deflating doll. My limbs are suddenly floppy and loose. My back bent. I press a clammy palm to my brow and straighten my knees. Hold myself up by the head.

"I just lost it, Tone," I say, and shudder as the words run across my tongue with the scuttling of a spider's footsteps. I hear it in my head as a tinny sound. Small. Like fingers on a keyboard. I cough, carry on. "When she walked in there, I just went mad."

"Yeah, mate," he says with a trace of a smile. "Kind of spotted that."

I smile back and breathe my way into a soft laugh. He joins me, and some of the tension leaves us both as we chuckle and shake our heads.

"Your newsdesk see it?"

"Doubt it," I say, shrugging. "Neil can't see his dick unless he breathes in. Can't see him going to the effort of turning his head to watch the TV screen. I haven't spoken to them yet. Didn't have a lot to tell them from the press conference."

"No, I'd imagine not. I managed to get a bit in for first edition. Front page appeal."

"You mention my little incident?"

"Referred to 'tensions running high at the emotional press conference'. That was about it. Radio Humbershite mentioned that one of the reporters had launched a personal attack on the senior officer, but nobody really bothered using it. TV people might do a bit later, for a bit of drama, like."

"Christ, how did it look? Really?"

"Like you lost it and flipped out. Relax, though, mate. People understood."

"What?" I ask, flinching as though somebody's tried to wake me by driving a needle into my eyeball. "You told them who Kerry was?"

"I had to," he says, putting his arms up as though about to defend himself, or like a wizard showing there's nothing up his sleeve. "What's better? Them thinking you just spazzed out or knowing you were hurt because Roper had your sister up there? That he did it cos he's a cunt and he wanted to show you up?"

I slump into the wall, forehead to the cool brick, and groan. "I know, but. Aw bollocks." I give up, knowing he's right.

"It's fine," he says, giving my shoulder a rub. He's tender.

"And Roper?"

"Loved it. Made a joke after you left. Something about another happy customer, or your aim being as accurate as your reporting, then banged on. We were out five minutes after you."

"How d'you cover it?"

"Well there was nothing more to it, once you'd gone. Kerry got upset as soon as she started speaking, once you'd fucked off. Got no sense out of her. Roper read a statement from her, but it was crap really. He wouldn't say anything about Petrovsky. Nothing about gang wars. I put in some of the stuff that I had but the newsdesk took it out. Dull as dishwater by the time it got through the subs. Just some shite about a 'caring and intelligent man' being brutally shot to death as part of a double murder, in which another man was bludgeoned beyond recognition. Lukewarm. Crap, as well. How do you shoot somebody in a non-brutal way? How do you kill somebody gently? Death of a thousand paper cuts?"

I rub the bridge of my nose and wander around to the water fountain. Take a swig that I feel trickling down into my belly. I swill my mouth out, feeling the agony in my gum shoot down my neck. Spit the unpleasantness into the silver bowl.

Slap.

I turn at the sound of a cricket ball landing in a fleshy palm.

Choudhury. Gliding. Light on his pins for a fat fuck. Turban like the prow of a ship, cutting through foggy waters. Oozing across the landing, fifteen feet away.

Stopping by the benches near the stairs to the canteen. A few words with a lumbering chap in a double-breasted blazer and threadbare cords. Choudhury leaning in. Words in his ear like he's kissing his neck. Reassuring squeeze of a forearm. Files falling to the floor. A look from Choudhury that could straighten the other's intestines.

Then a swish, and gone.

A couple of barristers stride past. Long legs and flowing robes. Solicitors behind them, pulling trolleys and riding coat-tails. The movement makes Tone and me look up, and as we do, Ella Butterworth's family come out of a consulting room. They bring the cold with them. Their pain and grief is written in blue neon. I watch as a room full of people draw their clothing a little tighter, and shiver to find them damp.

Mum smiles, politely, as she passes Tony and me, and heads to the courtroom. I try to nod encouragement, but the action stalls, like a gulp that can't be swallowed. And I'm just standing there. Seeing raindrops on muddy photo frames, and words blurring and blotting on slivers of card, wedged into wreaths that should have been wedding bouquets. I'm cowering on a beach, watching a tsunami, their oceanic swell of grief, and wishing it would wash me clean.

Thinking of Ella Butterworth and the look in her eyes in the moment the blade violated her tender, delicate skin.

Imagining the shadows that danced across the pale canvas of her face, like cave paintings in the firelight.

Wondering if the girl who dreamed of pumpkin carriages and fairy castles had time to mourn the shredding of her wedding dress, her princess's ballgown. Whether she spilled tears at the tearing of the expensive silk her family could ill-afford, before her mind turned to the business of opening her mouth, and screaming for her life.

34

It's 1.24.

Me and Tony are sitting by the fire in Ye Olde White Hart. He's on red wine. I'm onto my second pint of lager. Wired and drowsy all at once.

Decent pub, this. Proper pub. Dark. Leather studded seats. Hardwood floor, darkened and scuffed. Mahogany walls, almost black. Thick, frosted windows. An accountant and a solicitor propping up the bar, trying to make their lives more tolerable with two pints of Stella and a game of sudoku.

I'm feeling all right. Three hours of work. Three hours of doing what I'm good at. Scribbling, at just under 100 words per minute. Writing down what comes out of the mouths of people who, for today at least, are interesting. Watching, as Tin-Tin Choudhury just kicked a great big hole in the prosecution's case.

"I hate the twat, but he's a talent," I say, tipping a handful of peanuts into my palm, and proceeding to eat them individually, at junctures in my speech, as though devouring punctuation. "That really has to rate up there among my favourite days in court."

"I'm with you," says Tony H. His face lights up as he

recalls it, and in his dirty brown mac, he looks for a moment like one of his own cigars, being inhaled at the feet. "He spat him out, didn't he? Fuck, it really could go either way."

We sit in silence, brooding. Cadbury's acquittal would mean a scrum. It means national reporters in droves, flashing cheque books, sticking feet in doorways, pissing off the police. It means regional reporters like Tony and me looking like amateurs, trying to persuade people to talk to us without a fucking penny or a pint to entice them. It means our backgrounders are a waste of time. It means a whole new investigation. More work.

On a human level, it means we're living in a city where a man who hacked up a girl in her wedding dress is still wandering around.

It also means Roper has messed up.

But it has to be Cadbury. It has to be. If it isn't, there's evil among us. Evil free, and Jess missing.

"Wonder what he gets paid?" mutters Tony H. "More than me, no doubt."

"That kid at the bar earns more money than you."

"I'm in this for the love of it."

"Love? You?"

"You'll hurt my feelings."

"Feelings?"

"Yeah, they're new. Bought them off the internet. I'm not sure they fit."

We both laugh, then fall silent as we replay the morning's action, looking for the choicest of quotes. Thinking of Ella Butterworth's fiancé, and the way Choudhury had eviscerated him, and Roper's case.

It was clear from the outset that the lad was broken.

He had the air of a toy left outside in the rain, rusting to nothingness; never to be played with or enjoyed. He was too young to deal with any of this. Too young to hear the details of his sweetheart's violation, murder, decapitation. Nineteen years old, and done. Done in.

He'd been born to be mediocre, had Jamie. Decently mediocre. Five GCSEs. Flair for music and good at setting the timer on the video. Curious fold of skin at the back his neck which he was teased about at school. Three good shirts and a smart pair of shoes for baptisms and funerals. One suit, and he wore it when they buried his girl. Wore it when police interviewed him, under caution, for the third time. Wore it to job interviews for roles he hadn't got. Would never get. Something about him, now. An air of November. Of damp leaves and muddy turn-ups. Fogged breath, and wet eyes.

Jamie's life had ended when the knife went into Ella Butterworth. We could all see it as he pushed, then pulled, and pushed again at the wrong door to the courtroom, before stumbling into a room full of eyes and pity.

Eight steps up to the witness box.

Same suit, now loose at the shoulders. Burgundy shirt and an earring. Skinny. Smudge of stubble under his lower lip. Leather strap on his right wrist. Aggression, in his walk, his stance.

Had to be reminded to keep his voice up, as the prosecutor walked him gently through his evidence. No tears. No trembling lip. No emotion in his voice. Frequent sighs. Wringing his hands. Sipping water. Not letting himself look at Cadbury. Knowing he would only visualise what the monster had done to the petals of his rose. Probably thought of nothing else since the day she was taken.

Deep breaths through the nose, as though steadying his stomach, as he described their last words, their last moments together. Thinking of the last time he kissed her, held her hand, buried his nose in her belly button, like she liked.

And me, sitting there, feeling for the boy, but competitive. Convinced that my own pain was more real, my own misery more acute than that which racks him, devours him.

Me, wondering as his responses became more weary and his manner became aggressive, whether he'd ever raised a hand to her.

Watching, as steel entered his face, wire entered his jaw, mud entered his head. Questions. Times. Places. Dates. Words. Confirming a story he had told a thousand times.

Then showtime. Cross-examination. Tin-Tin rising to his feet, like a new island bubbling out of the sea. Jamie balling his fists, preparing himself for a fight that he would finish on his face, and with a fat barrister's cock in his arse.

Jamie didn't recognise himself in Choudhury's words. He didn't know the selfish, ambitious, ruthless and violent young man who had bullied Ella from the moment they met until the night he abandoned her to be filleted and fucked. Nor did he recognise the girl Tin-Tin described: the manipulative slut who'd cheated on him at her college Christmas party, had told her friends she wasn't sure if he was the man she wanted to grow old with, and whose appetite for al fresco sex and exhibitionism suggested she would have loved the thought of fucking a stranger against a garden fence in her wedding dress.

He spilled his water on the evidence bundle when Tin-Tin showed him the transcripts of Ella's outbox. The mobile text messages she had sent to her friend Tanya just four hours before she went missing, and which she hadn't thought to delete – saying it all felt false, that she was trying to act excited for her family's sake but that the wedding was coming around too soon. The message, too, from six months earlier, which Jamie had sent saying he would kill her if she ever looked at that bloke who had chatted her up in The Ship.

Ella's family stayed quiet. Wrestled with it all. Tongues were pressed hard against teeth. Jaws locked. Fingers gripped. They clung on to the image of the happy young couple that they had known; turned up the volume of their happy memories over the drone of Tin-Tin's lies. But they didn't look at Jamie as he left; hoarse, from shouting back at Choudhury around the ball of tears that wedged in his throat, from trying to defend his choices, his mistakes, his entire relationship. His life.

There was no nod from the public gallery as he shuffled by; smaller and greyer than when he walked in. No smile. No "it's over now" and an arm around the shoulder. They couldn't. Not yet. Not until they untangled what they knew, from what they had been told.

"Poor kid, though eh?" says Tony H, coming back from the bar with a whisky and dropping it noisily in front of me. "As if he hadn't been through enough."

"It's what Tin-Tin gets paid for. Just muddying the waters. He's not trying to suggest anything. Just create enough confusion to make any conviction unsafe. Does it well." Then, as an afterthought. "I'm still going to kill him though."

Tony H smiles as something funky comes on the CD player.

"How you going to cover the second witness, then?" I ask, turning back to Tony. "I've never seen anything like that in my life. Never thought Tin-Tin would meet his match in a Hull chav."

We share a smile, enjoying the memory. It had been a truly wonderful encounter. Tin-Tin Choudhury with his Oxford education, his twenty-five years at the bar, his Queen's Counsel stripes and his perfect enunciation, against Lewis, the ultimate little shit.

He came through the door in a fake Burberry baseball cap and a fake Fred Perry jumper, wearing skiing gloves that would be too big for a gorilla, still shouting at the usher who had interrupted his cigarette to shepherd him into Court One.

Five foot eight, but hunched. Kept his head down as he walked, so the peak of his hat always covered his face. CCTV generation.

He made Tony H look elegant. Pinched, sunken face. Hollow cheeks. Spots around his mouth and chin, hiding among the unruly stubble, growing in clumps and patches on his upper lip and pointed chin. Eyes the colour and consistency of French brie. Wiry, too. Skinny, but there's something under it. A chipolata sausage around a nine-inch nail.

Really, really didn't want to be there.

Aggressive, from the start. Didn't seem to realise that

Anderson wasn't the enemy. Didn't seem to realise he was there as a witness and not a defendant.

Didn't realise that when the judge told him to stop swearing, he fucking meant it.

Talking us through it in grunts and obscenities. That night. That fucking night.

He'd met Cadbury a couple of years back in a pub on the Orchard Park estate. Hit it off. Common interest in drinking and PlayStations, cannabis and wanking. No, he didn't have a job. No, he'd never had one, unless selling a bit of ecstasy counted. Yes, they were friends. Best friends? Aye, fuck it, whatever. Hung around. Went to each other's flats. Watched videos. Sometimes Cadbury's place, sometimes his. Usually three or four people there. Just watching telly and shit. Eating takeaways. Talking. Bullshitting.

Knew Cadbury had a temper though, he said. He'd seen it. Bit of a weirdo, really, he said. Girls didn't like him. Why? Ugly fucker, isn't he? Quiet, too. Just sat there, watching them. Watching until he started breathing deep. Then he'd try it on. Some awful line belched in their faces. Get a knock-back. Lose it. Just fucking lose it. Had seen him screaming in girls' faces before. Screaming that they were nothing, that they couldn't treat him like this, that they were just fucking sluts. He'd seen him smash himself in the face with a bottle of Carlsberg when some lass had said she didn't want a drink one night in The Sailmakers. Just Cadbury, though, wasn't it? He was a mate.

Then that night. The night they were all round Lewis's gaff, and Cadbury wasn't right. Hadn't been right for a few days. Quieter. Tenser. White knuckles and grinding teeth. Muttering about bitches, about never getting a fuck. He'd always had a thing about one of the local TV weathergirls, his favourite wank, but now he was telling stories about what he'd like to fuck her with; what he'd like to stick inside her. Wanted to see how much room there was in her arse.

And that night, the night he killed her...

Objection!

Well, he fucking did I'm telling yer...

Objection!

Yeah, whatever, that night, they was all at his place and Cadbury was giving out a harder time than usual. Could be mean when he'd been drinking, and he'd been drinking for days. Big lad with a temper, you put up with it, don't you? Not worth the fuss. But this night, he'd gone too far. Started taking the piss out of my lass, the fat fuck. Been seeing her a while. Good lass. Nice girl. Cared for her. Figured I could do worse. Told Cadbury and me other mate, Steve Venables, that cunt, told them I was thinking of fucking proposing, like. Steve wasn't bothered. Cadbury said nowt. Just sat there, drinking Lynx, eating a Chinky. We were watching some film. Cadbury's just sitting there, saying nowt, staring, eating, drinking, smoking, and then he goes off. Screaming and hollering about how she was a slut, how he'd shagged her, how Steve had shagged her, everybody had fucking shagged her and she was dirty, dirty like they all were, and he's in my face. Picks up this knife we'd been using to chop the gear...

Marijuana?

Aye, fucking weed, and he's got it to my eye, and he's nuts, just fucking crackers, and then he's gone. Just drops me and goes to the door.

And he took the knife?

Fucking must have.

And then what happened, Mr Lewis...

"...left it a bit, didn't I? Had fights before and always best to let him cool down. Just chilled for a bit. Then a few days later I reckon it's time to end it. Make up. Give him some weed and borrow a film or something, y'know? So I does. I goes round. Use me key, like always. Walk in. He's sat there in his living room in his boxer shorts. Pleased enough to see me. Watch a bit of telly. Have a crack. He goes to the bog and I remember about that film I wanted to borrow. I gets up to get it from his room, walk in, and there she fucking is. The girl from the telly. The one who's been missing. I shit myself. She's there, dead in his bed. Half-naked. Holes in her like she's a fishing net. So much blood I thought she was wearing a red dress. I'm puking and crying and gasping for breath, and I just run. I'm out of there. Cause he's killed her, hasn't he? Finally done what he always wanted, that sick fat fuck in the box over there. I just sprint for home, thinking he's behind me, and I get in and lock the door, and open a bottle and drink myself fucking sick. Then I wake up and puke and cry and puke some more, and then I phone the police. Then I'm getting fucking arrested, then bailed, and getting arrested again, and getting the shit kicked out of me by that flashy copper off the telly..."

Objection!

Smoke rising from notepads on the press bench. Sniffles and gasps from the gallery behind.

Cadbury, staring straight ahead, sucking his lower lip and rolling the rosary between a fat finger and thumb.

Then all of us, holding our breath, as Choudhury rises.

"You killed Ella Butterworth, Mr Lewis, didn't you?"

"Yeah. Yeah I did. Oh hang on a sec. No, now I think on, I didn't. It was that fat fucker behind you. That cunt who's wrecked my fucking life, you Paki bastard."

And that was the tone of it. Almost endless, the questions. Shot after shot, blow after blow from the fat man, and Lewis just batted them all away with barked obscenities and V-shaped fingers.

"*You had a key to Mr Cadbury's apartment. You stayed there when he was away, sometimes. That is what happened here, is it not? My client will contend that he did not even return to his home that week, that he indeed stayed at your property and you stayed at his. That it was he who returned home and found her dead in his bed, and that it was you who put a knife to his throat and said that if he did not take the blame, you would kill him and his family? You who held a knife to him and made him have sexual intercourse with her dead body.*"

"*What is wrong with you, mate?*"

"*You were feeling angry, about your failing relationship, about the fact that the girl you loved was interested in my client, and you took that anger out on the first girl you saw...*"

"*Can you hear the words that are coming out of your mouth? I've never killed owt. I don't even stand on spiders...*"

And it built. Built until something had to give.

"*In May of last year, Mr Lewis, you were in prison for a short time for selling drugs. Do you remember that?*"

"*Aye.*"

"*And do you remember sharing a cell with a gentleman named Minns? David Minns?*"

"*Bodybuilder.*"

"*Mr Minns contends that while you were his cellmate, you disclosed personal secrets to him. Do you remember that?*"

"*Told him I'd split up with my lass. Told him that copper had kicked my head in cause of that murder. Told him a mate of mine did it. No fucking secret. Everybody in there fucking knew I'd been questioned. Got my head kicked in twice before the rumours stopped.*"

"*You see, Mr Minns contends that while you were his cellmate, you told him that it was you who killed Ella Butterworth. That you tried to seduce her, she turned you down, and you plunged your knife repeatedly into her, then brought her body back to Mr Cadbury's flat, where you made him have sexual intercourse with her body to cover your tracks. That it was you who...*"

"*Minns is full of shit!! He'll say owt for steroids and smack. It weren't me, it was him – that fat bastard sitting there...*"

Wasn't easy to take down in shorthand.

Tony H and me sitting next to each other. Loving it all. Loving the abuse going Choudhury's way. The bare, raw indignation of a nasty little Hull shit who couldn't understand why anybody would think he had anything to do with all this; his wounded pride being spat out in swear words and rage.

A fun morning. Solid gold.

Erased my memory for a time. Blocked it out. All the shit. Jess. The bodies in the woods. Petrovsky. Kerry. Roper. The gun.

The gun in my inside pocket.

Hissing directly into my heart.

"Best file it in a sec," I say. "Don't think I'm going back for round two. You?"

"Reckon I'll see what's happening with the murder case. Give Roper a call. What do you reckon about what Lewis said? About getting his head kicked in? Bollocks?"

"I think he's capable of it. You've heard the stories about who he was before he got into character. We all are though. Capable of losing it."

"Well you proved that," he laughs, finishing his drink. "I'll catch up with you in a couple of hours. I'm going to work the phones a bit. I know a guy in the same nick as Petrovsky. Be nice to see what he's up to."

"Cool. Enjoy."

Tony pulls on his coat and gives me a slap on the shoulder as he leaves. A draught blows in as he pulls open the old oak door and I shiver into my jacket, my drink, my cigarette, my sudden, all-consuming loneliness.

Opening up my phone. Torturing myself. The image of Jess, asleep on her back, eyes closed, mouth hanging slightly open. Pink knickers and smooth legs. Soft, gentle fingers, always cold.

The phone chirrups into life.

I slam it shut, guiltily. Startled. Flustered.

Open it again, as the song continues.

And with Jess's body pressed to the side of my face, I say: "Hello".

A soft, accented voice.

"Mr Lee. I believe you may have killed a friend of mine. We have your sister."

His voice is lost amid the waves in my head.

And the whisper of the gun becomes a scream.

35

Tony H.
    Killing time.

Yellow eyes burning a hole through the tea-break quickie and waiting for the gobby cow to lock up the archives and click-clack her way home.

3 down. "Scum". Five letters.

No fucking idea.

He takes a sip of cold machine-tea. Swills it around his mouth and spits it back in the cup. Looks up, past the muddy shoes that are steaming on the desk.

Under his breath: "Leave, you bitch."

The newsroom's nicely busy. There's a pleasant buzz about the place: the early evening hubbub, when the junior reporters are looking at each other to see who's going to be the first to go home. They all finished their eight-hour shifts ages ago, but they think it will look bad if they leave the building, so they sit at their desks, reading stories on the internet and watching videos on YouTube, fiddling with backgrounders and bashing out fillers from the press releases and fliers that litter their desks.

Tony's sitting in the news editor's chair, feet in the boss's in-tray, stockinged feet dark grey with rain. He has a desk of his own, tucked away between the sports subs and the picture desk, but the cleaners made a stand several months ago and have refused to go near it until he unsticks some of the takeaway boxes and canteen dinner plates from the carpet under his chair, and a stand-off has developed. The keys on his computer are so encrusted with grime that he's been reduced to a four-letter alphabet, and he feels that even with his own inestimable talents, he'd struggle to craft a front page splash using only two vowels, an apostrophe and the number 9.

He gives up on the crossword. Puts it back on the pile of nationals. Stands up. Wanders around to the far side of the desk and leafs through the diary. Upcoming court dates. Inquests. Local authority meetings. Press calls and photo ops and parish councils by the bucketful. There are initials next to most of the entries: a reporter already tasked with spending their evenings sitting in draughty village halls listening to blue-blood wankers in cravats talk about ways to stop the neighbourhood children from enjoying themselves and pissing up the cricket pavilion. Tony's name isn't next to any of them. He does his own thing. The bosses know the score. He's left alone, and he delivers. The news editor, a panicky chap in his early forties who constantly looks like he's going to tear his clothes off and make a break for freedom, doesn't even like to talk to him. He knows this is Tony's manor. Tony's paper. The editor, bullet-headed southern cock that he is, has the power of veto on Tony's exclusives, but he doesn't use it. Doesn't want to upset his star man. He's happy to take the credit and bask in the awards. He has to endure the occasional angry phone call from people who don't like his methods, but it's a small price to pay for having a proper old-school hack on the team and valuable filth on the local great and good.

Tony knows his worth. Knows that if he ever decided to walk, there'd be an army of papers battling it out for his services.

He also knows he never fucking can.

He slumps back in the chair and opens up the newsdesk file on the news editor's PC. Looks at his watch, eyeing the door. Still no sign. Back to the computer. Double click with an ink-stained finger. A list of stories appear, all waiting to be assessed, digested, then sent onto the sub-editors to be chopped down to size and laid out for the morning's edition. He opens one at random. The upper class knobs out in one of the West Hull villages are moaning about plans for a new mobile phone mast. One of the young lasses has written it, and it's not badly put together. He looks around the newsroom and spots her. Twenty-two. Black hair and bangles. Bit of meat around her middle and a strong jaw. Not pretty, but interesting for the eyes. He searches his memory banks. Joined in September, straight out of university. Family from Leicestershire. Degree in East Mediterranean History. Lives with a photographer and a few other young professionals in a big house off Spring Bank. Drinks with the other reporters in one of the fancy wine bars on Princes Ave. Going to serve her two years as a junior, then fuck off to bigger and better things. Thinks that stories are things that come on pieces of paper with a logo and contact telephone number attached. Thinks she's being adventurous if she orders a half of cider on a school night. About as far from Tony's style of reporting as you can get. Her contacts are press officers and the occasional vocal councillor. Nobody in the gutter. Nobody wading through other people's shit and sifting out nuggets of copy. As far as he's concerned, there are two types of reporter. Those who know how far you can reach into a wheelie bin without toppling in, and those who don't.

Owen knows. Hates himself for it, the soft shite, but he knows how to get a story. Knows how to get people to open up. Willing to use his looks. His silver tongue. Even a bit of menace, if nowt else is working. Used to, anyway. Been fucking moping the past few months. Let his misfortune turn into misery. Started doubting himself and feeling guilty. Clamming up when he should be spouting. Staring at nothing when he should be smirking at the tasty juror on the back row and taking a baby-step towards rummaging in her drawers.

His nose wrinkles, a little ripple of anger that he can't keep down and which flashes across his face like the wake from a rowing boat. He wants to warn him. Wants to tell his mate that he's getting tiresome. That he's only where he is through Tony's own good graces. That he's sitting on what he knows because he likes the fucker. That the story can wait for years if Tony so decrees. That he doesn't have to destroy Owen, as long as the soft shite stops being so bloody maudlin and starts playing the game again.

The young reporter looks up and catches him scowling at her. She gives a nervous little smile, then turns away. He keeps looking. Stares until he knows she can feel it. Until she looks up again. Sees him still staring. She smiles at him again. He doesn't change his face. She looks away, and he looks back to the computer screen, smiling at his little victory.

He hates what's happening to the industry. Hates these twenty-somethings who can live on Daddy's money while they put in their two years in a town they know nothing about. That flows over them without touching. Always got one eye on the next step. All these Dick Whittingtons gazing at the bright lights of London and fantasising about the day they open *The Express* and see their by-line next to an in-depth analysis of the shadow foreign secretary's latest speech. Not Tony. He likes to take a city and wrap it around himself like candy floss around a stick. Make it his own. Take a paper and put his stamp on it. His brand. His rag. His paper: My Times.

He deletes the story that the lass has sent across and a few others at random. Looks for young Tom's by-line but can't see it anywhere in the file. He's annoyed. Wanted to drop in a few typos and spelling mistakes to get the good-looking bastard in trouble.

The screensaver comes up and he looks at his reflection in the dark screen. Long, lugubrious face. Teeth like widely-spaced cricket bats. Slicked back hair and eyes like smoker's fingers. Shakes his head as he feels it wash over him. The familiar feelings. He feels like lighting a cigar, just so the news editor will have to get up and ask him, in his faltering little squeak, to put it out. Stands up. Ambles over to the nearest empty desk and starts rifling through the press releases. Usual shit. Pubs re-opening under different names. Local businesses celebrating anniversaries. Political parties criticising their opponents for not fixing the potholes on the Longhill estate. Bollocks, really. Tony doesn't go near a story unless it's a potential splash. He doesn't do local news. He does news that happens to be local. Officially, he's the crime reporter, but it's a coat that buttons up tight over a multitude of sins. He does sleaze. Blood. Does anything juicy. If it doesn't come festooned in one or more bodily fluids, he's not interested.

He takes his phone out of his pocket. Nothing.

Pulls out the Batphone. 666999. It still makes him laugh.

One missed call and a voicemail.

Listens to the message and nods, a pen sliding into his palm, scribbling some names and numbers on the back of somebody else's notepad. Hangs up. Takes another sip of stone-cold tea.

Christ but he's bored.

Click-clack, click-clack.

He breathes out. About fucking time.

The librarian passes his desk, too-big slip-on shoes slapping against the soles of her feet. She gives him a smile.

"You gracing us with your presence?" she asks.

He gives her a grin. "I just love watching you leave," he says.

She's still talking as she walks away. Tony watches her ample backside swing. She's a plump lass in her fifties and her arse is enormous. Could balance a beer on her coccyx if you were so inclined. Couldn't fuck her on her knees though. Wouldn't get close.

He studies the computer screen for another few minutes. Visits past glories. Looks up his by-line on Google and reads some scoops from back in the day. A stabbing in Basildon. Pretty young blonde diced in a car park on her way home from the opticians where she worked. He remembers the story. Remembers the car park. The uneven tarmac with the big puddles of oily water that stained his socks. Detective inspector had tipped him the wink. He'd got there first when they were still scraping her up. Allowed him inside the tape. Killer had done a fucking job on her. More than eighty stab wounds. Fucking exhausting. Tony had followed the story for weeks. They arrested her boyfriend but it never got to court. Frittered away. Story was dead before the last petal fell from the mound of flowers laid at the scene. Poor lass. Had been pretty. Too pretty for him.

He stands and slips his feet back into his shoes. They're still wet, but it doesn't matter. Puts on his coat and heads for the door, a trail of muddy footprints on the soulless blue carpet.

A nod to the news editor, and a promise to call when he knows any more about the Country Park killings. Then out the door and into the stairwell. Down a flight of stairs. Another. It's dark beyond the frosted glass and the weather sounds ghastly as it hurls fistfuls of rain at the panes. *How would Owen describe it?* he asks himself, mockingly. Like soil on a coffin lid. Fingers twitching on a crystal whisky tumbler? Soft shite. He tries a metaphor of his own. Like piss on a metal urinal? Perfect.

The lights are off in the corridor that leads down to the archives, but Tony knows his way. Passes two closed office doors, then reaches out with his fingers to find the frame of the library door. Reaches into his pocket and pulls out a huge ring of keys. With a bit of wiggling, he can find one that will open just about any lock, and this one is familiar territory. By touch, he finds the key with the bit of masking tape around the stem, and slips it into the lock. A quick motion and he's in, pushing the door closed behind him before switching on the bank of striplights.

He breathes in. Savours the smell of old newspapers. Decades of copy, slowly turning yellow in manila folders and burgundy leather ring binders. Row after row of metal shelves, stacked with yesterday's news. The reporters upstairs treat it like a museum. Pop in on their first week to meet the librarian, say hello and marvel at the fact that somebody spends their day manually archiving every single story that's ever hit the streets of Hull. Then they fuck off back upstairs to use the computer database for background info on current cases, and forget this subterranean treasure trove even exists. Tony loves it down here. Gets on well with Gillian, the gobby, wide-arsed librarian who makes up for barely seeing a soul for forty hours of each week, by gabbling on about shit whenever somebody crosses her radar. Some days, when the snouts haven't rung and the coppers have got nothing more to offer than a half-hearted nonce, he comes down and picks a file at random. Holds it by the spine and lets it fall open. He always finds gold. A snippet from the Sixties about a drunk and disorderly. Young fella getting thirty days for pissing on a police horse outside Rayner's on Hessle Road. Easy enough to jot down the name and find out where they are now. That particular lad had grown up to be one of the bigwigs for British Gas, then become a magistrate when he retired. A phone call and a subtle letter, and Tony had another VIP in his pocket, drip-feeding him exclusives, opening up forbidden files, looking through court records to find phone numbers and contact details, only too happy to play ball and keep his name out of the papers.

Tony walks between the shelves, his fingers tracing the spines of the bulging folders. Pulls one out at random.

Selects a snippet of newsprint, glued on crumpled A4. A murder from 1963. Lad beaten to death at King George Dock. Body found in the water. Visiting seamen suspected. He makes a mental note to find out what happened, then carries on down to the far end of the room.

There's a bucket of stagnant water in the corner, next to the radiator. It's the *Hull Mail*'s answer to a humidifier and a vague attempt to protect these thousands of pieces of old paper from drying out and falling to bits. It's not working.

He finds the little step-ladder that Gillian uses to reach the top, dust-encrusted files, and climbs up. Selects the file he came here for.

A–C, 1921.

Nobody's looked in it for eighty-odd years. It had seemed the best place to hide his find.

He walks to Gillian's desk and sits down. Leafs through the old pages until his fingers seize on a plastic folder. Retrieves it and stares for a few moments at the headlines. The name. Pulls out the documents. Flicks through them. Finds the page that had first caught his eye. The face. Younger. So much younger. But still a handsome cunt, even at nine years old.

Tony spends a lot of time here. Enjoys many a quiet evening, when Gillian's gone home and he's got the place to himself: the chance to pan for gold in isolation. That's how it had been that day. When he yanked the file from the wall. Early Eighties. H through M. Skimmed dreary stories and speed-read through slow news days. And then saw the headline. The eyes. And then the name.

He wonders why it brings him such comfort. Wonders

why he takes such pleasure in knowing what his friend had once been. What he'd done. What it had cost him.

He reads the story again, although he could recite it from memory. Savours every adjective. Rolls every "horrific" and "bloodbath" around the mouth of his mind. Stares into the child's eyes and feels the connection. The spark. Sees something on the dark pupils, some spark of flame, some flicker of colour, that he finds at once alluring and familiar.

"That's never…"

Tony spins in his chair. Young Tom is standing behind him, brow furrowed, mouth slightly open, wet hair plastered to his pale face. "Is that…?"

Tony's arms embrace the cluster of documents and hold them to his chest. His heart is racing. How did the little fucker sneak up on him like that? How much did he see? What does he know? He's my story. He's mine.

"Tone, you were miles away…"

Tony tries to put a smile on his face, to pretend that he's been startled. Tries to laugh it off. He fails. His face betrays him. There's a fury in his eyes, something territorial and animal.

"Why are you down here?" His voice is dry paper.

"What? Oh, one of the subs reckoned he recognised a name from this kiddy-fiddler trial that starts tomorrow and the database was down so I popped in on the off-chance Gillian was still here. You were miles away. Anything good?"

Again, the attempt at a smile. He wants to force his face into a knowing smirk, to tap his nose with his forefinger and imply he's onto something big. But his hands are so tightly clenched around the folder, he can't seem to let go.

"I think she's gone," he croaks. "Must have forgotten to lock up."

"Yeah," says Tom, distantly, his eyes on the folder clutched to his chest.

"I've got what I came for anyway," says Tony, standing awkwardly, still holding the papers.

He knows, thinks Tony. *Fuck, he saw*.

"After you," says Tom, backing away.

Tony's knees are weak as he walks back between the filing cabinets, Tom a shadow at his shoulder.

"You leaving that?" asks Tom, all innocence, nodding at the folder. "Sacking offence to take them out, remember."

Tony does manage a smile, now. "I think they'll make allowances."

"Best not risk it."

For a moment, they stand there at the doorway, eyes locked, a battle of wills. Then Tom looks away. "Hear no evil, see no evil," he says, brightly.

"Good lad," says Tony. "You'll go far."

A pause.

A whisper.

One stinking foot on each path at the crossroads.

A gulp, and a smile.

And then, because somewhere inside him he knows that it will open a door that he would never have opened on his own, he reaches up and puts the folder on top of the nearest pile.

He feels like he's abandoning a child.

Tony walks back into the corridor, pupils expanding in the blackness. He's shaking. He listens for Tom's feet behind him on the linoleum floor, but hears nothing save the sound of rustling paper.

"You silly, silly bastard," he says, under his breath.

Turns the corridor and stops, leaning against the wall, eyes closed and chest heaving.

A wrinkle of his nose.

A Hamlet in his hand, placed to cold, wet lips.

Eyes aflame as he sucks on the burning cigar.

A shake of the head. Fears and doubts and second thoughts expelled in a plume of grey.

Decision made.

"Owen. You poor mad bastard."

36

L ater.
  Me.

Steps from home.

Scared and angry and desperate to do harm.

Through the big front door that faces onto the park and the theatre. Wincing, as if in pain, as the memories hit me like sharp stones.

I'm remembering. Jess and me looking out of our bedroom window at the crowds of theatre-goers on opera night; Jess looking at the pretty dresses and telling me which outfits didn't work. Me, impressing her with stories about Puccini and Bizet. Telling her the plots of *Carmen* and *Madame Butterfly*. Quoting lines that had managed to take lodgings in the soup of my head. Telling her love is a gypsy child who knows no laws. Her eyes sparkling like frost, and my hands on the cold, fragile bones of her hips. Promising to take her some day. Promising myself I would work up the enthusiasm to do so. Knowing she would cry when I did. So many tears, in one girl. Sometimes I feared she was melting from the inside out. Happy or sad, but still the same tears.

Nausea licking my throat.

Down the corridor to my left, and through the door. Up the stairs. One at a time, and each step heavy.

Remembering the day when we moved in. Trying to get a three-seater sofa up these fucking stairs. Dad and me, trying to pivot it around the curve. Unscrewing the feet to get it through the doors. Solving problems, together. We'd let him help because it made him feel good. It was a Dad thing. A father and son thing. Sweat and toil, and greasy muck on our forearms and back. Treated him to a sweet and sour chicken at the Chinese on Cottingham Road as a thank you. It was an escape for him. A night away from Mam. A night where he didn't have to look at the creature in the striped pyjamas and dressing gown, evaporating before him. The lump beneath the bedclothes getting smaller, as the shark in her tit devoured her. Dark shadows beneath her eyes. Veins snaking over her skin like tree roots, pulling her under the earth. Eating tinned fruit from a plastic spoon and Dad's hands. And Dad, giving it all so willingly, caring for her with such tenderness and fire. Strong. Still proud, despite the fall we'd all taken. Proud to still call her his wife, and me his son. Get her through it, then start on Kerry. Get round to me in the end. That was his plan. And now she's dead. And Kerry's dying in bite-size portions. And I'm a murderer. And Dad's lonely and small in a flat in Scarborough. Tying flies for a fishing trip he'll never take. Framing pictures, swapping frames, trying to find an outline that makes his family sparkle the way it used to. Before I did what I did.

Watching my feet, counting my steps. There's coffee stains on the blue-grey carpet. Adverts for yoga and Pilates on the noticeboard at the bend in the staircase. A sign from the caretaker, asking people not to smoke in the communal areas as there had been several holes burned in the carpet recently. Badly spelled, but heartfelt. Unlikely to mean much to the lawyers and teachers, the reporters and consultants, who believe, quite rightly, that £660 a month entitles you to shit in the fucking hallway should you feel the urge.

Open the door to my floor with a kick, and stomp on.

Everything slows. I can smell burning hair.

Seven, six, five…

My door opens inwards, and a figure steps out.

And I find myself smiling. Trying to make friends.

Tracksuit. Beard. Glasses. Scowl.

Gun held in a hand that could crush a baby's head.

Doing as I'm told. Stepping into my flat. Stepping out of myself.

Hearing the door close behind me with a click.

37

"Sir... sir, please, just a moment... look, have you seen this? The juvenile record? This is important, sir. Please, just listen, I'm not telling you how to do your job but this must be worth your time..."

Doug Roper smiles at his eager sergeant, holding the manila file, eyes wide with excitement and clothes damp from his quick run through the rain.

"I'm on it, sunbeam," says Roper, softly. "You'd be surprised how long this department managed to cope before you arrived. I thought I was pretty specific about what I wanted you to spend your time on..."

McAvoy seems too worked up to stop himself. He blunders on, clutching the folder like a shield.

"It was just a feeling, sir. I saw the report about the Vauxhall in the car park, and I know a mechanic from my rugby club, sir, and I gave him a bell and asked him who I would call to find out if anybody has ordered spare parts from this area for a Vauxhall in the past twelve months, and I worked the computer, and a name comes up that I recognise and I started digging sir, and well..."

"Good work, sergeant. But we're way ahead of you."

"We've got to have him in," says McAvoy, standing there

in his brown suit and white shirt and dull tie and ginger side-parting. Sensible shoes and a cheap watch.

"I appreciate your enthusiasm, sergeant," says Roper, leaning against the wall of the police interview room in the depths of the court building. He's just about out of patience with the new lad. Just about ready to feed him to the wolves. "Enthusiasm is a real asset. So is knowing how to read the signs. Look into my eyes, you big daft bastard. Read the fucking signs."

McAvoy arrived moments ago, panting and out of breath, ready to shoot his load and asked for a moment of his time. Roper, a bit sick of Flora trying to film him without him being prepared for it, was happy to step out of the police quarters of the court building and into a discreet advocates' interview room.

McAvoy stops. Takes a breath. Up close, he really is a hell of a size, though Roper has no doubt that he could put him on his backside and keep him there. He's taken down bigger.

McAvoy holds his gaze. Narrows his eyes. "Did you know about this? About his past?" There might be something accusing in his voice. Doug doesn't care either way.

"I know everything, son. Now you just leave it to me."

"But people could be in danger! He drives an old Vauxhall. His sister was girlfriend to one of the victims! The murder weapon's still missing. Have you seen the psychiatric report? Even the Butterworth case has some gaps he might be able to plug. We have to have him in!"

"The Butterworth case is solved."

"With respect, sir, I've been worrying about some aspects

of this for some time. I didn't want to speak up until I was sure but there are so many grey areas…"

"I spoke to Owen last night. It's in hand."

"Sir, I have to formally protest…"

"Protest away, son. But keep your fucking mouth shut."

He stands there for a minute, cheeks opening and closing like gills, torn between making a fuss and doing what he's told.

Then he turns away, dropping the file on the padded chair next to Roper. "Sorry sir," he mumbles. "Just enthusiastic."

"You'll go far," says Roper, smiling.

38

Shove in the back, and into the living room. Ducking as
I do so to avoid the gleaming Samurai sword that's still
embedded in the doorframe. I'm suddenly embarrassed
about the state of the place.

There's a man in a suit on my sofa, drinking an orange
and cranberry J2O. It's a good, chocolate-brown suit, but I
can't tell if he wears it well, because he's sitting down, with
one leg on the floor, and one stretched out on the cushions.
He's wearing a shoulder holster, over a grey shirt. No tie.
Delicate gold chain on his neck, with a medallion of some
kind. He's maybe forty. Large, wide face and a slightly
flattened nose. Three days' stubble. Scar in his eyebrow.
Smiling.

A silver gun on the cushion next to him. A copy of
the *Daily Express* in his lap. Seems a bit right wing for the
Eastern Bloc, but I don't like to pre-judge.

And there's my sister. Kerry. Not moving; pancaked on
the hardwood floor. Skinny legs poking out the end of my
coat. One sleeve rolled up. Eyes half-closed, mouth wide
open. Lying on her front, but twisted, so she's looking at the
door. Reminds me of a dead pigeon that's been left by a cat
as a treat for its owner.

She's breathing heavily. But breathing nonetheless.

"You write this?" he asks, brandishing the paper. His accent is thick. Russian-sounding. He's the man from the phone call.

I'm looking at him, then back at Kerry, and hearing the big man from the hallway breathe behind me, and I'm feeling as if I've spent an hour in a dentist's waiting room, grumbling about the delay, and then been told I'm definitely next, and suddenly don't want to be.

"What?"

"You write this?" he asks, again, infinitely patient.

I start to babble, my thoughts a swirl, my fingers shaking. "Oh, the *Express*? They carried it, have they? Haven't seen it yet. Probably used some of my copy, yeah."

He nods. Looks again at the page 15 lead, illustrated with a picture of poor, smiling Ella. "Sounds a nasty bastard," he says, with some authority. "Killing a young girl in her wedding dress. I have daughters. They mean everything to me. There should be no trial for this man. They should let the girl's father in a room with him. Cut his head off one day at a time. See how long it takes. You have seen this man. This Cadbury? Does he seem like a murderer? Like a man capable of this?"

I force myself to look at him. To get a hold of myself.

"I see a lot of murderers," I say, softly. "They all look capable of it, because when you look at them for the first time, you've already been told they're a murder suspect. It changes your perception. It plants a seed in your head. That's why pictures of paedophiles always look like pictures of paedophiles."

He nods. Pulls a face that suggests he's interested. He

puts the newspaper down, and then places his bottle on top of it, so as not to leave a ring on the floor. Then he stands up. He's a little taller than me, but there's a paunch, a faint middle-aged spread across the middle. He wears his belt tight to cover it, but I can tell the buckle will imprint on his flesh, and that he goes to sleep at night with *Levi's* written backwards on his gut.

He steps forward and extends his hand. The gun is still behind him, near the broken TV. The newspaper award, the giant Pegasus, has been pulled out of the wreckage and is sitting on the floor by the kitchen, next to my bedroom door.

"My name is Petruso."

A thousand witty retorts line up in my mind, but I just say: "Owen", and shake his hand.

He nods. Sighs. Gives me a look that suggests this is all out of his control, and looks over my shoulder at the bearded bear behind me. He gives a nod.

A fist slams into my right kidney.

I've never felt pain like it. I cry out, and all the air leaves my body in a rush. I'm already falling to one knee as another blow connects with my left shoulder. There's noise like somebody chopping through steak on a wooden block, and I'm done. Falling onto the floor. Wanting to roll into a ball, but I can't seem to get my legs up. Everything is tingling. I'm numb, but it still hurts.

The bear rolls me onto my back with his trainer. He's got a face on him like he's just been sick in his mouth.

And it's all about to come my way.

He pushes the trainer up under my jaw and stands on my Adam's apple. I'm gasping and gagging, struggling without strength; a puppy trying to swim up a waterfall. He's putting on just enough pressure to make it hurt, to render me useless. He's done it before.

Suddenly I don't care how I look. I don't give a shit that I'm losing the fight, or looking a fucking mug, or failing to help my sister. I don't remember the gun. Jess. The reasons why I am here.

The pressure eases for a moment, and his colossal fist slams into my chest. I half expect it to go straight through, to skewer me to the floor. I imagine his frustration as he tries to stand up and finds his progress impeded by a dead reporter on his wrist.

I'm clutching at my chest, coughing, snottering, as his hands go through my pockets. It only takes a moment, and I feel the gun being pulled firmly from my waistband.

Through the haze and the tears, I see him throw the gun across the room and I turn my head to follow its path. Petruso catches it, and looks at the handle. He slides out the clip and counts the bullets. He looks down at me, flapping on the floor like a goldfish on dry land.

The hands are on me again and I'm dragged into a sitting position, propped against the sofa. I feel the skin on my back shredding as I'm pulled over the broken glass and dented picture frames.

I've got my eyes shut. Screwed up tight. Too witless to be scared. Too overwhelmed to get angry.

Petruso is in front of me, crouching down. His face is inches from mine, and I can smell cigarettes and fruit juice, and see the specks of whatever he had for lunch between his bottom teeth. I can smell the damp on his jacket from the rainstorm outside. I can see the dark beneath his eyes, faint lines in his forehead that will become wrinkles when he speaks.

He takes a handful of my hair and points my face at where Kerry lies.

"This is your sister, yes?"

I nod and let my head loll onto my chest. I leave it there.

"That is a yes? Good, we have the right girl. It must pain you to see what she is. I think that perhaps she was a pretty girl, once. I think that perhaps, she was a clever, good girl. But the drugs, Mr Lee. They get inside you and they stay there, and they devour you, change you, rot you and make you ugly. I have seen it. I have seen strong, powerful men, transformed into frail old women by the shit they stick in their veins. It is a shame for many. But it is not a shame for me, or for the man who enables people like Kerry to take her daily rocket to outer space. It makes him rich. Makes me rich. I am not as rich as Mr Petrovsky, but I am still young."

Petruso stops himself after he says the name. I half expect him to genuflect. It's as if he's said the Lord's Prayer backwards in church and doesn't want to turn round in case God and the devil are about to hit him with a double clothesline.

I look up and open my eyes. They're heavy and everything hurts, but I'm paying attention. I want to know.

"You see, Mr Lee, I do not expect you to understand. You are not a part of this little world of ours. You are a decent man, a man who goes to work and pays the bills and flicks the channels looking for somebody to wank over while his girlfriend is out. You are an ordinary man, Mr Lee. And Mr Petrovsky is extraordinary. He has vision. He has respect. He has loyalty. And he has no problem with having people thinly sliced from the feet up. I do not call him my friend. I do not call him my employer. He is simply the man who says how things are. And he says that if you have killed our associate, then you must die."

I cough and try to speak but the pain in my back turns the words to a hiss of pain.

"Now I must make a decision, Mr Lee. I must decide if the creature snivelling on his back before me is capable of killing a man like Prescott. A man whom Mr Petrovsky has used time and time again, with impeccable success, to eliminate those who have chosen to stand in the way of his happiness. And I do not see that, Mr Lee. I do not see how you could do this thing."

"Nobody ever does," I say, spitting out the words in a spray.

I shuffle back against the sofa and sit up a little straighter. I'm starting to feel myself creeping back into my body. The monsters are testing the windows and giving the doors a gentle kick, as they look for a way in.

He stands up, and I hear his knees clicking.

"So, Mr Lee…"

"Call me Owen," I say, and manage to twist my grimace into a bloody smile.

Petruso smiles and snorts through his nose. He lights a cigarette, then drops it on the floor near my hand, as though he's feeding a dog a titbit. I take it, and inhale.

"Owen, then. Owen, I am in your shit-tip of a home, watching you cry, and I am being forced to breathe in the stench of your broken sister, because Mr Petrovsky has told me to. He is the only man who tells me what to do. You, have many. You have rules. I do not believe you killed our associate. However, you have his gun. The police suspect you were involved. Your car was parked at the woods where this thing happened. I have seen from your rather comical actions at the press conference that you have a temper like my own. And so I am here, to ask you, like a man, to tell me the truth."

I suck an inch off the cigarette. I smile, and choose my words carefully. "Fuck. Off."

Petruso shakes his head, a little smile on his face. "I admire you, Owen. You are being very... English. Very northern. Very stupid. You can show me the size of your testicles all you want, but I will still cut them off."

I try to think of some witty retort. Nothing comes. "You don't need an excuse to touch me, pal. You only have to ask."

Petruso lets out a slow breath, as though releasing the fluff from a dandelion clock.

Shrugs.

Looks past me.

Looks down at Kerry.

And picks up my gun.

Grabbing Kerry by the hair. Pulling her upwards as though yanking a turnip from hard earth. Her eyes remain closed, her face motionless, but her legs take her weight as Petruso stands her up in front of him and presses the barrel of my gun to the back of her neck.

"Did you kill my associate?"

I test the water by jumping in. "Fuck you."

Petruso pulls her face close in to his mouth and sniffs

her cheek, his mouth against her ear. Slowly, as if launching a paper-boat at the water's edge, he pushes her into the bear's grasp. He catches her before she falls. Something passes between animal and master. Unbidden. Wordless. Passionless. The bear tears her dress at the neck and pushes my coat from her shoulders. They puddle around legs that look like twigs stripped of bark. She stands there, naked and barely conscious.

The bear spins her back to Petruso, who hugs her in tight. He peers over her shoulder, her eyes still closed, and looks down at her body.

And he slides his gun through the ravaged crook of her arm, rubs it across her chest and then moves it down her body.

"Your sister's boyfriend stole from us, Mr Lee. He took our drugs to sell, and did not sell them. He used them. He was beaten for this, but we forgave him, because he was a man who could occasionally be useful. Then he got arrested. He was stupid, and he got caught. And he made a deal. A policeman friend of Mr Petrovsky's informed us that we were going to be betrayed. That Beatle was a dishonourable man. A rat. He was going to wear a tape recorder when we did business. So my associate was called. And he arranged to meet this piece of shit at a quiet, dark place. And he brought drugs and money as bait. Now they are both dead. The police think that you did it, or at least, they are starting to. I am starting to as well. Now, you will talk to me. You will tell me the truth, Mr Lee."

Kerry's eyes open, then close again, and she gives herself back to the world behind those eyelids.

"I will kill you," I say, say it so quietly I can feel the words on my lips like a kiss. "I will be the man that ends your life."

Petruso does't speak. He simply kicks her legs apart with the outside of his right boot.

"I am not enjoying this, Mr Lee."

I hear my own heart beating. I hear my blood roaring in my head.

"Yes," I say, breathing hard. "Yes, I killed him. I went for a walk in the woods and he was busy shooting somebody. Then he tried to shoot me. So I bashed his fucking brains in and took his gun and his money and his drugs. Who wouldn't have done that? Who would have acted differently? Would you? You'd have called the police, would you? Done the decent thing...?"

Petruso holds up a hand to silence me and puts the gun back against Kerry's head. He clicks his tongue against the roof of his mouth. "You killed him?"

"I had to..."

"And you have his money?"

"I don't even know what's there." I look at him hard, hoping to see some spark of humanity, something I can bargain with. "Leave Kerry be," I say, pleading. "She's no threat. Leave her be..."

Petruso looks at the bear.

"His money. Now." Petruso's tone is flat. Emotionless.

"Bedroom," I say, quietly "In the bed."

The bear turns and walks into the bedroom.

"I will kill you first," says Petruso. "As a courtesy."

"Don't do this..." I say. "It doesn't have to be this way..."

The big man re-emerges, shrugging. He says something

in a language I don't understand. Petruso looks puzzled, giving his associate more of his attention. Kerry opens her eyes, looks at me, then slams her head backwards into her captor's nose; blood exploding like a firework.

And I'm moving. Moving towards the big man. Reaching down as I go, and scooping my winged Pegasus from the floor. Swinging it upwards with all the force of all my rage. It connects with the side of the bear's jaw and I feel his head break, and hear it again as he slams against the wall.

I turn to face Petruso, hurl the Pegasus and it thumps into his chest, splintering ribs. As he falls he puts his foot on one of my toy cars, and his leg slides out to one side, snapping at the knee. It sticks out at a forty-five-degree angle, grotesquely bent, and he screams in pain as he writhes on the floor.

I pick up the Pegasus again. Bring it down two-handed on his head. Hit him again. Again. And when I've stopped, it's dark, and there is no head to hit anymore, and I can't feel my arms.

Lighting a cigarette with hands that can barely take its weight, and with fingers that turn the filter tip crimson.

And I search around inside myself for something good. Something decent. Something kind.

I find emptiness.

So I hold my sister tight. And pretend.

39

"And you're sure about this?" asks McAvoy, trying to keep his tone even. "He ordered it in August last year? And it would only fit that make of car, yes? Wonderful. Thank you."

McAvoy hangs up. He's alone in the office, save for a cleaner emptying waste-paper bins into black sacks. Everybody else in the pub or doing the rounds. They'd asked him, of course. Asked him to join them for a swift one. But they'd known he would say no, and he'd duly obliged. He couldn't think of anything worse than breathing in their cigarette smoke, their lager breath; hearing them talk about old cases and past glories, and how marvellous life seemed to be before he'd passed his exams and transferred over from uniform. Better to stay here. Work hard. Nose to the grindstone.

He sits back in his chair and breathes deeply. He can feel a bit of a cold coming on. A tickle in his throat and a sniffling in his nose.

Impulsively, he calls home. He tries to ration out these moments: perhaps one text in a morning, another in the afternoon, and a call as and when time allows. Roisin makes no such demands of him and doesn't hold herself to an equal standard. She calls when she's thinking of him, and she thinks of him a lot. She's spent most of her life in love with him. They met when she was still a child and he a green-as-grass police constable. She was briefly resident of a halting site outside Carlisle and he'd been sent with a sergeant to have a quiet chat with some of the lads. Things had gone bad. Roisin had got separated from her family. Bad men came. They began to hurt her. And more by luck than anything else, McAvoy came to her aid. He hurt the men so badly he cannot allow himself to look at the memory for fear of what he sees. But Roisin knew then that when she was old enough, she would marry the big, blushing police officer. She was seventeen when she saw him again. Arrested after being witness to an act of violence in Edinburgh at New Year's Eve, she refused to speak to anybody save McAvoy: then working as a trainee detective with Cumbria Police. In the days that followed, they fell in love. They found the parts of themselves that were missing. She fell pregnant, and he proposed with a borrowed ring. And now he is a detective sergeant and she is his wife, and every day he thanks the fates for bringing her into his life, and begs whatever force controls the universe that she never tire of him, or stop seeing the hero she claims lies beneath the blundering, clumsy exterior. She is absolute in her assertion that he is the only good person she has ever met. The thought shames him, now. Shames him, as he considers Shane Cadbury, and Doug Roper, and the fact that he is lying to himself because he is scared, and doesn't want to mess up his career or fall foul of a man who exudes charm and confidence and might, perhaps, be the devil.

"Hey you," she says, brightly, when she answers. "Was

just thinking of you. The boy rang your father. Had a nice wee chat. Wouldn't speak to me, of course, but I heard enough. Your brother's doing grand. Drinking less. Met somebody, actually. She used to be a nurse, so that's good, isn't it? Anyway, Fin's happy, so that makes me happy. How's you? Is it coming together? That trip to the Country Park all turned out OK, eh? Right place, right time. I can do some asking around, if you like. Somebody on the radio said it was maybe a drugs thing? I can ask Valentine, he knows about that stuff, and he dotes on you..."

McAvoy sits and listens. Lets her words wrap around him like a blanket. He wishes he could find the courage to write poems for her. He recites them, in his head, and hopes she hears them when her ear is pressed to his cheek.

"I'm panicking, Ro," he says, quietly. "They'll call me to give evidence, I know it. And I don't know what to say. Do I have doubts? Of course I do! If I show Roper I can be trusted then I'm in his good graces and we have a future that offers Fin the very best. And yet..."

"And yet you can't talk bollocks to save your life," she finishes, a smile in her voice. "Aye, life would be easier if you could lie, but you can't, and that's hardly a character flaw. Do what you think is right. Whatever that is, is the right thing to do. Don't worry your pretty head. I've baked, by the way. If you catch the killer before bedtime I'll stay up and make you a baked camembert. Is that the right way to say it? I camembert getting stuff wrong..."

He's laughing as he hangs up. Giggling, his shoulders shaking. He wonders what he would be without her. Wonders what he would be for.

He turns back to the computer, feeling equal to the task.

He's an investigator. A detective. It's his job to look into things. To find answers. Justice, if such a thing is possible.

I've got something, here. Worth following up. I'm in my own time now, he thinks. No harm in digging...

No point bothering Roper with it now, either. He's got his own way of working, anyway. Never tells anybody anything, but always brings in his man.

Sitting there, skin clammy, cold, he thinks of that day. When he'd found her. That poor girl, diced and violated. So much blood. And that smell. The smell that will never go away. Thinks of Cadbury's calm face. His words. "She was a gift," he'd said.

The thought, that has pervaded his dreams, denied his sleep, drumming again.

He didn't do it. He took her body and had his fun, but he didn't stick the knife in. There's somebody else. Somebody hateful, violent, broken-up inside. Somebody free.

He remembers Roper's arrival. Slick and polished and calm and hungry. Took a look at Ella. Pulled a face. Turned away. Spotted McAvoy, white-faced, staring at nothing, bile in his mouth, and told him he'd done well. That he'd go far. How he'd taken over. Spun plates and juggled balls.

No harm putting the name in the computer, see what it throws up.

No, he thinks. Roper's a strange one, but his way seems to work.

And this is my job. I'm good at it. I'll show him.

His fingers hit the keyboard.

Types.

O-w-e-n L-e-e.

*

The rain is turning from an irritation into a downpour; fat droplets exploding as they thump down from a leaden sky. The wind is sweeping in from the coast and one side of Tony's face is raw and stinging as he huddles inside his coat and scurries, stiff-legged, down the deserted street.

Ten miles from the city boundary, and a whole fucking world away. They've even got geese in the duck pond and there are no cock-and-balls spray-painted on the church door. Classy bastards, one and all.

Ripe for the picking, he thinks. *Plenty to lose.*

Although it's the only road in the village, there are no cars to turn the deep kerbside puddles into mucky spray. The street lights are on and the air is midnight black. Perfect conditions to duck and weave. To keep your head down, meet your source, and bribe her into handing over a folder full of gold.

He puts a hand on the door to the little pub. Takes a look over his shoulder. There's a little old woman on the far side of the street, pushing a tartan shopping trolley, but other than that, he's got the village to himself.

Tony doesn't really like it out here in middle England. He prefers a city. Likes the smell of exhaust fumes and industry. It's all too clean, this. The rain falls with a spirit of optimism, a poetic timbre, as if it still believes it can wash the filth away and make the world sparkly again by morning.

He pushes the cracked oak door and enters the gloom of the pub. A barmaid with rabbit teeth and David Hasselhoff hair is standing behind the bar, in conversation with an old boy who's leaning on a bar stool and drinking bitter. Tony gives the room a quick once-over. Tiny place. Two rooms in an L-shape. Oak beams. Old timbers and black-and-white Edwardian pictures showing how the village used to look when a double-barrelled surname meant something. Horse brasses and a copy of *Yorkshire Life* in the newspaper rack.

"Double Bells," he says, pleasantly, using his sleeve to dry his face and push back his hair. "No ice."

The barmaid pours his drink from the bottle and he gives an appreciative nod. He likes a lass who knows her measures. Doesn't need a fucking optic to tell her when she's reached 35 ml. He downs it, and asks for another. She pours, gives a smile, and pours another. It's larger than the last.

"Quiet today," he says, waving his glass.

"The weather's putting them off for now. We pick up after dinner time," she says, conversationally. "And usually get a good after-work crowd."

"Those that aren't retired," says the old boy, eager to get in on the conversation.

"Aye, it's an ageing population," says Tony, in his most understanding tone of voice. "You've got to feel for the young 'uns, trying to buy a house in this day and age. Ain't got a choice but to move to the city. It's no wonder places like this are losing their identity. Only people who can live here are outsiders."

There are nods from the old boy and the barmaid. Vague mutterings of agreement. A general consensus that the world is going to the dogs. Won't be long until somebody mentions Poles and darkies, thinks Tony.

"We were saying that," she says. "Poor Dan up on Tranby, he can trace his line back 300 years, but his son's having to get himself a flat in Selby because it's all he can afford."

"Dan Atkinson?" asks Tony, pretending to try and place him.

"No, Sheridan. Tall bloke with grey hair. Drives a Passat."

"Yeah I know him."

He files the information away. Will be worth a favour from Sue in the features team. An in-depth analysis piece on the loss of identity in East Yorkshire's most beloved villages. The sort of bollocks he would never read, but which he can write with his eyes shut.

They talk bollocks for a while longer. Rugby. The idiots on East Riding Council. Why it's up to the man in the street to sort out his recycling when they've already paid their bleeding council tax. He sinks three more whiskies and finds out the old boy was a prisoner of war in Greece during the Second World War. Keeps himself steady and dries himself on the fire, wishing Owen was here to help him take the piss out of the rich fuckers who occasionally scamper by the leaded glass.

Ah, Owen. You poor fuck.

At exactly 7 p.m., the door opens, and the woman he's waiting for walks in. He gives a satisfied smile, though he never had any doubts she would stand him up. They may be too good for him when it comes to hugs and kisses, but when he's got them by the balls, they're putty in his hands.

He gives a nod and a smug little smile. Orders her a glass of white wine without being asked.

The old boy gives him a look he's accustomed to. It says: *"You with her?"*

She takes a seat as far away from the bar as possible. Up near the toilets, in the draughty corner away from the open fire. Tony surveys her as he walks closer. She's forty-five at least. Brown hair cut into a neat, highlighted bob. Designer waterproof, stripy grey-and-black jumper and a scarf at her throat. Would have been pretty once, but she looks like she's lost interest. There are dark smudges beneath her eyes, and when she gives him a nervous smile, he sees lipstick on her teeth.

"Elle Dorcas, I presume," he says, placing the wine on the varnished table between them and taking his seat. He never lets go of his whisky tumbler.

She gives a nod. She loses control of it, and it becomes a shake, a rapid succession of jerks that she can't seem to stop.

"Relax," he says, sipping his drink. "You look like you've got malaria. Drink your drink."

She does. Takes a large pull. Coughs. Takes another. She looks him in the face, from beneath spider-leg eyelashes tangled with mascara.

Her voice, an urgent whisper: "You know what would happen to me…"

"Yes."

"And you don't care?"

"I care. Just not enough to spare you having to go through with this."

She sneers at him. Her voice becomes a hiss. "When you called, I felt like my world was collapsing. What you've put me through…"

"My heart bleeds. Keep your knickers on, and you won't have a problem."

She slumps back in her chair, staring into her glass. "And you won't tell a soul. That's it. You'll let it go."

"Cross my heart," he smiles.

Tony's enjoying this, getting off on her plummy, middle class accent. She sounds proper posh. A deputy head teacher at a village prep, perhaps. Head of the local Women's Institute and a whizz at lemon meringue pie. He knows what she's got to lose. That's why he's here.

"Do you want it now? Here?"

"Best all round," says Tony, taking another sip of his drink. He's feeling pleasantly light-headed, slightly pissed. Blood's rushing to places where it shouldn't, and he finds himself gazing at the little swirl of wrinkles at the base of her throat, and wondering if she smears herself in cream before she goes to bed; whether she wears high-necked nighties that accentuate her thick arms, her fleshy, round chin. He's got her address. Wonders if she keeps the curtains open at night...

"I hope it's worth it," she says, bitterly, and reaches into her bag. She pulls out a pale blue folder, fat with paper. She hesitates, takes a drink, then slides it across the table to Tony.

"It's all there?" he asks.

"Everything I could find. If there's more, I don't know where it is."

Tony nods, and pulls the folder towards himself. He savours the moment. Doesn't want to open the flap until he's got the privacy to properly enjoy the moment. He tries to keep himself calm. Tells himself he already has enough to turn this story into a fucking cracker when the time is right. But he wants the documents in the folder to be good. Wants them to measure up to his fantasies.

He stares at the file. At the name on the white tag.

Imagines what he'll find inside and senses his breathing becoming shallow.

He drags his eyes away. She's staring at him.

"Well?" she asks, her palms on the varnished table. He looks at her nails; manicured but bitten, the expensive French polish scored with teeth marks. Poor bitch must have been shitting herself, he thinks.

"Well what?" he asks, enjoying this.

"The pictures. The tape."

"Oh, don't worry about that," he laughs, distantly, wishing she'd just go away and leave him to enjoy this. "They're going on the fire tonight."

"That wasn't what we agreed," she says, desperately, her lip starting to tremble and her eyes filling with salt water.

He gives her a withering stare. "It doesn't work with me, pet," he says. "I've got a mate who would slice his bollocks off to stop you crying, but the whole thing just leaves me cold. If you hadn't been caught with your pants down, I wouldn't be here. If you'd been happy with what you've got at home, you wouldn't be in this situation. So don't blub. Don't fucking snotter and wail and expect me to give a shit. I don't."

A bubble of snot pops in her nose. She's a picture of misery. Her whole world has dissolved slowly inwards since the letter arrived at her work address. Second class stamp. Name in block capitals. One sheet of paper, stapled to a print-out of the message she'd posted on the internet dating site. Then a line of text, and the name of the man she'd allowed to fuck her in a farmer's field near Pocklington.

She hopes it's over, now. Now she's done what this feral

little man with the too-big teeth and the yellow eyes has asked of her. Now she's broken into her husband's office and stolen the file that he's caressing as if it were a lover.

"It was a one-off," she says, pitifully. "My husband works such long hours. It was a mistake…"

"Dry your eyes, councillor," he says, draining his drink and picking up her wine. "We all make mistakes."

She sniffs back more snot. Presses her knuckles to her eyes. "And this is over? I won't hear from you again?"

"Cross my heart," he says, finishing the wine. "Now, if you don't mind…"

She fumbles for her bag. Finds herself apologising for wasting his valuable time, as if this were a fundraiser and he was a benefactor. She doesn't want to upset him. Finds herself daring to hope that this will be it. That she's got away with it. Now she's robbed her husband, taken what this vile little man told her to take, and paid the price for her dalliance: her vicious orgasm, ground out against the wet plastic of a black-wrapped bale of hay, a man she only knows as Neptune133 pushing himself into her and calling her by his ex-wife's name.

She's almost at the door, when he says, without a trace of emotion, that he'll be in touch.

The door closes in a flood of tears and snifflings.

Tony sinks back into the chair. Makes the most of the moment. Stretches it out. Walks back to the bar and orders himself the same wine that the councillor had been drinking. A packet of scratchings and a bag of Scampi Fries. Sits down in front of the fire, and opens the file.

Twenty minutes later, he looks up, his drink untouched.

Begins to mutter as he circles key words in the psychiatric report on inmate HH539413.

Borderline personality disorder.

Hallucinations.

Visions.

RECURRING TALK OF CLASSICAL FEMALE FORM, CONDONING HIS "SINS".

No awareness of social conventions.

Capable of extreme violence without remorse.

Shows no regret for his actions, only for the repercussions on his family.

Recommend he remains under supervision for the foreseeable future.

Tony whistles. Smiles. Christ, but this has been worth the £50 he slipped the young lad in the petrol station when he heard him wittering about the old bird his brother had found on the web. He believes in serendipity. Owes his career to it.

"Owen, Owen, Owen," he says, savouring the wine. "You mad bastard."

He sits for another ten minutes. Familiarises himself

with the report. Begins to lay the story out in his head. Can see the name. The picture, then, and the picture, now. The same eyes. The same flame of dancing madness. The little boy, all grown up and handsome as fuck.

And then he's settling up and heading for the door, unsteady on his feet and hard in his pants, the file clutched beneath his coat.

Doing his second favourite thing.

40

6.14 p.m.

Asleep with my head on Kerry's belly.

She's freezing cold, and I should have dressed her or wrapped her up, but I haven't. I haven't moved in an hour.

I'm dreaming of Dad. I'm sat on his lap at the wheel of the jeep and he's letting me steer as we bounce up the rutted track towards the south field. It's our little secret. He's got a hand on mine and smells of cigarettes and rain, and there are scone crumbs on his damp, green jacket and his glasses are dirty. I'm nine. And we're talking about tortures, like we do. About the African tribes who would stake out trouble-makers on the jungle floor, cover their chests with sticky stuff and a dozen flesh-eating ants, and put a half a coconut shell over the top, and watch as they devoured them. He does lots of good noises and facial expressions as he tells me, and never takes his eyes off the dirty track that cuts through the green field. We're talking about football, and whether Paul Gascoigne will ever come back from his injury, and laughing at the way Mum always gets song lyrics wrong. And there is a sudden beating of wings and a flash of brown and red, and a pheasant bangs off the windscreen and I swerve the wheel and yelp, and we're suddenly flipping over and down and bouncing up, and the windows smash and I bang my head against Dad's face and then the roof, and the wheel, and we're bouncing down the hill, and there are strong arms around me, trying to hold me still, and I take a double-gulp of breath, without letting out the one I had, and I suck in something evil and chaotic and angry and resentful and wise and cruel and beautiful; something born in the broken glass and the torture and the violence, that will grow strong and loud and terrifying, that will be nurtured when I wake in a few days' time to see my parents arguing at the foot of my hospital bed, talking about how they are going to afford to pay Mr Blake for the broken jeep. Keeping my eyes closed, and listening to my mum telling my father to be a man, to stand up to him, to say 'no'. And hearing, for the first time, a whisper in the back of my mind, saying, in a rasping, sibilant tongue, "it's not fair..."

6.31 p.m.

My head hits the floor with a bump and I spin around and look up, hoping for violence. Kerry's sitting bolt upright, gasping, like she's just had a shot of adrenaline to the heart. She turns and in the half-darkness, she sees Petruso's body and cries out and pushes backwards, and her back bumps my face, and she looks at me and my mask of blood, and she squawks and pushes herself away from me and her skin is goose-pimpled and she's trembling and crying and I'm trying to hold her and she's fighting me and flailing her arms and I grab her wrists and I'm shushing her and trying to hold her and not to laugh, because it's funny and silly, and then I lose patience and hit her a good one and she falls still and doesn't move, and I think she's dead and I feel relief and then embarrassment, and then disappointment when she starts to stir, and I pick her up and carry her to the bathroom, and wash my face and my hands in the sink and turn the towels pink and then I run a bath with lots of Jess's special bubble bath and I fill it high and I lay Kerry in its embrace and stroke her face until she comes to, and she wakes and she's warm and safe and with her brother, and she smiles, and I see past the yellow teeth and cracked lips and bruised face and I see the little girl she used to be. I see Dad's little princess and Mum's little helper, and I see the girl who I used to swordfight with in the woods, and who used to carve her initials into Mum's pastry crusts, and who fixed the wing of the pheasant that almost killed her dad and her brother and who went off the rails when the family fell.

And she says, "I'm sorry."

6.48 p.m.

I'm wrapping a towel around her as she steps out of the tub, dripping, onto the bathroom floor. It's a fluffy beach towel, with stripes on it, and I smile as I remember how Jess used to say that she had to use it vertically, or it made her look fat, and I'm shaking my head as I rub Kerry dry, and telling myself that girls are stupid and men are thick.

She says: "Who were those men?"

And I say: "They were bad men. They killed Beatle. But I've killed them now and you're safe and don't need to worry."

And she says: "You killed them?"

And I say: "Yes."

And she cries again, and says: "Thank you."

And I tell her it's OK, and dress her in Jess's linen trousers and a tight T-shirt and a snuggly purple jumper, and I brush her hair. She likes it when I fuss over her, and I make her promise to keep her eyes closed as we walk through the living room because I can't be doing with another scene, and I steer her out the door, and pick up my coat and my gun from the floor, and I pop into the bedroom, and I pick up my sports bag and empty my top two drawers, and shove a handful of clothes and my electric razor and my picture of Dad inside, and I close the door to my flat and its ghosts and its memories and bodies, and we walk through the drizzle and the darkness and the pissy neon lights to the Royal Hotel by the railway station, and I book us in and we go upstairs, and she squeals as she sees the big bed and the comfy pillows, and we lie down and I hold her, and she falls asleep again, and I stare at the ceiling and wonder how long I have before this all catches up with me, and I watch a spider crawl from one side of the ceiling to another, then turn and walk back.

8.23 p.m.

Me, sitting on the edge of the bed, suit trousers and bare chest, dialling Tony H's number on the white plastic telephone on the bedside table. Press 9 for an outside line.

"Hello?"

"Tony. Owen."

Pause. Gets his brain in gear. Can hear him mentally squinting.

"Owen. Fuck. What are the headlines, mate? You're

having quite the day. You went right off the radar this afternoon. More bad news?"

"Something like that. Sorry mate."

"Listen, mate, I'm a prick but even I don't like to see somebody's life go completely down the fucking bog, unless there's something in it for me. You're going to have to get it together. I rang your newsdesk and said you had an emergency and filed some copy for you, so you're not in too much bother at work, but they sounded like they'd heard about the press conference incident, so you've probably got some explaining to do, and everybody's trying to get a chat with your sister, but nobody can track her down."

"She's with me." I say it quietly, partly so as not to wake her, and partly because I'm feeling a little floaty. Light-headed. Peculiar. So hungry I'm sick with it.

"She OK?"

"I haven't pushed her for the exclusive, yet, Tone," I say, meaningfully.

"Amateur," he says, and gives a little laugh. "I had a long chat with Roper a couple of hours back."

"And?"

"You're definitely the itchiest of his haemorrhoids, mate. Be fair to say he's got a bee in his bonnet about you."

"Was it the press conference?"

There's a pause, while he decides whether or not to voice the thoughts and theories that have been breeding in his pickled walnut of a brain for the past twelve hours. "It's a good job I know you so well," he says, lightly. "Anybody else might have you down as a suspect."

I close my eyes and breathe out heavily through my nose.

"Cheers mate," I say sarcastically.

"Well come on," he says, urging me to follow him down this fatal path. "I'm not daft enough to think it, but one of the victims was your sister's boyfriend, and I know for a fact you weren't a fan. Secondly, a car just like yours was parked nearby when it happened. Third, you're a hard bastard and you could probably do it. Fourthly, you've just shown the local press pack what a temper you've got, and most importantly – and you know I'd never say this to anybody else – you've got quite a colourful mental and criminal history. Maybe Roper has you down as suspect number one." He rattles to a halt, and we both realise at the same moment that there are too many coincidences and it's all too neat, and that I'm a killer, and that Roper knows it.

"Fuck, Owen," he breathes, and I can hear the whiff of humanity and friendship in his voice. "What are you going to do? Fuck, I need to see you, mate. You need to see me. Give it an hour, yeah? See you in Sandy, yeah? Sandringham about nine-ish? Fuck, Owen. What are you going to do?"

Rat-tat-tat.

I chuck the receiver on the bed and hear Tony's tinny voice get smaller as I cross to the door. I open it a crack and it's a waiter in a white shirt and a badly tied tie, holding a bottle of Chardonnay on a tray. I smile, and sign for it, and give him a quid, and I'm turning away from the door when I see the big lad with the bleached blonde hair and the stud in his lip stepping into the lift at the end of the corridor. My mate from the café. The one who thinks I'm ace. He's in gym gear, carrying a holdall.

"Gym still open, is it?" I ask the waiter. "I told my mate I'd maybe join him for a swim."

"Until ten," he replies. "Wouldn't fancy taking him on in an arm wrestle. Probably going stir crazy after a day staring at the wall."

I look at him, feigning understanding. "Where would we be without room service, eh?"

"That's the joy of the company credit card, eh? Are you one of Mr Choudhury's clients too?"

I keep my face inscrutable. Smile. Nod. I close the door softly and pad back to the bed. Open the wine and take a swig from the bottle. I pick up the phone. Tony's gone.

8.37 p.m.

Staring at my face in the mirror.

It's too bright in here. The light is bouncing off the brilliant white tiles and the pain in my jaw is working its way up to my temples, where a migraine is starting to throb. I can't really see myself. I feel like I'm nose to nose with somebody pretty, unable to separate or distinguish between eyes, mouth, nose, jawline, but knowing that the picture will be beautiful if I back away.

There's a voice in there somewhere, barely audible above the squeals and cackles that pound behind my eyes, and it's telling me I don't have to be like this; that I beat this once before and if I just pick up the phone and call Mill View Court they'll let me in and give me a room and I'll get assessed again and given the pills that will make me stop feeling like this, and I'll get a care plan, and doctors will tell me that I'm not to be ashamed and that it's an illness like any other, and it's the chemicals in my head that make the monsters and the desires and the rages, and that one pill a day can make it right.

I rub my face and my back suddenly hurts again, and I wipe the dribble from my chin from the wound in my gum, and I see that the saliva on my hand is pink and frothy.

And then I put the pieces together. The bodybuilder. The court case. The cellmate. *Minns*.

I pick up my bag and grab a towel from the bathroom. T-shirt, tracky bottoms and some running shoes. Blue and orange Bermuda shorts that show off my tan.

Kiss Kerry's cheek, and out the door.

41

Me. Stripping down in the cold.

Conscious and proud of my scrapes and scars, my bleeding medals, the stripes on my skin, the mottling at my throat and kidneys.

Just shadows in the half-light, this bruised air.

My skin, goose-pimpled, as I undress in the dark changing room, lit only by the street lamp in the car park, with its windows that won't shut, its solitary bulb that won't light; my bare feet in a puddle of icy water.

Naked, now. Naked and shivering.

Minnsy, he's called.

He's busy talking to the assistant. Excited. Voice muffling for a moment as he pulls his shirt over his head. Eager to get naked.

"Really good to see you again," he says to me, grinning. "You gave me a hell of a start. Was going to come back to the caff tomorrow. Was just thinking about you and then you're here."

"Small city. Not many gyms. You got me thinking I should get back in shape," I say, smiling. "Need to burn off a bit of fat and a shit-load of energy."

"I'm your man," he says.

The gym assistant is young and plump. Curly brown. He's wearing tracksuit trousers and a blue T-shirt, and doesn't look like he should be the face of a gymnasium.

"You're the only ones tonight, lads," he says. "Last of the night, I reckon."

"Well, you make the place so welcoming," I say, sarcastic, indicating the bare walls and pools of cold water. "You got a heavy bag in there?"

"No, sorry."

"Have to hang you from the ceiling," I say, to my new friend.

The assistant gives us a little smile and disappears for a cup of tea and a Mars bar.

I'm alone in the dark with a man twice my size. He's naked, with a towel over his shoulder, and he's rubbing the muscles on his forearms.

"You'd expect better for a three-star, wouldn't you?" he says, gesturing at the cold and graceless changing rooms. Then: "Have a swim and a sauna first, yeah?"

"Right behind you," I say, smiling.

I wrap a towel around my nakedness and head past the lockers and the showers to the door at the far end of the room. He falls in behind me and I hold the door open to let him go first down the stairs bathed in darkness and slippery underfoot.

"Used to be the place to be, this," I say, chattily. "Really posh. Had a bad fire a few years ago and was never quite the same. Apparently the manager of the place sent all of the guests to Marks and Sparks in the middle of the night to get replacement clothes, and picked up the tab. That's class. Don't get that anymore, do you?"

"There's no bars on the windows," he says. "That's a step up for me."

"You're a guest, then?" I ask as he plods down the stairs, two steps ahead of me.

"Yeah and bored to tears with it. Under strict instructions to keep myself to myself."

"Sounds interesting," I say, although it isn't really. "You local? I hear an accent."

"Gilberdyke. On the way to Goole, y'know. Land of the Coneheads. No forks in the family tree. Twenty kids in a class and only three surnames. I've heard all the jokes…"

He pushes open the door to the pool room and I follow him in. It's dark, but invitingly so. Petrol blue tinge to the light as it emanates from behind the closed door of the steam room. I place my feet carefully, gripping the cold wet tiles with my toes. Minnsy seems at home. Even in the darkness I can see the definition in his calf muscles as he walks, the broadness in his shoulders and the strength in his back, tapering to a taut waist. He's stronger than me.

Ahead, the pool is perfectly still; a sheet of smoked glass reflecting the light as it flickers around our shadows. The darkness bends and distorts around us as we pull open the door to the steam room and the wave of intense heats grabs us in its fist and pulls us inside.

I look around, enjoying the sudden wash of heat. Wood panels, gaudy blue light, tray of hot rocks, a ladle and a bucket of water. Condensation on every surface, and the slats in the benches look as inviting as a spitting griddle pan.

My new friend steps on the first bench and pulls himself up to the back, where the heat is most savage. I sit on the bench below, and feel the warmth seep into my skin.

"Bit naughty this, isn't it?" he asks. "Haven't earned it. Normally need to do 500 crunches before I even consider treating myself to one of these."

"Fuck it," I say. "You're not exactly out of condition." We sit in silence, then out of politeness, and because I can't think of anything suggestive, I say: "What line of work you in, then?"

He sucks his teeth. "Used to do telesales. Got out of that racket, though. Can only be told to piss off so many times before it gets to you. Nah, this is more a business trip. An opportunity." He says it enigmatically, like he wants me to think he's something more than he is. "Could be a nice little earner."

I rub my hand over my face and down onto my chest and realise I'm already dripping with sweat.

"Yeah? Go on."

"Can't, mate," he says, shaking his head and pulling his lips down over his teeth. "All very hush-hush."

"Fair play," I say, backing off and raising my hands. "None of my business."

I push myself back against the wall and turn to face him. "You been in here before?" I ask.

"Few times, past couple of days. Not much else to do. Not so bad as prison but not much better. Another day or so to wait it out, then I'm out of here. Take my money and offski."

"All sounds very intriguing," I say, and pander to his

ego again. Journalistic habit. "You seem like a man worth knowing."

"Got a bit of clout," he says, feigning humility. "Lot of people would love to be this close to me right now. Coppers. Crims. Journalists. Family of that poor lass." He stops and looks away again, then shakes away whatever thought just fluttered into his mind. He seems to drop a bit of the attitude, and he slumps back against the wall. "Big day tomorrow," he adds.

"Yeah?"

"Fucking big."

"Yeah?"

"Yeah."

A breath.

Another glance at my body, my scars, and he decides to unburden himself. I think he probably needs a friend as much as I do.

"You read the papers?" he asks.

"When I get the chance."

"You read the locals? *Hull Mail*, all that shit?"

"I'm not local, mate. Hotel, remember?"

"But you heard the radio? Trial going on at the moment. Big trial. Few months ago a lass in a wedding dress got cut up. Butchered, she was. Raped. Done in the arse. Real sweetie, too. Fucking terrible. Psycho shit."

"I remember," I say. "Big deal when she was missing. They've got someone though, yeah? I heard he had coughed to it."

"Trial's going on, now. Wrong man, though."

"Yeah?"

"Yeah. I know the guy that really done it. And tomorrow I'm telling the court. Star witness, me. Gonna get an innocent man off, I am. Hero of the hour. Put that little shit Lewis away instead."

Me. Holding on. Trying to control it.

"Christ," I say, and my voice sounds like there's a foot on my throat. "Wrong man? How did they fuck that up? I thought they found her in his flat, or something? Yeah, I remember it now. They'll have DNA and forensics and stuff. Hard to see how they got that wrong."

He bristles, giving me a pissed-off look. "Well, they did. I know who did it. He confessed when we were pad-mates."

A drip falls from the ceiling. I say nothing. Let the silence build.

"The barrister who's defending the guy in the dock. Big rich prick in a turban. He's paying for the hotel and keeping me happy."

"Sweet deal," I say. I give him a nudge, sweaty skin on sweaty skin. "Who was it then?"

"Lad I knew inside."

"You done time?"

"In and out, y'know. Bad boy, me."

"Looks like it will be the making of you though. You play this court case right you'll be getting well fed."

"That's what I'm thinking."

"Did he really confess, then, this lad you know?"

"Yep. Laughing he was, in our cell. Little ratty fucker. Laughing, about how his mate was going to go down for it, and he was the one who sliced her up."

"Must have been hard not to tear his throat out."

Drip.

"Had to keep my nose clean," he says. "In for drugs, I was. As ever. Couldn't add GBH to the list. Getting him now, though, ain't I?"

"Suppose so. Christ, the lad in the dock will think you're his knight in shining armour."

"I am."

"Good lad, is he? The one you'll be getting off."

"Oh yeah. Been stitched up."

"What about the DNA though. Plant that, did they?"

"Must have. You know coppers."

"Yeah, I do."

Silence, again. He rubs at his big arms, clearly brooding, then snaps a hard look at me. "Don't need you making me feel shit about it. He said it. That's all that matters."

"Whatever you say, mate. None of my business."

He's shaking his head now. Something's bothering him. "You're one of them, aren't you? A bloody journalist…"

"What are you talking about?" I ask, indignant. "I don't know you from Adam."

"Did he send you? Choudhury?"

"Choudhury who, mate?"

"Or are you one of the copper's lads? That slick prick? He said he'd get me. Said I would regret it…"

"You can piss off with your accusations, mate – I only wanted a bit of down-time. You stay in here with your paranoia…"

I start to stand and he closes his huge great hand around my calf and digs his nails in to the muscle. A pain like nothing I've experienced before rips through my left leg and I lash out with my right: instinct taking over.

It's a decent kick, knocking his head back against the

wooden wall, but he keeps hold of my leg and I fall with him as he slips from the bench and down onto the wet tiles. We crumple on the sodden floor – hands slipping off oily skin, fighting for purchase, a meaty forearm hitting my jaw, and I claw myself up his body, reaching for his thick neck.

"Get the fuck off…" he hisses, and catches me in the face with a hard right hand. I hit him back. Slam his head against the tiles.

He pushes again. He's far too strong, and I fall to my left onto the wooden bench, sprawling on the hot wet wood.

He's pushing himself away from me now, and as he opens the door the cold and the dark flood in. He turns back and tries to stamp on me but I throw myself forward, arms around his waist, and he falls on the hard tiles with me on top of him; half in and half out of the sauna door, between light and dark.

I let go. Raise my hands, and back away. Slither backwards, and feel the cool, wet glass of the door upon my back. Minns scrambles to his feet. Turns. Runs for the stairs.

He slips in a puddle of his own sweat. Skids right and falls like a tree. His head hits the tiles so hard that it bounces.

And I'm sitting there, staring into wide, open eyes, watching them fill with blood; watching the dark water fill with red.

Feeling nothing.

Not even pain.

It's suddenly all just funny. These bodies. These people who keep dying around me, like I'm a fucking plague. It's fucking hysterical.

So I start to laugh. Laugh like a lunatic.

I'm still laughing as I slip Minns's body into the ice-cold plunge pool, and head up the stairs.

The gun is calling like a siren.

42

8.54 p.m.

Owen Lee the Lonely, sliding between two metal barriers and onto the tarmac of Ferensway. One lane closed for the workmen to play with tomorrow. Climbing over the metal rail in the centre of the road, waiting for a gap in the traffic, then scurrying to the far side.

I don't look at the hotel or the gym as I go. They're behind me, fewer than fifty feet, but I'll look that way when I've done what I need to do, and I can head back to Kerry, free of distraction.

The adrenaline is leaving my system. I'm shivering, rubbing my arms and stamping my feet as I stomp through the insipid drizzle that turns the city lights into an abstract painting of reds, golds and strips of white.

Shitty end of a shitty city centre. Tattoo parlours and greasy spoons, cheap package holidays and a circle of drunks around the war memorial and its cold rendition of a Tommy rescuing his mate.

The smell of chips and curry sauce from the dirty grills and bright lights of the takeaway.

Me, hands in fists.

Fists in pockets.

And I'm coughing as I push open the door to the Sandringham.

Tony H smiles, but doesn't show his teeth.

He's alone in the bar. Alone. No staff. No customers. Just vague half lights, illuminating the tiny bar that only got rid of the sawdust on the floor when the landlord found a nest. Only food is pickled eggs. Clientele usually share three tawny yellow teeth between them. No posters on the walls. No cushions on the chairs. The till isn't electrical and they don't do receipts.

Tony H, standing by the bar. No drink in front of him. No cigarette.

His face the colour of a notebook.

The notebook on the bar in front of him.

With his eyes he says sorry.

With a shake of his head, he apologises for what he's about to do.

With a nod, he points behind me.

I hear sudden movement. Waterproof coats rubbing together. Heavy steps. A camera clicking. A director whispering 'action'.

And I don't even turn around as Roper puts his hand on my shoulder, bends my arms at the elbow, and a second set of hands cuffs my wrists together.

"Owen Lee, I'm arresting you on suspicion of the murder of..."

Me, just staring.

Tony looks away first.

I don't notice his eyes leave mine, or him scribbling in his notebook, or the flashbulb in my face.

I'm staring at the hole in his head that only I can see.

43

11.18 p.m.

Me.

Sitting on a mattress no thicker than a sandwich, shivering in a paper suit.

Black ink on my fingertips. My photo in a file.

It's all shrunken down, like the TV we had when I was small, with its picture that gradually dwindled down to a tiny dot in the centre of the screen when you pulled the plug from the socket.

I'm inside the dot now. A prisoner in a pixel. Stuck in a full stop.

Trapped in here, in this room with its pale green walls and its white tiles and its black graffiti and its wet floors and dripping ceiling, and the weak light that dribbles through the hole in the metal door.

I sit and hold my bare feet with fingers that don't remember warmth, and I lose myself in the rocking, the rocking, the rocking back and forth.

44

Boots. Voices. Darkness suddenly darker.
Keys. Metal. Chains.

Iron on steel.

A scraping, like nails on unvarnished clay, like teeth on wool.

Light, filling the room in increments with its pissy yellow glow.

The corridor coughing illumination into my cell.

A shape against the light.

Roper.

Stepping forward.

Face obscured by the glare.

The sound of a smile. The rasping creak of a smirk creasing stubbled skin.

Me, dressed in paper and pimpled flesh.

Huddled and folded, holding my feet and rocking, rocking, rocking...

Darkness again.

Another figure in the doorway.

Larger. Something in its hand.

Me, raising a hand to my brow as if in salute.

My own thin elbows in my ribs.

Trying to find the style to smile.

A step…

Roper's face in mine, now.

Breath soft, like a lover's.

Gently swaying in time with my rocking as he bores through my irises and pushes on.

He steps back.

Brings his arm up and under. Up, then down.

Hard.

The snarl on his face as ugly as the smile now glinting in his eyes.

And I'm on the wet floor with my suit in shreds and blood in my mouth.

Sprawled out and looking up as he stands over me, a telephone book in his right hand.

Thoughts crashing into each other like a pile-up on the motorway. Everything coming to a halt, save for spinning wheels and blinking lights and the first whimpered cries.

He squats down over me, one loafer on my right wrist.

"Sticks and stones may break your bones but names can never hurt you."

Takes a look at the book in his palm and the blood on my chin.

"Depends how many names."

McAvoy, rounding the corner, sensible shoes beating a rhythm on the lino: a sound like stampeding horses. Still got his pyjama top on under his sweater and jacket. Got him, he's thinking. This is it. He followed my lead, he says to himself. Went out and got him. Don't expect a thank you but this could be the start of something. Least he can do is let me in on the interview. I deserve it.

He'd come sprinting into the station the moment he heard the report on the radio that he kept by the bed, turned low, like classical music, soft as Roisin's gentle breathing...

And then he hears it. The unmistakable, crunching sound of violence and laughter.

A growl, emanating from the belly of the station. Animal and ugly.

He stops. Slows.

There's rotting meat in his nostrils, bile climbing in his throat.

And stepping out of the cell like the devil himself: smiling wide.

Roper.

45

I'm dragged back onto the bunk.

The young blonde copper's grabbing the skin beneath my armpits as he manhandles me into a sitting position. There's more pain – a sharp, precise sting through the throbbing agony in my neck and crown – and I hear him snigger as I twist in his arms.

"Look at me."

Roper, standing astride me, in a silver two-tone suit, grey shirt and oxblood tie. Leather coat. Black gloves.

"Look at me."

I raise my head, pain shooting from my neck to my toes and back again.

He brings the phone book down again on the back of my head, spine first.

I sprawl onto the floor.

Blondie picks me up. Puts me back on the cot.

Roper hits me again.

Takes off his coat in a graceful shrug of rustling leather and a cloud of Aramis.

Pulls his extendable baton from a pocket. A flick of the wrist and it's two-foot long.

A nod to Blondie. Grabs me and sits on my chest, holding

my left leg with his strong hands as I squirm and struggle to breathe.

Directs my foot over the end of the cot, bare toes twisting and curling as though trying to make their own escape.

Wet cloth in my face, pressure on my chest and jaw, pain everywhere.

Wham.

I hear it before I feel it.

Flash brings the baton down across the knuckles of my toes with a sound like a branch breaking in two.

The pain comes. White hot and sickening.

I kick and roar and clench my fists and bite down hard with bleeding teeth as I struggle to shift Blondie. I need to see the damage. Need to squeeze my broken toes with my hands and roll into a ball and sob.

The pressure subsides as Blondie steps down.

I roll into a ball, my legs drawn up, my toes hot and throbbing in my palm, my teeth biting into the mattress. There's snot and blood on my chin.

Three loud bangs on the cell door. A *tssk* of irritation from Roper.

A big red face at the window: eyes that can't quite believe what they are seeing.

Me, hoping against hope that I still deserve help.

46

"Happy now, Sergeant?" asks Roper, enjoying the look on McAvoy's face. "Your hunch was right. Not that we needed it, of course, but at least your instincts are correct."

They're standing in the corridor outside the cell.

"You don't need to do that," McAvoy says, quietly. "There's enough evidence…"

"I don't need to. I just fucking want to," says Roper, astonished that there are people in this world who won't kick somebody if they are down. "When you've been here a few more years, you'll want to as well. And even if you don't, you'll know when to shut the fuck up about those who do."

"You'll kill him," says McAvoy. His stomach hurts, and his fingers are numb. He can smell rotting food.

"Nah," says Roper, listening to the grunts. "We're very experienced."

"I can't be a party to this," says McAvoy, and he finds there is a pain in his throat.

"But it is quite a party. Go on in. Give him a prod. You can learn a lot from me."

"I want nothing from you."

"Come on, sunbeam," says Roper, enjoying every minute. "God loves a sinner."

47

Keys. Metal. Chains.

Light, filling the room in increments with its pissy yellow glow.

Me, braced for it. Up on my haunches: coiled.

Roper.

He steps in front of me, and gives me a nod, as one professional to another. He takes the lit cigarillo out of his mouth and proffers it. There's a suit carrier draped like a deflated skin over his right arm.

I hesitate, reach up, take the cigarillo and inhale. It feels good. Warming, somehow.

He extends a hand and I take that too, and he hauls me to my feet, and I stand naked, bruised and bleeding, in the middle of the cell. He gestures to the bed and I take a painful step, then sit down on the mattress.

He takes off his coat, puts it around my shoulders, and retreats.

He stands with his back to the door, and the back of his head blocking the spy-hole.

He says nothing for a while. Lights another cigarillo and watches me like a stud watches the dancefloor.

My hands start to twitch.

"Why did you do it?" he asks, his head on one side and an eyebrow raised theatrically.

I smile, weakly, and say: "Fuck. Off."

Roper smiles at the gesture. Nods. Has a moment of inner dialogue that I can't fathom, then nods again, as if making his mind up.

"I'm only asking, because from now on, you're not going to have much to say in this conversation," he says, softly. "I'm going to tell you things, you're going to nod, and when we're done, you and I will be friends again, and I won't have to worry about you being a silly boy."

I try to say something clever, but any fight that's still within me is saving itself.

"Good lad," he says, and pushes off from the door. Four steps, and he sits down next to me, his legs touching mine. Slings an arm around my shoulder and leans in. He whispers in my ear until I'm warm.

"I've never actually got round to thanking you, Owen. I must be honest, when you broke that story about me as a kid and the world found out I wasn't just Doug Roper, it really did change my life. I won't say I wasn't furious with you at the time, but look at how far I've come since then. But I'm nowt compared to you, son. You're a better story than I am. I'm good at knowing who to poke around inside, if you'll forgive the double-meaning. You always did seem a little bit different to the rest of the herd. So I had a look into your life. Your past. The things you did. You'll never guess what I found. I put you away in my back pocket. Got to know you. Liked what I saw. And I kept your secrets secret. I'm good at that, at keeping something back for when you need it. I've got half this force stitched up with secrets. I've got a lot of favours to cash. I'm untouchable, lad. Got very big plans, got a future doing whatever I choose to do, all thanks to you. And I still get to put villains away."

He pauses. Sighs: the weight of the world on his shoulders.

"Thing is Owen, I've still got a job to do. I'm still a copper. I've still got baddies to catch and crimes to solve. I do that well, you know. I may put the boot in, but I do catch people who need to be caught. Famous for it, when all is said and done. That's why this week has been so very hard. The Butterworth case. The Chocolate Boy, as you lot call him. An evil fucking sadist kills an angel in her wedding dress and cuts her head off so he can fuck her better. No real grey areas, there, son. Not much middle ground. Kind of case you lot like. Kind of case that needs a good strong conviction. That's what I need too. One hundred per cent clean-up rate, Owen. One hundred per cent! I'm proud of that. This documentary, Owen, in which you are going to play such a part, will set me in stone, son. Life for Cadbury, justice for the Butterworths, all thanks to me. He was what? Hunting a double murderer at the same time? Fuck. Who wouldn't watch that? I'm going to be up in lights, lad, for doing my job and doing it with style. I'll be a superhero, son. Trouble is, Owen, that if I don't get the conviction I need, I'm snookered. And truth be told, I'm worried. This witness of Choudhury's, this fucking cellmate. That's strong evidence. It's a worry. I couldn't get to him, you see. He was inside, and Choudhury had him sewn up like a duck's arse. By the time he appeared on the scene, I'd already charged Cadbury. I've been trying to iron it out ever since.

"Then bang! Boom-shack-a-lack, we've got a double murder on the first day of the trial, and most importantly, on the first day of the documentary. I'm a busy boy, but I take it. And there it is. My solution. My salvation. I let Tony H into the incident room. Let him see the pictures, and the boy does a double-take when he sees the shot of the lad with the bullet in his head. Almost loath to tell me he is, but he's a greedy little weasel and he knows I remember a favour, so he tells all. It's only Owen Lee's least favourite human being, his sister's drug-addicted boyfriend. Really, I say. She into that scene, is she? Oh yeah, says Tony. She's a smackhead. Lives in a bedsit, spreads her legs for cash, never been the same since, well, since you did what you did. And it all crystallises in my head, Owen. All the little pieces come together. I see a way out, and I see a way to thank you properly for what you did for me.

"So here's where we're at, laddo. Here's the deal. You killed Beatle. And the other one. Prescott. Your car was in the car park at the time. You've got quite the history and quite the motive. You killed them both. Personally, factually, I doubt it. That other one was a real star. Hard as nails. Doubt you could have offed him, but juries are more easily persuaded than I am, and the most important thing is, I can make it stick. Almost as good as the Butterworth case. But that's the word. *Almost*. It isn't going to set the world alight, is it? Half-decent journalist offs his sister's boyfriend and his mate. Page 15 of the Telegraph, if I'm lucky.

"I'm a bright boy, though, Owen. And it comes to me. Two birds, one stone. Two cases, one lucky bugger. That's you, by the way. I've got to get the conviction in the Butterworth case. Got to. No argument. What's the sticking point? What's the obstacle? The cellmate. The witness. He has to go away, Owen. He has to leave the picture. How do I make that happen? I need somebody to make him disappear. Who can do that, I ask? I've got a lot of people I can call upon in said circumstances, but none of them I could trust to truly shut the fuck up in an interview room. Nobody who wouldn't save their own skins by flaying mine. Of course, I could do it myself, but it's a bit tricky getting time to indulge yourself when there's a TV crew following you around twenty-four seven.

"No, what I need is somebody who's fucked already. Somebody who's capable of doing the job and then keeping their mouth shut. Somebody with a past to die for, a present that's a gift. I need you, Owen. We both know I'm going to get you for Beatle's death. That's a given. But I can hang fire for a day or two. We'll do a 'no comment' interview, and I'll bail you. Set you free. Give you a change of clothes, and an address. A room number, in fact. A room at a rather plush hotel where the infamous cellmate is staying, and you're going to kill him. Then I'm going to arrest you, for three counts of murder. The two in the woods, and the cellmate. Minns. Big fucker, but you've got a pedigree. Maybe a couple more, if needs be.

"And we're going to have quite the time, you and I. Some wonderful dialogue in the interview room. You'll be a serial killer, Owen. And I'll be the man to catch you. It's hard to avoid the word 'nemesis' isn't it? We're aiming for primetime, here, Owen. I know you're the sort of guy who'll play nicely with me, despite what we both know you're capable of. I doubt you'll mention this little chat, because your sister, who seemed so very taken with me, will still be on the outside, with me. I don't have to go through the cliché of threatening her life, do I? You get it, I'm sure.

"So there we are. An interview, we go through the motions, and I let you out. You find him, and you kill him. Use this. It's one of a pair and it's taken life before so you'll get on famously. I'll slip the bullets in your pocket as you leave. Don't think of getting cute. He's a big guy. Use your looks, what's left of them. Then you can run, if you like. I'll catch you, and the chase will be good TV. Or you can just hang around until I feel like bringing you in. Then we do the interview properly, we charge you, and after that, your future's whatever you want it to be. I'd end it all, if I was you, but there's no pressure. You do whatever makes you happy. Just don't confess too early, yeah? I want them to see me break you. Are we clear, here? Any questions that won't irritate me?"

I try to hold his gaze. Cough. Spit blood. I ask: "How much did Tony know?" My voice is so weak as to be little more than a smoker's last breath.

He smiles at that. "Tony knows what I tell him. He told me where he was meeting you, and I thought the arrest would make good TV. I promised him the exclusive, and I've kept my word. Anything else?"

"Jess?"

"Your girl? Interesting. We got a report on her early this morning. Friend of hers said she was still missing. Said you were the last person to see her alive. Don't worry, I've taken over the investigation. Leave it all to me. I'm sure she's fit as a fiddle. What d'you reckon? Now get dressed. Remember, 'no comment' answers to every question. Then out the door, and do what you've got to do. Console yourself with the fact you're giving justice to the Butterworths. They're a nice family, like yours were once. And try not to read the papers. They'll just upset you."

And he's up. Opening the suit carrier and tossing me a black suit, black shirt, and my own muddy boots. He pulls my rings and chain from a pocket and drops them on the floor. Then he hands me a gun.

"Suit's my spare," he nods. "I want to be a part of this."

He pulls open the door.

I'm just sitting digesting it all.

Holding a gun in my hand.

Cold and metallic and oh so familiar.

There's a half-smile on my face.

He wants me to kill a dead man.

And he doesn't know.

About the gun.

About the others.

About the six beautiful shots or the bodies I've left behind.

He's opening the door and giving me another chance.

A chance to make a difference.

Put things right.

48

At 6.58 a.m. two uniformed officers come into my cell and bang their palms against the metal door to wake me up. I'm already dressed, but they tell me to get ready, so I lick the last of the ink off my fingertips and rub my hands on my trousers and check my watch and they walk me to the front desk.

The breakfast show is playing Radio Humbershite and I catch the news headlines while I'm signing my bail form. *A twenty-nine-year-old local man was arrested last night on suspicion of carrying out the horrific double murder at the Humber Bridge Country Park. Detective Chief Superintendent Doug Roper is understood to have made the arrest and is currently interviewing the...*

They tell me to come back in the morning and walk me from the belly of the police station through corridors and up green-painted stairs with their posters and noticeboards and damp patches, and we stand aside as a figure in a good suit jogs briskly up the stairs, then it's on, up, on to the large double-fronted glass doors and the white-painted lobby and its smiling desk sergeant and its rain-mottled windows and the darkness beyond, and I nod a thank you as they punch a code into a keypad and disappear back into the station and I fold the bail papers and put them in my inside pocket where they tuck themselves behind a tin of cigarillos.

The doors open as I walk towards them, and then the cold and the dark and the rain take me into their embrace and I walk down the steps and into Queen's Gardens, across the well-tended lawns and barren flowerbeds and frozen earth that serve as the city centre's lungs in summer and which attract the tramps and the teenagers and the drunks and the office workers whenever the sun shows its smile and we sprawl on the grass and read books and drink cider and ogle cleavages and throw a rugby ball and which make us northerners feel like we live in London.

Up the steps at the far side, past the duck pond with its year-round algae and its matted reeds, and look up at the towering apartment building, which seems to be growing all the time, as if craning its neck for a view of something more palatable.

It's not until I've passed the fountains and the benches and I'm scampering across the main road past the slumbering, half-lit hulk of the shopping precinct that I reach into my trouser pocket and feel the cold, metal object that Roper slipped to me as we passed on the stairs.

One more. One more chance. One more opportunity.

Enough!

Walking briskly on the wet pavements and skirting dirty puddles, watching Hull coughing itself into life with the early morning farts and belches and retches of engines revved, voices raised, buses vibrating, beer kegs dropping down cellar stairs, street lights humming, mumbles into mobile phones...

The rain is so fine as to be barely visible, but it's the kind that chills to the bone and makes your bruises sing with pain, and I'm huddled inside my suit jacket and almost running as I pass the big screen and its fifteen-foot blonde newsreader telling me they've caught someone on suspicion of an horrific double murder...

Consumed with minutiae and tedium. Wondering which photos of me they'll pull out. Which papers will have the balls to name me. Which of my friends will even try to call and get a quote, and which will simply tell their news editors they tried but my phone was switched off. Wondering how many people will be surprised. Whether they will be telling each other that they always knew there was something dark about me, that they always believed me to be capable of anything.

Cold and wet and with my heartbeat sounding in my head, I creak up the front stairs to the Royal Hotel and into the warm and walk briskly across the red carpet of the lobby to the lift. I push the button, and the brass doors open. I step inside, nod to the waiter in his black-and-white tweeds as he heels his breakfast trolley out into the lobby, then hit three, and lean back against the wall as I'm carried upwards, staring at my reflection in the glass doors; a reflection cut in two when they open, and I step onto the landing with the image of my bruised features and grazed, burned hands dividing and separating like a tattoo on the insides of my eyes.

Down the corridor.

I knock on the door until my hands hurt and hiss Kerry's name through the hinge and the crack at the base, but there's no answer and no sound. I tell myself she must be asleep still, but it's common sense tinged with panic and I'm running through all sorts of hysterical scenarios in my head when the maid comes along with the trolley and loans me her pass-card, and I swipe the lock and it doesn't work, then swipe it again, and the light by the handle turns green and I push the door open and hold it with my foot, and pass the card back to the maid with a grateful smile and a wink that will keep her going 'til lunchtime, then turn into the room, and see my sister laid out on the bed in the thick white dressing gown, with her eyes wide and staring at me and a goatee of blood and froth around her chin and mouth. The veins in her face are purple and pronounced against the clammy white pallor of her skin. Legs, like lengths of rope, stick out from the robe. One skinny arm hangs over the edge of the bed, clawed hand almost reaching the carpet. The other is at her side, open handed, displaying the polythene bag she has found in my coat pocket. A 'comments' card she has ripped in half and rolled into a tube to snort the poison while she waited for her brother to return and make it all right, has unrolled itself and lies, curved like a bridge, on the pillow next to her face.

Around her, across the bed, the floor, the pillow, the cabinet, are £20 notes. Each rectangle of paper touches the corner of the next, forming a pattern that looks like a child's depiction of a giant snowflake. They have clearly fallen at random, fluttering down from the sky like dead leaves, after my sister, the only girl I ever really loved, found an unopened packet of cash and a bag of powder in her big brother's pockets, thought her life was about to change, and threw it in the air as she bounced on the bed, excited as a little girl on Christmas Eve, then celebrated with a goodbye toot of poisoned crack; falling into death on a mattress of money.

And I cry until there's nothing left.

49

An hour goes by, and I get up and take a piss, and squeeze an entire miniature tube of toothpaste into my mouth and swill it out repeatedly, brushing my teeth with my thumb, feeling my tongue go numb and tasting coppery blood through the minty foam; looking at my reflection in the bathroom mirror every time I raise my head from spitting, and never once seeing myself whole. Always disjointed. Fragmented. Sometimes just eyes and a mouth, sometimes a bruise and a sneer. Now just a faceless head. Now an open mouth with a grinning gecko on its tongue.

Back to the bedroom, and Kerry.

I open the bedside table, and there on Gideon's favourite story, is the gun.

I pick it up and hold it on my palm, as though weighing a fish.

I place my other hand on top of it, as if making a benediction.

Feel its weight, enjoy its power.

Hear its song.

I hold it in my right hand and with my left, pull its twin from my waist.

There is no explosion, no riot of colour, no chorus of

circling demons holding ribbons of flesh and banners of bone. But the sensation of metal in my spine and steel in my fingers grows harsh and hard as I close my palms around the two handles, flick the bullets from the clip, take the clip from my pocket and divide the rounds between the two handguns.

It feels wonderfully precise, all oil and grease and smoothness, and I feel good doing it, the way you feel when you sharpen a pencil with a knife or saw a bit of wood in half without straying from the pencil line.

I lie down, and remember…

June 1991. The day of the shoot.

When I first pulled the trigger.

Kerry asking Mam why the sky was azure blue overhead, but clear by the time it reached the grass.

Mam and Kerry sitting on a blanket at the top of the east field. Kerry in a Liverpool shirt with a gymkhana rosette stuck on the emblem and big pink knickers, slurping home-made lemonade from a beaker. Mam, brown hair tied back, in a floaty gingham dress and bare feet, shielding her eyes from the sun as they stared down at the shooting party below.

Me, watching it all a few feet away, staring at the collection of rich bastards drinking Pimm's and carrying shotguns and adjusting the angle of their peaked caps, muttering about what an oaf Blake was until he waddled in their direction and they greeted him with smiles and sweaty handshakes. They seemed absorbent. They seemed to have sucked up the water in their last cool bath and retained it in vast rolls of soggy flesh, like camels.

And among them, bowing, scraping, almost curtsying, scampered my father. Handing out drinks. Fetching and carrying. Waving instructions to the beaters in the woods. Never looking up. Knuckles white and cheeks pink. Scurrying wherever Blake pointed his flabby finger.

Me, watching.

Tuning out Kerry's laughter and Mam's giggles and jokes. Ignoring their pleas for me to come and sit with them.

Watching, as the fat men took their places and raised their guns and the air was suddenly alive with flapping and feathers and calls, and bang after bang after bang.

I could smell blood and gunpowder even before it drifted across to me in a ghost of smoke that danced for a moment with the lady in the ballgown before it floated on and over the slopes.

I stayed until they had taken their six shots each, and stood as the last of the pheasant thumped onto the hard earth.

Then Dad put down his gun. Slotted it into the spike on the ground, and strode onto the field to collect the dead birds.

And then I stood, and felt so many eyes upon me and tentacles like cobwebs on my skin, and I felt the dry, rasping kiss of the lady in the ballgown upon my cheek, and I walked down the slope and into the throng of fat men, and I smelled the sulphur and saltpetre and the feathers and the blood and I ignored the hellos of the fat fools and brushed past hands that tried to ruffle my hair and dogs that whined as I passed, and I picked up Dad's gun, and felt its weight, familiar and pleasant and powerful and so full of promise.

Reaching into the pocket of my dark trousers.

Pulling out a cartridge.

Cracking the gun and breathing its sharp, metallic tang.

Slotting in the cartridge.

Snapping it shut.

Walking, calmly, to where Blake stood, surveying his empire, sweating on his lands.

Standing three feet in front of him, eyes locked.

Watching the puzzled look spread across his jowls, as though he were stifling a burp.

Hearing the cackles.

The excited hissing and yelping of the demons who dance on his shoulders.

Seeing the lady in the ballgown and the look of ecstasy, of unsullied lust on a face that was no longer beautiful.

Hearing my dad shouting my name.

My own voice.

Saying "I'm better than you."

Her, moaning in ecstasy.

Raising the gun.

Pulling the trigger.

Bang.

Hearing the screaming start.

The thud as he collapses back.

The wet blood sizzling as it hits the sweat of my brow.

And feeling the ground lurch.

As I begin to fall.

50

Out the door and into the swirling rain.

Through the barriers, the dust and the diggers, the yellow road signs and blinking lights. Newspaper under my arm, keys jangling in my hand, two hanguns tucked in my waistband.

Three bounds, up the stairs, a turn of the key, along the corridor, another turn, and I'm back in the flat.

He's still lying there, is Petruso. His blood has run as far as the kitchen, and shards of glass and fragments of skull float like islands in the deep claret sea.

The other man lies where he fell, by the bedroom door.

I lean down, and pick up the picture of Jess and me. Hold it close to my face, as if I can breathe her in. I put it in my inside pocket. Flop down on the sofa and open my phone.

Close my eyes and hold back tears as I scroll through the numbers and select the name I should have called days ago.

She answers on the second ring, her voice tremulous and small.

"Owen," says Jess. "Owen, what's happening?"

Her voice is a blanket. I tie myself up in it, and feel as if swaddled.

"I'm so sorry, Jess," I say, and am stunned by the honesty of the statement. "I miss you so much."

She pauses, then the words come out in a rush. "I've had so many messages. Saying things about you. Saying you're in trouble. Lenny won't leave me alone, she thinks you've done me in, and she's twisted my brain around so I don't know what I'm thinking and she says you've been manipulating me and treating me wrong and maybe you have and maybe you haven't but I can't stand this being apart when I can feel how much you need me there with you, and it wasn't meant to be like this, Owen, it wasn't…"

"Where are you? People have been worrying." Then, truthful: "*I've* been worrying."

"I needed to get away. To think. To decide what I really want."

"You told nobody? Just ran?"

"My mind was everywhere. I couldn't tell Lenny. You know how she feels about you…"

"She really thinks I hurt you…"

"Owen, that's crazy." There is real shock, there. Incredulity. "That's crazy. You won't even hug me too hard for fear of breaking me!"

"Mud sticks."

Silence. Tears, and snot. The air heavy with the enormity of it all. Then I say: "You answered my call. I wasn't sure…"

"It's what I've been waiting for."

"I need to see you. There are things I need to tell you. Things I want you to hear from me and nobody else."

"I knew you would call. Eventually."

"I suppose I knew you would answer."

"I told you I would. I told you all you had to do was find

it in yourself to let me in. To think about what you wanted and decide if it was me…"

"It shouldn't be me making this decision, Jess. It shouldn't be me agreeing to love you. You shouldn't even breathe the same air as me. I'm poison. You're an angel…"

"No, Owen! No." There is anger, and hurt. "I'm not. I'm a woman. A grown up. Not a child. Not a pet. Not an angel. I'm not here to be protected and pretty. I love you and ache for you and want you, but I can't grow old with a projection. A character. The bits of yourself you let me see. I want it all. Better and worse. Sickness and health. Darkness and light."

"You made that one up."

"I was going to put it in our vows."

Silence, again. I want to climb inside the phone. Be kissed. Held.

"I told Len you'd gone to Nottingham. Was I right?"

"No. I've been at Bridlington. Crappy bed and breakfast. Just been sitting in my room, staring at my phone, trying to work it all out."

I feel bubbles in my blood. Almost intoxicated by the nearness of our embrace. Giddy and girly with the sensations of being loved, properly. Suddenly feeling able to offer the same in return.

"I'll come to you."

51

Ten minutes later.

Up and out, with a bounce in my stride.

Dropping today's *Hull Daily Mail*, with its picture of a good-looking, smirking journalist and Tony H's by-line, onto the mangled mess of Petruso's head.

MAN WHO KILLED AS A CHILD HELD OVER DOUBLE MURDER

Exclusive

By Tony Halthwaite

A MAN who killed a Yorkshire landowner with a shotgun when he was just nine years old is being held on suspicion of the horrific double murder at the Humber Bridge Country Park, the *Mail* can reveal.

The bodies of Darren Norton and Alfred Prescott were discovered on Monday morning at the popular beauty spot in the heart of East Yorkshire. Mr Prescott, from West Yorkshire, had been beaten to death and Darren, a city man, had been shot.

Owen Lee, 29, was arrested at the Sandringham Hotel in the city centre last night by well-known policeman and the detective in charge of the case, Det Supt Doug Roper, following assistance from this newspaper.

For more details, turn to page 2…

I do. I turn it slowly, wondering which words I would have cut from the intro if I'd been sat on newsdesk when Tony filed the piece. Good tabloid read, I admit.

Lee, who lives in a city centre flat and who recently broke off his engagement to a long-term partner, is a reporter with the Press Association and had been covering the case for the news agency prior to his arrest.

He shocked other reporters at a press conference at Priory Road police station yesterday with an outburst aimed at Det Supt Roper, 39. He fled the scene when the girlfriend of one of the victims was brought in to read a statement. It is understood by this newspaper that the witness is Lee's sister, Kerry Lee, and that the two had an especially close relationship.

The *Hull Daily Mail* can exclusively reveal that Lee spent many of his teenage years in a succession of mental hospitals, seeing his family only at weekends and attending a special school, before eventually joining his family in Scarborough, where he changed his name and gained a place at university due to good 'A' level results – secured while just 13 years old – and a high IQ.

Lee was committed to an institution by mental health chiefs following the death of respected landowner and fishing fleet owner, Tom Blake, 58, on the Drayton Manor estate, near South Cave, in 1991.

Blake was killed with a shotgun blast to the face during a pheasant shoot on his land. This newspaper understands that Lee, whose father was gamekeeper on the estate and whose family lived in one of the farm cottages, was said at the time to have harboured a grudge against Mr Blake for his attitude towards his father, and for disciplining him in front of party guests.

He is said to have walked calmly up to Mr Blake carrying his father's gun, spoken briefly to him, and then shot him.

Because of his young age, Lee was never charged, but the incident made headlines around the world. Lee remained in the care of the mental health authorities for many years, and was only allowed occasional visits to his family's new home.

After continued scrutiny from journalists, the family changed their name to Lee, from the original, Swainson.

His father, at his home on a run-down estate in Scarborough, last night declined to comment, but appeared visibly shaken. The suspect's mother died in 2010, and his sister, Lee, 27, is helping police with their enquiries. It is understood Owen disapproved of his sister's relationship with Mr Norton, a known drug user. The suspect also drives a car similar to that spotted on CCTV at the Humber Bridge car park on the night of the deaths.

Lee was last night described as being a "very dark and brooding person", who did not get on with fellow journalists, and whose career appeared to have flatlined following a promising start. He was also said to be a very heavy drinker, and is understood to still be on medication to control his mood swings, manic depression and violent temper...

52

Detective Superintendent Doug Roper puts a warm arm around Sergeant McAvoy's shoulder and raises his coffee mug to his lips. Together, they pretend to have a conversation about the case, while the camera rolls. There is much earnest nodding of heads.

"You ever mention this, and I'll fuck your youngest," says Roper, who's feeling better than ever.

The response is mumbled, made insensible by the sickness in McAvoy's throat. The fog in his eyes. "You're worse than he is. Worse than any of them."

"Nah, sunbeam," he says, pointing at McAvoy's computer screen as though discovering a new piece of evidence. "I'm a fucking star."

"It isn't your world."

Roper smiles expansively and gestures at himself. "It's more mine than anybody else's."

He hears Flora shout 'cut' and gives McAvoy a smile. "You could still be part of my team," he says "I would like to keep you close. You've got a future."

"You haven't," says McAvoy, getting up. His skin is goose-pimpled, his face white. He looks like the sole survivor of an atrocity. "You're going to hell."

"The place could do with a new broom," laughs Roper, and pulls on his coat.

A swish of leather, a cloud of Aramis, then back to court.

53

He's standing in the entrance of the church across the street, zipped up against the slanting drizzle inside a well-worn waterproof jacket. His pale, freckly face as grey as the dreary bricks that frame him.

Hair, darkened by rain, plastered across his forehead, like something plastic has been melted across his skull. His hands are in his pockets and there's something under his arm. He looks like a farmer, all weather-beaten skin and strong arms beneath cheap fabrics.

The copper.

The barrel-chested Scot who shook my hand and froze at the contact.

McAvoy.

Me, scowling as the big man approaches, fingers becoming fists: not sure if I want him to hit me in the jaw or pick me up in a bear-hug and tell me everything is going to be OK.

He towers over me, looking lost. There are pink spots on his cheeks: spheres of colour against the slate of his face. He looks feverish.

"Mr Lee."

He stops, falters, battling with himself. I wait, squinting into the cold, damp air, wondering how long it is since any of us saw the sun.

"I think we need to talk," he says, at last.

"I got the message last night," I say, not breaking eye contact.

McAvoy looks momentarily pained, as if he's just heard a story about a cancer survivor being killed in a hit-and-run.

I don't know why he's here. What he wants. I know he can't be allowed inside the apartment – not now, not with the bodies bleeding out onto the carpet.

I test the waters. "Tell Roper I'm on it," I say, weakly. "Being taken care of. He needn't waste the manpower."

"This isn't Roper," he begins, then stops himself. "Well, it is. But not like that. This is about him. He's why I'm here, but he doesn't know I am."

I hold his gaze, make him squirm. Examine him properly. Big and broad-shouldered, open-faced. Clever eyes and huge hands, the knuckles sunk beneath ridged, rough skin. There's something else. Some spark in his gaze, some flicker in his expression, that I take as being fuelled by a rapidly moving mind. Could be a thinker, this one. Could go far.

"You had a tiff with your fearless leader?" I ask.

McAvoy closes his mouth and purses his lips until it seems they are shaded in pencil.

"I need to know what's happening. What he wants you to do. What he's done to you." He pauses. Seems to make a decision. "I think he knows Shane Cadbury didn't kill that girl."

Despite the blood in my nostrils and the heavy scent of the wet air, I can suddenly smell burning. For a moment, it seems that the metal of the guns is searing into my flesh...

54

I sit in the front pew of the church, colder in here than I was on the street. Eight gaudily-attired stone bishops gaze down from plinths behind the altar, faces serene, halos golden. One is captured mid-blessing, his hand raised, three fingers extended. He looks like he's lost his glove-puppet. Fat angels and unfeasibly clean shepherds stretch towards the white clouds and perfect sunrise that crowns the masterful painting on the far wall. It seems to shimmer in the pin-pricks of heat that rise from the candles, and Jesus, sat atop the mural like a fairy on a cake, looks at once beatific and sinister in the rippling air.

It's a magnificent church: a splendid, gorgeous, ornate celebration of a religion I don't understand. If this place were on the continent, it would be full of tourists. It's not. It's empty, save the rumpled copper genuflecting before the cross, and the good-looking, battered journalist in the front row.

He finishes his ritual and takes a seat behind me, so I have to swivel to talk to him. He looks wild-eyed and earnest. I can't help myself. I take pity on the poor sod and open the conversation.

"Catholic, I presume?"

He pulls a face, apologetic. "Yes and no. Free Church of Scotland, as a child, but Mother's new husband was a Catholic, and I had to convert to get into the school he wanted me to go to. Some of it's stuck. All must seem rather disingenuous, I suppose."

I twist in my seat and give him a hard stare. "You're not like the other coppers on Roper's team, I can tell. You're not like many other coppers, period."

"I've heard that before."

We sit in silence for a moment. I run through what I know about him and feel a sickness in my gut as I remember where our paths crossed before.

"You found her," I say, softly. "Ella."

McAvoy nods, looks down.

"Thought I remembered you. You know I covered it, don't you? I was on the scene an hour after they found her. I'd done plenty on the search, like. Got a tip something had come up. You were uniform, then."

"I was busy taking the sergeants' exams around the same time. Hadn't been long in Hull. Got a CID posting a few months back. First available sergeant job."

"Straight onto the golden boy's team? Lucky for you."

He looks up at the church roof, as if expecting to see something. Gulps, as though swallowing a half-pint. "I'm not one of them," he says. "Not properly. It doesn't bother me, you understand. I'm not out to make friends, though I don't like not being liked. Who does? But it's not the blokey talk or the drinking or the talking about girls. That's the same in any workplace. I can do all that. I'm a farmer's boy, for pity's sake. I can swear with the best of them. It's something else. Something they seem to have accepted and

I can't bring myself to. They reckon that 'good enough' will do. They whinge about lack of resources and manpower and money, and they laugh when the official figures come out and they show that there's about a five per cent chance of actually getting caught if you do something wrong. 'That's life', they say. 'Ain't got the lads'."

"You out to catch every shoplifter in Hull, are you?" I ask, and can't keep the sneer out of my voice.

"It's not that," he says, shaking his head. "It's not about crime figures. Or being seen to do everything you can. That's all just a show. It's about right and wrong. About doing something wrong, and paying for it."

"Justice?" I ask, trying not to laugh.

His face folds in on itself and it's hard not to reach back and hug the big lump until he feels better. He's so miserable and confused it's like looking in a mirror.

"I just know how she smelled when we found her. How she looked. Just a body, a headless mannequin, her white dress stained red. Skin like orange peel. Her private parts exposed…"

I don't speak. I don't want to visualise what he's telling me, but I can't help it.

"He just stood there beside me," he's saying, his world turned inwards, watching his memories. "Said she was a gift. That he'd found her. I couldn't even breathe. Couldn't think. And then Roper's there, and he's taking over and taking charge and it's like he's floating above us, untouched by it all. We went home with her stink on our clothes and he walked out of there smelling like a film star. It's me who wakes up retching. Me who scares my son with my nightmares. 'Work through it', they said. 'Been through something terrible'. Catch the bad guys, put them away. Make the streets safe. Do your job. And that's what I've been doing. Trying to catch the villains and lock away the dangerous people and find some kind of ending for the people who loved her…"

"But you are, mate," I say, comfortingly, wanting to tell him it will be OK. "They've got the Chocolate Boy and he's going to go down."

He looks up and through me, eyes seamed red. "It wasn't him. I stood there next to him and he told me what he had done to her and it didn't bother him for a second. There was regret in his eyes, but it wasn't for what he had done. It was for what he hadn't. He hadn't been the one to kill her. Wasn't the one to stick the knife in, and the thought upset him. I convinced myself otherwise. I was too busy trying not to let my mind unravel. But the more I think about it, the more I think he's still out there. The person who killed her."

We sit in silence, growing cold, breath forming into ghosts on the chill air.

"You're sure?" I ask, eventually.

"No," he says, soft, with a faint, hopeless smile. "I could be wrong. But I don't think so. I think Roper took the easy option. And I think he wants you to help keep it that way."

I can't help but probe for more. "So who do you think did it?" I ask.

"Until last night, I thought it was you."

Eventually, I say: "And now?"

"I don't think so."

"Why?"

"I watched you take your beating. Through the window in the cell door. You took it like you wanted it. There was nothing in your eyes. No anger or disgust. No venom. You found your release in your own pain, not the pain of others. The man on the floor in the cell couldn't do those things to her. To Ella. I saw hatred in your eyes, but it wasn't for anybody else. The man who did this has a rage turned outwards…"

"The headlines might disagree," I say, and my voice catches. I feel tired, suddenly. Tired and cold and empty.

"I know what you did," he says, softly. "But you were a child. A child who had access to guns. You had opportunity and motive, and in the eyes of the law, you were too young to know what you were doing. And by God, you've suffered enough."

"Justice, right?"

"You're the only person I can think of who might begin to understand something about what it really means."

More silence, save the rain on the stained glass, the drip of water onto stone flags from the hem of McAvoy's soaked clothes.

"He wants me to kill him," I say, and the words are out of my mouth before I can stop them. "The witness. Roper gave me a gun and let me go, and told me to make sure Cadbury went down. Then it's night-night for me. Prison, maybe. More likely, he knows I'd do myself in and tidy up the loose ends. And, do you know, I'd do it. Go out on a high. Do something that mattered, then end it all." I stop, angry and accusing. "Even that's gone now. I can't even help Ella. Can't even send the right man down…"

"You can still help make it right," says McAvoy, staring into me, hard. "I don't know how to play this game of his. Of Roper's. But I know you're a pawn. I think I am too. He's moving us where he wants us. Toying with us like we're puppets and this city is his stage. You need to get out of the city. Anything happens to the witness, he'll be straight after you." He stops, as his thoughts tumble into one another. "The bodies in the woods."

I'm so far gone now there's no turning back. I need to tell somebody. Need to rid myself of all these carcinogenic truths.

"I did one of them," I say, flatly. "Prescott. I walked into the middle of it. He'd just killed the younger lad, and then he tried to kill me. I stopped him."

He doesn't react. "What else?"

I feel myself growing lighter as the weight of the dead lifts from my chest. "There are more. I got caught up in something. I'm still in it. People have died because of it."

"Your girlfriend? The one the papers say is missing?"

"I don't know if she's still my girlfriend, but she's alive. I'm a bastard to live with, mate. Treat her like a trained pet, so she says. It all got too much, and she left me, but she couldn't get me to leave her thoughts, so she went away. Told me to get in touch when I was ready to be loved. I wasn't. I went to chuck myself off a bridge and ended up mucky to the eyes in other people's blood."

I realise I'm panting, eyes cold, fingers shaking, lighter than air.

McAvoy, nodding, sniffing back snot, making fists as he deals with thoughts unfamiliar and anger undirected. He takes a folder from inside his jacket, and starts pulling out pieces of paper. Crime reports. Probation documents. Psychological evaluations. Even a few newspaper clippings. Black-and-white photocopies of colour photographs. He starts holding them up for me, like props, then laying them out on the pew beside him. He starts talking quickly.

"I don't take any notice of hunches. Feelings, even. Maybe if you get an inkling that somebody deserves a closer look than others, you follow it through, but I don't do things like that. I build. Put the pieces together and see what emerges. I've been a detective a few months, and the lads are probably right when they say I know nothing. But I reckon that if there are this many grey areas, then the picture probably isn't perfect."

"Go on."

"I took a call, meant for Roper. London technological expert. Asking how he managed to shush up the stuff that didn't fit. The report on her phone? I suppose it got me thinking. Remember, I'd been there. Seen him. Looked into his eyes when she was still lying on the bed. And it just started from there. This gnawing sensation in my head. A feeling we hadn't got the right person. That Roper had taken the easy option..."

"Pretty cut and dry, though, isn't it?" I say, trying to be a voice of reason. "I mean, they found her in his flat. They've got his semen inside her head. You don't get much more unequivocal than that. Was hardly worth pleading not guilty."

"Look, there's so much stuff here," he says, mania creeping into his voice as he jabs his finger into the papers. "There are other cases, some solved, some not, going back years. Stabbings of young girls. Did you know Ella had reported a stalker outside her house only a few weeks before this happened?"

"Tony and me heard something but it was bollocks," I protest.

"No, it wasn't!" He's hissing through gritted teeth. "I went back through the computer database. Contacted every complainant who logged a call in the windows of time I'd been given. Checked them against the hard copies we keep on file in the basement. There was a discrepancy. On the official log, one log number related to a complaint about a group of yobs making a racket outside a house in north Ferriby. But the sergeant's logbook, the one that keeps a record of where the different cars are sent, it had the same number for a despatch to a house on Bransholme. A complaint about a prowler. Somebody staring in through the windows at the house. The address matched the Butterworths'. Somebody took it out of the official log. Didn't want people knowing about it…"

"Yeah, but that doesn't mean…"

"There's more. The other girls. Look, this is basic stuff. Basic investigative procedure. I put together a profile of what we knew about the murder, up to the point Cadbury claims he found the body. Young, pretty girl. Dark alley. Vicious, frenzied stab wounds. Right handed. Nothing taken. No witnesses. Previous reports of prowler or stalker. The computer started churning out lots of cases, mostly London, some further north, going back to the early 1990s. Some had been put to bed. Solved, so to speak. Druggies put away for losing their temper. Robberies gone wrong. Unhappy or jealous boyfriends. But there were plenty still open. Some where the victim died, some where they didn't. All young, attractive women. Half a dozen had made previous reports of suspicious characters following them or showing up at their home. Some had received letters, full of fantasy stuff. Grim, sexual stuff. Some had reported having personal items taken. Some had made complaints before the attacks. Others, this all came out afterwards. There was a pattern that nobody else seemed to be following up."

"And Ella? She'd had things taken, had she? She'd had messages?" I can feel the ice I'm standing on starting to splinter.

"Messages, yes. There's a report in there on her mobile phone. The boffins dug back into the memory and found the ghost of some old messages. Nothing too sinister, just messages that didn't have a name attached. It was just a number. A pay-as-you-go. Things like 'you look good in yellow' and 'that colour brings out your eyes'. The way I read it, this was somebody telling her they were watching…"

I'm scowling, unsure what I want to be true: feeling my brain protest at being forced to consider new truths so late in the game. "That's a leap," I mumble, but I realise that his words are striking home. There's something in his passion that's infectious. He doesn't seem capable of lies.

"Maybe, but it's something that needs to be investigated. I've been going through the interview boxes and these questions weren't asked. There was no attempt to ask the family if anything was missing. No contact made with the phone provider."

"But if the phone isn't contract…"

"But it's still active! I dialled it. There was no answer, but it's still in service. There are ways, if you have the resources, to triangulate the signal, to make a GPS reference for which phone mast is being used to transmit the signal. There are things that can be done if the investigation is done properly."

"What else?"

"Whoever did this, had to be covered in blood. That

means, they can't have been on the streets for very long after the incident. So they either lived nearby, or were parked nearby. I've gone back through the CCTV footage of all the streets within a two-minute walk of the crime scene. I got a list of all the registered users and whittled that down to the people who aren't local to the area. Left me with two dozen." He looks at me. "You were one of them. You were there."

I smile, tiredly. "So I'm back in the frame?"

"No, I told you. I believe you."

"Who else?"

"Half a dozen with known form. Two fleet cars from the *Hull Daily Mail*…"

"Yeah, we were having a drink. A few of us…"

"I know."

"Who else?"

"Her fiancé. Jamie." He stops, almost pained to be saying it.

"He's already said, he was having a beer at The Ship…"

"Then why park there? Two streets from your girlfriend's house? Why not park outside? Or at the pub?"

"So your money's on him?"

"No! But these are things that should be followed up. Roper's just trimmed away all the stuff he doesn't want to hear. That means we have a man in the dock who's far from innocent but who may not be guilty! This is a hate crime. It has the hallmarks of an obsessive. Somebody who saw a pretty girl, fell for her, stalked her, drove themselves crazy over her, then killed her. Then Cadbury found her. His gift. Took her and did what he wanted. But the person who did it is free. The person who may have done all these girls. There's a serial obsessive. A serial stalker. A killer! And Roper doesn't want to know."

He falls silent, breathing heavy.

"So why me?" I ask, at last. "Are you wanting to expose this? Tony's your man. I don't know for certain, but I rather doubt my newsdesk are taking my calls."

McAvoy opens his mouth to speak. Closes his eyes, as if trying to find the right words written on the inside of his head. He looks ill and frantic. Lost.

"You can do something," he says, eventually. "Roper's got you as one of his pawns. I don't want you to be. I don't know the rules of his game, but I know that if you move somewhere he isn't expecting, it could change everything." Then, softly. "I know he has to go."

"And I'm the man to make that happen? You and me? Are you insane? Look at where I am! At what my future holds…"

McAvoy folds in on himself. Then, staring at his feet: "All I have are vague ideas. Bits and pieces. He's Roper. The celebrity copper. He's got everything sewn up."

"And you want me to unpick the stitches? How?"

He pauses. Looks up at the mural of saints and seraphim. "You could give evidence. Explain what he's done to you. That he gave you a gun and told you to kill a witness."

My face tells its own story.

"And you think that case would get to trial, do you? Me, accusing Roper of dirty tricks. I'm not in any rush to prolong my life, mate, but I'm not going to let Roper be the one to end it."

McAvoy visibly crumbling, like a statue eroded by the elements. He looks broken. Disappointed. Hollowed out.

I hear McAvoy, softly, saying: "So what will you do?"

"I don't care," I say, quietly. "I never have, much, but now it's all boiled down to this, some bits are making sense. I know I need to hold Jess again. After that, whatever happens, happens. A few days back, I was ready to kill myself. End it all. Chuck myself off a bridge rather than let a beautiful girl see I'm as vulnerable and scared and useless as she is. Today, look at me. I got a gift. A second chance, and here I am. Wanted. Hunted. The middle of something I can't change."

"But you can!" He grabs a hold of my words like a branch. "It all comes down to Roper. We get him, we can start looking for some real truth. Real justice."

"We? I'll be in a cell. Or dead. Dead at the hands of a man I can't stand."

McAvoy's suddenly picking up the documents, thrusting them towards me. "Read them," he's saying. "There's a killer who needs to be caught. Look, I can contact another force, start an official investigation. You just have to go on record. You can put it right," he begins, starting to stand. "Do something good. It might make a difference…"

"To you."

I hear myself panting, feel myself stand, papers clutched to my chest. Files and reports, phone numbers and statements. "This is the way I am. The way I have to be. Always will be."

McAvoy stands, raindrops scattering outwards from his wet clothes. "I can make you," he says, and drops his eyes, as if he's unaccustomed to dishing out threats and doesn't want to see how I respond to his rookie attempt.

I stare back, twice as hard. "You can fucking try."

"I can arrest you," he says.

"And take me where?"

"I can do this without your help. I just thought I saw something in you that would want to be involved. To put things right. Remove Roper. Do things properly. Find the truth for Ella's family."

"Then you've backed the wrong horse," I say, and I feel like an absolute devil for saying it. I'm breaking McAvoy's heart here.

He breathes out, slowly, and the breath seems to contain the ghost of every hope he has held inside him since he saw Ella Butterworth's corpse.

Looks at his feet.

Up at the heavenly mural.

"Owen Lee, I am arresting you for the murder of Alfred Prescott…"

He's barely said more than the name when I'm pulling the gun from my waistband.

It's the twin.

The one Roper handed me.

McAvoy freezes as he sees it, words drying in his throat.

My finger on the trigger, the sound of an onrushing train in my head. Getting closer. Closer.

McAvoy seems about to move, to stagger backwards, to beg for his life, but he holds it in check. He just stands still. Looks at the gun, and me, then the skies. He says a name: Roisin…

I know that I can't.

Instead, I hurl the gun high into the air. McAvoy's head swivels to follow its path and I lunge forward, shove him in the chest and watch as he topples backwards onto the pew.

Then I'm running. Sprinting, a blur of angels on either side.

Hearing the gun clatter onto the stone flags.

Pushing open the wooden double-doors.

And disappearing into the rain.

55

It's mid-morning by the time I see the sea. It's a strip of sluggish movement, the colour of fresh-fried chips, reaching up with mucky fingers to tickle the sagging belly of the fat, low clouds.

Bridlington manages a kind of shabby eloquence when the sun shines. When families from West Yorkshire tell themselves that they don't need to go abroad to have fun and book themselves into a B&B for a long weekend; their days wrapped up warm on the demerara-coloured sand or feeding cash into slot machines; their nights on the promenade, eating chips, sipping tea, daring each other to test their strength on the arcade attractions or to take a ride on one of the feeble big dippers run by the gypsies down at the harbour. Eating candy floss and sugar dummies, because that's what you're supposed to do.

Here, in winter, the place belongs to the natives. Most of the chip shops and toffee-apple shacks shut up shop. The guesthouse owners nip away for their own holidays to somewhere more appealing. The thick floral curtains are pulled across single-glazed windows and the 'No Vacancies' sign is spun. The trawlers that offer boat rides around the bay from Easter to September either tie up or head to middle waters, looking for the crab and lobster that have slowly turned the resort into the biggest shellfish port in Europe without seeming to bring any money to the town.

The old car glides down gusty roads, polystyrene chip cartons dancing on the wind, past boarded-up shops and dilapidated guesthouses bearing names like Avalon and Edelweiss. "*Come as guests, leave as friends.*"

Down to the seafront.

The keening of gulls.

The insistent rustle of the sea as it pans for shiny pebbles in the shallows.

Computer games bleeping from the neon-fronted arcades.

Metal shutters banging open, as a smattering of tattooed shopkeepers decide it might be worth trading, even if it's only for a few hours.

I park up on the hill. Townhouses and guesthouses, three and four storeys, gazing out on a view sketched in different shades of brown and grey. Step out onto wet concrete, leaving the crumpled documents on the front seat. I half hope the wind will carry them away as I open the door.

And then I'm walking down the hill, listening to the tide, the swish of the occasional car as it slices past and throws mucky water up my trouser leg.

I look at my watch. Mid-morning. We're meeting in the fancy ice cream parlour on the promenade. I turn right into the harbour, lighting a cigarette. There's no cloud as I breath out. The smoke is the same colour as the sky.

Listening. The hulls of wooden pleasure boats knocking together like chimes. The slap of water against peeling hulls. The shouts of fishermen, unloading empty pots from greasy decks, their luminous waterproofs and rubber-soled boots squeaking on the damp, worm-eaten wood.

Up the steps, to the promenade. Most of the shops are shut. Only a few kiosks stand open, selling kites and knick-knacks, imitation shells and kiss-me-quick hats, staffed by miserable teenagers texting on mobile phones or grizzled old women who look like they have been standing in the same place their whole lives.

I try to smile. There's excitement in me. Exhilaration at the thought of Jess. Her embrace. Her kiss. Fear, too. At opening up. Telling all. Telling her the bits she doesn't know.

On, down to the amusements, boots leaving an unbroken trail of chocolate-brown mud on the wet red pavement. The prom is almost deserted. One man studies the tide charts, another trains binoculars on a lonely shoreline bird.

Down to the ice cream parlour. She's not there, yet. Three staff members in black T-shirts and trousers stand chatting, one leaning on a broom. Its theme is 1950s America, all polished chrome and mirrors painted with knickerbocker glories. It looks like the cast from *Grease* should walk through the door and order cherry sodas and thick milkshakes, but the only customers are two old ladies, sipping coffee from mugs that are too heavy for their shaking hands.

How do I tell her... How?

I sense her before she speaks. The air behind me feels suddenly softer. Warmer.

"Hey you."

She's standing by the sea wall. A sensible purple coat over jeans and sandals, painted nails. Blonde, fluffy hair and hands in pockets. Her face, cold but flushed. Her smile, reaching all the way to her eyes.

I try to speak but nothing happens, so we just stare at each other, until the wind blows her hair in front of her face and I step forward and brush it behind her ear, resting her cool cheek against my warm palm, and rub the tip of my nose against hers, and then her eyes increase, blur and fill as we move together and goose pimples appear on her chest, and mine, and we're kissing.

And nothing else really matters, for a while.

56

McAvoy wonders if this is how killers feel. If, in this raw moment of despair and anger, he is sharing a bond with the men and women it is his job to bring to justice.

He adds guilt to the cocktail of emotions sloshing in his system and turning his face a flushed and livid red.

He feels like a creationist being eaten by a dinosaur. All of his beliefs, the anchors that make him what he knows to be a good man, seem suddenly silly and insubstantial in the face of his desire to cause harm.

Is it just circumstances that turn anger into murder? He thinks of jealous husbands, out to scare, acting in rage, strangling their cheating spouses for a second longer than they intended, and suddenly finding themselves astride a corpse? Thinks of pub fights. Men in drink, pulling a pen knife from a pocket and sticking it in the belly of the bloke who has spilled their pint and failed to apologise.

He is seeing in shades of grey, and it scares him.

Until today, he believed there were murderers and victims. Decent people and evil people.

He finds his fingers curling themselves into fists.

He shakes the steam from his eyes. The computer screen

keeps blurring. He can feel a migraine edging into his head, encircling his brain with cold, numbing tentacles.

More than anything in the world, he wants to run home. Sprint down the stairs, take a patrol car, and screech home. Hold her. Hold the baby. Pack a bag and run. Put miles between himself and this place. These people.

He sits at his neatly ordered desk in the empty CID suite. A civilian officer is doing something with files at the far end of the room, but save for her shuffling of paper, he is alone. The team are either at Roper's side or hunting the man of the hour.

The call came through mid-morning. The body of a man thought to be the missing witness from the Cadbury trial found in the plunge pool at a city hotel. Prime suspect, Owen Lee. Recently bailed on suspicion of two other murders. Detective in charge, Doug Roper. Suspect considered armed and dangerous. Firearms officers have been put on alert. Media informed. This is a priority case...

The men and women in the shiny suits had scrambled. Taken Roper's individual calls and hustled out of the office, pulling on matching raincoats and picking up umbrellas carrying the insignias of cars they can't afford. Despatched to likely hideouts. A team of uniforms sent to his home address. Called in moments later to alert the control room to two more bodies. Brains bashed in. Fucking bloodbath...

Later, the call from the team at the hotel. The suspect's sister has been found. No pulse. Suspected overdose. Drugs in abundance. Signs she had been assaulted shortly before death...

McAvoy, in the middle of it all, not moving. Just sitting

at his desk, waiting to be given something to do, trying to keep the tears from his eyes and his feet firm on the carpet. Making his tongue bleed as he clamped his teeth upon it. Longing to run. Longing to run.

He doesn't know how much of what Owen told him is true. Wonders how many times self defence will work as mitigation. Whether anybody saw him, standing outside the apartment block, talking to the country's most wanted murderer in the rain, ushering him into the church. If there were witnesses as Owen fled the scene, putting distance between himself and the duty McAvoy had so believed he would perform.

Obsession.

McAvoy knows that is the key to it all. It is the fuel that is keeping him here. Fixing his eyes on the screen. Burning in his gut and belching bile into his mouth.

How to stop Roper?

How to stop his lies?

How to find the killer? The person who took a shine to a pretty girl, frightened her, followed her, and killed her in an alleyway within view of her house. Who left her body to be found by a pervert, who took it as a gift, and used it for his own unspeakable lusts.

He logs onto websites he has visited time and again. Cross-references log-numbers and statistics, profiles and callouts, with the bundle of paperwork and photocopied notes by his right hand. Spills his mug of cold tea and does not even stop to mop up. Begins picking up the documents in his fist rather than his fingertips. Finds his hands in his hair. His jaw aching as he grinds his teeth, and watches the screen flicker, and wonders what to do, what to do, as the radio fizzles with static, more reports, updates, lies, lies, lies...

...Attention all units, the trial of Shane Cadbury has been adjourned following the discovery of the body at the hotel. Whether it will resume after the weekend is unknown, but indications are it will be declared a mistrial. The judge has been briefed about developments and the Crown Prosecution Service is holding off on any decision about whether to progress with the case until the involvement of Owen Lee has been fully investigated...

McAvoy kicks the waste-paper bin and slams his arm on the desk. He doesn't know who he is anymore. Last night he stood dumb as a suspect was beaten in a cell. This morning he sat in the Lord's house with a killer.

Roper will stitch it all together again, he thinks. He'll ensure Owen is either shot, or dismissed as a lunatic and fantasist. He'll get a retrial for Cadbury, without the hassle of the defence witness. He'll probably find out about McAvoy's little meeting with the prime suspect, and then he'll either put him in his back pocket, or have him go away.

And Ella's family will go home and curse the wrong man. They'll sit in a house surrounded by flowers and cards and her picture, and they'll loathe Shane Cadbury, when the man who stabbed their daughter, and the man who let him go, are walking around, and preparing to do it again.

He tries to focus.

Somebody who knew her.

Wanted her.

Fantasised over her and wouldn't let go.

Running through suspects in his head.

Realising he has none.

All he has is a deeply-held belief that the investigation was carried out improperly. He doesn't even know who to tell.

He looks at the phone again, and the number on the paper in front of him.

He wants to phone her family. Tell them everything. Explain to the Butterworths that they've been lied to. That the copper with the dazzling smile is a chancer and a villain, more dangerous than the man the whole police force is hunting.

Tries typing the mobile phone number into a search engine. Gets gobbledygook and accounts for an Australian air-conditioning firm.

Puts her name in.

E-l-l-a B-u-t-t-e-r-w-o-r-t-h

Page after page of news stories. Online versions of papers, TV reports, radio bulletins. Snatches of sympathy and opening lines.

Sees Roper's name among most of them.

Puts it in the search engine.

Profiles and interviews, story after story, case after case. Even an entry on Wikipedia and Who's Who. Pictures. Sometimes smiling, sometimes overflowing with saccharine concern.

A fraud, thinks McAvoy. A liar. A conman.

He scrolls through site after site, sneering at the screen. Finds himself back where he started. The *Hull Daily Mail*.

A story by Tony Halthwaite on the search for a missing

girl. Disappeared in her wedding dress having spilled wine on it and raced to her auntie's house for help. Family very concerned. Never done anything like this before. Detective Superintendent Doug Roper understood to be personally handling the investigation.

The picture that accompanies the story is the one that the city would come to know in the weeks and months that followed. That would accompany every update and bulletin. Ella. Captured in a broad smile. Large hooped earrings, halter-neck black top. Flushed cheeks and sparkle in her eyes.

But it's not just a headshot. It hasn't been cropped.

In this, the first chapter of the Ella Butterworth story, the picture is printed in its entirety. She stands on a stage, in front of the *Search For A Star* banner, bouquet of flowers in her grip.

An arm around her shoulders.

The hand, almost imperceptibly, curving down onto the slope of her breast.

Family and friends around her, celebrating her triumph in the heats of the talent contest she would never have a chance to win.

And staring out at him, with a leer, a familiar face.

57

She's done the hard work for me. Told me what she knows. Said it while staring out over the sea wall, hands on the wet brick, eyes on the horizon, filling the air with my misdeeds.

Blake.

She'd always known, she said. Dad had mentioned something to her about him having done something bad in the past, and she'd pieced it together from there. Got other bits from Kerry when she was off her face. She just wanted to hear it from me, she said. Have me trust her enough to open up.

"You were a child," she says to me, still looking out at the grey waters. "You didn't know what you were doing."

She tells me she understands the demons, too. That I sometimes talk to them in my sleep. That I fight and kick against invisible things in the moments before I give in to unconsciousness. That she's found my prescriptions, and the pills.

Always known, she says. Just waiting for me to tell her.

So I tell her the rest.

The men in the woods.

Kerry's flat.

Our home, and the Russians.

The sauna.

Kerry.

Roper.

McAvoy.

I share it all, between gasps of cigarette smoke. When she turns to face me, I don't know whether the water on her cheeks is from her eyes or the sky.

When she holds me, she's trembling, but the embrace is strong.

I didn't know I needed to be forgiven until she said that she did.

And then my floodgates open, and the tears that fall from my eyes are twenty years old, and roar to earth with the intensity of a storm.

58

McAvoy is trying not to run. His shoes are squeaking on the plastic-covered floor as he moves quickly down the corridor and into the darkened PNC room.

Punches his code into the keypad and steps inside.

A uniformed officer is sitting at one of the two large terminals. He looks up, gives a gruff "all right?" then returns to his work.

McAvoy sits down in front of the screen and logs on. He entertains the notion of using somebody else's ID, but he is past caring. Evidence trails don't seem to matter. Roper can make things look however he wants to.

Excitement making his fingers tremble, he puts the name into the database.

There is a pause. The screen turns black, and McAvoy finds himself digging his nails into his palm and chewing at his cheek.

Unsure what he wants the criminal record check to find...

And then it begins.

A catalogue of mugshots, going back twenty years. Unmistakably, the man in the photograph.

The familiar face.

Cautions for shoplifting.

Affray.

Then a dwelling burglary.

Another.

Threats to kill.

Indecent exposure.

Five more, inside two years.

Burglary.

Indecent assault on a minor.

Assault.

Rape.

Carrying an offensive weapon.

A decade of arrest and conviction, and then ten years of almost nothing.

He's got better.

Found out how to do it properly, and not get caught.

McAvoy looks in his notebook. At the cases in London, and further north.

The addresses match.

So does the photo.

He's trembling, now. Excited, but angry, too. Angry that this man could have been caught, if only Roper had cared enough to do things properly when Ella's body was found.

An obsessive, with a violent past, whose previous addresses match with the dates of the murders and woundings of half a dozen attractive young women.

Aector McAvoy breathes out, and wonders what to do next.

He's just found a killer.

59

We stroll hand in hand to the car, no longer caring about the rain, or the vehicles that splash water from the deep muddy kerbs up our trouser legs. We stop once in a while to kiss. For her to ask another question. For me to feel lighter with each truth spilled.

She's nodding a lot. Taking it all in.

It helps, talking about it. Laying it out chronologically. All that has happened since she told me this was my last chance. Since I set off to the bridge to spite her, and smashed a rock through the skull of a man who was trying to kill me.

"Why this area, though?" she's asking. "After you got out. Why not start again somewhere else? Why surround yourself with memories of what you did?"

"Because I didn't deserve a fresh start. I didn't deserve to live calmly and peacefully. I needed to be here. So I could never forget. Never put it behind me. Never condone it."

"It sounds like those Catholics who whip themselves," she says, biting her lip. "Who wear those things around their thighs that dig into the skin so they're always reminded of Jesus's suffering. Is it like that?"

"I wear mine on the inside," I say, looking away, watching the gulls and the waves and feeling my heart race as I dare to believe that she does, truly, understand. That she gets it. Gets me. And it's not too late to make a difference.

"But to become a journalist? In the area where you were born?"

"I've only ever been good at a few things, Jess. Boxing, writing, and talking to people. The hospital I was in, it was more like a centre for troubled teens, it had a boxing club and I didn't have much else to do with my time other than getting back in the ring. I knew I'd never be able to box professionally. Too notorious. But I made it a decent club. Had a proper coach and everything. Ended up with kids who weren't even residents at the centre coming along for training. And our best boxers started entering competitions. Just little stuff, but I reckoned they deserved some credit so I started sending in match reports to the paper. *York Press* was the nearest. They liked my style. And I told enough lies to get a freelance job, sending stuff in over the phone, making a few quid. And then when the shrinks reckoned I could go out into the big bad world without shooting anybody, it became a proper job.

"Nobody was more surprised than me. It was like everything I'd done had been atoned for and forgotten. The world had given me a normal life. A job. A wage. There was only me who didn't feel like I deserved it. Who kept waiting for the world to give me the skinning I deserved. But it didn't come. I found you. I found a chance at happiness. All the stuff with Dad and Kerry, that was bad, but it wasn't my punishment. It wasn't justice, I suppose. And then you got pregnant. And I found my atonement. Our baby died. I poisoned it. And I wasn't even strong enough to hold you…"

"No," she cries, her hands rising to her mouth as though

she fears she'll be sick. "No, Owen, that wasn't it! That wasn't your fault. It was nobody's fault. It just happened."

"It happened because of me."

"Why not me?"

"Because you're an angel. You're perfect. You've never hurt anybody."

"I've hurt you every day we've been together. I haven't been what the man I love needs. Why wasn't us losing the baby all down to me? Why not my fault?"

"No, Jess, I was poison in you…"

"You were my goodness, Owen. Even now, you're the only good man I've ever known."

I see myself reflecting back in her eyes. They're the only mirrors I can tolerate.

We hold each other. Touch each other as if for the first time.

Eventually, she speaks again.

"But you must have torn yourself open, not knowing what would happen. Not knowing if you had a real future. Every moment, not knowing if somebody would recognise you from an old picture…"

"Tony did. He knows. Saw me in the files and told me he knew everything. It was a weird feeling. Like being found out, but being relieved that somebody else knew, all at the same time. Maybe that's why I couldn't tell you. I had a confidante who didn't share my bed. I could talk to him about it without worrying that I'd scare him away. How could I lie there with you? Telling you about how it felt to pull the trigger. What I'm seeing when the lights go out. How it feels to spend most of your life trying not to flinch when goblins start chucking daggers in your face…"

She puts a hand on my cheek. Pulls me close. "That's what love is, Owen. That's what your kind of love is, anyway. It's taking somebody else's sadness. Using everything in your power to make their every moment a perfect one, even if it means making yourself miserable. It's caring more for somebody else than you do for yourself."

I feel myself fragmenting. Coming apart. I can't see properly, through the tears and the rain and the endless images that spill over one another as I try to make sense of who I am. "I'm a fool," I say, and it doesn't seem like enough.

"You are," she agrees, and we find it in ourselves to laugh.

I tell her about Roper. About how he works. What he's done. Show her my bruises.

She shakes her head. Reacts as if I'm telling her about an unpleasant boss. Tells me not to worry. That he's probably jealous. That he'll get his in the end.

Then I'm spilling all of it. Tony. Ella.

As the words spew into the low cloud, it becomes harder and harder to look at Jess. In her, I see another life. Another person. Another Owen.

I suddenly can't argue with any of it. McAvoy's right.

Ella needs justice.

They all do.

And I have to pay for what I've done.

We climb inside the car, and sit, silently, watching the steam rise from our clothes and the rain on the windowpane.

Her: "We could run."

Me: "I have to go back."

Both of us, horrified at the words of the other. Then folding into a smile and another embrace.

"Will they catch you? How much money did you take?"

"I never counted it."

I pull out the roll, and her lips move as she counts the £20 notes. "Just under £2,000," she says.

It doesn't seem very much.

"The gun?"

I pull it from my waistband and pass it to her. She holds it. Weighs it. She passes it back with a shudder. "I don't like it," she says.

I put it back where it belongs.

She reaches underneath herself and pulls out the wad of documents McAvoy had thrust at me. She starts sifting through them.

"It is important," she says, softly, almost to herself. "Not just that somebody gets put away. But that the right person does. I suppose ordinary people just need to know that somebody has gone to prison for doing something wrong. It's the people who are caught up in it, who are directly involved, that need something more than that. Some proof, deep down, that the world makes sense. That if you do something dreadful, it'll catch up with you."

All I can do is nod, and try not to look at the papers in her hand.

"This Ella," she says, looking at a potted biography of the deceased. "She was a good person?"

"She never hurt anyone. She was a sweet girl, who died for no reason."

"Would it make a difference if she had done something wrong?"

"I don't know," I say, honestly. "That's my job, isn't it? I deal with death almost every day. I see people at their most raw and exposed. You can come to convince yourself the world is chock-full of blood unless you find a way to reconcile it. So, yeah, if some hooker's been found dead, you tell yourself she knew the risks and shouldn't have been out. A bloke's been kicked to death after a night out, you tell yourself he probably said the wrong thing, and what was he doing out on a weeknight when he had a baby at home? That's what you do. You find a way to tell yourself that they would still be alive if they hadn't been playing silly beggars. That way you can write about them and it doesn't touch you. You can say they were fabulous people, without the burden of having an emotional connection to them. It was different with Ella. None of us knew why it had happened. None of us could find a bad word about her. Not even Tony. It was new for all of us. The whole pack. She was a good, decent person, and she was killed in such a horrible way."

"What if she was seeing somebody else? If she was a bully at school? If she went on internet chat rooms and talked dirty with strangers? If she was a human and not a bloody angel?" Jess's eyes flash fire. It's as if she's jealous of a dead girl.

"I don't know," I say, again, and it sounds so pitiful I want to bite it back. I try again. "It would be easier, yes. Easier for Tony, anyway. I've never known him so bloody respectful as on this case. Barely went near the family. Wasn't at many of the press conferences. You know what he's like. Can get the family to tell him their pin number inside five minutes, most days. This one, he even gave the backgrounder to young Tom. I think it troubled him. Giving a shit."

Jess scoffs. "Him? Care? The only way you could find that dirty sod's heart is with a metal detector."

I find myself smiling, because it's a phrase I made up and she's taken to copying. I should have known better than to mention his name. She likes me to have friends, but would rather I share a bolthole with Osama bin Laden than a pint with Tony H.

I switch on the windscreen wipers for something to do, and a jumbled, opaque landscape appears on the glass. Wet. Desolate. Miserable. It occurs to me that all I want is in this car.

I take the sheet of paper from Jess.

Lean in and kiss her.

Pull back.

To stop myself crying again, I look down at the documents, gulping hard.

The sheaf of papers is open on a report from the technology division. The history of Ella's mobile phone. Calls in. Calls Out. Texts and pictures.

I look at the number that McAvoy has ringed in his sturdy, steady hand.

666999.

The Batphone.

60

Through the double doors. Past security and up the stairs.

A swirl of raindrops flying from his coat, McAvoy pushes through the throng of suits, and into the police room. He's out of breath, but he's keeping it controlled. He's gulping down his panic. Stilling his heart. Knows this is important. Too important to mess up with excitement, silliness and panic.

He's made a decision.

He's elected to trust in the goodness of people. His belief that if you dig far enough, you will find even the worst person's limit.

Roper's sitting at the back of the room. He has an arm around Wendy Butterworth's shoulders and he's talking in a soft, hushed voice.

Two other detectives are talking gently into mobile phones in the rear of the shot, looking business-like and efficient. On the case.

They look up as McAvoy enters, and just manage to stop themselves from groaning.

Wendy does not even raise her eyes. She is too far gone. Her existence too terrible. She has not experienced any

374

happiness since her daughter was taken, save for the grim satisfaction that the man who did it will be locked away. Now that small glimmer of comfort is in doubt. Nothing makes any sense anymore. She would take her own life, were it not for anguish at knowing that her daughter's killer would have claimed another victim.

Roper catches McAvoy's eye, remembers he's on camera, and smiles. "Yes, Sergeant? Any developments?"

"A moment of your time, sir," he says. Calm. Even. Then nods towards the cameras, and shakes his head.

Roper looks puzzled. Angry, for a second, then accepting. He excuses himself, and steps lightly to McAvoy's side.

"Well?" His tone is light and mocking. Smug and amused.

"Cadbury, sir. What's happening?"

Roper rolls his eyes. "He's in the cells. They're probably going to call a halt to the trial. We'll be back here in a few months doing it again, all being well."

"And Lee?"

"Oh there's a school of thought that he had something to do with Ella's murder but I can't see that coming to much. Not much need, neither. We'll get him on all the others. No point tagging Ella on as well. Big case like that, needs its own hearing. No, we'll get Owen for this week's little trail of destruction and Cadbury for Ella. Job's a good 'un."

McAvoy nods. Tries not to let the anger into his face.

"Does it matter to you, sir? Whether or not they really are guilty?"

Roper snorts. "You getting holier than thou, son?"

"I am holier than thou. I've never met anybody less holy than thou."

"Very good," says Roper, smiling. Then he moves in a

little closer. "What is it this time, laddo? What's chafing at your nethers?"

"It wasn't Cadbury," he replies, calmly. "I never thought it was, and you know that. But I know who did it. He met her when he was judging the singing contest. He's got a record as long as your arm. He's a violent obsessive. Done time for it, years ago. The *Mail* reporter. Tony Halthwaite."

Roper giggles. Shakes his head. "Tony H?"

McAvoy meets the other man's gaze. "Yes."

The moment stretches.

McAvoy waits for Roper's mask to slip. For some humanity to smile out.

Roper drops his voice to little more than a whisper.

Then smiles.

"I know Tony H, son. Know him well. He's a nasty little bastard. I know all about his fucking record. Checked him out the second he got the crime brief at the *Mail*. Filed it away in the old upstairs. A thing worth knowing. A trump card. But he's got fuck all to do with this case."

"That's not true, sir. We know somebody was prowling around the Butterworths' house not long before she died. That she'd had dubious messages on her phone. I checked the computer and the CCTV records and there was a *Hull Mail* fleet car in the area, both on the night of the sighting at her house, and the night she was killed."

"Circumstantial," he tuts.

"But enough to investigate. This is what I keep saying. It's not about convictions, sir. It's about truth." McAvoy tries to stop his voice rising, but his angry hiss still prompts looks from the film crew and the other officers.

Roper treats them all to his best smile. Puts his mouth close to McAvoy's ear.

"Fuck truth, son. Fuck it all. Fuck you, and Owen Lee and fuck Ella Butterworth. Silly slag probably had it coming. Maybe Tony H stabbed her. Maybe he didn't. I don't care. There's enough on Cadbury to make it stick, so that'll do. And Owen? Armed and dangerous, isn't he? He won't see the morning. Done me a good turn and drowned the chap who was becoming a problem. Didn't even use the gun, which is fucking ungrateful, given what a bitch it was to get him out of the station with it in his grubby mitt. Tony's my friendly face at the *Hull Mail*. He's useful. He might have some demons, but haven't we all? And as for you, laddo? You're out of my department. You can go where you fucking like, but it's not even funny watching you waste your time anymore."

McAvoy rubs his hand across his forehead. He feels faint. Sick to his stomach. There's blood thundering in his head.

"But he might do it again…" his voice has no strength.

"I always find the right man," laughs Roper.

They look at one another. McAvoy, although taller, is stooped and weakened, so has to stare upwards to see into Roper's eyes. They are black and lifeless. Nothing comes back save his own, uninspiring reflection.

McAvoy wants to say something clever. Make a threat. Make a scene.

But it will do no good.

Nothing will.

Nothing save the gun in his pocket.

The one Owen gave him, to put things right.

McAvoy closes his eyes, and mouths an apology to the pictures of the people in his head.

Tears sting his eyes and his chest is fit to burst.

His head is full of hot snakes and cold anger.

His fingers close on the gun.

Pictures the hole the bullet will make in the skull of the smirking demon who stands before him, clad in leather and the air of the untouchable.

Begins to pull the weapon free...

...the door bursts open, knocking him off guard.

A uniformed officer, his nose bloodied, calls for help. Shouts and screams emanate from the court building down the hall.

Swearing, switching off phones and pulling batons from their coats, the two officers race into the corridor and down towards the main body of the court. Roper, blowing McAvoy a kiss, follows behind them. The camera crew, mindful of the ban on filming inside the precincts of the court, shimmer with frustration as they crane their necks to see what is happening.

His breath coming in stutters, the tension draining out of him, McAvoy wills his feet to move.

Near blind with tears and frustration.

He fumbles at the door and pulls it open, the gun, hot and guilty in his pocket.

Stumbles down the corridor and into the wide, circular body of the court building.

Three officers are holding back Ella Butterworth's father. He is struggling in their grasp, roaring like an animal, his hands and face, spattered with flecks of blood.

McAvoy pushes through the press of bodies.

Ushers.

Court clerks.

Solicitors.

The innocent and the guilty, waiting to be judged.

On the floor, like a whale beached on umber sands, Choudhury is sprawled, not moving. An island in the rich sea of his long, flowing, barrister robes.

Two uniformed officers tend to the wounds on his face. His turban is askew on his head. Long hair, snaking from his colossal round head, puddles on the floor. One of his polished shoes has come off. He looks like a slain sultan. A fat, rich crook, beaten bloody by a weak old man.

"He was laughing," screams the man with blood on his hands and the toes of his shoes. "About getting paid twice! Said he'd be back next time. Nice little fucking payday! That's my daughter, you bastard! My daughter! Dead! Murdered! And you're making money from the man who did it!"

As he folds in on himself and gives in to great racking sobs, McAvoy slips away.

The emptiness inside him is dissipating. The guilt, at his own weakness, his feeble inaction, his naïve belief in the goodness of those around him, turning to smoke on the fire of his sudden sense of what must be done.

He's filling up.

Gorging himself on righteous rage.

And visions of what must be done.

Out to find a killer.

61

The air-conditioning is on in the internet café and Tony H is shivering. The only spare terminal was directly under the blower, and the breeze on his cold clothes is making him feel snappy and irritable. He keeps sniffing, and his bones are starting to ache as if he's coming down with something.

He wants a cigar, but there's no chance in a place like this. It's all nerds, geeks, students and foreigners. They don't know who he is, or that he's used to being an exception to the rules.

He logs on to his own website. *Hull Daily Mail*. The late edition hasn't hit the streets yet but the website is usually updated first, and he's eager to see how the silly bollocks on newsdesk have treated his copy.

Clicks on the top story and reads the words he sent through before lunch, his phone tucked under his chin as he sat, warm and dry, in the front seat of Roper's sports car.

He smiles as he reads it. They've left well alone. Put the exclusive tag on it and left in the meat.

Poor fucker, thinks Tony, as he reads the hatchet job he's done on his best pal.

The guilt has gone, as he knew it would. He tells himself

that Owen would have done the same were the situation reversed. That he'll forgive him. Let him off. Probably even send him a visiting order and invite him over for a spot of company at the nick. Not that he'll go. He doesn't like prisons. Never has. It's been over a decade since he last lay on a prison-issue mattress: his nostrils full of bleach and body odour, stewed food and the shit-bucket. He hadn't coped well inside. The other inmates had him down as a nonce, and he took his fair share of kickings before he toughened up and started hitting back. He wonders if Owen will fare any better. If he'll have to suck a cock before he's allowed to get a good night's sleep.

He reads the story again, for the sake of completeness. Wonders if Owen will ever get to see it. If he'll mind the description of his sister as a "city prostitute".

Tony had been surprised to learn just how many bodies his friend had been able to rack up. Even with his fucked-up history, he didn't have Owen down as a killer. Too bloody soft. Feels sorry for people, and himself most of all. Always trying to pull somebody out of the shit. His girlfriend. His sister. Poor Kerry. Seven stone of poison, puncture wounds and crumbling bones. She'd been pretty when he'd first met her. He'd even thought about pursuing it. But the smack had grabbed her quicker and firmer than he could, and soon she wasn't worth his time.

Vaguely, not really thinking about it, he logs onto a porn site. He keeps the sound down so as not to alert the other users, and watches one of his favourite little videos. It doesn't get him hard, but he likes to watch it. Nothing really gets him hard. Not when they give it up so easily. When they offer themselves so freely. When pretty things are willing to let an ugly bastard like him inside them. He can't fuck something he doesn't respect. For Tony, it's about the thrill of the chase. Finding somebody perfect, angelic and beautiful. Watching over them. Becoming a part of their lives. The shadow behind them. The handprint on the window. The words in the condensation on the bathroom mirror. When they shiver, and wonder if he's watching. That's when he knows he's inside. And when the knife goes in, and his image is burned into their dying eyes; that's when he knows he has mattered more to them than all the dirty bastards combined.

The air-conditioning starts making a clicking noise and Tony feels like he's sitting in a wind tunnel, so he logs off and stands up. Stares through the window at the half-dark street and shudders at the thought of going out in the dreadful weather. It seems to have been like this ever since he moved to Hull. He can't remember what the sun feels like. The people seem wraith-like. Their skins pale and unhealthy. Grey-green, like a wet headstone. It had been hard to find somebody beautiful. Somebody worth getting himself in a lather about. He's always been at his happiest when a woman's got under his skin. Somebody worth making up fantasies about. Painting mental pictures of possibilities and perversions. Ella had been like that. Somebody with sparkle. Effervescence. Charm. A smile that from the first moment she flashed it at him, he had wanted to split with his cock. More than that. He'd desired her more than sexually. Wanted to hold her hand and kiss her hair as she fell asleep. Wanted to embrace her, stroke her skin. Sniff her feet…

He'd got carried away, of course. Gone too far, like always. Wound himself up to breaking point. He knew she would never have looked at a man like him. That it was obscene to even hope. Got his kicks another way. Being close. Watching her sleep. Taking the little things that belonged to her and which, he fancied, still smelled of her scent. Revved his engine until he couldn't take it anymore. Had to end it. Had to stop her from debasing herself with an obscenity like him. Had to save her from herself.

Standing in the doorway, watching the rain, he indulges himself in the memory of their association. The time he managed to nab a pair of her tights from the wash basket and found that they were still warm. Still carried an unmistakable scent. Or the yelp of fear when she saw his shadow at the window. He half wishes he could have kept it at that. Let the thrill plateau, and stayed there. But he wasn't that way inclined. He needed stronger hits. He climbed the ladder of adrenaline, until only violence could excite him. Until every part of his body was buzzing with a need to hurt her. To punish her for being so pretty. For being so unobtainable.

So he killed her.

Watched her run from the house in her bare feet and wedding gown. The red stain, spreading across the pure white, somehow a portent of what he would do.

He followed her.

Stood in the alleyway, the knife in one hand, his exposed dick in the other.

Remembered past glories.

Other times.

Other snotty slags.

Saw her coming back. Her tears glistening in the shadowy yellow light. Her face cold and raw from the wind.

And he stepped out.

Gave her a wink.

Then bared his teeth.

Enjoyed the moment of recognition. Her understanding of what he intended.

Then he showed her the blade.

Let her scream.

Then took what he wanted. Scared himself with the ferocity with which he attacked her.

He hadn't realised until then just how much he wanted this one. Just how angry he was with her for being so fucking pretty.

Slag.

Slag.

Slag.

Then she was dead. And he was taking great, exhausted breaths. Bathed in blood which was growing cold from the gale.

And somebody was coming. A hulking lad that Tony would later dub The Chocolate Boy.

So he ran.

Rode his luck.

Got away with it.

Tony ducks into the street and heads for the car. It's mid-afternoon and the story's changing by the minute. More and more national reporters are arriving on his patch, and he's in two minds about going and joining the pack outside Owen's flat, where forensics investigators are picking over the mutilated bodies of two unnamed men. There might be something juicy for him to pick up, but if the TV crews catch him on camera, he fears there's always a chance some old lag will recognise him as the flasher from E-wing, and burst the bubble, like last time. When he had to get the fuck out of Birmingham and head north, for another fresh start. It's one of Tony's constant regrets that his journalistic star will never shine on a national scale, because his face has just a little too much history in it.

He climbs inside the car and feels a vibration in his pocket. Smiles with smug contentment as he realises it's the Batphone, and somebody's about to tell him something exclusive and delicious.

He looks at the screen, and his leg starts to jiggle with shock and excitement as he takes in the number.

Fucking hell…

"Well, well, well," says Tony, as he opens the phone. "The man of the hour."

62

I can't hear his voice at first, over the rushing of blood. It's like driving too fast with the window down. I force myself to sound right. To keep it together. I chew the end of my cigarette. Taste blood and tar.

"What are the headlines?" I ask.

Tony gives a snort of laughter. "This is something of a surprise, Owen," he says. "I mean, I appreciate the call, but I figured you'd have pressing engagements. Like fucking off."

"I've always got time for you, Tone. Least I could do, after all the loyalty you've shown me." I say it sarcastically, keeping the anger out of my voice. I can't give too much away.

"Now, now," he says, jokily, and I hear his soft exhalation as he lights a Hamlet. "You know the job. What was I going to do? Sit on it? I didn't enjoy it, if it makes you feel any better."

Now it's my turn to laugh. "Yes you did. You loved it, mate. I can picture you, tumescent with fricking glee."

He gives a giggle, and we're suddenly two old friends again. "Maybe a bit," he concedes. "Still, it's the job, isn't it? Worse to come tomorrow too. Last call I took from Roper and some lass has come forward saying you and her have been meeting up regular as clockwork at that same spot in the Country Park. One of Roper's tame informants, no doubt, but she'll stick to the story if it gets her in his good graces. He's got it sewn up, mate, unless you've any bright ideas. After what happened at court, he'll need a result."

"At court?" I ask, unable to help it. "Cadbury?"

"The Scottish detective – looks like an advert for Quaker Oats and always seems to be about to burst into tears. Went back on his statement, didn't he? Said he had grave misgivings about Cadbury's guilt. If he survives the night he's definitely worth having a dig-around. I'd heard there was a copper married to some pikey princess but it sounded too outlandish. I reckon we need to bring it all into the light, eh?"

I shake my head, unable to find the right words. Then: "Leave him be, Tone. He's doing his damnedest. Can you imagine what it took to do the right thing?"

Tony laughs, full and throaty. "Of course I can't," he says. Then: "Where are you?"

"Million dollar question," I say, drily. "Apparently, a few people are quite keen to have a chat with me. It seems they're under the impression I've killed half of Hull."

"Dunno where they got that idea," he says. "Maybe the bodies all over the city?"

"Aye, maybe."

"So what's the plan?" he asks, genuinely fascinated to know what I'm going to do next.

I turn my head and the picture before me slows down and comes apart. Suddenly my vision is full of purples and reds. Claws. Tails. Talons. Faces. Each one uglier than the last, intertwining, conjoining, twisting, building, growing: a writhing throne on which she sits, golden and serene.

"I'm coming in," I say, quietly. "There's nowhere to run. Nowhere to go."

"Roper will be pleased," he enthuses.

"Last thing I fucking want," I growl. "That's what I need you for. He can't get the credit if he's fuck all to do with the collar. And he can't have me fall down the stairs if you document the bruises that are on me before I go in. You can orchestrate the lot. Have the whole pack there, if you like. There to see me, getting out of your car. I'll give you chapter and verse."

"Fuck."

"Fuck indeed." Then, to seal it: "Despite everything, you're the only one I can trust not to sell me out."

There's a pause, heavy with excitement and desire. I can hear Tony's brain whirring. Working in headlines. Opening paragraphs. Images of celebrity. The solidification of his legend. And then the obstacles. The pitfalls of being seen. Of stepping out from behind the by-line and into the glare of the media with the country's most wanted murderer on his arm.

Greed wins.

"Where do you want to meet?"

63

McAvoy chews on a cardamom seed, and holds a handkerchief, containing a crushed sprig of lemon thyme, to his nose. Breathes deep, his eyes closed. Roisin gave him one to settle his stomach, the other to mask the stench of rotting meat that seems to be again spilling up from his throat and into his mouth.

The smell of Ella Butterworth's body.

Fetid and decomposing.

Headless, but still somehow accusatory in its stare.

He sits at the kitchen table and listens as his wife fusses over their child in the playroom upstairs. It is a happy sound. Roisin's songs. Fin's laughter. Footsteps, unusually heavy and thudding for such a small frame, thudding on the hardwood floors of the blue-painted room.

Here, in the house they are renting until they save for a future. Three-bedroomed, thin-walled, and characterless. An interchangeable landmark in an ocean of bland housing. Utterly unremarkable.

He stares at the phone, tasting the bitter seed, breathing in the herbs, concentrating.

In.

Out.

Soft.

Slow.

The nervousness bubbling in his stomach.

The gun on the table.

You've done it, he tells himself. *No going back now.*

He makes a fist and hears the thyme rustle through the cotton. The smell grows stronger, and the retch of decay seems to recede.

Perhaps it isn't the herbs, he thinks. Perhaps it's having somebody to give them to you. To stroke your hand. To tell you to do what you must. That she believes in you. That you're a good man.

He tries to stop shaking: the adrenaline, still rich in his body.

He's made the call.

Said what he must.

And they've said they'll come. Hear what he has to say.

Help him.

He crosses to the window. There's little view, save the houses across the street and the fly-curtains of rain. No children playing. No cars swishing by. Just homes, like a bleak Lowry, and a sky the colour of his father's hair.

His telephone rings, and he composes himself. Wonders if it's them. Ringing back. Confirming details of their appointment. Checking he hasn't lost his nerve.

He answers it to a hysterical female voice.

Shouting, against the sound of a storm.

He can pick out only a smattering of words, as she snotters and cries.

"He's going to kill him!"

And then, as he asks her to say it again...

"Tony H. He killed Ella Butterworth. And Owen knows!"

64

The Humber Bridge Country Park.

Back where it all began.

Owen Lee Swainson, leaning against a silvery tree.

Watching…

The gale pulls at the tails of the fluttering garrotte, yanking it tight around the trunk of the half-dead sycamore. It is a noose of blue-and-white police tape, and it seems ravenous as it chews through the rotten bark and into the living flesh of the tree.

I force myself to look away. It makes no difference. I can still visualise the tightening knot; the bubbles of oozing sap.

Breathless, fingers making fists, I snatch a glance at my watch, wiping rain from its face and my own. Jerk my head skywards. Damp leaves and rotten branches form a ragged canopy above this patch of woodland where the ground is too rocky for the trees to grow. Beyond, the sky is all ripped tissue and hard slate.

I look down, the smell of blood inside my face.

Amid the mulch of timber and twigs, there is evidence that this place has seen violence. Polythene evidence bags. The page of a notebook, littered with crossings-out. The prints of size-ten shoes, forming fish-shaped hollows in the mud. They took pictures. Maybe one of the men and women in white suits asked why they couldn't find anything. More likely they didn't care.

Even now, even at the last, I don't know what I intend. I don't know what I want to happen. I don't know how far I'm willing to go. I've done terrible things but I still don't know if I'm a bad man. I just know I'm not a good one, and that there are people so very much worse.

Through the trees comes a charcoal figure: skinny and small, as if made of twists of tarred, knotted rope. He's hunched up inside a dirty, camel-coloured raincoat and the thin cigar at his lips is unlit. He sucks on it anyway, turning the stub into a mulch of tobacco, brown paper and spit.

"Fucking hell, Owen," shouts Tony, as his feet slurp at the path. "This is bloody horrible. Where you planning for the summer? Self-catering in Helmand?"

I look at him as if seeing him for the first time.

Tony has never been attractive. He's a rat in a raincoat; all bad skin and yellow teeth. His whole being seems to have taken on the hue of a chain-smoker's fingers. Here, now, I finally see the truth of him. Tony is more than ugly. He has a feral quality to him. His movements are those of a half-mad animal, a thing raised on violence and nourished on scraps of rotten meat.

And I'm thinking: *Do it now! Grab him. Smash your fist into his nasty little face. Make it make sense...*

I smile. Wave.

Tony comes closer, seemingly a little unsure whether to stick out his hand. He settles on a smile and a gesture at the heavens.

"Lovely day for it," he says.

"You alone?" I ask, quietly.

"Who the hell else would be out on a day like today?"

"All quiet again, eh? You'd never know it had happened, would you? Never know there were two bodies laid out over there a couple of days ago."

He shrugs, sucking spit and raindrops through his teeth. "The world keeps turning, lad. There'll be flowers, soon enough. Your sister will probably bring a wreath."

I shake my head. "She won't. Dead. OD'd."

He looks genuinely sad to hear it. "Bad week you're having, innit?" he says, trying to lighten the mood. "Got a trick up your sleeve to put things right?"

I nod and feel the rain run down my face.

I force myself to meet his eyes. Stare into him. Through him. Through Tony H. Through the man who killed her. *Ella*. Who killed them all. For a moment it feels that if I just stare hard enough, I'll see it playing out in the little man's eyes. See his confession. His fantasies. His memories of what he did.

I shiver. Feel myself coming apart inside my skin.

"We gonna get under a tree or something?" Tony asks. "Got a few questions for you. Weird place to meet. I'd have chosen somewhere with fewer memories."

"I'll bet," I say, and I can barely hear the words.

"You're not looking well," Tony adds. "You OK?"

Then I begin. I say the thing that I need to say – to make the accusation so at least he knows what he has done to deserve all that is about to happen.

"You killed Ella Butterworth," I say, in a spray of mist.

Then, more forcefully: "I know, Tone. I know what you've been doing."

"What?"

"How many more?"

"What are you talking about?"

"Your old number. It was in her phone. Messages about watching her. Liking what she was wearing. You killed her. How many more?"

Tony's face, so practiced in deception, twists into a mask of confusion. He looks baffled. Hurt.

The words come spilling out now. I can't stop myself. Don't even try to.

"Was it because she wouldn't go near you? She looked at you and saw a dirty ugly bastard and decided not to let you near her? You were freelancing in every city where they died. You couldn't resist it. I've seen the aliases you used for the by-lines. I've seen the addresses where the cheques were sent. It was you, you fuck. She was beautiful, Tony. But you couldn't just look, could you. You had to have her. And when she said no you started hating her, like so many others. You stalked her. You sent her anonymous messages from a phone that only a few people know you own. And you hunted her down. You never thought I'd put the pieces together. But I know. That copper – the big one, McAvoy – he showed me her mobile phone history. He doesn't believe Cadbury killed her any more than I do. I recognised the number, you prick!"

I'm grinding my teeth, now. Pressing my nails into my palms so deeply that I score through the skin: crimson trickles over my fingers and wrist as stigmata.

"She'd done nothing," I spit. "Nothing!"

I glare into his eyes: inkwells filled with a darkness that doesn't just swallow the light but seems to deny its very existence. I see myself, staring back. See the swaying trees and the warring branches and the tumbling, tumbling rain…

"Owen, wait…"

"You dirty, dirty bastard."

"Easy now…"

"You didn't deserve to touch her. To breathe the same air. For you to be the last thing she saw…"

And then Tony unleashes the killer within. Drops of red explode like dying stars in his eyes, as blood vessels burst with the enormity of his fury.

He thuds into my bruised ribs with a strength that he does not look as though he possesses. Tony's body is a pestilent, fragile thing; all tissue and twigs. But there is a venom inside him that makes him strong. The breath escapes from my lungs in a rush. My hands fly up. I bite my tongue and taste old coins. The gun lands wetly on the sodden path as we thump onto the ground, my head smacking back with a dizzying thud.

Tony is astride me, forearm beneath my chin, pushing down on my windpipe, staring into me.

Then deeper.

A more terrible aspect to his face than anything my mind has ever conjured.

Spitting poison, spraying rage.

"You're right, you soft cunt! I didn't deserve to touch her. Didn't deserve to touch any of them. Not like you. Not like a handsome bastard who doesn't know what he's got. Not worth fucking trying because I can already see it in their eyes. That knowledge that they're better than me. They think it's a game. Winding me up. Getting me going. Slagging around in their short skirts with their tits out, begging the world to look at them. Well, I looked. I fell for it, time and again. And then I ended it. Became something more important than a fuck. Whatever happens, the most important thing anybody will remember about these pretty girls is the way they died. And every time their deaths are spoken of, they'll be talking about me. Nobody else can ever have that. Nobody!"

Spit froths from Tony's purplish, blubbery lips and lands among the raindrops on my face as hands tighten around my throat and squeeze the breath from my body and the thoughts from my mind. Thunder roars in my skull.

My vision dwindles to a point, like an old TV being switched off; everything spiralling down into one tiny blob of colour.

Desperately, I reach around on the forest floor, fingers scrabbling for a branch. For something solid.

Tony slams his spare hand down on my forehead.

Again.

Again.

It seems as though my own tongue is halfway down my throat, as though my eyes are going to explode. I desperately try to get an arm free but there's nothing to hit. Tony's all bony elbows and sharp fists, wet clothes and loose skin. It's like fighting a long-dead corpse.

There is a solid meaty thump, and then the pressure is gone; the figure on my chest suddenly absent; the pain dissipating like blood beneath rain.

And I'm on my knees, retching, massaging my throat.

Through blurred, watery eyes, I see him. See Tony pulling himself to his feet. He's reaching inside his dirty, sodden coat.

Pulling out the murder weapon.

It's a kukri: a curved blade used by the Gurkhas of the Nepalese Armed Forces. Pictures of it have been appearing in the *Hull Mail* for months. Tony wrote most of the articles.

I stare. Glassy-eyed at the weapon. See Ella Butterworth's blood on the blade.

I turn at the sound behind me.

He's sprawled out like a fallen statue, trying to find his feet on the sloping, slippery surface, a look of panic on his broad face...

McAvoy.

For a second, Tony seems unsure which direction to advance, whether to finish off the copper who pulled him from his prey, or gut me, his best friend, before I can get my breath.

McAvoy finds his feet and hauls himself up, emerging from the puddles and the dirt and the leaves. He's big enough to snap Tony in two. Seems almost big enough to pull one of the oaks from the ground and smash it on the murderer's ratty head.

"Stop," he shouts.

He's holding the gun in a massive white fist. The barrel shakes and trembles. There is absolute terror in his eyes.

I drink him in. Focus my whole being on the vision of the earnest policeman, with his red hair and his cheap suit and the look of willingness in his eyes. Among the pain and the hate, I feel compassion. Sorrow, for what it must be like to tread the path of righteousness when darkness and light are such imposters. He doesn't belong here in the blood and filth where people like Tony and me wade.

And I know, to my very bones, that it is not in McAvoy's nature to pull the trigger.

Tony laughs. Gives me a glance and a wink, as if we're still old pals in the press room making fun of the new boy. Then he runs at McAvoy.

He slashes down with the kukri. McAvoy raises his hands in a boxer's stance and the blade hits the metal of the gun. It falls from his hand. He steps back and loses his footing as Tony hacks at him. The blade digs into his collarbone like an axe into firewood. Tony has to yank it hard to get it free. McAvoy is falling onto on his back, a look of broken-hearted bewilderment upon his big, trusting face. Tony chops down again.

McAvoy jerks like a dying fish as the rainbow of thick blood arcs upwards and patters onto the earth.

I feel the fight run out of me. Feel nothing but an overwhelming sadness as I watch the dying, gulping breaths of the only good man I've ever known.

Tony turns back to me, his face crimson, eyes wide and terrible.

He picks up the gun.

He points it at my chest.

Gives a shrug that could almost be apology.

Pulls the trigger.

The bullet thuds into the tree trunk and Tony yells as he totters off balance. McAvoy's shove in the back of the knees has cost him his shot.

I watch the gun as it pinwheels through the rain and bounces off a branch to nestle on a pillow of sycamore leaves. I sprint forward, planting my feet in the blood and rain and earth and dive for the weapon, my damp hands clutching at the metal. I turn, triumphant. Focus on the man who has taken everything from me.

Tony stands, motionless. Slowly, he looks down at McAvoy. Changes his grip on the kukri. Something flickers in his gaze: a flash of teeth and tail, shadows and blood. He lurches forward, ready to plunge the blade into McAvoy's heart as if planting a flag in hard earth.

I pull the trigger.

Tony's mouth opens as his eyes turn black and for a moment he has the look of a shark, crashing upwards through sea and spray to close his jaws around something fragile. Then his knees give way.

He collapses amid the mulch of the clearing, a dark stain spreading outwards from the ruination beneath his belly, as he clutches himself and hisses on the forest floor. Blood seeps through his fingers through the ragged, hanging wound between his legs.

For a moment, there is just the sound of pain, and running blood, and the savage swish of the branches overhead.

Then I'm crawling to where McAvoy kneels, one hand pressed to the gash at his collarbone. His face is a mess: more meat than skin.

"Is he dead?" McAvoy asks, and the effort seems to lighten his skin tone by several shades. He is the colour of dirty chalk.

"No," I say, trying to work out which wound to press my hands to. "Not yet."

"You didn't kill him?"

"No."

"Why?"

"Why didn't you?"

"I don't think I'm a killer. Not really."

McAvoy's breathing begins to sound unnatural. He blinks, furiously, as the rain hits his staring eyes. I wonder what the big man can see, here in this place between life and death.

"You'll be OK," I say, and hope that it's true. "Where's your phone? Your radio?"

McAvoy says nothing, and I realise I'm scrabbling through his pockets, like a battlefield magpie searching the pockets of the dead. I find his phone in the inside pocket of his jacket. Pull it out with fingers dripping blood. I dial 999. Look down at the dying policeman and wonder if Doug Roper will give a damn.

We sit in the rain, wind tearing at our skin, our wounds, listening to Tony's sobs.

After a while, I hold up McAvoy's phone. The picture on the screensaver is a beautiful, dark-haired girl with hooped earrings and too much lip gloss. If I knew her name I would call her.

I press my hand to the ugly trench of ruptured skin on McAvoy's front. Feel splintered bone. A thought, quick as a whip. A sudden, selfish, disloyal question: what will happen to me? Only McAvoy believed me. Only McAvoy could help me clear my name. But McAvoy is dying. And Doug Roper wants me in the ground.

I take a moment for myself. Think of all the lives taken, the broken bones, the grief-weighted tears, the good people corrupted by the bad and the bad people masquerading as agents of justice. And I realise it's all lies. All pretence.

All fiction. There's just us. Just people. And we're fucking awful.

I feel a hand gripping my arm. There's strength there. Immense strength. I look down and he's glaring up at me, his face all blood and beard and desperate, tear-filled eyes.

He shakes his head.

"No," he growls. "Not here. Not like this. Not without her…"

And like a great wounded bear, he begins to haul himself to his feet. He drapes an arm around my shoulders and I stagger under the weight of him. He stands. Arches his back. Straightens his tie, even as the blood pours down his front.

He says it again. "No."

He fumbles in his pocket. Hands me a small plastic recording device, and nods, meaningfully.

I press 'Play'.

Roper's voice.

Tinny, but unmistakable.

"*Fuck truth, son. Fuck it all. Fuck you, and Owen Lee and fuck Ella Butterworth. Silly slag probably had it coming. Maybe Tony H stabbed her. Maybe he didn't. I don't care. There's enough on Cadbury to make it stick, so that'll do. And Owen? Armed and dangerous, isn't he? He won't see the morning. Done me a good turn and drowned the chap who was becoming a problem. Didn't even use the gun, which is fucking ungrateful, given what a bitch it was to get him out of the station with in his grubby mitt. Tony's my friendly face at the* Hull Mail. *He's useful. He might have some demons, but haven't we all? And as for you, laddo? You're out of my department. You can go where you fucking like, but it's not even funny watching you waste your time anymore."*

He stares past me. Whatever he sees, whatever image his mind is projecting, it brings a flash of smile to his face.

And I can do nothing but hold him, and feel his blood mingle with mine.

65

Lights flashing, sirens blaring, ambulance pulling up as close to the entrance to the woods as the driver can manage: its crew leaping out in green overalls, dragging equipment, barking instructions, questions, cursing the rain...

Police cars. Roper's Jag in the lead, tyres screeching on the tarmac. A cameraman sitting in his passenger seat. Roper driving. Face stone.

The press. Satellite dishes on roofs. Reporters in fleet cars. Photographers. Journalists, tucking shirts into their trousers and pulling Wellingtons from car boots.

I turn away.

Watch the procession.

They see us, and run forward in a scrum. The uniformed officers try to marshal the press, but this one's too big, and they're greeted with universal suggestions to fuck off.

The guns are on the table in front of us. Knife, too.

On the floor at our feet, Tony Halthwaite, grey with pain and loss of blood, rolling in the gutter, one arm handcuffed to the leg of the picnic table, red palm turned upwards, still spitting pink froth onto his chin, chewing at his face as he gutters the word "slags" over and over and over...

Elbowing his way to the front, young blonde copper bustling people out of the way, comes Roper.

"Owen Lee," he begins, when he's sure that his documentary crew are behind him. "I am arresting you..."

Me and McAvoy, pale and bloodied, turn to one another and give a smile, which turns into a laugh. "Well done," I say. "You got me."

He snarls, flustered. Begins again. "I am arresting you..."

"You're not, pal," I say. "McAvoy here's already done it."

"What?" Roper's trying to stay calm, but a vein in his head is starting to pulse.

The faces in the crowd are starting to turn to him. One or two people I recognise are twitching into smiles.

"I'm going to come quietly," I say. "Unlike your missus, who's a real screamer."

There are sniggers at that, and I fancy, for a moment, that the sun is starting to peek through a hole in the cloud. I wince in the unfamiliar wink of golden light, and just as suddenly, it's gone.

"McAvoy," he says, unsure which mask to wear. He smiles. Frowns. Plays along, gives up. "Sergeant, please explain..."

McAvoy gives a sigh through pursed lips, then peers through a space in the crowd. Another car has pulled up. A uniformed senior officer steps out. Chief constable material, by the look of him.

Heads turn.

We stand. McAvoy's arm on mine, his grip just solid enough to make sure I don't say anything smart. He needn't. I'm out of ammo.

The man comes through the crowd, other uniforms on

either side. I recognise the face. Long, haughty, and utterly joyless. Top cop. Head of Humberside Police.

Roper looks confused. Lost. The ground beneath his feet is splintering.

"Sergeant McAvoy," says the senior officer, with a nod. He seems uncomfortable in the glare of the press.

"Sir, things are very much in hand…" begins Roper, but falls silent with a glare from his commanding officer.

The cameras catch it all.

"And this is Owen Lee?"

I nod. Don't know if I should extend my hand.

"In the car," he says, and his officers move forward. I put my wrists up and allow myself to be cuffed. I smile while they do it.

"Sir, this has been my investigation," says Roper, and he's a petulant child. Cameramen rub raindrops from lenses. I'm led through the crowd to the squad car. Behind me, I hear Tony groaning as the paramedics begin tending him.

The uniforms suddenly get the situation into some semblance of order and start to move the press back.

I slide into the warm car, and shiver as I lay my head back. I'm suddenly dog-tired, but I can't help wishing I was with the pack, covering this, as it happens to somebody else.

Another copper slides in beside me. Doesn't even look in my direction.

Outside, the Chief Constable is talking to Roper. Supercop's head is bowed. Anger is radiating off him.

I just nod. Chew the inside of my cheek for a while. Rub tiredness from my face with muddy, bloody hands.

I look out at Roper again, and wish I could catch his eye. There might be something in them, at last.

He doesn't turn around. I can only see the face of his young puppet. The blonde copper who wanted to be my friend and who beat the shit out of me in a prison cell. The lad who looks baffled and scared, and who's standing on his own.

And then I lean back and close my eyes.

Feel the pleasant constriction of the cuffs on my wrists.

The knowledge I have nowhere to be and nobody to kill.

And I think of Jess.

I don't doubt she'll forgive me, and I hope she won't have to wait for me for very long.

Kerry.

I can feel nothing but sadness, there. Nothing but empty, cold pain. I couldn't save her. I helped her fall. Sadness, that on the day my dad heard he'd lost his daughter, he'll hear his son has been arrested for murder.

Ella.

Just regret. That we never met. That I could not know her in life, the way I have understood her in death.

And then we're moving.

Out of the car park. Past the cameras and the flashbulbs.

The rain somehow less ferocious on the windowpane.

Up at the sky.

Six spears of sunlight forming a constellation in the canopy of grey.

Epilogue

June, 2012

It's a ghastly day. Although the fog has not taken this part of the east coast in its fist, the sky is an endless smear of grey and the air is speckled with a misty rain; a billion tiny raindrops hovering like flies. Despite this, it's warm. Sweaty. The sky may be the colour of white clothes washed alongside a funeral shroud, but the air has a moist pestilence about it, as though a great damp beast has been laid invisibly over the city. Roisin McAvoy feels perfectly within her rights to lie out on a sun-lounger in the front garden of her terraced house on the Kingswood estate.

Standing at the sink, staring through the window and more than enjoying the view, Aector McAvoy wonders whether his wife is breaking any laws in looking so extraordinarily beautiful. She's wearing a leopard-print bikini, pulled down to avoid tan-lines, and she's holding a baking tray to ensure that the occasional moments of sunlight help her fill in the gaps in her tan. She has earned this moment. She rarely considers what she does or doesn't deserve, but her husband has made it plain that whatever she wants, she has earned.

Inside the little semi-detached on the Kingswood estate, Aector McAvoy, alive despite his best efforts, is thinking about his mum. He has spoken to his mother four times in the past five years – once to tell her about the birth of her grandson, and the others to put her mind at rest about rumours of his demise. She had been pleased about Fin. Hadn't been aware, on any of the other occasions, that he had been in any kind of danger. *You're a policeman*, she had said, as if this explained everything. *Isn't that what happens?* McAvoy had found himself agreeing with her. Played down his injuries. Asked after her health and that of her husband and stepchildren. She had, in turn, asked after 'the Irish girl and the baby'. McAvoy had kept his temper. Were he to lose it, he would never find it again.

He considers his son. The lad is asleep. Dead to the world, snoring contentedly. He's going to be a big brother soon. He needs his rest.

It's June 2012. McAvoy has been on sick leave since February. In the immediate aftermath of his encounter with Tony Halthwaite, his heart stopped twice. McAvoy would love to be able to tell his wife that he saw white light and perfection. He did not. In the moments between life and death he saw Ella Butterworth. Saw the girl taken before her time. Somehow, the wounds she sustained in Tony Halthwaite's attack had been repaired. She was peaceful. She was serene. There was a moment's connection, as she evaporated into fragments. And then there was only

Aector McAvoy, half-dead on the damp ground of the Humber Bridge Country Park. He'd been given the chance to become something else. Something other. To pass on and be done with the complications of life and the people within it. He'd fought for life as if he were drowning. He does not know what lies beyond, but unless it contains Roisin and Fin, it holds no attraction.

He sits at the kitchen table. The radio is playing one of his favourites. It's 'Roll Away Your Stone' by Mumford and Sons. There's a new album out soon. Roisin knows a guy who knows a guy who robbed a guy. There will be tickets for the new tour in his car when his birthday arrives next month. He'll be thirty years old. A third of the way through his life, and still no fucking clue what it's all about.

He looks at the phone on the kitchen table as if it were a bomb. It is almost twenty minutes since he hung up on the newly appointed Detective Superintendent Patricia Pharaoh. She wants him on her team. She's taking over the rebranded Major Crimes Unit. It will be known as Serious and Organised. He feels as though he fits both descriptions well enough to qualify.

The door swings open. Roisin is glorious: glazed in sweat and sun cream. Her sunglasses, knock-off Pradas, reflect McAvoy back upon himself. Barefoot, she crosses to where he sits. Slides, guilelessly, onto his lap, and drapes herself around him like a scarf.

"Tell me," she says, into his ear. "I can take it."

He swallows. Gooseflesh rises upon his exposed flesh. He feels her press her forehead to his. Feels her make him well, the way she has made him well these past months.

"Serious and Organised," he says, his lips brushing her earlobe. "She says she trusts me. Understands."

He hears her laugh against his neck. "The one with the blue eyes and the big tits? Yeah, she's seen something in you, no doubt."

"They're all gone," he says, quietly. "The whole team. Roper's lot. Scattered to the four winds. Stace. Slater. All the DCs. All gone."

"Fresh start," says Roisin. "New beginnings."

"It's still on the table," says McAvoy. "The offer. Full pension. Disability pay-out…"

"And what would you be, if not this?" asks Roisin, quietly. "What would you be for?"

He thinks about it. Casts around for an answer that works. "I'm not brave, Roisin. Not a hero. I just blunder around and somehow it's worked out. But Mum was right. She asked me whether I was ready to do something that could actually make a difference. Christ, I'd do more good going back to the croft…"

"Whatever you choose," says Roisin, and she squeezes his forearm. "You'd let me be whatever I wanted. It's not mad to expect the same in return."

"I expect nothing," he says, and tries to keep the tears from his voice. "I just want to make you proud."

Roisin shakes her head. Smiles into his neck. "She'll be so fucking proud, Aector," she says, and her small, warm hand finds his big, cold fist. She places his palm on her belly. "This time," she says, and there is a ferocity to her voice. "Your girl. Your Lilah. She's a fighter, this one. She's you, and she's me, and she's herself too."

McAvoy pulls her closer. "He got away with it," he mutters. "Roper. Handed in his notice, took his pension. Working for a consultancy in London, making a fortune. And Owen – they got him. Put him away while I was dead to the world…"

"You nearly died," says Roisin. "And there's nothing gone wrong you can't put right."

McAvoy can't find the words. Just holds her, close, and wishes there were a way to make her see that there is nothing in his life worth anything if she weren't there to help him put himself back together.

"I nearly lost you," says Roisin, softly, her lips brushing his skin. "I felt your heart stop. Truly. I felt the world break. And I called out, and you came back…"

"Roisin…" he begins. He can't find a way to end the sentence. Feels tears spill. Feels her, kneading her fingers through his hair, his beard, cupping his big scarred face as if it were made of fine china.

"This Pharaoh," she says, sitting back and looking into his damp, glazed eyes. "You know she fancies you, yeah? You only got the job because she wants to rattle your bones?"

"Roisin…" he begins, and he feels her love as if it were a second layer of skin.

She grins. Kisses him. "Keep it professional. You'll do good."

He says nothing. Lets her kiss him. Feels everything else drift away.

"*Me gamau dut…*" says Roisin. Then adds, for his benefit: "*For ever.*"

He can't find the words to reply. He just knows that here, now, life seems like something worth protecting.

He wonders whether, in the depths of the dark winter, he will find his way towards the light.

About the Author

DAVID MARK spent more than fifteen years as a journalist, including seven years as a crime reporter with the *Yorkshire Post*. His writing is heavily influenced by the court cases he covered: the defeatist and jaded police officers; the competent and incompetent investigators; the inertia of the justice system and the sheer raw grief of those touched by savagery and tragedy. He writes the McAvoy series, historical novels and psychological suspense thrillers.

Dark Winter was selected for the Harrogate New Blood panel (where he was Reader in Residence) and was a Richard & Judy pick and a *Sunday Times* bestseller. He has also written for the stage, for a Radio 4 drama (*A Marriage of Inconvenience*) and has contributed articles and reviews to several national and international publications. He is a regular performer at literary festivals and also teaches creative writing.

David also starts to get all squirmy and self-conscious when he looks at stuff like this, so we'll leave it there.

@davidmarkwriter www.davidmarkwriter.co.uk